STAR REAPER

CHRIS TURNER

CHAPTER 1

I thought I'd seen the last of Sharki. I was wrong.

They say misery loves company. That bad things come in threes. I say it's a load of bollocks.

We were holed up on Sharki's hijacked cargo ship, a U56 junker, the *Trident*, out on the outskirts of nowhere, trying to find some safe haven to tuck tail in and hide. Or at least keep a low profile. Our trio was nothing more than a band of haggard outlaws, fugitives. Not in the classic sense, as in escaping the law, or the lofty powers of justice, but fleeing very sinister crime lords, criminal scumbags, who ran the Beryl Station at Thetis. Dregs of dregs, who would skin us alive or boil our intestines in vats.

The three of us: Marty, Deidra and I, were fleeing Sharki's wrath. We needed to get food and water together or starve out here in the hinterlands.

No one ever said an outlaw vagabond's life would be easy...

There seemed to be a problem with our engines. Occasionally there'd be this little bird-like chirp from somewhere down in the engine room, like the harried cry of a swallow chased by a sparrowhawk. Then the console would do this little skip, a weird twitch as if we were in some bad virtual reality video game.

Better drop out of hyperdrive, Rusco. Give these tired beryl-core engines a break.

I had this sinking feeling they would conk out in the middle of space, maybe put us in limbo, never to materialize in human form again. That, or strand us somewhere outside communicable range of any habitable planets.

I sidestepped that morbid thought. The premonition I ignored. Instead I turned my attention back to the scanners, and our problem.

Marty was his usual self, pacing the bridge: a warthog of a man strutting back and forth. He was the stocky, bulldog type, right out of a B bulldog holo flick, egging us on into some unsound con or the other.

"Listen, Rusco, in spite of our ship's handicap, the darkweb index says there's an outpost orbiting Tylas worth checking out. It's minimally manned. Some scumbag raiders' hub, I'd guess." He gestured to a schematic of a dingy space station 20k miles in slow orbit around a blue-gray planet. He'd been studying it while noodling around in the database. "Looks ripe for plunder. Not expecting guests or tricks. Hell, I've seen more guns on a toy tinman. We could make it there in under half an hour, if the engines hold out."

"It's suicide, Marty. See that tronic booster?" I stabbed a finger at the parabolic gun on the blueprint. "Tachyons'd tag our guidance systems. One roving patrol's alerted and we're toast." It was like explaining the birds and bees to a child.

"We gotta eat somehow."

"Yeah, but we can't do that if we're dead."

Deidra turned in the seat beside him. "Go chew on an old shoe or something, Marty."

She was restless as ever. Gnawing on her knuckles as she moaned on about Sharki. Whether dear old gangster Sharki would come and kill us, if he hadn't already bit it back on the fireball that was Thetis 3. I'd caught a glimpse of her as she turned to palm-slap at the nav sensor. Her face was flushed; a thick tangle of wavy rosy-blonde hair brushed at her shoulders. A pall of dark worry hovered over her like a cloud.

"Three ships limped away," she muttered. "Three bloody vessels, any one of which Sharki could have been on and now—"

"Possibly," I corrected. "Dee, they were just blips on the radar. At best dodgy confirmation he was alive, considering the EMF magnitude of the blast."

"You don't know that, Rusco." She gave her head a furious shake. "You don't know Sharki like I do."

"I do," I snarled. "He's a scumbag and a cutthroat. Bastard should be knifed and drowned in his own piss for what it's worth. Doesn't merit the words we're wasting on him."

What more to say? I shook off my anger. I'd seen too many thugs and crime lords in my day. Too many years of struggle, too many memories of blaster fights, knife duels, con jobs turned to sour milk.

"Sharki always survives," Deidra moaned. "Nothing can kill him."

"Yeah, what is he, superman?"

A tremor brushed at my solar plexus. I knew what the man could do. Seen it with my own eyes. The dozen he'd killed, left in crimson pools. Back there at the salvage yard outside of Tyrone City while Marty and I were trying to shield Deidra from his wrath—it had started to go wrong early on and all those innocent yard workers had died. Marty and I had made it downtown, trying to spring her out of that neon-lit cathouse that he had enslaved her in. The one where she'd been forced to do her pole climbing routine, naked as Eve, to the jeers of blue-collar-men and young hoods who roamed the city.

Memories like that were hard to forget.

Some old geezer who worked a vape shop on the city fringes, took me aside when I pumped him for information. He'd given me some nuggets about Sharki. That he grew up on a backward slave planet, Xizon. Only mines and swamps. Sharki was no more than a distempered orphan at the time, snatched up and turned to work the mines with the rest of the waifs. An abused kid, no doubt an odd survivor who learned 'an eye for an eye, spade for a spade'. Survived his share of years. Clawed his way out of the mines. Killed his way up to the top. Cut the balls off anyone who crossed him or offered him the slightest offense. Got revenge on every son of a bitch who'd ever done him a disservice as he rose from gangsterdom to kingpin. Made it his mission.

He was rewarded for his efforts. He showered his loyal followers with riches and power. Started with small holdings then moved on to ships, then mineral rights; finally snatched up larger enterprises. He became master of the Thetis 3 Mining Station. Brought in millions of yols per year. Became the #1 supplier for beryl-based drive systems in the Vala sector. The mining station that Marty, me and Deidra helped destroy...

Never humiliate the Shark. It was an unspoken anthem among thieves, whispered from dive bar to dive. Earn an enemy for life.

That included Marty, me and Deidra, a ragtag crew aboard a battered ship...

We planned to hyper into Ulso—a minor sun spawning a pioneer planet on the fringe—near Perseus somewhere, the Wasteland Zone. A beautiful place for rebels, outsiders and criminals.

Or so, we'd heard. Its cities, grounds for hovels, dirt and vice. Certainly no utopia. But as good as place as any to lay low, trade in this ship and look for a better future settling somewhere else. We'd gotten wind of it from word of mouth chatter Marty and I'd heard in seedy casinos and saloons spread here and there across the galaxy. I'm sure there were poppy fields and pleasant lakes and rivers scattered somewhere throughout the backwoods of the planet. Beauty incarnate in the terraformed worlds of what were life-giving planets.

"We're going to have to get to the next planet, this Tylas," Marty said flatly. "Get some supplies and grub."

"Yeah, and with what money?" I turned my attention back to the nav.

Marty hunched forward. "We'll figure that out when we get there." He inclined his head toward Deidra. "We can always rent this filly out by the hour," he joked.

"Keep on talking, wise guy," Deidra said, rising to her feet. "Might be your hide bent over a sawhorse getting ridden by some ranchies before the end of the day."

"Quiet down. Your fantasies don't interest me."

"Alright already, enough banter." I stepped in between them. "We've got to stay sharp. We have to beat out a plan and get ourselves out of this mess." I stared hard at Marty. "No impulsiveness." I matched his beady-eyed stare. Right. Like telling a barn cat not to catch birds.

Marty. The quintessential brawler and bully boy. He'd been like that since he dropped out of the womb. Bullet head. Brush cut. Stocky muscular build. 5' 3". Natural fighter. As subtle as a bucket full of nails dropped on a marble floor. No, you'd not want to cross Marty in a back alley.

My eyes shifted back to Deidra who glowered next to him, an altogether different beast. I stared not without silent admiration at the animal curve of her hip, the upslant of the taut breasts easily contoured under her light-brown leathers. Strawberry blonde. Wavy shoulder-length hair. Each strand glistening in the artificial light, as fine as silk. A body at full height standing as high as my chin. Classic proportions, not too small, not too large. A challenging, if not sultry look in the slightly greenish eyes. An arrogant tilt to rounded chin. A lazy lean to her lissome frame as she sat assessing me coolly, left butt cheek pressed to the starboard console. No less inspiring to the imagination in terms of bedroom parkour than the average beauty queen. I dragged my attention away from the pleasant stirrings.

And me? A rawboned drifter. Six foot, lanky build. Purple dyed hair. Part of a program and long-running gag to camouflage myself from the demons who chased me. Hair side-cropped, prickly at top, long at back, giving me a retro mullet look. A man too often waking in the morning to stare at a face of mild irony in the mirror with faint traces of laugh lines bracketing the eyes: the eternal jaded space rebel.

All said, the satirical part of me was capable of a passable mirth. An odd, quixotic, nice-guy tendency to defend the downtrodden—at least when I wasn't too busy trying to save my ass from a frying pan and put food on the table.

I snapped out of my cynical reverie. I motioned to the nav. "Planetary Index says this sector hasn't got a lot going for it."

"So, what else is new?" Marty gestured at the star chart. "Should we waltz back to Tyrone City and try our luck there?"

"No, Marty. Just saying. You got the terraformed world Tylas, then our gas giant, Ovon, then—wait for it—nothing."

"Okay, so how does this help us?"

"Index says there's a lot of masterless space rogues lurking around this region. Also a massive asteroid belt. Looks like we're only on the fringe of it."

"Again, this helps us how—"

The ship gave a menacing shudder. There came a massive boom to our ears, then an ear-splitting crack, as if the hull were about to implode...

CHAPTER 2

PVellgrvk Asteroid Belt, *Urvvik* region. 997 Sol years prior...

A ring-shaped ship nudged itself out of its safe huddle within an array of smaller ships. These were insectoid, aphid-shaped vessels— lightfighters, which formed a protective shield around the much larger, more advanced ship and its mysteries and terrors. The captain of the ship wished to have the Ring Station's might displayed. At this history-making moment, every movement and nuance was crucial, if not significant.

The Zikri war host who faced them kept a respectful distance, awaiting the first sign of hostile activity. The superior numbers of the insectoid enemy clustering around the Ring Station did not faze them. These Zikri were almost too eager to unleash their age-old hatred upon the Mentera race.

Nonetheless the 3000 aphid-like lightfighters posed a necessary barrier to that half grounded ambition. The Zikri had only half as many orb-like vessels in their defense, though all were three times a lightfighter's size and supported more weaponry. Spikes and scopes protruded from their black, plated outerbodies like prongs of a fishing barb.

The Zikri had pursued their quarry to the far edge of the charted universe and now the tables had turned. The hunter was now the hunted. Space rock floated among the Orbs and the insectoid lightfighters. They ranged in size from boulders to small, frost-crystalled mountains.

The Zikri stood steadfast. The random space rock meant nothing to them. Nor was it a tactical disadvantage. It was a last stand, a standoff: an ambitious hope to end the unceasing aggressions of the more clever Mentera race. The Zikri called them *Vokern*, or *Druuvk*, a blasphemous and insulting term for 'vermin' on their home planet— the mongrel hybrids hatched in the frozen ponds of the barren wastes of distant Kraetoria. The standoff was yet another skirmish in a long line of battles between the two enemy races over the eons.

This one was different though. The Ring Station superseded anything in creation ever built by the insectoid Mentera, those four-foot high quasi-hominids. It was a wonder they had not used it at once to crush all the races: Zikri and human alike.

The past had now met the present. A red line had been drawn in the sand, marking the long history of struggle between the two races. The insectoids knew it. The Zikri now dreaded it. They were scavengers and raiders spanning the centuries, creatures of stealth and ambush. The Mentera were slavers, collecting victims of all known races they could get their pincers into. Many squid-like Zikri had fallen prey to their nets and traps, fodder for their life generators. Likewise, many Mentera vessels had been waylaid by the Zikri, and scavenged, and the pirated technology incorporated into their own ships. Although they had not reverse engineered all the Mentera secrets—such as that sheltered aboard the Ring Station—they had done much to increase the breadth of their technology. The ships massed before them were gathered to decide once and for all who would be masters of the galaxy.

This faceoff was nothing as compared to the strange ritual at play aboard the Ring Station. Under the supervision of a team of Mentera scientists, an alien plant with sucker pods, central stalks, petals and purple leaves was being plunged into a massive glass tank filled with a pale green solution.

This was no ordinary glass tank. Nor was it an ordinary liquid. The vessel assumed the shape of an ancient telephone booth of Old Earth. Four sides were closed at the top, but for a circular valve now open to admit the 'specimen'. Immersed within at the half way point, the alien plant floated toward a captive Zikri, rotating ever more slowly in the liquid medium; its six squid-like motilators splayed passively alongside its umber, mottled body.

The creature was not dead. It was not drowned or drugged, as would a bystander assume. An oleaginous, rheumy eye fluttered open from a misshapen head. The organ inspected the intruder plant with an almost dopey curiosity, perhaps lackadaisical wonder.

The tentacles twitched then reached out. The alien creature navigated toward the plant, in a slow-motion circle. The petal leaves likewise opened, as the squidish Zikri sank deeper in the brine toward the bottom, and the two met in a silent, seminal embrace, even though the plant was only half as large as its host.

The insectoid scientists gathered around, looked on with hope. They bobbed and gawked, clicked chitinous pincers among themselves. There ensued an indescribable bonding of alien flora with quasi-carnivorous Zikri. It was a strange metamorphosis, one with flashes of silver, blue and purple rippling through the crude squid-like Zikri body. The petal leaves writhed about the Zikri's motilators. New ones sprouted from the tentacles' tips as the leaves wrapped around the rubbery flesh in a peculiar caress. Almost as if plant and animal had become a single symbiotic unity.

The insectoid scientists screaked ever more wildly. Satisfaction lit their almond-shaped greenish eyes. The volume of their tones doubled.

"Marvelous!" they chorused.

From the base of the tank ran a thin, almost imperceptible silk-like strand. It was a fine, most subtle, fiber-optic of creation, connecting organic being to the light drive system buried deep in the bowels of the ship…down, down, far below the thick plates of metal and the lumo-reinforced bulkheads, for reasons only the insectoid scientists knew… It was as if to proclaim a most brazen truth: that the Mentera had tapped into the life energies of organic beings and could somehow feed it into the propulsion system that drove their miraculous ship.

In this way, they had dared to defy nature.

It happened in a flash, before either side became aware. Within the aphid-like horde, the Ring Station made an unusual fractional rotation, its hull emitted an invisible beam of rarefied energy: a strange, powerful carrier wave powered by the alchemic bio-resonance within the tank. A new form of energy.

Seconds later one of the lead Zikri Orbs jerked out of formation. From its port cannon came a spat of fire bombs that came smashing down on two of its neighboring ships, blasting them to oblivion.

Other Zikri ships rose to defend. They aimed cannons at the rogue Orb. Crimson rays licked out and struck its outer plates, blasting it from many angles. The offending ship turned orange, then red then exploded into chunks of incandescent metal.

Staccato orders were jabbered among the commanders of the Zikri vessels.

Zikri General Zokorg paused and peered out from his flagship's bridge with something of incredulity. He raised his foremost squid-like motilators, balled them into oily clumps and smacked them hard on his skull-like carapace. "What is this?" he roared in his guttural tongue. "Some kind of rogue technology that can commandeer an enemy ship's weapons' systems and turn it on itself?" Three orbs had been obliterated in seconds!

In that fleeting instant, the Zikri knew they had lost before they had begun.

The Orbs moved forward, not shirking their enemy in a backward collective rout, though doom was upon them. Like their forefathers, the Zikri were not cowards even when outnumbered.

The voice of the imperial Mentera commander chirruped eerily over the airwaves, fresh from the Ring Station. "Rein in your war dogs, Zokorg! We have your Emperor Hyrgop with us now. He is looking out from behind the glass of his new home right now." A video clip flashed over the com, the captive Zikri, now morphed into half plant, rotating ever slowly in the magical brine. "He will pay for his crimes against our race." The imperial commander's greenish eyes lingered speculatively upon the macabre scene. "We will have safe passage to the life-bearing planet past the Belt of this minor sun."

The general of the giant flagship Orb bit back his anger. His reply came in staccato bursts through the universal translator. "We cannot comply! You would enslave all the lifeforms on the planet and then turn on us. You would create yet another outpost from which to rule the galaxy."

"And you would do no less," came the equally stilted response. "We are at an impasse, General. My advice is to leave! Or face the wrath of our new Ring Station. The weaponry aboard this vessel you cannot conceive of. Nor can you stand against it. You have witnessed but a tiny sample."

The general's reply was neither civil nor restrained. "We will have WAR! You are posturers. We will shove war down your throats!"

"So be it." The imperial commander cut the channel. And with the last word of that transmission the captains geared up for their grisly activities. They issued commands to their squadrons; they awaited the bloodshed to come.

The Zikri vanguard launched the first offensive in the form of sinkers and bombs. Lurid ruby-red globes sprayed down upon the aphid horde.

From the Ring Station came a pale, violet ray, which swept out in a spiral pattern, then circled the Zikri Orbs and came starfishing down in the form of a net. Another of the larger commanding Orbs turned yellow, then orange, then burst into a million crimson fragments. Shrapnel whipped against neighboring hulls, flinging red-hot metallic charges almost bursting the Zikri's shields.

In a last kamikaze rush, over a thousand Zikri ships plunged headlong into the aphid host. They aimed straight for the central Ring Station, heedless of destruction.

The aphid vessels impulsed forth to meet them, swerving in and looping overhead of the oncoming horde like a swarm of bees.

The Ring Station shifted.

Rainbow-colored light starfished out from its core in all directions.

Then all hell broke loose.

CHAPTER 3

Vala System, the edge of the Belt.

Trident lurched again and I was knocked out of my seat and flung against Deidra. I snatched at the nav console but my full weight came crashing down upon her. She was cursing and fuming underneath my bulk.

Marty was scrambling at our side five feet away, finally wobbling to his feet.

"Light drive died," he said.

"No kidding."

"Get off me!" Deidra squirmed from under my dead weight.

There was another pitched groan, a disturbing clunk and grating from below like a grinding of gears as our ship was thrown back into regular space time. The damage in our last dogfight fleeing Thetis 3 had at last taken its toll.

My eyes focused. From the scanners I saw we cruised at impulse power, far below light speed. This was near stationary in terms of relative speed. But at least stable. Yet with a sinking dread, I knew we were in fact, stranded.

A trio of space rocks whizzed by our starboard side.

No more than the size of boulders, but enough to make mincemeat of our hull.

"We came too close to that damn asteroid belt," Deidra cried.

"Nav system must have gotten fried somewhere." I motioned to the viewport. "We with it too. The gods must be looking after us."

Deidra shook her head. "How are we still alive, Rusco?"

"A miracle."

"Where the hell are we?"

"Dunno. Looks like Tylas down there—" I jerked my head toward the smallish blue-gray disc that floated like a solitary ghost.

A voice popped up behind my shoulder, *"It's a class B planet. Indeed Tylas. Daedalus sector, to be exact."*

I turned around and saw a metallic object the size of a cantaloupe hovering a few feet away with three aerials sticking up from its silvery skullish outerbody like porcupine quills.

"What the hell is this?"

Marty just tottered forward and scowled.

"It's a utility drone," said Deidra. "Many of the miners on Thetis installed them on board."

"Why?"

"An extension of the onboard computer. The units offered useful advice and statistics. Helped combat loneliness aboard on the longer runs. This is a new Mark 6 model, I think—" She frowned curiously as she leaned in to reach up a hand.

Mark 6 or not, the thing must have come online on high alert when the main drive crashed.

"We gotta get out of this system, Rusco," Deidra muttered.

"Not with this ship we don't." I hustled to the readout panel and did not like what I saw on the engine gauges. "We'll be lucky to get to the next planet. With this snail pace at 1/30 impulse power."

"Must have been from the blast back at Thetis."

"You think?"

Deidra stiffened. "Sharki fixed it so the mining crews couldn't steal his ships—or at least get very far before he caught up with them."

Marty bared his teeth. "If I ever see that bastard again I'm going to shit down his throat. We're barely a hop skip out of Dodge and now—"

"It's a big bad world out there, Marty," I grumbled. "What do you expect? Party hats and fanfares?"

The bot interjected an erudite observation, *"Trident is experiencing structural fatigue. She must be overhauled immediately."* The silver-black outerbody hovered an in-my-face foot over my shoulders.

"Tell us something we don't know."

"The Vala system supports two habitable planets, Tylas and Tyrone. Altus, which is nearest to the sun, is being terraformed and will currently——"

"Very nice, Mark 6. It's old news. We've already been to Tyrone."

"Indeed. Thank you, Jet Rusco. Shall I try again?"

I knuckled my eyes in defeat.

"Altus has been terraformed for the past 5.21 earth years. She is slated for completion in 3.56 earth years. Tylas, on the other hand, is only one third water, centered at the poles. The bulk of her is land, one of the few earthlike worlds that has required little terraforming. She is a dry world. Water is of course, a precious commodity and citizens are urged to conserve it. The arid environment makes the planet best suited for raising livestock and supporting crops of wheat and hay. There are many ranches and farmsteads and few cities and settlements. The largest commercial center is Tylas City, known as New Port, under dominion of the Free Scutzers Union, which is at best a moniker for cattlemen and space cowboys. Its population is under 100k inhabitants. There is a copious asteroid belt in proximity to Tylas. Asteroids here are rich in precious minerals, like Beryl, Astraliad and Iridium. Proximity to the inner planets supports mining infrastructure, a healthy base for bands of locators, who in the vernacular of the Interspacial Scutzer Zone, 'breed like flies, many crossing the line between raider and cutthroat'."

Deidra gave a dry click of tongue. "Great. Just what we need."

I peered slantwise at her. Out in the viewport I saw another stray asteroid drift by in the distance. I rubbed the back of my neck. "Maybe a perfect cover for us. We can join one of these hungry, hopeful gold digger bands out for riches and wealth."

"With a ship like this?" Marty cried.

"Why not? Not all of us are expected to have the perfect rigs. For all they know, Marty, this could have been a junker we picked up from a chop shop anywhere from here to Vega."

Marty waved a hand. "So? If this ship even makes it to the next fireman's ball, I'll eat my shirt."

Famous last words. Sensors started to ping. The collision sensor's warning red light flashed on the main console.

The Mark 6 chorused in a metallic tone, *"Danger, danger! Perilous object at 240 degrees!"*

The ship shuddered and the starboard vane came perilously close to another of those hill-sized *roids* of space rock, rolling forward on a menacing angle. Luckily the ship's auto nav kicked in and thrust us out of range within a few yards of collision.

I gripped the controls and grimaced while steering her away. *Trident's* nose dipped toward the distant planet. Out of the viewport, dozens of more space rock were drifting as silently as ghosts, as they had been for eons in ceaseless orbit around the faraway sun. I studied the harbingers of death as they revolved in slow, drugged motion. I gave wide berth to the other slowly spinning rocks.

I glared at the semi-useless Mark 6. For an 'advanced warning device' it seemed incredibly inept. "Let's draw straws to see who drowns our 'Eye of Newt' in the commode."

"Very droll, Jet. You got a name for me too?" Deidra fluttered her eyelids demurely.

"You're 'the Countess'. You like?"

She whipped back the bangs of her strawberry-blond hair. "How touching."

"What about me?" Marty drawled.

"'Warthog'."

"Has a ring to it." He popped another Myscol in his mouth.

"Save some for the fish," I warned him.

"There's some for you too, flyboy, so don't get too zipped up."

Deidra turned impatiently in her seat. "Okay, can we start getting a plan together here, people?"

"Keep your panties on."

Newt piped up, *"There's a 91% chance of failure if crew does not work as a team."*

I jerked around to see the floating eye a foot from my nose;

evidently the bot liked his habit of breathing down my neck.

"Why would anybody install one these stupid, ugly devices on board?"

"I told you," Deidra said querulously, "the miners were lonely. They wanted to stave off cabin fever while they hauled ore between worlds. They found the crew was bonding with the bots."

"Yeah, well, not much bonding going on here. Newtie can clam the hell up for all I care."

"Example of hostility is proof of earlier warning."

I shook my head and peered at Deidra. "Is this going to be a problem?"

"Only if you make it. Just ignore the damn thing if you want to stay sane."

Marty's mouth worked in a mocking grin. "What she means is the more you egg it on, Rusco, the more tutorial he gets."

"I'll get right on it."

"Hostility and anger reaching apex, Jet Rusco! Eye of Newt predicts 93.5% chance of mutiny before—"

Marty whipped out his blaster and cracked off a shot. The flare missed Newt as it careened sideways and ducked behind my chair.

The blast ricocheted off the bridge post and left a smoking hole in the farthest wall.

I ducked in time to avoid any backlash and sent a glare at Marty. "You fucking asshole. You could have breached our hull. What're you thinking?"

"Sorry, bro. It's a bad habit. That chatterbox's unnerving me."

"Yeah, well, close your ears, you dumb bastard. Apology not accepted. Think first, shoot second. Classic Marty. Always the way, isn't it?"

"Never mind, you idiots," Deidra snapped. "There are blips on the radar. Could be ships."

"Could be anything." Marty slapped his blaster back at his hip.

I hitched myself forward, squinted through the viewport. "Doesn't look like ships."

"Escape pods, gangsters, what does it matter?" Deidra muttered.

We leveled out and turned to face our new arrivals.

Turned out it wasn't ships. Only more roids. Sizable ones. Averaging 20 miles in diameter, about 10-15 miles away.

And something more interesting…

CHAPTER 4

I hunched in, eyes glued to the auxiliary display and saw glints of metal and machinery speckled on the barren surfaces of those roids. Some organized operation out in the hinterlands. A minor outpost?

The largest roid was an ugly ovoid-shaped brownish-gray chunk I estimated at 40 miles in diameter. Buildings and equipment soon took form. A human enterprise. The outpost appeared unmanned, not government or company run, given no presence of flag or banner. A terminus of some sort?

Eye of Newt swirled closer. *"My databanks register no record of this installation."* The bot did a half twirl which I interpreted as startlement. *"Technically the outpost does not exist."*

I scowled. Why did that not surprise me?

We had nothing to lose by checking the roids out. I impulsed closer with whatever remained of *Trident's* drive, which was nothing to write home about. A dozen thoughts entered my mind. What could draw humans out into this no man's land? Certainly there was not enough ore to merit such efforts?

I increased the magnification on the viewscope. Closer inspection revealed gunmetal-gray mining machines sprawled over a distance of about 6 square miles. This, on the largest roid. I guessed the whole complex was confined to an area that seemed to have been blasted to a level surface. Irregular features pocked the immediate surroundings: a grayish-brown terrain, mostly barren ridges with upthrust rocky crags and dark-shadowed burrows that looked like gullies.

Drill towers pricked the immediate foreground. Many of them rose up and down like the dinosaur oil derricks on Old Earth.

An asteroid mining operation... and what appeared to be a fully-automated low-yield station. Red and yellow rigs worked the nearest roids. The larger derrick-like drills installed had the potential to extract significant ore. I turned my attention back to the largest roid. I saw some square-post grav-stabilizers positioned around the perimeter to keep objects where they should be, instead of floating off in space.

I zoomed in again, using the magnifier to best advantage. I saw an odd-looking piece of equipment dead center. It looked like a cross between an oil derrick and a tall mining tower.

"It's a Telebractor, Jet Rusco. The smaller drill-like structures are Tricons. The circular outbuilding to the left is a crushing mill. Beside it, those airtight vats are used for leaching ore and—"

I grunted my thanks, disliking the excitement with which Newt relayed this bit of information. I could discern a hammer-head with a *Crestar* logo on the telebractor's top: a half moon with a white-red flare over its side.

Egg-shaped robotic loaders were hauling fresh ore from the tower to a nearby storage area several hundred yards away. Likely to be shipped to the nearby planet, Tylas. Feeders shaped like old-world gravel pit conveyors transported the excess rubble from deep underground to the storage area.

"Well, son of a bitch," Marty hawed. "Just your everyday drilling operation out in space, nothing to see here, folks."

"What do you think they're mining?" Deidra asked. "Beryl?"

"Maybe, or Begrium," I suggested.

"It is Beryl and Iridium," Newt said. *"Why does nobody ask me?"*

"Because nobody likes you, Newt, so please buzz off."

Movement stirred along the edge of the eerie compound. From behind the giant tower, a long submarine shape emerged. It was an old QT Scout which seemed to be overseeing the operation. But in a kind of lackadaisical way, in my estimation, making a slow tour of the premises, as well as keeping an eye on the smaller asteroids being mined. Its interest though, appeared to be the main telebractor.

And now us.

A sharp voice burst over the com. "Where the hell're you bastards heading? This is a restricted area. Move along. Get the hell away from here or face—"

Before I could respond, two more vessels came shooting out from behind the dark side of the roid. Their black armored plates were fire-worn and scored. Their intentions did not look peaceful. Their odd, misshapen hulls cast blue-black shadows across the ghostly rock.

The lead ship veered off to face the QT Scout. Doubtless some transmissions were traded before it became clear that hostility was about to erupt.

I impulsed closer to see what was up. "Send a signal to them!" I rasped at Deidra.

She opened a channel. "U56 Hauler to unknown vessel! Request identification and terms. We come in peace. We're sending a Mayday. Repeat. A Mayday. Our drive is—"

One of the ships, the nearest with the armored hull and turtle-like prow, nosed our way. A splash of menacing crimson shot out from her port. Our hull shuddered at the impact. Another blast knocked our shields down another notch.

"What the fuck?" I smacked a fist at the console. "Why are the bastards firing at us?"

"Must have thought we were part of that space outfitter rig," Marty grumbled.

"What a silly thing to assume. Can't they see we're just casual observers?"

"It's a silly ass universe, Rusco."

"Thanks, Marty, for the reminder." I hopped over to my seat at the central weapons' console. "Man the port cannon, Dee. Marty, you take starboard. I'll take the main—" Another blast shook our hull, nearly knocking us two more points to the red.

"For shit's sake!"

I steadied myself and reached for the weapons' grid. "This

junker's going nowhere fast."

But it did have a decent weapons' arsenal. No doubt Sharki's provisioning. I gripped hard on the main autolock toggle and set the autotack to heat-seeking lethality. Maximum damage.

White fire flew from our front cannon.

A flutter of ion fire licked out like the tail of a greased eel and scraped the nearest marauder's underbelly. It sent her into a fishtail. Deidra and Marty's coordinated shots hit her tail fin, sent her wobble into a spin. She went nose down, hooked beak into the gray surface below and crumpled like a ball of lead before she burst into flames.

Marty rasped out a hurrah.

The defender ship, the QT Scout, had mobilized her guns and engaged the other armored craft, keeping well away from the main telebractor.

But not before the turtle-prowed ship raked the surface of the compound with wicked white streaks. Such firepower obliterated one of the smaller drills; the unidentified enemy was ready to do more. What did these space rogues want? Were they after the equipment? Maybe out to destroy the operation? Why, though? Maybe some beef with the mining company, this Crestar, or the operators of the QT?

"Last thing we need is to get mixed up in a feud, Rusco," Marty warned. He sucked in a breath.

"Too late for that. These raiders have gone beyond the point of friendly fire."

"We lost our light drive, Rusco. If things go south or more of these reavers show up, we're done."

I hated it when Marty went all optimistic on us.

I had no time to stew. Another viper, with heavy steel plates, set in on us, slipping over the rim of the roid. The vessel had come from nowhere, out from behind those rugged contours on the other side of the space rock. It hurtled across the gray landscape like wildfire.

I guessed he'd been lying in wait for us, for a cue from one his allies, maybe as backup. He dogged our tail like a wildcat and pumped us full of fury, plugging fire up our asses. Our shields dipped into the red zone. Reverberations sounded throughout the bridge, and now a foul smoke drifted from the ceiling.

For crap's sake, who are these animals?

I dipped *Trident* down and took her in steep dive toward the drills and the telebractor, in line with the ore storage area, hoping to dodge our enemy.

A narrow lane of possibility ran between the twin rows of drills. I slid down at 4 o'clock, tilted her sideways. We squeezed through the narrow gap, hoping to gain some time. Only a few seconds of grace, before we had to nose our way up again and fight her in open sky.

Marty swiveled the starboard cannon back to align with our pursuing craft. He ripped a streak of ion fire across her hull. Missed by a foot's breadth. The ship eeled away toward the nearest telebractor. I banked upward on an improbable angle. I was trying to use the main tower as cover before the superior speed of our enemy had its way. Deidra punched at the controls and loosed an incessant stream of fire across her coal-dark flank.

Three hits smote her port cannon. They smashed away the cowling and fuselage, rendered the gun useless. The marauder now rode impotent—and she knew it—an ugly, turreted war machine, useless as a giant paperweight, but for maybe one last crazy kamikaze rush. I doubted she would do that, but one can never tell.

The pilot tried to make a dash for it out in open space, but I zeroed in and bird-dogged his ass and gave the front cannon its head. I pegged him full of holes. The craft went spinning off into space on a haywire angle, trailing fire.

The QT Silver Scout came abreast us. I prepared to engage her, but a gravelly voice crackled over the com.

"Hot damn, boys. That was some fine shooting!" An old grizzled face came over the com's vid-link wearing a broken-toothed grin. "Where and when did you get that rustbucket? One of the old mining haulers?"

"A little bird gave it to us," I murmured. "What gives with the riffraff and the pyrotechnics?"

"That was Brex's Boys from the *Beryl Bratts*. Reckon they were up for some rustling, but things went bad for them." He lifted a hand to the viewport. "Nothing but space dust. Now they're in Davey Jones' Locker."

"Could've been us too."

He gave his head a fretful shake. "Trying to make trouble for us. Sabotage our rig. A gang of no-good swamp rats scooping up spoils as they can. Wrecking and ruining competing rigs. Bastards. Devil spawn, if you ask me. Where you coming from? What brings you to Trito Station?"

"Engine trouble. Light drive conked out. We almost got clipped by some of your space rock as we were jarred out of hyperdrive."

He winced at that. "You got trouble then. You'd best impulse to Tylas. Nothing much out here to help you, I'm afraid. Ask around for a good repair shop. Try the *Four Dog Salvage* in Tylas City. Just mention the name 'Barrel Ox'. They'll take care of you."

"Thanks for the tip, sir. I'm Rusco and this rustbucket is *Trident*. I'd say you owe us your ass, thanks to the gunmanship of Marty and Deidra here."

"That so?" His gray eyes narrowed at what I guessed was the image of our ship as seen through his viewport. I wondered how much he guessed at *Trident's* origin and the erstwhile Thetis 3.

"One thing for sure, Iron's going to hear about *Trident* and its skipper's crew. Might even be some perks in it for you. General Iron's a generous man. Just mention the name Ox to him if you cross paths. Him or any of the Star Reapers in the city. They'll do you right."

"Thanks, Ox. I appreciate the gesture. We may just do that."

My eyes traveled from the smoke billowing from our ceiling panels to the clouds of blue vapor rising off the foremost drill below. "You suffered some damage."

"Nothing serious. Crestar'll bring in some maintenance crew to run repairs on the drill. My boss'll have his wrists slapped for allowing such tomfoolery in the first place. He'll send in some reinforcements to help watch the compound. I could use the company, so it'll all work out for the best, I reckon."

"You're a tolerant man, Ox."

"Have to be at my age. Out here in the boonies, nothing to see but the stark blackness of space. Enough to drive a man batshit. That or slit his throat."

They were hyperbolic words, but I understood.

Something else was bothering me. I toyed with how to broach it. "A question."

"What?"

"Why's this installation not registered?"

He frowned. "Crestar likely keeps it off the books for good reason. Probably less chance of sly rogues coming looking if the location's not on public record."

It made sense. The fact told me much about the treacherous nature of this corner of the star system.

We traded some more inconsequential talk before we took our leave. My thoughts turned darker as I churned over the new information.

It turned out Marty had been right. These raiders thought *Trident'd* been sent up by this General Iron to guard this mining operation. To protect it against rogues such as the likes of them. Funny how fate brings seemingly innocent bystanders pursuit and peril.

Or was it just my own imagination and magnet-for-trouble karma at work again?

CHAPTER 5

It took us two days limping on impulse to get down to Tylas. We couldn't trust the nav either after it had dumped us so perilously here in the fringe of this roid belt. We limped on under manual control, the old-fashioned way. Worst case: we could be holed up or stranded out in nowheres-ville with no drive to speak of. A spacer's nightmare.

The very same had happened in my earlier years while fighting against the Skurgs. A vicious dogfight ending with three of them blowing out my rear thruster and jamming my hyperdrive. I'd blown two of them out of the sky before I'd been disabled; luckily I'd incapacitated the other. Had I not gotten off a mayday when I did, I would have been a skeleton in a drifting coffin.

A moon base somewhere in the vicinity of Vagus had picked up my signal. Relayed it on to Pegamon. Sure enough, when I was at the end of my reserves, a transport carrier had loomed up on my port. She'd found me two weeks after I'd been shanghaied by those mutants.

One cannot pick and choose his brushes with death.

I kneaded the stubble on my chin. How I wished I could forget those years...

I set *Trident's* nose aiming for a major land mass that banded the planet at its middle. Gliding through the atmosphere and down, I leveled her out just below the clouds and we studied the images of the surface below us. Only empty countryside. No airports or ships to be seen.

"Looks like any one of the many low tech worlds on the fringe," I mused idly.

"You were expecting something different?" Marty said.

We swung low, our engines roaring—over rolling landscape of cattle ranches. Big-horned sheep, or some cross between big horns and cattle, roamed in tight herds.

"We should land soon," Marty advised. "We don't know how long this bucket is going to last."

I shrugged. "We have to get to the city, like Barrel Ox said."

"We're not going to make it to any 'city'."

Deidra nodded her agreement. That was when the impulse drive sputtered out.

Try as I might to level out our flight, we fell fast through the last low-lying clouds and the surface loomed up at us much too quickly. I tried to reduce our speed, but only so much is possible given the laws of physics. "Strap in! We're in for a rough ride."

We shrugged into our shoulder harnesses. We braced ourselves and I managed to coax some life out of the impulse engines just before they completely died. I reversed the ion jets as much as they'd allow and took her in a shallow dive, nose lifted.

The latter was what saved us.

Trident's rear struck and dragged, slowing us. We bounced and wobbled, fell sideways as our underbelly skidded across the golden sun-baked field, gouging a 100-foot long trench in the ground. Tumultuous noise raked our ears. Terrible g's assailed our bodies as solid earth pummeled our steel-plated sides. We were like straw puppets in a mixer.

The ship ground to a halt. All was quiet, but for the buzz of the ship's warning systems, the hiss of air escaping the reserve tanks.

I unhitched myself from my harness and staggered over to the nav. Through blurry eyes I scanned the controls. Electrical and backup systems seemed to be operational, but both drives were kaput. The rest of the controls seemed dead.

A snarl formed in my throat. What good was a ship without a drive?

I shook off my daze and watched the others uncrinkle themselves from their command posts. None of us was seriously injured, but we stumbled like zombies toward the hatch. Newt chose to chatter on about probable causes of failures and whatnot. *"68% degradation in warp ring mechanism! Three inductor systems are severely compromised, Jet Rusco, from the impulse conduit and—"*

I whipped out my gun and smacked the barrel across his gleaming outerbody. The Mark 6 tumbled away. He made a mad scramble toward the utility bay.

In a foul mood, I yanked open the circular hatch and jerked my lanky frame out. I squinted in the bright sunlight, sucked in a breath of air. The tart fragrance of country wildflowers filled my nose, a welcome respite from the recycled air of the ship. The sun was too bright here. It could only hurt my sensitive eyes. I rubbed my jaw, not without a small bit of wonder that we were still alive. Now in something of a fix. *Trident's* hull lay canted on a disturbing angle, plumes of dust fanning out behind her. We'd skidded to a stop in a featureless plain carpeted with yellow-brown grasses with tufts of green here and there. The slow roll of the land led to a low copse about a mile distant that looked like young sycamores. Between the treetop-gaps, ghosts of hills of smoky pale blue color rose in the distance.

I squinted further into the sun and thought to see birds. But no, just heat shimmer on the horizon with all the qualities and falseness of a desert mirage on a hot summer day. My eyes shifted back to the girth of the ship, dismayed to see a thickening trail of smoke curling high on the slate-colored fuselage. It wafted higher, just above the long tempered-steel barrel of the port cannons that stretched like bazookas. They were now scratched and battered, a signature of all clunkers from that era. Higher still, the faded, fork-like insignia 'T R I D E N T' was placarded in rusted lettering. This ship might once have been a beauty, something a captain could be proud of. Now she was worn out and looking like a step away from the junkyard.

"What are those?" Deidra's hand went out to a herd of grazing beasts a few stones' throw away. They had come around the other side of the ship in curiosity. Maybe hostility? I wasn't sure. Evidently the crash had somehow attracted them rather than driven them away.

I shrugged. "Dunno. They look like cattle—or some kind of pseudo-buffalo."

"Ain't no cattle I've seen before," Marty grumbled. "Too ugly for that. Ain't no frigging hybrid buffalo either."

"So what are they then?" I scoffed. "Let's hear it, since you're such an expert on extra-planetary critters."

"Don't know, Rusco. Ask Newt…and dial it back, please."

"Just pissed, that's all."

"I can see that. And who isn't? We're about 100 miles away from any city and in the middle of nowhere."

"So what now?" Deidra hissed.

"We make the best of it. We walk."

"To where?" Deidra scoffed. "The nearest five-and-dime or steer watering hole perhaps?"

"Funny, Dee."

I touched the R1 at my waist. I scanned the countryside, looking around with sinking hopes. I was comforted only by the presence of the smooth stock in my hand. I doubted there would be trouble here, but one could never be sure. Being marooned in an unknown place brought restlessness. Worse, the loss of a ship was something that unsettled a man—big time.

We watched the herd wander closer. They stared at us with moony eyes, as if we were intruders in their domain. Which we were. The glint in those eyes was edged with the beginnings of threat. We'd disturbed a sacred space.

One of the larger males—a mean muscular hulk—trotted closer and tossed his big horned head at us, showing shiny pointed whalebone-white horns.

"Don't like the posturing of that one, Rusco," Deidra whispered. "Dangerous, you think?"

"Let's find out." Marty shuffled over and shot me a grin. "Why don't you go over and pet him, Rusco, feel out the territory?"

"Better idea, why don't you, Mar, since it's your idea?"

"Ah, that pipsqueak ain't going to do anything," he said confidently.

The animal let out a bawling roar. Front hooves stomped, then he came a hop and skip closer, only to lumber straight at us in a bow-legged strut.

The herd of horned creatures lifted their heads in curiosity as they chewed their cud. The alpha male snorted and huffed in closer. I saw it was much larger than it first appeared. Definitely not to be provoked.

Marty licked his lips. He sprang back, R1 spitting out a defensive volley. The bull stopped short, vexed by the stink of grass smoldering before its massive front hooves.

It glared then backtracked at a trot toward the herd. It nudged the dozen or so of the smaller beasts away toward the distant field. A foul wet steam blew from its flared nostrils.

"Ugly mother."

"Look who's talking," Deidra murmured.

The bull turned back to us and began to paw at the grass. It lowered its head, snorting displeasure, then swung its horns to and fro in challenge. Its matted gray-black hide reeked of urine and sweat, buzzing with flies. Even at this distance, its ox-eyes were full of menace and it dug its front hooves again into the turf.

"Not getting a good feeling about this, Marty." I reached for my R1. Cautiously I edged around the side of the ship toward the hatch.

The bull didn't seem to take kindly to my surreptitious movements. It charged.

I skipped back as it smashed its heavy horns headlong into the side of the ship.

The animal swung its head side to side, raising its blackish snout and bellowed fearsome challenges as it staggered back on wobbly legs.

Marty guffawed. "He don't look too happy to be alive, does he, Rus? Maybe his young heifers over there can't stand the stench of him?"

The bull seemed to take offense at the remark. Snapping out of its dizziness, it came barreling at Marty in a blood mad charge.

"Motherfuck." He grabbed at his holster and aimed his blaster, nailed the beast between the eyes.

The black-gray armadillo of a hulk went down, silver horns ripping at the sun-baked ground. Its neck lay twisted. The once fearsome hide smoked where Marty pegged it again for good measure. A soft gray-blue eye glared up at us with anything but love.

I moved over to its side and bit my lip. The foul hide reeked worse than ever. I was just about to say something pithy when a blur of black motion came fluttering around the back of the ship.

Another brute hidden from sight... In some sly way the beast'd cut us off from the hatch.

Marty was closer to it than me. The young bull rushed.

I saw it as in a dream. One minute it was a stationary mass of flesh, the next, a lumbering rush of living muscle.

Marty lifted his blaster, whipped off a shot.

Too slow. The blip only grazed the bull high in the shoulder. It loosed an angry bellow, incensed at the charred section of its hide and kept coming at him like a battering ram.

I aimed my weapon but realized no fire power would do any good with that amount of momentum.

The beast would plow into Marty and smash him to pulp. Once those U-tonged horns found flesh, there could only be one aftermath.

I did the next best thing possible. I hotfooted it toward the bull, waving my arms frantically and roaring at the top of my lungs. I raced right into its perimeter, distracting it.

The beast swiveled its head my way but not before its left foreshank nicked Marty and sent him spinning away. The beast turned and came galloping straight at me.

"That's right, you big bastard! Come and get me!"

I lunged to the side just before it could spear those nasty horns into my belly. I rolled twice for dear life while grabbing my blaster and got off two quick shots that basically did nothing but rip some more burnt patches into its thick hide. Dull echoes erupted from somewhere behind me. To my surprise, I realized it was Deidra. She'd fired and caught the raging animal in the hind legs.

It gave a tortured bellow of pain before it half-bucked, half-skittered its way out of range behind *Trident*.

Deidra came running toward me, her hair bouncing, blaster raised in a steady hand.

"What the hell are you thinking, Rusco?"

"People aren't too smart when they're looking at death, I suppose." I picked myself up and gave a painful groan. I was more shell-shocked than anything. Only some bruises and scrapes. Blood dripped from my left forearm where I'd skidded off stones in the grass.

Marty had landed in a rolling heap and for a long time he lay there, strange noises coming from his throat. Then he picked himself up, clutching his left side and wheezing. I'm surprised the bastard hadn't broken some bones. Maybe he had, but he was not showing it. Scraped and bruised all to hell, the wind knocked out of him and maybe a cracked rib or two.

He licked his lips and wiped sweat from his brow. "Friendly buggers." He hitched himself over to kick at the corpse he had shot. He fell, then got up again, wincing. He clutched at his side and spat. "I'm treating this as a very bad omen, Rusco. Us crashlanding on this planet."

"Maybe. But we still have to somehow get out of this mess."

He tottered our way as we craned our necks, looking for signs of another lurking threat. "We got a busted ship and mean-ass animals ready to stick us like pigs." He lifted an arm. "Nothing out here but steers and sun." He mopped at his brow again. "Damn it's hot."

CHAPTER 6

Most of the herd had scattered. Its loyalty and courage had been dulled by the smell of burnt hide that lingered in the air. Some of the younger bulls huddled on the periphery, out of range of our guns, wary of the enormous ship. A few looked as if they wanted to attack, but they did not relish losing a game against fire sticks.

I could understand some of this. I lowered my barrel and respected their instinct to cling to life.

The faraway sound of a motor hummed from somewhere east of us. I cocked my head toward it.

The sound grew louder. Definitely the burl of an engine. About a mile away, I soon discerned a small red four-wheeler buzzing over the small rise.

More trouble, I expected.

We squinted into the sun and saw the brightly-painted vehicle come bouncing down the vestiges of a trail outlined in the parched grass.

The driver came sputtering toward us. He looked up at the ship, jaw-agape. He cut the engine and jumped off, all cowboy hat and denim overalls. He swept off his dusty stetson and waved it at us in fury.

"You can't park that piece of crud here! Move it offen my land. You're scaring my herd of gleers."

"Sure thing," Marty gave him a friendly wave. "Except we can't, Chief. Left vane's toast. Drive broke too."

The lank-limbed man was engrossed enough with the ship that he hardly heard Marty's words. Nor did he notice the dead gleer sprawled to the side. I could see, upon closer inspection, he looked as if he'd had more meat on him at one time, but the ravage of advancing years had shrunken the slabs of hard muscle to loose gristle and string. He blew out his cheeks in an exasperated breath. He pulled at his chin, as if presented with a grade school problem beyond his capacity. "I should think to charge you strangers a flat fee for parking here."

"It ain't parked," said Marty. "Marooned. And you could, but pretty hard to collect monies from folks who have none." He spread his palms in a glib way and put on his best panhandler's smile.

The herder's shoulders sagged a notch. "No yols?"

"That's what we said, Chief."

"Quit calling me 'Chief', you wiseass."

"How would you like to be called then, friend?"

"Name's Hoss. I run this here ranch." He spread his arms like a deacon. "Orchard Grove, Mesquite Swallows Township. My Grandpappy had it before my Daddy did, then he left it to me."

"That's very nice." I lifted a hand. "This is Marty and this here's Deidra. I'm Rusco. Sorry to intrude on your—"

He interrupted me as he appraised us with an irascible look, his gnarled, red-knuckled hand coming up to brush at his whiskered chin. "Hoss Garner's my full name." His big doe eyes passed over us with critical regard. The sun shone through scudding white cloud, casting long running shadows over the gleer-chomped grass. "My cousin Ethber told me any stranger showing up unannounced means trouble. Three, and you got yourself a jinx."

I looked over at my comrades, who were trying to hold back smiles. "That so?"

"Now if I had the proper tools and inclination I might be able to fix your young'uns' ride—" He gave a sharp look at Deidra "—But I don't."

Marty grinned while Deidra's eyes moved restlessly back to the wandering herd. Her gaze shifted up to the clouds as if expecting Sharki to drop out of the sky and put her back in his cathouse.

The idea seemed as farfetched as its possibility.

Hoss gave Deidra a once over and his gaze lingered on her tantalizing curves more than I cared for.

His eyes rounded on the twisted carcass beside the ship. His jaw hinged open. The sight, all horn and hide and its net of blue bottle flies, had him putting two and two together. He gave a hoarse shout, "What are you, a bunch of good-for-nothing rustlers?" His eyes beetled from our beached ship to the blasters at our hips. "Son of a bitch! You buggers owe me for one dead gleer. A hundred yols each for a good hide of mylar flesh like that."

"Now wait a minute," I said. "That critter near—"

"I don't care." His hollow cheeks burned red now. "I'm gonna round up the local posse and run you shitbags out of town. They'll tar and feather you, if I don't do it myself!" He reached for the leaden piece tucked at his belt.

My fingers instinctively spidered to the butt of my own R1. A part of me wondered whether it would be expedient to cap him now before matters got out of hand.

But I opted for the more peaceable approach. No sense having a Hatfield-McCoy feud out here in hicksville for nothing more than a dead gleer. "No worries, Hoss. We'll work off our debt. Riding the range, hog-tying steers, whatever you wish." I motioned back to the place where he had come, unable to hide a begrudging hitch in my voice.

He grumbled out a note of acceptance. I nudged at Deidra: my cue for her to put on some charm. Maybe ease us out of this mess.

She flashed me a petulant look then gave a complacent shrug. She sidled over to him and put an arm around his bony shoulders.

"We're rightly sorry, Mr. Hoss. Anything we can do to help, it's our pleasure."

The man's brows softened. The creases on his cheeks and brow seemed to fill out. "Well, seeing as you folks are near shipwrecked, I might make an exception."

Deidra pretended relief. She clapped palms on cheeks as she

flashed me a quick glance. He stepped gamely from foot to foot, grumbled quietly as she lifted a hand to let her finger trail over his hollow cheekbones. The little coo she let out was a little overdone, like a teenage girl, but my philosophy was, 'if it ain't broke, don't fix it'.

That, and a few more tried-and-true gestures seemed to soothe, if not embolden our cowboy some more. "Well…Bessy's simmering stew on the cook stove this afternoon—possum methinks, which she'll pour into a pie. It'd be mighty unneighborly of me not to invite you people along…seeing as you're here and all."

I smiled tautly, the first since stepping off that wrecked craft. "Sure. We're more than happy to accept."

He waved us on toward his ride as he piled on the quad. "Come on. Let's haul ass. Time's a-wasting." He sparked up the machine and was ready to head to the farmhouse.

"Hey, wait. What about our ship?" Marty demanded.

He spat out a wad of tobacco. "That shitbox don't look like it's going anywhere but the scrapyard."

"What you calling junk?" Marty said. He hunched forward, a growl in his throat.

Hoss chewed a bit longer on his wad. "First off, I'll get Nils or Big Nanda to come out and take a look at it. Maybe tow it, if that's the best option. Could be it's worth the scrap in weight. Nanda runs the salvage yard down at Gleer Corners, just past the old ford by Oxbridge. Might be able to help you people out."

"Sure. As long as repairs are the first order of business," I said tersely as I turned the idea over in my mind.

Hoss pulled off his cowboy hat and flicked back a ruff of dog-brown hair. He made the call on his handheld, jawing out some idle talk while he chatted to the people he knew there.

As we waited for the tug to arrive, Hoss buzzed around on his four wheeler scouting the immediate vicinity to check in on his herd of gleer. They'd gone off to a nearby watering hole, heads down, ears up, looking lost with the absence of their protector. Hoss motored his way back to us, his jaw hard, lips mumbling some harsh words about another grievous injury to one of his bulls. He screwed up his mouth in distaste while gazing at the dead bull once again. Muttering to himself, he motored back to the farmhouse, undeterred by the heat of the afternoon, to return some time later with an attached trailer and several sharp machetes in the back. He carved off the beast's head, then its forelimbs and hindquarters. Lastly he made a show of slicing off some choice slabs from the haunch. He slapped them all in the back of the trailer under a tarp. The smell of oozing blood and the squishy sounds of his butchering filled the air.

Deidra looked as if she was going to puke. Marty looked on in fascination. I spent most of my time scanning the skies, wondering how much this 'fixup job' was going to cost us. Were these 'salvagers' going to shaft us and we'd never see *Trident* again?

Hoss spoke to my unvoiced thoughts, "No worries, Rusco. They're trustworthy. Not to fret."

When he'd retrieved the last of the fresh meat, he tossed spades at Marty and me. He told us to hop to work. "Start digging, boys. Five feet deep."

Digging we did, though I was of mind to let Marty do the lion's share since it was he who'd killed the bull.

When it was all said and done, and by the time we'd tamped the last sod patches over the crude hole filled with gleer guts, the sun was well past its zenith. I was bathed in sweat and could feel my shoulder muscles begin to burn. There'd be more burning to come. I was tempted to dowse the contents of Hoss's water jug over my head, but refrained. I took a long drawn-out swig instead.

Before long a ship's low roar drifted our way. A couple of big *mercators,* leadpipe bronze with toad-like hulls, grew larger and soon hovered directly overhead. They didn't even assess *Trident* for damages. Thick cables dropped down to plunk on top of her belltop bridge. A technician slid down the wire on a jerry strap and affixed them to tow rings on *Trident's* bow and stern.

With grass blades stuck between our front teeth, we watched as the cable-guy gave a high five to the pilots above and we watched our rig being pried out of the soil and hauled away by the two big *mercator* tugs. They flew away with our ride. In a half dream I expected the boy wonder to come flying after to adjust the bat cables.

I stared long at the shallow crater of the crash site where *Trident* had lain. So much for making distance from Sharki and his burnt out crib on Thetis.

Hoss fired up his quad. He did a sharp turn, tires spitting grass and dirt and was off.

Marty intercepted and hopped in the trailer beside the fresh meat. He sat there grinning at Deidra and me as we hoofed it, trying to catch up.

We were chasing in Hoss's wake at a generous dogtrot, huffing and puffing and I snatched a glance to the north and saw remnants of the scattered herd a few stones' throws away. A cow and a calf and several yearlings hunkered in the grass. Farther out in the yellow-green grasses some straggling steers grazed.

I caught up and jogged beside Hoss as he clutched the wheel with a purposeful intensity. I shouted at him over the noise of the engine, "Aren't you afraid one of your big pets is going take a swipe at your little tractor?"

"I can outrun the gleers. Dodge them, if needed. The bulls get feisty. That's why I got these here goads in case one of 'em gets too feisty." He reached a hand over and pulled a four foot-long gunmetal cattle prod fastened to the side of the quad. "300 V of juice'll send any one of those critters hoofing it with tail between his legs. The frame and bumper are electrically wired. I can turn it off and on. Just in case I need to play bumper sports. Get what I'm saying?" He grinned and toggled a switch on the dash.

"What if one sneaks up on you or gets past your shield?"

"Then guess you're up shit creek." I saw his lips spread in an ever-widening grin.

CHAPTER 7

We arrived sweating and panting before the hardwood gate of Hoss's ranch. My undershirt and leather jacket were soaked. Deidra didn't seem to be as fazed as me. Only a pleasant flush to her skin and the scent of ripe young female on her. The advantage of youth and being in good shape.

Hoss parked the four-wheeler in a flat-roofed storage shed past the barn and white sycamore log house. Deidra and I followed dutifully with more modest strides. I saw him haul the tarp-wrapped meat over to the side in a gloomy corner.

"I'll deal with that later. Time for a sarsaparilla," he said.

Three more ATV's with big balloony tires sat holed up in the back. I didn't see any other vehicles outside of a dusty air speeder whose brown, rusty nose was peeking out of a nearby outbuilding. I assumed these were Hoss's family's only means of transportation. A two-treaded track snaked dustily away from the farmhouse and the backyard into the miles of flat pastureland beyond.

Orchard Swallows was an impressive holding, I had to admit. A beautiful two acre garden stretched behind the house, full of flowering and leafy green vegetables. A sprawling tree sat in the front yard. Its leaves were ocher-tinted and rustled in the breeze. Pastureland galore with pockets of horned mylar roamed free off in the distance.

"Beautiful, ain't it?" Hoss spread an arm proudly. "I could live here forever." He extended his palm. "Don't eat the ossem berries on that there tree." He gestured to the big sycamore. "Make yourself sicker than a dog. If you don't know how to boil them right and soak them in vinegar, you're in trouble."

"Good to know." I gave Hoss a salute and an inward ironic grin. *Because I was just about to go out there and eat a handful of poison berries.*

To his credit he was hospitable enough to let us stay at his ranch while our ship was being repaired. He fetched some gauze from the shed and offered it to Marty for his busted ribs which we taped up to minimize movement. Marty winced and grunted, hand going from time to time to his side. Nothing could be done. Time would heal it. We'd forgotten to grab the regen on *Trident* which could have accelerated his healing.

To sum up our initiation, it seemed we were to spend many a stiff and sore moment helping Hoss around the ranch with chores.

That aside, the place was a marvel. It was good to see people living like this. In some corners of the universe there still existed paradise. I sucked in a healthy breath. Clean, country air. Wholesome living.

A pleasant dryness touched this corner of the planet. Soothed a man who was looking to hunker down on a patch of land, get himself closer to the earth. There was tranquility here. The warm sun shone down and brought a blush to my skin. Streamers of high cirrus stretched along the northern horizon. My jangled nerves felt relaxed; momentarily I could put behind the harrowing battles of the past.

But it was dangerously easy to forget the scumbags out there just at arms' reach, crawling out of the shadows. Rogues who would not hesitate to pop a man for his ship or his shirt.

A stout figure came to stand in the shade of the veranda, her arms akimbo.

"Hoss, that you?"

"Got ourselves some visitors, Ma," Hoss bawled at his wife as she'd lifted her voice in inquiry.

Dressed in white apron and heavy green-and-red plaid gingham trailing down to the ankles, she blinked in the hot sun, the apron doing little to hide her plump frame. "Well, I'll be a horny toad. Been a long while since we had company, Hoss." She took one look at

Deidra and gave a small cry of pleasure. "Heaven's, girl! You need to put some meat on those bones. A man likes his woman with something that he can hold on to."

Obviously starved for female company, she set to fussing over Deidra. Deidra stood stunned, a deer in the headlights. Last seen, Bessy had set her up in the barn, milking a goat and teaching her to braid twine. Earning her keep, and to work up an appetite, I imagined.

A smile touched my lips. Deidra was bonding with the farm woman. I thought such labor a practical application of her pent-up energies. She was a wayward, restless woman. One needing to be kept busy and out of trouble.

As anticipated, Hoss had set us to work early on. He got us fixing some fencing and gathering up odds and ends around the yard, moving them to the barn for storage. The gleers had taken objection to a particular section of the rail fence. I looked gloomily at the 5-inch lightweight aluminum piping that stretched from the cement well back of the barn, around the drive sheds and toward the garden. I knew in my gut that a lot of work was in order. We'd be stiff and sore after a few days of such chores. Sure enough, our next task was to connect the irrigation pipes from the cement well, all the way out to the barley crop, and then getting the new sprinkler system working.

Marty didn't see any sunny side to rural living and he ticked off points on his fingers. "Rusco, this is how much I hate doing odd jobs." Before he could elaborate, he nicked his thumb on the edge of a metal ring as he haplessly tried to screw on the gasket. "Fucker. I should smash this bitch-eyed piece of crap—" He lifted his hammer to hardnose the ring into place but I grabbed his arm.

"Relax, buddy. You're going to chop it to shit. This is delicate stuff, like knitting a sweater or caressing a woman."

"Not how I do it, Rusco."

"I don't doubt it. Explains why you don't get laid."

I noticed Hoss had been away for some time now. I looked

around and saw neither hide nor hair of him. Bessy's tuneless voice drifted over the sounds of bees in the nearby shrubbery by the house. I could make out the woman's humming a down-home country melody from the open window which in turn brought the waft of fresh oven baked pies.

Marty and I hunkered down, struggling to assemble the irrigation piping for the garden. Out of the corner of my eye, I saw Deidra come sauntering out of the barn. Her hair was mussed up and she was flushed faced and wearing the ghost of a spritely smile.

I didn't like that.

"What's with you?" I queried. "Had a little tussle in the hay with our cowpoke?"

"No, our little cowpoke's got his nose rubbed in the dirt though. Tried to get fresh with me and had to teach him the error of his ways."

I stood frozen for a moment.

Deidra kept on toward the house, her hips full of swing and with an extra leggy grace. An oily grin was pasted on her face as she tossed a capricious look back at me. My stomach still rumbled at the whiff of the home-baked crabapple pies coming from Bessy's open window.

"Wonder how long it'll take Bessy to put two and two together," Deidra mused, "realize that old Hoss's a philandering goat. My, my, when she sees him lying there yanking his crank beside the flowers he picked for me..." She slapped her thigh in amusement.

"We're their guests, Dee," I hissed. "Quiet down. You can't be going around saying—"

"I can and will, Rusco. Now if Bessy's a smart gal, she'll get it, and maybe that'll teach that lousy bastard to put his hands where he shouldn't."

"Right," I said. "Looks like I'll have to smooth this over myself." I cracked my knuckles and eased myself over to the barn.

"Don't do it, Rusco," Deidra warned.

I peered over at Marty.

"I'm kind of favoring Deidra," Marty said.

I shook my head. "You two are a couple of lamebrains."

I whisked open the barn door and set feet in the quasi gloom.

Hoss was lying on his side by the milking stalls. A nanny goat looming over his torso. Its woolly head was lowered enough to rake a raspy tongue over his flushed cheek. A half filled pail of milk sat by his leg.

Hoss's shirt was pulled over his head so he couldn't see too well. His back was bare. The flowers—a bouquet of once nice white, yellow and red ones—lay crushed where he lay, bindertwined at ankles and wrists. He squirmed a little once he saw me. For some weird reason the man was snuffling as if he were tongue-tied.

I discovered the reason for this soon enough. I pulled the gag out of his mouth. He sputtered.

"Damn it, Rusco! You gotta control that she-devil of yours. See what she done to me? It's not neighborly."

I frowned, trying my best to look serious. "From my vantage, Hoss, you picked the wrong girl to tango with. For shame. What were you thinking?" I pulled out my bowie knife and made a slow show of cutting his bonds.

He cursed and got to his knees like a jerky steer. He flicked me a lamprey's grin. "I reckon." Now his smile grew slightly conspiratorial. "Not a word of this to Bessy, you hear?"

I looked away with a frown, as if struggling with a moral dilemma. "I don't know about that, Hoss. Dee's got some strong feelings about what happened here. Don't know if I can hide this under the barrel."

"Come on," he pleaded. "You know how women get."

I did, and I gazed at him with a pretended stern countenance. "Well, as I'm seeing it, you've been caught with your pants down in a scene that could easily ruin a solid marriage, but as I'm a peaceable sort, I might choose to ignore this one little incident."

"Sure, sure, whatever. You're a pal, Rus!" He shook my hand, patted my back, his eyes lit up like a bulb. "We're pals, ain't we?"

"We sure are, Hoss." I made a zippering motion across my lips. "Mum's the word."

He nodded and clunked out of the barn, somewhat mollified. I ambled behind at a more leisurely gait. We made our way over to see how Marty was faring with the pipes. Turned out he wasn't faring too well. He had nicked his other thumb and now had bitched up the ring.

Deidra fixed Hoss a chill stare as he passed by Marty. He grunted at Marty to keep up the good work then stalked off to the house to check on Bessy and her pies.

I crouched to help Marty fasten the two segments of pipe together. Deidra waltzed over with her voice pitched slightly more irascibly than usual. "Seriously, Rusco, you had to let him go free? He was due for another hour squirming in the straw before Bessy found him. Every man looks at me and sees an easy grab. I'm sick of it. They think they can take anything they want! No bloody way. Had to deal with this shit my whole life. It's very bloody annoying."

"I can imagine, Deidra. It sucks to be you."

A petulant snarl stuck in her throat. "You'll never understand, Rusco."

"Oh, I understand, Dee. Too much attention on the physical body, it makes one cynical—and a hater of men. Am I getting close?"

"Crabby and violent too," Marty put in.

Deidra went off in a huff. She slumped in the shade under the shagbark sycamore. A gleer lowed in the distance. I could see the young one lift its head and swish its tail to ward off flies.

"Aren't you going to help us?" Marty bawled over at her.

She ignored the request and stuck a blade of grass between her teeth. She looked off into the field.

Marty'd begun to feel the heat and slouched back with a restless grunt. "I'm done, Rusco." He popped another white pill in his mouth. "Tell, Hoss, it's time for a siesta."

"Easy there, Mar. How many of those've you inhaled?"

"Not enough." He wet his lips as if to ward off a bad taste. "I belong in a ship, Rusco, not out squeezing udders and repairing some damn irrigation pipe."

"Yeah, well, life's sometimes not to our preference."

He shook his head and winced. "Have a hit, Ruzbo. Stop babbling."

I gave my head a grave shake. "No, not into the stuff. Trying to quit the habit."

"Sure." Marty guffawed. "Like pigs fly."

I looked away. Marty was right. I'd had my battles with Myscol—most of them I'd lost.

Within a few moments, his eyes started to dilate and his voice took on a pseudo obnoxious monotone which anyone not on Myscol took exception to.

It was getting on toward sunset and the end of the planet's long 33 hour day. Vala hung low in the sky, casting a wan, golden honey-like glow over the heat-shimmering fields.

Hoss called over to us and we made our way to the patio and settled down at a wide, wood-carved table overlooking the garden. Plants and shrubs were burnished gold, just catching the last rays of sunlight.

Of the incident in the barn not a word was mentioned.

I helped myself to a healthy slab of beef on the center platter with ears of fresh corn.

"There are sweet peas, possum pie and my specialty, leafy bitters," Bessy announced. "I use only family recipes of long standing. Help yourself, Mr. Rusco."

"Thank you, ma'am. I reckon I will."

Hoss smiled and cupped Bessy's hand. "It's all scrumptious as usual, Bessy." His thumb traced a circle on her wrist while he wore that deceitful, two-timing grin of his. "This meal's even better than your own fricasseed chicken and candied apple dumplings."

She sighed and made a small sound of pleasure in her throat. Her round, plump cheeks blushed.

Deidra swallowed a catch in her throat as she sat in cool,

phlegmatic silence.

Hoss made sure to avoid those eyes of hers, given what had gone down in the barn. I still chuckled inwardly at the whole thing, as unfortunate as it had been. Hoss droned on in his drawl, of affairs of the neighboring farms, the burdens of the farmer, the long hours of herding gleers and the hazards of the change of season when the winter squalls'd come to bend the trees and lift the shingles off the roofs.

Marty was all grins and chuckles, flying higher than a kite. Unusually though, he kept his mouth shut—at least when he wasn't shoveling forkfuls of roast gleer and baked yams into it. "This is mighty fine chow, Bessy!"

"Slow down, cowboy," Hoss warned him. "Looks as if you haven't eaten for a week. Damn you Rusco, don't you feed your crew on that rig of yours?" He lifted a grease-smeared finger my way.

"Haven't had much of good meals lately, truth be told," Marty remarked. He chewed loudly and dramatically, his grouper-like mouth hanging open.

Bessy winked and gave a honk of a laugh. "Ain't nothing more pleasing to a woman than a man with a healthy appetite, ain't that right, Hoss?"

"You betcha, Bessy dear."

I cleared my throat. I thought to take a tug on my sarsaparilla and stole a glance at Deidra who was doing her best not to chuck her plate at him.

There was a stamping of feet, a sliding door opening and closing then a long sigh as a gangly figure ducked under the low clearance. He swept off his dark brown sombrero and rubbed his tanned brow. He had a sun-raw look to him and a guileless look of innocence.

Hoss's face gleamed. "Hey there, stranger. This here's Slapper. He lives out back in the farthest outbuilding. Takes care of the derrick back of our property. Here, fella," he said heartily. "Grab yourself a chair. Sit down and eat. Bessy's saved you a plate."

Bessy got up to ladle meat onto a square platter for him.

"Thankee, Hoss. Thankee, Bessy."

The young man plopped himself down in the chair beside me and Marty. Lean, beanpole tall, a rust-colored mop of hair brushing his angular shoulders. A lazy lean to his sidle. A thin sheet of sweat beading his long, sloping forehead. He looked the image of a regular boy scout.

Hoss cleared his throat. "If you'd sauntered by at a more decent hour, Slappy, we could actually sit down and have a decent conversation sometime."

"Well you know how it is, Hoss. Out at the derrick all day. Dang thing ain't going to look after itself. Rustlers use it for parts. To nip tanks of oil when they can and Iron's told me to be vigilant." He gave us a meaningful look. "Lest I want to lose an arm, that is."

I turned my fervent gaze on him. "Iron?"

"Yes sir, that's what I said. Iron. General of the Reapers."

I mused, "We ran into a fellow out in space, helped him out in a certain...difficulty. As luck would have it, he said that if we ever want to call in a favor, then we should seek out Iron."

Slapper clapped his thighs. "You don't say? Iron? I can take you to his favorite sarsaparilla watering hole, down at Casino Row."

"Later, Slapper," Hoss intoned. "Let's all celebrate after dinner over at the local karaoke, rather than run out to the big city."

"Old Town's got nothing on Tylas, Hoss. You know that."

"Count me out." Bessy frowned and rose to gather up the dishes. "Truth is, I've got my night-watering to do. And you know how I like getting an early rise."

"I know, Bessy, I know, and I respect that."

Slapper gazed moodily at us. One eye seemed to be out of true with the other, giving him a slightly goggle-eyed look. Few visitors came to Orchard Grove and it seemed even Slapper was up for a good night of karaoke.

Hoss inclined his head. "Jet Rusco and his friends are having some ship trouble. Fact of the matter is, their hauler's over at Nanda's right now, awaiting an estimate for tomorrow. She'll likely give them a reasonable deal, I reckon."

One of Slapper's eyebrows went up. "What kind of rig you got?"

"A U56 hauler. One of the old breed salvage feeders manufactured by Bright West Star. From sometime in the last century. Her name's *Trident*. Not a very pretty lady but she gets the job done."

Slapper gave his head a thoughtful bob. His mind seemed to be working overtime. Faster than I would have expected for a country rube with an Aw-Shucks, downhome demeanor. "Why, you want to buy it?" I half joked.

"No, I ain't got money for that—just thinking of how she'd cruise out there out among the roids."

Bessy started. "Now, Slapper don't you be going getting any hare-brained ideas."

"It's just fanciful musings, Bessy. Not to worry."

"Well, let's keep it at that."

Hoss changed the subject. His nose looked a shade redder from all the ale he'd been drinking. "So, you folks up for some karaoke?"

I admit I was not, but I didn't want to be a Debby Downer.

"A bunch of us locals meet down at Smilly's at the corner. We drink beers, have a lot of laughs. Some of us get into some singing now and then. At least when we've got enough juice in us." He play-elbowed me in the ribs, thinking that was pretty funny.

Deidra fidgeted, pleading fatigue.

"Aw, come on, people," Slapper grumbled. "Let's not be party poopers."

I sucked in a breath, finally gave a slow nod. "Sounds like fun, Slappy. Lead on."

"Good."

Marty was all grins. Especially after popping another Myscol.

I quietly warned him about the volume of his intake. But you know Marty. All nods and giggles when it came to intoxicants.

I gave a heavy-shouldered shrug. Why in the end should I give a damn about his addiction? It was his life.

As it happened, we got roped into the karaoke in the big metropolis of Old Town. A place past Tiliwack. What to lose? Maybe a couple hours of sleep?

What harm could come of such an outing?

CHAPTER 8

We piled into Hoss's air speeder and took to the west as dusk was falling like a dirty blanket across the night sky. Something tugged at the back of my mind. A vague worry about what could go wrong at such a venture.

I shook it off.

Crickets sang in the grasslands. The western horizon fringed a dull red. We cruised at fifty feet off the ground with an airspeed of one fifty mph.

Old Town was nothing much to speak of. A few hundred residents, mainly a cluster of adobe-clay houses with small or no back yards. A couple of crossroads leading to nowhere. Two-lane dirt tracks grooved by four wheelers heading out to various parts of the lonely prairies.

Smilly's Bar sat on the main corner, all lit up in red and white like a pizza box. We parked our rig somewhere out back and with the other dozen or so quads and speeders we seemed to fit right in. Hoss eyed Deidra with wary introspection as we moved toward the entrance. He kept his distance from her. We pushed our way inside, past the saloon-like doors.

There was clearly a heady din in progress and a crowd gathered in a roomy, squarish hall. Larger than life photos of wranglers, gleers, beer cans, rodeos and rifles caked the walls. There came a clinking of glasses, the muffled laughter of rowdy men, the carrying voice of the DJ from the PA system. Most eyes were glued to the stage. A stocky, muscular woman was now clutching the mic on the low stage with cowboy hat angled over her sunburnt face. She had sandy curls and large fake lashes and began scratching out a mournful honky-tonk tune at the top of her lungs.

Fortunately the DJ had dimmed the volume to a level not geared to blow out everyone's eardrums. A gang of the singer's 'fans' crowded close, stomping their feet and clapping their hands in time with the beat, cheering her on.

It was nice to have an entourage.

We threaded our way through other bunched groups and past a few tables to sit perched on stools at the bar. We watched a succession of locals take the stage—the usual line of drunken wannabes doing their version of *Cry Me A River* or *Ranch Life* or *Rawhide Sunset* or some other assorted golden oldie. They gave it their best. No one could fault them for passion. Some renditions were painful to the ears, others not so bad.

Slapper left us to put in his request to the DJ.

The locals had attempted to modernize the setup. A big screen poised front and center, looming behind the singer, for the benefit of all at the back. The AI module accompanying the screen had taken the video feed, processed it, decked out the singers in star-spangled gear, teased up their hair, botoxed their lips and juiced up their bodies while putting them before a fantastic backdrop of a dramatic waterfall or high cliff or mountain peak. Very creative.

I guessed some whiz kid had installed a digital signal processor somewhere in the mix to adjust the off-key voices of the worst-sounding singers to sound much better than they were.

All part of the show.

About an hour in, I watched an alluring brown-skinned girl move up to the dance area before the stage and start up a fierce jitterbug. Crickets, could she move! Jumping and swiveling, dancing up a storm. Almost nose to jowl with the singer on stage at the mic. Entertaining, but weird. Endless energy. She was a gal in her tweens. An individual in her own world, a veritable, living breathing tour de force, gyrating, gesticulating with facial gestures to match, oblivious to everyone else. She must have been flaming on Myscol or some new street mix. Marty would know all about it.

She was an ice queen though. When one of the bolder regulars tried to cozy up to her, get an angle and some touchy-feelies, blurt out some witty come-on, she kept on dancing, ignoring him and others as if they were sand fleas. That dance routine of hers, it was savage. Naked arms snaking out in multi-armed dervishness, pelvis whirling with ample hip action. Head down, head back, throwing in a few high kicks to mix it up, just in case anyone thought there was some pattern to her calypso.

I had to laugh. There was something outlandish about it all and I was soon near rolling in laughter on the floor. Marty offered me a Myscol before he slugged back the rest of the pill box. Figured I'd be doing the sod a favor, so I took the capsule, sparing him an excess or an OD.

I offered it to Deidra but she declined. She seemed moody and taciturn, toying with her gin and sarsaparilla. She stared from the stage to the smallish dance floor, at the mixed breed of patrons, the oversize puffy ranch hats, the clinking beer mugs, the cheers, the catcalls directed at the girl. Deidra was looking without seeing. Maybe the stage reminded her of that striptease-turned-casino cathouse Sharki had put her in back on Tyrone. It was not too long ago she'd been holed up climbing poles and half naked before a bunch of ogling men.

Yeah, that would probably make me blank out too.

Marty elbowed me in the ribs. "Whyn't you try your luck with that swing-a-thing, Rusco?" He motioned toward the dancer. "There's something of a challenge for you."

"I dare you, Marty."

"Not me. Ugly mongrel like me gets nowhere with chicks like that."

"You have a point. What you think, Dee?" I brushed her on the arm.

She cast me a withering glance. "Whatever tickles your funny bone, Rus. Why don't you two gagsters tag team up, see who wins?"

Marty and I blinked at each other. Why not?

With the uninhibitedness of the pills settling in, I lumbered off my stool and made my way to the dance floor. I was just about to try something stupid when the DJ caught my eye and waved me over.

I sauntered his way, the few drinks already washing down the Myscol and mellowing me out some. I veered over to his little booth setup, to the squat, barrel-shaped guy with nose rings and ear bangles.

"You look like you know what you're doing, bro. You want to request a song?"

"Sure." I gave an affable shrug. "You got any *Axels'* tunes?"

"No."

"How about *Hungry Ghosts?*"

"Nope."

"*Roughing It Out at Hogs?*"

"Nada."

"So what about *Goon Squad?*"

"No and no."

"Shit, then, what do you have here?" I blew out a frustrated breath.

"We got some *Gilber Thorp*, some *Thorn* and *Mistletoe Country.*"

I held up a hand. "How about *Fanstar?* You must have some *Fanstar.*"

"We got *Fanstar.*" He screwed up his eyes in thought. "We also have some—"

"Skip it. Put me in for some *Fanstar*. Name's Jet."

"As you wish, Jet. Expect to be up in, about half an hour. And there's going to be a vote at the end of the night. See who's our best singer. You're in. Get your pals to cheer for you and vote. Wait, the only two *Fanstar* tunes we got are—'Fixer' and 'Filth Pig'. What'll it be? 'Filth Pig' needs—"

"Yeah, I know. Backup." I started to tell him *Fixer* then I opted for *Filth Pig*.

I whispered another name in his ear and some instructions and he nodded, his lips curved in a knowing smile.

Yay, I was going to be a karaoke star. Hell, yes! JR against the local cowpokes. Space hero goes to escape gangsters and ends up in a karaoke showdown! You just can't make this shit up.

I sauntered back to my stool, with a silly, lame grin on my face, wondering how this evening was going to play out. Probably not very gracefully. I hoped to hell that some other people would be chuckling it up as much as me before it was all over.

That said, I used to be something of a rocker back in the day. A bit crackly around the edges now, likely fudging some of the high notes and rusty with the moves, but what the hay?

Upon some more reflection, I decided it seemed a bit on the heavy side of irony for me singing up there to the tune of cheesy musical accompaniment. I say that because I used to do professional gigs back in the day. Was lead singer and played a mean synth-guitar. Gave that all up when I became an outlaw, wandering about the hinterlands of the galaxy. Old man rocker Rusco reminisces about the good old days.

I had to laugh. The lighted stage. The colored lights. The cheers. The roaring fans. High drama. Women galore.

It was a surreal moment, one of nostalgia. It was gone as quickly as it came.

I looked at Deidra and saw her slim profile caught in the gaudy red glare of the karaoke lamps. Her eyes were unusually expressive. She had that kind of stunning that could rip out your heart if you let her. Long-bodied, lean, with gentle but clear curves even in her loose spacer's outfit. She had a sexual magnetism that was hard to define, oftentimes that had me pausing for breath.

Wide hips but not too wide. Not too leggy or showy or one trying too hard. Wide-spaced gray-green eyes. A pleasing combo of all round elegant female.

I gained my seat as the lights went down, lending a coppery ruddiness to her skin.

I shook my head, chastised my romanticism. You fantasize too much, Rusco. She's just another young female of the human-animal species, like the millions out there ready to mess up your head.

I rubbed my chin and gave a wry laugh.

Marty and Slapper had been going at it, battling at the archaic table soccer game in the corner. Now they wandered back to the bar. Hoss had settled into his drink, tapping his foot to the music from time to time, beaming, enjoying the ambiance. Deidra looked bored and was looking for an excuse to quit this joint. She was on my mind and I couldn't shake her out, much as I would have liked. I found it a bit disconcerting. I was about to invite her outside for some fresh air when the dancer caught my eye again. She was lip-syncing the words of every song with powerful, almost painful passion. Not just one or two songs but all of them. It was the damnedest thing I ever saw. This tween knew them all by heart. Every word. Uncanny.

Okay, just an anomaly, Rusco, some freak of nature.

"Who is she?" I asked Slapper who hadn't said or done much this evening.

"Dunno." He too was studying her sweaty figure with interest, if not lascivious intent. "First time I've seen her."

Deidra saw who we were fixated on and scoffed. "Time to come up for air, boys—leave some fodder for the other suckers. I don't know why you're so enamored with that loon. She seems off, or something's not quite right with her."

"Or simply a woman's jealousy?" I said.

"Jealous? *Please.* You can jizz your pants all you want for all I care."

Marty grinned. He leaned in and whispered in a slurry voice, "She likes you."

I let out a whistling sneer. "She's harder to crack than a petrified nut."

Marty just kept on grinning.

I knew Deidra's crabbiness wasn't that. Sharki had done a number on her in that damn casino. Scarred her deeply.

The PA blared. "And for our next number, we have—Wait for it—the hit single, *Filth Pig*—sung by the illustrious Jet Rusco and the one and only, Deerdree!"

Marty slapped me on the back. "You're up, Rusco. Break a leg."

There came a heady applause. As no one knew who Deerdree or Rusco was, it came as a surprise. Or maybe the prairie folk were just welcoming of new talent on the stage.

Deidra stared around in odd confusion. "Wha—"?

"I put your name on a card and picked a random song and handed it to the DJ earlier without you knowing."

"Bastard!"

"You're up, Deerd." Slapper pushed her forward. "Hope you're ready."

"Ready for what? I don't even know the song. Or how to sing."

"Doesn't matter," I said. "Half these amateurs don't know either. You just read the words from the cue-card monitor in front of you."

"Sure, but—"

"Look, I'm going to go up with you, Dee. It'll be something of a duet anyway."

Marty uttered a strangled snicker.

Deidra shook with anger. "Screw that, Rusco. You can stick your duet up your ass. I'm not—"

"You are." I grabbed her arm and hauled her up onto the stage. She struggled, but I wasn't about to let her squirm her way out of it. I practically had to strongarm her the rest of the way up the steps.

She glared at me as we stood before the mics. Her face was flushed, fingers curled. Half of the crowd was having a good giggle at our supposed domestic quarrel. A little lover's spat.

"I'm going to murder you, Rusco," she seethed between her teeth.

"Good. Let's wait until after the song." I matched her fire for fire, meeting the deep, wild gleam in her eye.

But with all the heat of the lamps and all the eyes on us and the reality that we were now up there, she realized there was no way to opt out.

The DJ with the ear-bangles got the music going. The first

italicized lines slipped across the screen at our feet in green liquid motion. I hammered up the drama, jumping around with my head tilted back, hitting the high notes with an affectionate screech. The lows were not so good.

Deidra mouthed her lines, reading the script from the monitor. She clutched the mic in an eagle talon's grip. She looked ready to throttle anyone who looked sideways at her.

She flubbed some of the words but I slipped an arm about her waist and helped her navigate the difficult passages.

She was warming to it. She was holding her own, damn it, now rising to the occasion. Her voice was a bit hoarse around the edges and raw at times. But one thing she didn't like was to look a fool, so she was doing her best to improvise. To step it up. Then the weirdest thing…she suddenly underwent a personality transformation. All self-confidence and swagger. She began to strut like the dancer she had been, a stage glow settling around her.

The swarthy young groupie stood a few feet in front of us and had too upped the ante: going wild, hair flying, sweat flowing off her brow. Bare brown arms waved as she belted out the words,

"Paid my dues, now I sing the blues! Filth Pig!
Over and over, it's never better! Filth Pig!"

I belted out the next stanza,

"You only got so much you before you can't give any more! Yeah, yeah, yeah,
yeah!
There's more to come but you ain't having your heart tore! Yeah, yeah, yeah,
yeah!"

I dipped low, swung an imaginary synth-guitar back and forth, hips swiveling in rhythm with the catchy beat. The crowd was digging it, many in the front going ballistic. Deidra was on fire. Others were dancing about, catching the wave, swirling up in the energy of it.

They rode the crest, and were now trying to compete with our crazed dancer.

This scene was almost too good to be real. If I had a camera and could snatch a moment in time, this would be it.

We ended on a high note, wailing in harmony, hands in the air, with a final cheesy refrain, *"I'm a fool, you're a fool. Filth Pig!"*

The DJ did a wild wrap up and called for a show of hands.

Our duet got close to a standing ovation.

Good stuff, cheese-dog stuff, but whatever it was, it'd galvanized the crowd, got everyone on their feet, kept the beer flowing. Management was happy. Everybody loved us.

There were catcalls for an encore but Deidra had had enough. Truth be told, so had I, but not before some last-minute theatrics. Our 'duet' had stoked the dancer to a frenzy. She was sweating and puffing like a steam engine. Mouthing syllables, yelling words in a language neither I nor Deidra could understand. I don't think anyone else could either.

I clopped down the steps to allow the next singer up, but halted, squared myself before her. Even before the next number, sung by another heavyset cowgirl, a bawdy, coarse-voiced tune about love and death and all things in between, I started matching the dancer's moves, step for step, trying to imitate her high-kicking fling, a half cross between a Cossack-like dance and a Vegasian sex-walk. She seemed to be responding to my energy. I could feel a visible heat pouring off her as she stared into my eyes and tried to engage me.

A couple of ham drunks who'd been trying to get an angle on her earlier sauntered up and broke up our little ensemble. For no reason other than simple malice due to the obvious rapport I shared with her, they tried to horn in, get a piece of the action.

The dancer wasn't having any of it. She swatted at the first lug with the sombrero and the greasy smile who tried to paw-grab at her arm. Meanwhile his mate, a skull-faced baldy with bandanna and bared tattooed arms with anchors and spaceships, made a move on Deidra who was trying to escape back to her stool at the bar by

Marty.

Marty skipped in with a sweaty grin. "I think you should leggo the lady, Chief, while you have a chance."

I dropped my routine, alarmed where this was heading, and came over to assess Baldy narrowly.

"Yeah, what are you going to do about it?" he slurred.

"I'm not going to do anything about it, friend. It's more what she's going to do."

"This pussycat?" He scoffed. He grabbed Deidra's left arm and pulled her toward him. "I might take her for a spin on the dance floor. What's it to you? See if I like her dancing as much as I like her voice."

His buddy who'd kitty-cornered the dancer gave a sneering guffaw. "Yeah, Ned, let's pair up. This one's a dancer, the other's a singer. Two birds for the price of one. Pretend like we're doing our thing round the fire at the local corn roast." He laughed, a coarse gust of ale-drenched breath wafting my way that reeked of local barley malt.

The dancer punched out her elbows to block the lug's advance. Sombrero-man was slow on the draw. The movement caught him in the face and had his head snapping back. It was a movement almost too militarily precise for one of such girlishness in my opinion. Nevertheless, it brought tears stinging the man's eyes...and only served to amuse the bravo who clutched at Deidra. He tightened his grip and whispered something indecent in her ear.

Deidra twisted and smacked his cheek, ducked under his snaking arm. He regained his hold on her and pulled her in closer. "Now then, kitten, no need to fight."

She ducked out of his steely grip and elbowed him in the teeth then knuckled his eyebrow.

"Damn you, bitch!" He pawed at his left eye and came at her, all hairy paws and sweaty torso.

Deidra lashed out her right leg. Her knee caught him in the testicles. His eyes went funny, a vivid white color, as he doubled over, clutching at his groin.

I grinned and gave my head a shake. "Told you, Pops. Don't mess with her."

His buddy came over to sneer at me and try to bitchslap Deidra. I caught his wrist and twisted it, eliciting a painful yelp. He wrenched his arm free, and as his other fist came up with aim to become intimate with my face. I jerked aside, gazing at him in curious amazement.

He spat, "You guys can take Puss n' Boots here and suck—"

"Language," Marty warned. He pushed in, swinging back a calloused hand and smacked him hard in the face. The man's head whipped back and he staggered sideways a step.

"Beat it, bullet head." He licked the blood off his face. "Come back when you've grown a foot." He came charging in, thumbing his bloody nose. Marty cracked his knuckles, flexed his biceps.

It doesn't pay to get Marty angry. I winced as his hammer fist lashed out, a mallet blow that drove the man four feet backward. Yes, for a guy half wasted on street Myscol, Marty was no slouch.

I watched as the man's head smacked on the wooden floor. He was out cold.

There were growls and yells from the motley gathering. Some of his buddies surged forward. Now it was a full out hoe down. Four bravos came leaping at Marty and me, fists flying. Slappy and Hoss gulped down their drinks and swept in, shouldering blows and roars in their throats. With fists balled, sleeves pulled up, they took some of the heat for us.

I nailed one grease-bear high on the shoulder, landed a chop to his neck. He fell, gasping for air. Marty kicked out the knees of another, shoved him back into his buddies. Deidra ducked and skipped in only at the last minute to land a meaty kick in an aggressor's midriff.

Another swept in low like an ape, arms swinging wide to side-grapple me. Deidra was good with those kicks. Her boot found the man's left knee, sending him to the floor with a howl. I skull-clapped another who'd crept up behind Marty and caught him in a headlock and threw him to the floor. Marty swaggered to his feet and returned me a grim nod of gratitude.

The dancer had stepped back from the action, having prised free from her stalker. I caught a glimpse of her standing statue-still several feet back, hands tucked at her sides. She assessed me with a look of anything but loonishness. No, it was much too clinical and calculating as she edged back behind the other bar flies with an air of calm authority. I rubbed at my temples. No more the speed demon or the furious jitterbug.

The old spidey sixth sense was prickling. It was trying to tell me something, but I could not quite peg it. No matter. I had other fish to fry.

Management was leaping over the bar. In my inattention, I'd missed a vengeful left jab and was backpedaling dizzily only to crash backwards over a table.

Somebody drew a piece and aimed it at my head but Deidra kicked it away and I kitty-crawled up to get air back in my lungs. Except now, one of the feisty girlfriends or wives of the brawlers had skipped over and tried to cat scrap with Deidra.

"You, Sister?" Deidra shook her head. "You don't know what you're getting into." She caught the wrist and the woman's squawk was loud as Deidra pinned her arm behind her back and shoved her flying six feet forward.

The music had cut out, courtesy of DJ Bangles. The stocky woman still holding the mic just stood there, like a gap-toothed hound.

The next man who'd gotten Marty in a headlock made a fatal mistake. Marty's bullet head twisted aside and his horse teeth chomped down hard on the back of the man's hand. He fell back roaring, clutching at his mangled hand.

Slapper lunged to steady me on my feet. "Think it's time to skedaddle, Rusco. Unless you want to be sitting in a hospital ward for the summer?"

"No, not especially." I shook out my bleary, crossed-eyed vision and wiped a bloody lip.

Marty, Deidra and I made a hasty exit. Only too happy to do so. Out in the fresh air, Slappy and Hoss joined us, their chests heaving. The chill night air helped take the fog out of my brain.

I sucked in some more air while Hoss got the speeder hatch open and we hustled ourselves in. Slapper fired up the engine. We all tumbled into our seats and we rose high over the neon lights of Smilly's, banking east back to the ranch.

We were a pretty sullen crowd on the ride back.

A surly chill was in Deidra's mutter as she broke the silence. "I told you not to mess with that woman."

"Seems as if you were egging Marty and I on about her, if I recall. Thought you'd have been a little more appreciative after we ran interference on those two bozos for you back there."

Deidra gave a small chuckle of amusement. "You knock out a couple of pipsqueaks and expect a medal?"

I grinned. "Thought you'd be impressed."

We were still nursing our bruises when we arrived at the ranch. Bessy had kept a light on for us and the front windows glowed a soft, orange that resembled cats' eyes in the dark.

Hoss offered to put us up for the night in the parlor off the kitchen. Marty and I helped him drag in a fold out bed to complement the two couches set against the west and south walls. Marty flopped on the nearest one and rolled on his side. As much as I wanted to crash, I needed to cool off a bit. I invited Slapper to take a walk with me out in the night air. Deidra oddly decided to tag along. Hoss sat out on the porch smoking a noisome cigar. I could already hear Marty's heavy snoring through the screen door and I imagined the bully boy with an arm draped over his eyes and fingers trailing down to the floor.

We crossed the lawn, angling toward the barn. I brushed Slapper's shoulder. "You were saying you could get us to your man, Iron?"

"Tonight?"

"Not this instant, bro, relax. But soon."

"Sure. Next couple of days maybe."

I gave a brisk nod.

Hoss yelled out at us, "Mind the field shrews out there. They're nasty this time of night. Bite at the shins."

I gave him a thumb's up.

The sound of cicadas chirping from the shrubbery created an ambiance. The leaves too rustling in the ancient sycamore. Overhead a welter of stars sprayed the sky: the Muridon Belt shone a faint amber diagonally across the northern sky.

"What's that bright light up there?" Deidra asked. "It's too small to be a planet or moon. Too big to be a star."

"Terminus," Slapper replied. "A lone planetoid. We call it the *Ghost Star*."

Hoss, sensing some of Slapper's reverence, called out from across the lawn. "Only roughnecks and scutzers out there at Terminus! Steer clear of it."

Deidra pointed hesitantly 30 degrees west. "What's that other one? Tyrone? Looks half as big."

"It is Tyrone."

My memories of Tyrone City were not pleasant, given Sharki's brutality. Speaking of which, I wondered where the gangster was. Was he still out there somewhere searching for us?

Not to worry, Rusco. We'll get *Trident* up and running again, chalk up these gleerboys and gals and their hokey karaoke as a minor blip on the horizon. One day you'l look back at all this and it'll be a fuzzy dream.

CHAPTER 9

The next morning Hoss fired up the air speeder and took Marty, Deidra and me across the plains over to the salvage repair shop. Bright sunshine glared down, promising another scorcher. Not a cloud in the sky. The golden plains stretched endlessly in timeless synchrony.

"How far is it?" I asked.

"Next town over. Near Greely's Ford where the old nickel mine is." Hoss pointed to an onboard mapfinder.

I was curious as to why they called the owner 'Big Nanda'. I guess I would find out soon enough.

We landed in a rough-packed gravel yard crowded with junk speeders and other vehicles of all sizes. I saw the two *mercators* that had hauled away *Trident* lined up to the side by a squarish garage-like hangar. Two sturdy vessels were waiting for pickup. Not bad rigs, I thought—easily could have traded them for our U56. It wouldn't require any twisting of my arm to make the transaction.

Hoss left the engine running while the three of us stepped out. Our boots crunched on the gravel.

It didn't take long to find *Trident* tucked off to the side looking sorrier than a gut-shot coyote. Three grease-covered figures were staring back at us from the darkened mouth of the garage. We walked over to greet them, me all smiles and warm howdies.

"You owners of that rig?" Big Nanda tapped her knuckles under her double chin and sucked on her upper lip.

"None other."

She was no more than five feet tall and all thunder thighs and knotted biceps. Baggy coveralls. Oil smears on her bared, beefy forearms. Dark tan, hooded eyes, bushy brows and the closest to a shrewd human ape I'd ever seen.

"Warp coils are busted. It's gonna cost you."

"How much?"

"About 5 grand."

I licked my lips. It was a thousand less than I expected. "We're going to have to tuck into Tylas to acquire funds like that."

"You do what you need to do, cowboy." She shrugged, lips peeled back in a country smile. "You can choke your chicken as much as you want, just as long as you pay me my money. The deal's this, 200 up front, the rest when the work's done. I keep the ship on retainer. If something goes wrong, meaning if you people don't pay up, I say, thank you for the ship." She gave me another cheese-eating smile.

I returned a grim nod. Nanda, the sumo-wrestler's wet dream, worked a sharp deal. She was not someone just off the boat.

I drew Deidra and Marty aside. "We're going to have to rustle up some funds fast," I whispered harshly. "I don't want that bathing beauty, Nanda to snap up our ship. Any ideas?"

Marty jibed, "Might have to rent her out for a bit of fun to interested parties."

"Who, Big Nanda?" I cried.

"No, you fool, Deidra here."

"Very funny." Deidra shot him a violent look.

"No, Mar. Maybe you're onto something." I stroked my chin. "We can check out some of the joints on Tylas then—"

Deidra slapped me hard on the cheek.

I jerked back, offended. "It's not like you're thinking, Miss Shrewster. We can work some of the cons I used at the casinos in the old days. I can use you guys as extras."

Deidra's teeth bared in a skeptical grimace. "We could always also work at Hoss's."

"Doing what, shoveling shit?" Marty sneered. "It'll take us

forever."

"No, you're not listening," I grabbed at the back of my neck in frustration. "There may be a better way. As I said earlier, always chickens for the plucking."

"We don't even know the town or the people."

"Doesn't matter. Always suckers and marks on the loose."

Marty's grunt indicated he was warming to the idea. But maybe not as totally as I required. It was up to me to convince him, ease him like a newborn chick back into the hen house, until I planted the seed so deep in his little brain that he was just begging to be part of the plan.

Two days later, after a crimson-gold sunset, we set out with Slapper in Hoss's air speeder for Tylas City. On the pretext of bumping into Iron. It was a journey of no more than 60 miles, cruising at about 150 mph, which took us under a half hour.

We gave wide berth to the near-deserted spaceport tucked to the north and its huddle of space yachts and freighters. We banked down at 100 feet. I caught my first glimpse of the planetary city. A small checkerboard of lights, not organized in any grid pattern as one might expect. The place looked like an old frontier town grown up from its cowboy days into a quasi-commercial center. And still used the same routes as the old goat paths that had once made its name and its main streets. No tall buildings graced the city horizon; the highest were no more than 50 feet. Houses, shops and an impressive, large central zocalo made for a pleasing sprawl. I guessed the place housed no more than 50k inhabitants.

We banked lower and flew over the miners' mansions: large adobe brick and local slate-roofed dwellings owned by the super rich. Some poorer areas lingered to the south beyond the seedy night life central core. Hotels and run-down guest houses for itinerant workers and layabouts were its principal highlights.

Bars and casinos sprouted up in neon, their signage arcing like gaudy billboards. About a dozen other ships crowded the air space.

Several mini speeders skimmed over the streets, cruising for night action. Their little white, yellow and red taillights gave them the semblance of electric fireflies or a medley of goldfish.

I jerked my head to port and was surprised to hear the heavy drone of engines and the hiss of ship fire. I craned my neck to see two BEL eagle scouts clip by our hull. They had narrow hulls and short flared wings. One chased the other in what appeared a mock dogfight.

Slapper banked off to the right to the lighted district. "Don't worry about them, Rusco. A bit of roughhousing and friendly fire between scutzers. Some fun before a night on the town carousing with the local gangs. Their shields'll take the brunt at such low doses." He chuckled at the slant of my arched brows.

"Don't the local police frown upon such antics?" I asked.

"If there were local police to speak of."

I narrowed my eyelids.

"Yes, welcome to the wild frontier."

Marty gave an offhand snort. "No sheriffs or rangers. Hire your own goons or militia to take care of your own."

Slapper nodded. "Sums it up."

Knowing the lawlessness of the most of the galaxy, this did not surprise me.

Our first priority was to conjure up yols. I wondered about making connections with our scutzer, Iron. If we bumped into him, it'd be a bonus, but we'd be wary.

I caught Deidra in a sullen, reflective moment slumped in the back seat, arms draped around her middle as if she were not relishing the risks.

"Iron'll fix you up. You'll see." Slapper's face shone with excitement as he brought us in closer to the brazen luminosity of the red light district and the bars. His face beamed upon mention of Iron. "We'll scour New Town. We'll cruise all the joints. I know where he mostly hangs out."

I gave a curt nod. It seemed as good a plan as any.

"Two places I recommend," Slapper announced. "'The Tidal Wave' or 'The Rip'. Your choice."

"How about *The Rip*?" I suggested.

"*The Rip* it is. The first place I'd go looking for action. Some folks call it the Hellodrome. A hell-of-a-place, if you get my meaning."

Slapper circled west and I started to make out more details of the town. The place had a novo-world chill, land-and-city-of-the-free feel, somewhat dreamy and disarming in its superficial appearance of normalcy, without the oppressive presence of roving police patrols and heavy regulations. Yet I could feel the threat of danger lurking here, in the cracks of the shadowy night life and the seedy crannies.

We banked lower and blitzed the casino of interest, our curiosity piqued.

The place was enormous. A squat cinderblock, maybe 30 feet high but many times over as wide and long. Tacked up top, a larger-than-life emblem lit in crimson neon. No words like, 'The Rip' or 'Casino'. Just a single ancient galleon, like one of the old wooden wonders from Old Earth. Modern thrusters sat at her stern, hurtling her through space, with a few twinkling stars behind. The bright, brassy colors did not dispel the unsavory aura of the place.

We set down in a parking lot the size of a hopball field. I was tempted to direct Slapper to another more inconspicuous place further away from the hubbub, but I hesitated, thinking it better to stay close should we need to make a hasty retreat. Experience had taught me not to err on the side of caution.

I peered long at the ugly cinderblock and pictured a rough and ready crowd inside, packed like peas in a pod: a motley crew mesmerized by slot machines and gambling boards. Noisy, dark and fun.

We parked in a tight corner between a couple of scuffed-up speeders. We stepped out, all four of us. The slightly humid night air relaxed our limbs. We were all geared to go in together but I put an arm out to slow Slapper's eager-beaver rush.

"We go in separately, Slappy. Let's meet at the bar."

"Why? Aren't we here to see Iron?"

"We are and we aren't. Let's play it by ear."

Slapper's lips tightened, but he said nothing.

Marty gave a knowing nod. He was smart enough to know that if scams were on our minds, we didn't want to get pegged as consorting with each other.

We were out a hundred or more yards from the entrance, which was still in much shadow, when I inclined my head at Slappy. "Any weapons' check in there?"

"There's an unwritten rule: thou shalt have the right to bear arms. This is the wild west, as I told you."

"Okay." I gave a satisfied grunt. I was packing my short-barrel R1 and my fingers reached reassuringly to its smooth butt nestled at the jut of my hip. Marty and Deidra were carrying sidearms too.

Slapper's eyes roved over the parked ships. They settled on a couple of hulls with wide bellies and black-tinted viewports. "Some of Iron's scutzers. He's parked here, or at least some of his men are."

I noticed those ships Slapper motioned to had a grim black reaper logo hefting a pickaxe instead of scythe, just back of the nose and its curved fuselage.

"What's with the morbid signage?"

Slapper shrugged. "To tell friends from enemies, who knows? Look, are we here to philosophize or look for Iron? Enough of this time-wasting talk."

"Sure."

I noticed toward the east end of the building, off to the right, some renovations were in process. Scaffolding hiked all the way up to a flat-topped roof. Couple of load lifters and cement mixers. Not just repairing a bit of cracked concrete, but installing a whole new set of pilings.

I let Marty and Dee go first, told them to wander about a bit in different directions then meet back at the bar. I counted 50 steamboats before I pushed off myself, past the front glass double doors where I was hit with a wall of noise.

The place was rocking; I reckoned about 250 to 300 people wandering about. High, cathedral ceilings. Rancheros playing darts. Brassy women over by the craps tables. A couple shooting lewd stares at two men in oversize cowboy hats who they seemed to be sizing up for a grease-down.

For such a big place it seemed mighty stuffy. The air buzzed with the intensity and glitter of lively activity. There were the age-old gambler addictions, the deep laughter of gamesters and cons rubbing shoulders, the staccato clink of glasses, the bawl of an unhappy drunk who'd lost hard and who hadn't the heart or courage to break the sad news to wifey and kiddies that the family farm was forfeit. Truly a carny atmosphere rather than a man's night-out-on-the town place. I scratched my head, felt the stubble on my jaw. I bit back the sour taste in my mouth. I tilted my light brown sombrero—the one Hoss'd given me as a cheap souvenir from the farm, and psyched myself up to make the best go of it, for whatever it was worth.

I prodded my way on through the throng and as I made my way to the bar, I pondered the fact that on the surface, it could have been any casino from one end of the galaxy to the other. But there was an even seedier flavor of corruption here and lost fortunes burning brighter than most joints. I could hear it echoed in the harsh jangle of the betters' voices, the forced animation of their exaggerated gestures: the promise of bright riches to be had under the colored lights and wall of noise, with an equal undertone of exploitation and greed hanging heavier still. A drunken man's worst nightmares, one who loses everything in one bet on a bad night.

Money moved here. The joint was run by some of the scutzers we'd heard of, the hombres high up in the food chain. It had all the hints and trappings of organized effort, the regular workings of a money chain making its way to the proper channels. Also the place where they'd take you out in the back and break your legs if they ever caught you working a system.

The prospect sent a thrill through my bones. The hell-bent-for-leather part of me dared to defy these cheeseheads.

I grinned. The trick, of course, was not to get caught.

The lulling drawl of country music piped through the sound system was starting to annoy me. I discerned a bandstand to the far left, obscured now by dark velvet curtains. No band tonight—I guessed it must be a side attraction, so as not to distract the gamblers from their addictions: the pumping of much money into the voracious machines and piling chips onto gaming tables.

I met the others over at the bar as planned. Slapper's head was bobbing like a bird dog's looking for Iron. A young lady on elevator heels shoved a complimentary drink in my hand. She pulled two more from the tray she was wielding to give to Deidra and Slapper the instant he'd turned to signal the bartender. The waitress had ocher-tinted skin and was almost as tall as I was, but she shooed on by with her long legs before Marty had a chance to grab one off the tray himself.

"Where's Iron?" I grunted at Slapper.

Slapper took a big swig from his complimentary sarsaparilla. "Not here, is he?"

"Very witty, Slap. Now I thought you said he'd—"

"I'm not his keeper. Nor his shoe-shiner or valet either. It's still early, Rusco. He might show."

I chewed my lip. This simplified things. Plan B. I was slightly disappointed in Slapper, but then the no-show was not his fault.

Slapper inclined his head, jaw outthrust. "If we can track him down, I wouldn't be surprised if he offers you a commission."

"What's the catch?" Marty's frown deepened.

"Meaning?"

"What stake do you have?"

"You got a ship, right?"

I glared. "Yeah, we got a ship."

In one gulp he downed his drink. "That's all needs be said. You gotta take me with you. I need off this planet."

I rubbed my jaw. Did we really need another wiseass on our junker, even if we could get it repaired? Likely just more baggage. We could maybe use friend Slapper as some extra manpower, if it came down to a cat scrap in some back alley or a cheap dive out in the boondocks. He could hold his own, at least with fists, booze and information.

"Can you work the controls? Like fire port?"

Slapper looked at me as if I were insulting him. "Do dogs have fleas? Iron'll show. We got all night."

"Sure, Slapper, sure," I said. I took a sip of my complimentary drink.

I noted management had changed most of the games from the standard fare of craps and roulette to three large rainbow-colored wagon wheels with numbers and motifs on them that suckers could bet on before they could spin. Some water chutes too, bearing colored balls and sailboat-like toys that cascaded down a beguiling obstacle course to land in a pool littered on the bottom with numbered squares and assorted coins. Exotic goldfishes swam about. I was still wondering how the betting process worked, but it wasn't rocket science. It was unique, I'd give them that. Creative buggers. Mixing it up to guard against wise-guys like me working systems on the tried-and-trued games. I cracked a smile.

Slapper took me aside and whispered in an excited voice. "There, over at the wheels. A couple of Iron's men. Reapers. You'll want to pay attention to them. I've a mind to go over, pay my respects, catch wind if Iron's coming."

I looked over and saw two heavy-tattooed, biker-type bruisers in blue leather jackets with chains and studs at wrist and hip. One had a brush cut, the other a heavy mustache with long goatee.

"Good plan, Slappy. Glad that we have you around to choreograph things."

Slapper inhaled a sharp breath. He seemed to take offense at the remark. "You'll want to tread lightly around those guys. Iron's a moody man."

"No worry, Slapper, I'm not out for glamour."

His head gave a little bird-like shake. "You've been warned."

"Not getting a good feeling about this, Rusco," Deidra murmured.

"I got this covered, Deidra. Relax."

CHAPTER 10

While Slapper went over to talk to our Reaper friends, I made a mental inventory of the surroundings. I paid no heed to the slick series of crap tables upgraded for the new century. Too much probability and math theory required. The more bets you made, the higher chance the house'd clean you out. Unless you had horseshoes up your ass. Better to play the games of bluff and bluster with the moneyed guests in the back rooms. There was a world of human adversaries there from which to chose from with foibles and foils.

In casinos like this there seemed to be a lot of activity with purpose. I'd seen it in dozens of other outfits across the star systems. A certain practiced fervor of placing bets, knocking back tall boys with muffled laughter and guffaws and cheap puns and jokes on the side with all the raw, fun-time melodrama to go with it. But under the glitter and glam, there's something dingy and dead about it all. The soulless ritual of man against machine, man against the unseen house which never loses. With plenty of intrepid folk daring to try their luck again against the house, the ones who dared to disbelieve.

I scanned the upper tiers and tried to pinpoint where in those gloomy shadows, spyholes existed. Where the cameras trained down or some shrewd operators telescoped on persons of interest. I noticed the stance of aggressive-looking undercover bouncers posted here and there—some of them were gambling, or pretending to gamble, whether losing or winning, it did not matter. From loud boys to quiet easy boys, posing as friends of friends, having a few drinks and yukking it up with the crowd, trained to be on the watch for trouble or cons. Easy for experienced eyes to spot, but they didn't fool me. Once a person was pegged as working a system, one or more of those 'friendly' people would casually walk up, escort you outside to the parking lot for a date with their boots and their fists. Worse yet, a date back at some dank corridor or back room for a fireside chat of illimitable horror with the manager.

The bigger the installation, the more fluid the enforcement was. It would take a crafty con to hose this place for even twice the yols he came in with, or even chisel 5C off some of the regular sharks gadding about the back rooms. I had my doubts whether I was such a slick operator, but with Iron nowhere in sight, and me not relishing traipsing all over town looking for him, I began to grow impatient. Such is the simplistic binary logic that leads a man to doom.

I conversed in low tones with Deidra and Marty and we decided to skip the wagon wheel gimmicks and the water runs and meet at the gaming tables to the side where the big fish hung out. The place where the big money was to be made. The wheels were for the small-money five and dimers.

I turned my attention upon this quieter section of the casino. Set against the west wall were several tables where groups of 4 to 8 people could play, invariably throwing dice or dominoes or dealing cards. There was subdued light here, like a hooker's parlor. Quieter music too, an ever-present quasi gloom intimating privacy and indiscretion, but allowing gamblers to bet big and loose. Behind the tables, in the darker shadows, loomed a steel door, locked shut.

"There's where we want to be," I whispered to Deidra. The area was roped off, behind which a navy blue-suited monitor stood in polished black shoes. He only let approved people pass. Beyond the roped area, I saw 4 tables holding 5-7 players each.

Deidra mused, "Something tells me we can't just waltz in there, Rusco, without an invitation."

"How about my fist for an invitation," Marty sneered. He planted a heavy fist in his palm and began to hunch his way forward.

I held him back. "Relax. It hasn't come to that yet, Tiger, and that won't work here. We have to split up, so it doesn't look like we're together. I'll start off at the warm-up tables over there, then worm my way into the VIP section, if I can. You guys go—"

"Rusco, whyn't we just stick to the small fry section at the water chutes," Marty said, "earn enough to—"

"No. It'll take all night over there. Be lucky to make 100 yols. Better that we aim big. At the highballer tables—one win and we've got enough pocket change to pay off Nanda and hold us for a few months while we get our feet back on the ground, make some headway in some other star system. We could be eating steak dinners every night, Mar, whatever else we want."

His lip curled, cheering at the prospect. "Okay, but if things go sour—"

"They're not going to go sour, relax. Not if we do this right. Look—" I slapped him on the shoulder "—you go piss around at the water wheel. Make it good, blow some money, show some anger, some astounded fury, make it look less obvious that we're here to score some big coin."

"Screw that," Marty hissed back at me. "You fuck around with that shit, not me. I wanna—"

"No, not you. You're too direct. You'll blow our cover. Remember that con that went bad on Vestra?"

His jaw sagged.

"One wrong fist or bootheel and the house of cards comes crashing down. Our con is basically this: we pretend to be something we're not. Businessmen, entrepreneurs, rich cats out for some fun. Deidra, you're the decoy. Always some blowhard out there with a bucket of cash waiting for us to give us all his chips."

"Who's going to give you all his chips, Rusco?" Marty whined.

"Not me. Her—" I jerked a thumb at Deidra. "She schmoozes some of those fatcats over there with her feminine wiles. Charms her way into their inner circle while I swarm in and scoop up the spoils."

"That easy, huh?"

"Yes, easy as taking candy from a baby, Mar."

He gave an ear-to-ear smile, bordering on a grimace. And I knew

Marty liked the idea.

"Like that guy—" I did a little head roll toward a heavyset, square box of a man tucked in the shadows at the head of the second table. He wore a posh blue and red plaid suspender and pants combo with white shirt and bow tie, black shoes like an old-world plantation owner. Little gold pins and decorations like medals stuck on the front that tinkled when he moved. Real classy guy.

"See, Fatso there looks like he's got an eye for the ladies and money to burn. Here's the deal—Deidra you go in over there, pretend to be busted—you know, all broke and teary-eyed. You had a good streak, then blew it. Fat Stuff'll be making moon eyes at you and offering drinks, offering to cover you, expecting a little something back in return." I grinned and gave her the wink.

She winced but I wouldn't let her speak. "Play it up, Dee. You know the drill."

She wrinkled her nose. "That hog? Having his ham hands all over me makes me want to puke."

"I doubt it'll come to that."

"You doubt?"

Slapper had returned, his eyes gleaming, his lanky body near squirming with restlessness. "Iron's not here. At least not yet." The youth's lips parted in a scowl. "You know who that is over at the table you're eyeing? Brex, Captain of the Beryl Bratts."

"So? I'm supposed to care?"

"No…" He frowned slowly. "Just saying." He knuckled his forehead, flustered, trying to blubber out some excuse as if rationale for Iron's absence. "What's Brex doing here? Him and Iron are sworn enemies. Brex is one third owner with the boss, Piggy, and some other bigwig nobody knows about. But with connections to *Damocles*, shadiest mining company this side of Terminus."

"Which means more money in his pocket," Mar said.

"Oh joy," muttered Deidra.

Slapper took a gulp of his newly-ordered drink.

I frowned. "How is that Iron can even set foot in this place if he and Brex're ready to tear each other's throats out?"

Slapper flipped a palm. "It's an odd custom. The casinos are neutral ground. The Captains perform their little ritual of civility and save their battles for space."

"Sounds very professional," Marty said.

My frown deepened. "Also illogical."

"It is. If it were me, I'd kill that bastard Brex first chance I got."

"Well, seems all's not well in the little henhouse," Marty mused.

Slapper nodded gloomily. "All's I'm trying to say, Rusco, you'd better be wary of that man. Have a care."

"Care's for old ladies, kid," Marty grumbled.

Slapper looked away. "I say you're playing with fire."

"That's our middle name, Slappy, don't you get it?" Marty drawled. "Be a good boy and go introduce us to Brex, or better yet buy us a round of drinks." He laughed.

"Make that sodas," I grunted.

Slapper screwed up his face in a frown. "You guys insane? You want to get killed or laughed out of town?"

"Just do it." I whacked him on the arm and he sauntered off. I shouldered Deidra forward. "Off you go too, Dee. Time to earn your keep."

"Wait," I grabbed at her arm. "Introduce me as Retro. Jive Retro. If you get in there, I should come to your table soon enough."

"You're joking, right?"

"No, I'm not." I grinned. "I'm an old friend, acquaintance. Be creative."

She glared back at me. "Sure, Rusco. Or Retro. As you wish. It's your head in a noose."

"Another thing, If you catch a glance of a big hand by the big boys when you're all snugged up close comfy cozy, blink twice with those gorgeous eyes of yours and say something about the heat in here."

She gave a curt nod and sashayed over. Not surprisingly, she slipped by the monitor at the roped-off area without a hitch. The scowly stuffed suit initially hooked out an arm to stop her, but she bent and whispered something in his ear until he was all grins and waved an arm to let her pass. That was the advantage of being a curvy woman. Good looking, flirty women were all exempt from certain 'rules' and 'regulations'. They could always jump the gate.

Slapper returned with our drinks, his face sullen and curled into a somber mask. When he saw Deidra past the rope, he grumbled, "Don't want any part of this, Rusco."

I tried to coddle him, but it was clear he'd caught the drift of what we were up to.

"My advice: let's clear this place and look for Iron at *The Tidal Wave*."

"Later, Slapper. We got some things happening here."

He scratched his ear. "Good luck with that. Gonna go and try my luck at the craps tables. You're on your own."

I shrugged. "You do that."

I was somewhat relieved. Slappy didn't have it in him for these cons. Better he stayed back at the speeder like a good little boy. Couldn't fault him. The boy was more straight shooter than any of us.

CHAPTER 11

While Marty was working the wheel and Deidra was strutting her stuff, it gave me time to revisit my strategy. I was not going to get by rope boy that easily. It'd take a little more work than what Deidra had accomplished in 30 seconds. Even with some funds scavenged from the cheap seats this side of the rope and some preplanned gambits, it might not be enough. What then? A diversion? Some muscle?

Wouldn't work.

A distraction gave me pause. An older woman had snorted with disgust at the slot machines she was working. I saw her saunter back out to the common area. She passed me and stared hard at the floor as if she could not break stride fast enough to get out of here. A vape stuck in the side of her mouth. She mouthed curses, grousing about her night of bad luck.

Tough break, sister, the world's a rough place.

It gave me a sudden idea.

I caught up with her and headed her off before she took the last steps to the exit. She stopped and surveyed me with red-eyed suspicion.

I gave her a winning smile, trying not to look too sleazy or desperate. She had short dirty brown hair, cropped short at the ear. A sombrero was perched on her oval of a head, a small frayed one, pulled tight at her jaw by a thin leather cord. She was not a small woman. I caught the pungent odor of sweat and cheap perfume waft off her dry rouge-pasted skin, almost as subtle and appealing as buck musk.

"How'd you like to earn some yols, Sister?"

I saw dirt caked under the nails as keen dove-gray eyes sized me up and flashed a suggestive look at my crotch. Whether due to the alcohol in her system or her frank nature, I wasn't sure.

"Nothing like that, Luv," I said with a forced smile.

"So what then?" She frowned. "You in for a threesome? Want me to scout you out a man?"

She was imaginative. I liked that and I resisted the urge to box her ears. I just smiled. "Let's say you come back in exactly 30 minutes. I'll be sitting over there at the warm-up tables. Probably yukking it up with the other men, maybe winning a bet or two, maybe losing. If I give you a signal, say a tug on my left ear, you come running and break up the party, you hear?"

She flicked me a conspiratorial wink. "What's in it for me?"

"Enough to merit your time."

"What if you don't give me a signal?"

"Then you take the money I give you and walk out 20 yols richer." I pulled out some coins and waved them before her face. She reached out a calloused hand, but I pulled back before her grubby fingers could snatch them.

"Remember, you don't know me," I warned.

"Yeah, yeah, nobody knows anybody." Her voice cracked, her lips pursed. Deep pits cratered the round cheeks, likely the aftermath of a bout of teenage acne. "Help me out here, friend. Give me some details. I'm not getting a clear picture. Is this some kind of weird hustle?"

I rocked back on my heels. She was not a pretty woman. Dark circles ringed her small, suspicious eyes. A gaudy bracelet manacled her left wrist. Several large dark red and dull green rings collared the fingers of the right hand.

"Think of it like girls' night out. A drunken blind date gone wrong. You pretend you're tanked. Put on your best karaoke voice, sing some loud tunes, start up a fuss, lots of schmooze and sass. Sit in the first guy's lap, talk in a brassy voice, whisper some lewd and imaginative hints in his ear. Get him to buy you some drinks, a beer, soda whatever. It's not an exercise in military exactness. You getting the picture?"

"Yeah, so, what's the angle?"

"If I told you, it might implicate you. Better not to know."

"Oh." She nodded. She stuck the vape back between her lips and puffed. A ruff of coarse hair dangled into her eyes, which she quickly brushed away with a cough in her throat.

"Ham it up," I said. "Make it look real."

"Why?"

"Let's just say it's a private joke of sorts, a bit of personal amusement among old friends."

"Right."

"Get security to escort you out, if need be. I likely won't be sticking around to backslap it up with you or the others." I gave her the 20. "A hundred more if you do a good job. Remember, you don't know me. Never saw me."

"I get it." With a last long stare, she turned back toward the slot machines.

I was hoping the carrot of an extra hundred would inspire her to follow through, rather than stiffing me the twenty.

The music was getting tired. Three-chord monotony with cheesy lyrics. The twang and thump of lukewarm instruments that wore at the nerves. Instruments out of style a half century ago.

Suck it up, Russie. You getting old?

I chanced to look back at the wagon wheels by the bar, seeing if Marty was crushing it with his bare hands.

I recognized the oval face at once. The hair was blond this time, the skin toned a lighter shade perhaps, almost olive-white, but it was sure as rain, her.

Prickles formed at the back of my neck. The girl from the karaoke bar. The dancer.

An eerie feeling of deja vu hit me like a hammer. Of being in some place from some time long ago.

No.

Coincidence?

Unlikely. My sixth sense was pinging, but I could not figure out what the connection was.

I made quick steps to seek her out, but something must have pricked her radar for she'd turned on her heel and merged into the crowd without a trace.

I got to the place of milling people with held breath, but she was nowhere in sight. I looked around the restrooms, the bar, the slot machines, the water tubes but there was no sign.

A ghost, as if she had never been. A trick of the light? Maybe I'd just imagined her?

No, Rusco, don't be a fool.

I recalled the relaxed look on her face, the full lips, the hot blue eyes and the shapely haunch and thighs. Attractive in the best of ways, but harboring a spark of mysterious, dangerous energy. She defied profiling. A certain sensual vacuity, if not indifference remained in the expression of the eyes. A contrived detachment. Very incongruous in the hell-bent dancing jitterbug of the other night.

A hand plopped down on my shoulder. I whirled, ready to pounce, only to see Marty.

"What's up, Rus, lost your calculator-watch?" He thrust a drink in my hand.

"Damnedest thing. Remember that manic tween, the one back at the karaoke bar in Old Town? The crazy dancer?"

"Yeah, so what?"

"She was here. I just spotted her."

"No way."

"Yes way."

He swore and wet his lip. "So, what does it mean?"

I shrugged. "Could be anything." I spread my palms. "Following us? Keeping tabs. A stalker?"

I touched the post where she'd last been, the same curved metal around which she'd wrapped a seductive arm as she blew smoke from her vape.

Almost at once, a sudden chilling idea formed in my brain. For a frozen instant I was pushed back in time to that place in the opulent marble Temple on Riga. The Temple of the Moon. Another woman, a young acolyte, had pulled at my arm, pleading with me to tell her the whereabouts of the *artifact*, the one that I secretly carried in my body—the one I was charged to keep and guard secret. That woman I'd thought an ally, but she was anything but.

So could this other girl—

An icy hand clawed along the base of my spine. Ghosts of the past. I'd acquired for some time the power to see the pattern in the past and future. The *weave* as they called it. A gift given to me, and taken from me by the alien artifact. The plaything of the Masters. Some nonsense about me being the 'Chosen One'. Now, a sudden flash of insight hit me that the artifact's power was returning. It had just lain dormant. For years, I'd been running, thinking I'd lost it. Trying to stay away from powerful forces that wanted to recruit me, or see me dead. I thought I'd been careful, but maybe not careful enough.

I thrust the train of thought from my brain and branded myself a lunatic. No, it was too wild a conjecture to entertain.

And yet...

Marty's rough hand came sliding down on my shoulder again. "Fat Boy's looking a bit antsy there, Rusco. Best get back to the tables before Deidra loses her momentum."

"Yeah, good plan, Marty." I gave a quick nod. "Keep your eyes open."

He slurped his whiskey then sauntered back to the wagon wheel.

CHAPTER 12

I moseyed back to the warm-up tables. Sure enough, looking past the rope in the shadowy interior, I saw it had taken no prodding for Fat Boy to warm up to Deidra. He was leaning in his chair, teetering toward her, talking big, slapping bright red chips on the table.

I tore my gaze back to the first group of men at the tables on my side of the ropeway. Four rough-bearded fellows were playing a version of Dice and Dominoes. One throw to get the numbers, the second to see what lined up. Snap and rattle of dice. Tinkle of dominoes. Tip of glasses. The cheers rose heavily when there was a big win; the grumbles and whines surged mournfully when there were losses. I gave my little foursome a cursory glance and inserted myself without ado. I did my jolly routine, humoring them with 'Geez guys, life is hard when Little Minnie, my partner, just left me for a wandering scutzer, took all the money and now I'm just out to booze it up and maybe win some dough, but don't care if I blow some too'.

They were more than happy to share their table, take my money, clink glasses, engage in some backslapping. Especially when I started to babble on and lose at some simple bets that even a primary grader should not have lost.

Boy, was I a card.

I snatched the odd glance over at Deidra. She had a glow on her face and looked pleased. I too was pleased to see further evidences of her softening up Fat Stuff. Little touchy-feelies here and there on the arm and some reciprocal snickers and grins by old Fat Stuff himself. Some louder than necessary guffaws and red-cheeked grins from the other good old boys at the table.

I couldn't see Marty. I was hoping he'd stayed the hell away from violence and trouble at the wagon wheels. Only took one little trigger incident to have fists flying.

A dozen hands had gone by and I'd slowly accumulated some winnings. I was up to 450 in chips, more than what I'd expected in that space of time. Maybe I hadn't lost my touch.

"I'm out," wheezed a big sandy-haired fellow. He tossed down his dominoes in disgust. He turned to me, his cheeks red from too much sarsaparilla. "That's some neat purple hair you got, friend. Once you get over this Minnie thing, you think you might try taking up locating?"

"Maybe. My cousin was in it some time back. You a locator?" I asked.

"Was, once."

I nodded sagely. "I might try it for a little while. See what it brings."

"Yeah, which outfit you thinking, Gravediggers?"

"Couldn't say. Heard the Reapers are a fair choice these days."

The big man upended his sarsaparilla and winced. "There's been a rash of incidents out in the roids."

"Oh?"

"Skurgs have gotten wind of the fruits of our labors, so to speak. Coming in like sand fleas. From what I hear, they could be a major problem in a year or two. Who knows where they're coming from."

His smiley-faced comrade piped up, "Sonni ran into a threesome off the Pegasoid Roid. Near got his head blown off, his ship scuttled."

The news jarred me.

"Ah, shit, Lace. You're a better story teller than a domino player."

"No, really, Quin. They scoop up claims, those that have the brains to waylay cunning men and the ability to communicate in our language. They register their finds at the claims office. Others scavenge men and ships like there's no tomorrow, grubs all around.

Who knows where they take them?" He took another pull on his whiskey, grimacing.

I had an idea where the Skurgs took them, but I could not speak of that, unless I wanted to blow my cover. A cold chill ran down my back. "I might reconsider scutzing, after hearing all this talk of Skurgs."

"Just don't get yourself on the wrong side of them," the other growled. "We're from the Scags, way out on the fringe. We try to drive those bastards out whenever we spot them."

The other jeered. "Like blow their spike-bedeviled ships to kingdom come."

I shook my head in startlement. "Sounds like you boys're building up for a full blown war. You don't want to go messing with Skurgs."

"No kidding, friend. But it's getting like it's not possible to avoid them."

I changed the subject. "Why you call that other outfit Gravediggers?"

He gave a bassoony laugh. "It's an old joke, you know. 'Gravediggers', cuz so many of them died out there on those uncharted roids prospecting, they might as well have been digging their own graves."

I turned my head. There was a commotion over by the water wheels. The sound of a shrill warning beeping, like somebody had set off an alarm. A troublemaker must have violated protocol. Who could it be? I could not deal with the fact that it might be Marty.

A half hour was up and right on cue, sombrero lady strolled over and leaned her hefty haunch on the edge of the table, busying herself with her vape. I tugged at my ear—remembering my instructions, *Make a scene, get yourself escorted out...*

She started jabbering on, then plopped her big behind in the nearest man's lap, working up a big fuss. She did all of what I asked for and more. Just the diversion I needed. If I could have paid the lady 8000 yols for the sweet way she did it, I would have.

But I was getting ahead of myself. I slipped away like an eel.

Some of the security staff were in the midst of hustling over.

Something must have alerted our rope monitor for his head jerked my way. A flutter of fabric maybe or my purple hair dangling, not perfectly hidden under Hoss's goofy sombrero.

"Push off, buddy," he grunted. "These are reserved seats. Only the big players."

"Don't see any sign saying so."

"Minimum bet's 100. Doesn't look like you can even manage 20."

I flashed four hundred in chips in his face. "That enough for you?"

He reached out to spot check the fifties and I snake-thrust out thumb and two fingers and clutched his left elbow, digging hard into a nerve. I thrust the chips in my pocket then grabbed his other elbow and found a nerve there too that had him buckling at the knees. His face twisted in pain. I released my grip, tucked my other arm around the small of his back and pressed on another pressure point back of the neck. I hissed in his ear, "A word of warning, friend. A world of more pain is coming your way if you don't let me past this rope. You're not going to squeal to any superintendent or jackass manager or this pain is coming back three-fold. For your time, maybe I'll give you one or two of these red chips here and you can have some fun down at the water wheel. Sound good?"

He opened his mouth as if to squeak out a warning to some buddy bouncer, but I dug fingers deeper into the nerve chain back of his neck and the man nearly passed out.

I let up and he gave a vigorous nod, gasping.

"Attaboy."

I marched on and when I looked back, the monitor was smoothing out his arm, face ghost pale, and massaging his elbow under the trim blue jacket. Sweat trickled down his sunken cheeks.

That martial arts-shiatsu trickery I'd learned back on Kramala 2 had come in handy.

I was almost 500 to the good, which I could now use to reel in some bigger fish. Was it enough?

As I approached the second table, Fat Stuff was wearing a brighter color on his cheeks. His medallions seemed tipped a bit higher on his flabby chest than I remembered.

Deidra sat perched with a coppery glow about her. She was the life of the party, beaming and twisting and jawing on, flirting with the other men at the table, the good old boys.

She was an effective enough distraction to be used to disarm these sharks, but I'd never used her before in a game like this and I wasn't sure whether we could work in harmony. The heavy lifting was up to me.

I plopped myself down in the padded seat opposite Fat Stuff and tipped my hat at them all. "Evening, Gents. What game we playing?"

They all glared at me.

"Who are you?" Fat stuff bawled, "How'd you get past Bask?"

"Oh, Bask was just plum peachy to let me through.

"Yeah, why's that?"

I shrugged. "Showed him my stash."

Deidra chimed in, "This here's Mr. Retro. A fine gentleman who I met some time ago at the wheel. He spotted me some chips and a drink when I was having a streak of bad luck. I don't even think I paid you back, did I, Mr. Retro?"

"No, don't think you did, ma'am. Wasn't going to remind you."

Fat Stuff glowered. "Don't seem to recall you, Mr. Retro, and I've been here most nights."

"I'm not here that often."

"We play a sharp game of Shiastro here, Mr. Retro. Novas and Deuces high, Stars random. Our first bet is capping at 8 grand and starting at 200. Can you handle that?"

"I think I can."

He gave me a quick, hard look. "Well then, giddyap. Ease back in that chair, Mr. Retro. We can always use more money in the pot."

"Call me Jive."

"No, think I'll call you Mr. Retro, if you don't mind. And you can you call me Mr. Alf. How does that sound?"

"Sure, Mr. Alf." I shrugged. "All the same to me."

He lifted a pudgy hand. "This here's Davish and that there's Captain Konrad."

"Gentlemen." I gave them a two-fingered salute.

They returned me wary nods. Konrad was of middle age with a ruff of ginger hair and bushy beard. Mournful folds of skin padded his jowls. Davish was only slightly younger, a wiry-built man with black hair clipped to the bottom of the ear. He had a squirrel-like quickness to his movements, the turn of head and the fingering of his chips.

Deidra clapped her hands. "Well, Geez! Looks as if I'm out of chips again, Alf. Be a dear, whyn't you spot me some more? I'd like to give back some to my friend here. I feel bad I couldn't pay him back that night. Think this is going to be an exciting evening!" She rubbed her hands briskly.

I grinned. Good old Deidra.

Alf assumed his usual amiable self. "Well, how can we deny a good samaritan like Mr. Retro here a place at our table. That, and a sizable stash of chips?"

I grinned more heartily. Why indeed?

The big man counted out the chips: five big black hundreds. He pushed them with slow ceremony over the plush green-clothed table to my side. "Have a care that you hold on to these, Mr. Retro. They tend to slip away like greased wheel bearings in a hailstorm in the thick of the moment."

"I'll take that into consideration."

Deidra's face was pasted with a cat-like grin. Her cheeks were puffed out, flushed like an artless schoolgirl. I marveled. The woman was a natural at this art. I was admiring her from a distance, secretly proud of her for her flair for the dramatic, though somewhat jealous of her flirting with these weasels.

There was some rough words exchanged at the table next to us, some coin transactions rendered and chips changed hands. A hulking man with barrel-chest, the one Slapper had referred to as 'Brex', rose, stroked his beard and with a rugged, cheshire grin, came and settled into the chair beside Captain Konrad. Eased is a better word for it, like a big lazy tiger—and Konrad did his best, all deference and nods and head bows, to push his chair away to accommodate the burly man.

Alf gazed ponderously at the stack of chips that Brex had laid down. "Well, Brex, I see you've been doing well."

"Can't complain." The man snapped his jaw and inclined his head. "Iron never showed?"

"Nope. Haven't seen him yet."

Iron? I licked my lips.

Brex made no comment. He flicked a hundred down to roll into the center of the table. Decked out in scutzer's garb, a long trenchcoat of black buffed leather, he was an impressive sight. "Start." His big gray-brown eyes rolled in my direction. There was something more than curiosity there. A suspicion bordering on menace. He hadn't inquired as to my presence. Yet.

I noted his fine-chiseled square jaw gave his face character. He was handsome in a rugged way. But it was the steely, hawk eyes that signaled 'mess with me at your peril'. Proud, belligerent, ruthless. Where Alf was all soft, fatty tissue, Brex was hard brawn and muscle. A natural tan showed on his arms bared to the elbow; also in the round, full cheeks. The half-inch brown, whiskey-colored whiskers showed no gray. Though the lines crisscrossing brow and jowl were starting to show. The clear gray-brown eyes rarely blinked. A proud, stubborn man, I concluded. I could see the uncompromising nature writ in his face and what was to be the beginnings of a rocky association between us.

Big Alf motioned for a round of drinks. Some curt and laconic introductions meanwhile were traded. The waitress flitted by in her skimpy getup, pom-poms and elf-princess red fluff around her middle. I opted for a plain sarsaparilla. Deidra took some gin while the others opted for double-shots of the local rot-gut rye whiskey.

The first round went predictably badly. The dominoes did not line up as nicely as I would have liked. I lost my big blind and was now down 80 yols from the 950 I'd vowed to keep quite solid.

Shiastro was a stepped-up variation of the game me and the scutzers'd played at the warm-up tables. Instead of rolling dice, players were dealt cards then pulled dominoes from a stack on each draw from the deck. A player could use the numbers on the dominoes to add to his or her hand: the only catch being that when rivals interlocked their dominoes with yours, they could block your face values and in the end, only those numbers on the outer edges of the domino chain could be used to complement hands.

Deidra put on a big show of losing after she'd dropped ten fivers and three twenties. Big Alf was all charm and benevolence. He put a beefy hand on her shoulder to comfort her. "Don't pout there, doll." He slid her over two more big black chips and some twenties in change. "Always room for a pretty girl at our table, ain't that right, Brex?" He nudged her in the ribs.

Deidra swept a wisp of hair back from her brow to block Big Alf from making another pass.

"Sure thing, Alf." She put a hand on his fingers and gave it a squeeze. "You're the best." She ran a fingertip suggestively over the back of his knuckles.

I studied his lascivious frog-like grin with a detached resentment. He was all salamander eyes and warty cheeks. His oily manner was fueled by the slimy assumption that the more she lost, the more she would owe in bedtime favors in the heat of the night.

I chomped back my ire and thought of the brighter future: hosing these shysters for every yol they had while I got away with the girl.

Brex seemed to study Alf's interplay with something of lazy, clinical interest but I knew there was a darker undertone of emotion simmering under the surface: a desire for the girl. He was all eyes for Deidra. Had been the moment he sat down at the table, entranced by this tall, sweet, flirty strawberry blonde popping up out of nowhere. Though the bastard was trying not to show it.

I nursed a silent sneer. It wasn't all so simple. They would get their dues, when all their chips were in my pocket.

Who are you trying to kid, Rusco? You just lost another 150. What universe are you living in?

Brex quirked his elbow toward my sarsaparilla. "Mr. Retro, you not a drinker?" His tone assumed a nasty sweetness that I did not like.

"Trying to abstain." I took a frugal sip of my drink. "At least when I'm at the table."

"Smart man."

Deidra blinked her eyes in girlish innocence.

"Well, we can order you a mango lassi or a soda water, next time round, if you'd like. Wouldn't want you to get too thirsty."

I gave an aw-shucks smile. "It is a bit stuffy in here, Brex, and I appreciate the sentiment."

The cards and dominoes were dealt. I saw twin Roids in my hand and a pair of Comets. Dominoes slipped from the other player's hands. I saw two of them matched the Comets in my hand. That was a good turn. I knocked the table for a pass, smiled as I bluffed my way through, drawing attention away from my killer hand. I ended up winning 1200 in that round. The last cards and dominoes turned over by the weasel-faced dealer Davish, had fallen in my favor.

Alf chuffed out a sound of disgust as he forfeited seven of his hundreds plus some in change.

Konrad gloated. "Looks like your deuces ain't so high, eh Alf?"

"Nor your threes," Alf said icily.

"Might have to start calling you Little Alf." Davish let out a smug laugh.

Little? Shit, looked like that snouthog couldn't get his fat ass into the back of a meat truck.

I thought to try a risky bluff, emboldened with my last success but with only a high Nova in my hand. It didn't work. Brex called it out and I ended up losing all that I'd won plus 300 more—much to Alfie's delight.

There was talk at the rope barrier. Bask ushered a large,

commanding figure into the VIP section. He was wearing a stiff-brimmed stetson and dark mahogany leathers with silver chains dangling from vest pockets and belt. His right fist was balled. His expression was like granite as he twirled his walrus-like mustache that framed his long face.

He thumped over and stood there beside the table. Alf turned and acknowledged the man with a sullen stare then a nod. "Iron."

The man frowned and looked down at the chips and dominoes in mid game. "Told you bastards to wait up for me." He sank heavily down in a chair beside Davish.

Konrad and Davish each flapped a hand. "We had itchy fingers."

"Why're you late?" Brex growled.

"Had business to attend to."

"A courtesy call would have been nice."

"Ain't no courtesy between us."

Brex's mouth did not move.

Iron scanned the group, staring hard as he counted heads. Even when he sat, he towered a good three inches over all of us, and a foot over Alf, the shortest of the lot.

"Who's this?" His shaggy head swung my way.

"Jive Retro. A new addition to the table," Brex offered.

"Who is 300 in the hole," announced Davish as he stole an ironic glance at Konrad.

"That so? Just waltzes in here to our section like that?" He pulled out a fat cigar from his breast pocket and bit into its end and gave me a frank stare.

I took in his muscular torso—250 pounds if he was 50—and registered the rest of him with mounting unease: the broad shoulders, hard gaze, grizzled gray seeping into his whiskers. Inwardly I cursed. Why the hell couldn't he have shown up a half hour earlier? Would've been more convenient in the overall scheme of things. Maybe I should have heeded Slapper's advice to wait for him. I gnawed at my lower lip. Now I was embroiled here in this vipers' nest.

This gambling gig was going sour. I knew the moment Brex had turned up that it was already looking highly suspect. And now Iron's presence complicated matters. How could I introduce myself as my real self after this charade?

My mind churned on how this new twist could be turned to advantage.

"And the pretty lady?" Iron asked with considerably more graciousness.

Deidra planted hands on her hips. "This pretty lady's name is Deidra." She held out a hand.

"Pleasure to meet you, ma'am." He took her hand and his thumb lingered on the back of her hand for longer than I liked.

She flashed him a coy glance that neither Alf nor Brex liked.

Did I care? No. I felt no sympathy for any of them.

Brex glared and drummed a domino on the table. Iron leveled his unblinking gaze on Brex. "You called this gambling meet for a purpose. What is it?"

"A proposal."

Iron's thick arms crossed on his barrel chest. "Well?"

Brex waved a hand. "In good time, Iron. Sit. Let's have some play first, quaff a few whiskeys and chat. Like all us scutzers do. Or have you forgotten our time-honored customs?"

Iron rolled his shoulders, showing what he thought of old customs.

A strange ritual among these scutzers who were sworn enemies, yet could sit down at a table, play games and parley.

Iron gave a curt nod. "Deal me in."

CHAPTER 13

The good news, I was holding my own. I'd won back 150 calling a bluff by Alf who'd cast me a distant, dog-like stare as I collected his chips. Deidra lost the next round, fluffing it off with a girlish titter, knowing full well it was not her money. Brex seemed to find the whole thing entertaining. He was like a quiet mummy-faced, stone-jowled fixture along for the ride, betting the minimum, taking no large risks.

I folded on the next round. I watched Brex close out Iron in a close call with two dominoes up, black flush down. Brex's lips formed in a loose snicker. "Tough break, Iron. Unlucky in cards, unlucky in scutzing."

The veins popped out in the older man's temples. "You and me have some unfinished business." Iron pulled up a sleeve to reveal bulging biceps. "Things not said are in need of saying, Brex. I reckon we'll see it out before long, out in space somewhere."

"Could be. Stranger things have happened. I'll remind you, this is a neutral zone."

"Huh, right. Neutral zone. What's the idea of taking out Zavius 6 and tossing it like it was a kid's crib?"

Brex's eyes widened. "You must have me confused with someone else." Lips puckered, he looked the figure of innocence.

"Sure. And that shithead comedy bloodbath on Protius 3A? Twenty men up and disappear after I sent reinforcements to that roid. Six ships just plain disappear into the ethers. Blown to smithereens."

Brex did his best to conceal his astonishment. "That was quite the mystery."

"Sure, if you're into vaudeville and slapstick gore."

The briefest flush of rancor tinted Brex's cheeks. "If you have any evidence of my involvement, Iron, please produce it, otherwise shut your yap."

"Evidence? What evidence do I need, you lying bastard. Got your bloody, sadistic signature all over the scene."

"Don't be going and fouling up what has been a good fellowship up till now. The last few turns around Vala, we've been civil."

Iron gave a chuckle of disgust. "If that's what you call 'civil', then you've got your head screwed on wrong."

"Talking raw facts, Iron. How many ships have we lost feuding? A few hundred, maybe a thousand? How many men? How much blood spilt and yols down the tube?"

A smug smile touched Iron's lips as he lay down his dominoes. "You, my friend, just lost two thousand. Three Spacers up, two down, and a pair of Roids, all black."

Brex's smile was just a shade more sinister. "Sorry, Chief. My Roids match your Spacers, and I have a Nova as the deciding high card."

Iron just threw down his cards and smashed a fist on the table. Chips and dominoes scattered every which way. He jumped to his feet. "I smell cheat!" His big fist came angling at Brex's face.

Brex slapped the fist away and leapt up, cheeks darkened with anger.

A brisk motion over by the roped off area had Iron turning. "Aw shit." He swore and looked away as Bask came hustling over.

"Now gentlemen, this is a game-friendly zone," Bask began, still pale faced in his blue suit and polished black shoes. "No roughhousing. Let's break it up before it comes to blows."

Iron turned on him. "We're just having a friendly conversation, bunny. Go run along to those peeping Toms and your chicken-livered manager hiding in the back somewhere with his spy camera."

The monitor's thin face flushed. He clenched a hand into a fist at his side. "Now, listen here—"

"No, you 'listen' here—" Iron flexed his bear-like arms and upended the monitor with a swift uppercut. Bask landed on his back with a loud thump. He stayed down for about five steamboats before he tried painfully rising to his knees.

Big Alf gave a thin chuckle. "Looks like Piggy's going to have to hire himself a new gatekeeper."

Iron snarled, "You and your pork-face Piggy who run this joint, need more than that. I'm down two grand and as much as I hate to leave this fine establishment, I'm afraid I don't much like the company here."

Konrad and Davish kept eyes glued to the table, each hoping to stay out of the brawl.

Play had resumed, but Iron kept standing, his jaw clamped.

Brex's low mutter broke the silence. "Sit down, General. The round's not finished."

"You called this gambling meet for a reason. Spill it." Iron glared hard at him.

"What I have to say is better left for private ears." He motioned to me and Deidra.

Iron gave a smiling laugh. "I think Retro and Deidra look reasonable enough people." He flicked Deidra an admiring glance. "Not too dangerous or wayward as to leak out state secrets. I'll bet a 100 they aren't going to burn down the house." He gave a mocking laugh.

Brex's lip twitched in annoyance. "Sure, if that's the way you want it." I could see him battling indecision. "I'm proposing an alliance. A merger between our scutzers."

Iron reached out and took a swig, swirled his whiskey around in his cheeks a few times before he spat it out. "Am I hearing you? You're trying to make peace?"

Brex held up a hand. "There's much to be gained. We spend too much time shooting each other's scutzers full of holes."

"You think? What possible gain's there for me?" Iron growled.

"A million yols."

Iron paused. "That's some mighty high price tag for a truce. Why you being so magnanimous, Brex?"

He spread his palms. "I'm just a generous man."

"Sure you are." Iron's eyes raked the sleepy, poker faces of the other players. "There can't be two of us."

"That's why I'm recommending that you leave Tylas as part of the deal. For some other star system far from here, where they've never heard of you."

Iron gave a crooked smile which gave way to a low chuckle. "So, that's it. Trying to get rid of me. I get it. While you reap all the rewards. Sew up all the contracts of Crestar, Damocles, and the other mining scum. You'll buy out all the rival scutzers too, the Gravediggers, the Scags, the Mongers. Get rich in the process."

Brex mustered a faint grunt. "If that's the way you want to put it, yes."

Iron ground his teeth. "No deal. I'll burn in hell before I give up all that I've worked for. For you and your scumbuckets or anyone else. A monopoly, is what you're scheming. Give you rights to make millions off the Mining Corps. You're a megalomaniac and a treacherous hound."

Brex's mouth worked as his fists whitened. "Sorry to hear that, Iron."

"Bet you are." Iron clapped his empty glass down on the table. He threw down the rest of his chips in disgust. "I'm out of here. Gotta bleed my lizard anyway. Sick of this place."

Davish stood up to stop him. But thought better of it.

"Get some better quality control here, Brex. This place is stuffy as a hog pen."

Brex tipped two fingers to his ear. "Right on it, Iron."

Iron stomped out, leaving his chips behind.

Alf tented his fingers and peered at his fellows. "Well, that went over well." He picked gamely at his tooth.

Brex chose not to respond. He scowled and mouthed expletives.

He looked away, then turned to me as if my presence were a scourge on the world. "Well, Mr. Jive Retro. Seems you've jinxed this table. Looks like it's your turn to deal. You're down to your last hundred—and that from the last 2k you just borrowed on the house." His voice was low and menacing. "You in or out?"

I gave Deidra something of an ominous glance, a glance of threadbare optimism.

Hard, stony faces stared from left and right. Enemies, all of them, ugly and impatient, and all sensing as if something was not quite right with the new kids on the block.

"Looks like Mr. Jive is near busted, Brex," Davish crooned. "Don't think he's going to be in for much of anything tonight."

Alf picked at his hangnail, his mocking malice palpable.

I silently screamed at Iron's exit. Deidra felt it too. She flashed me a quick warning glance as she wet her lips. Time to up the ante. We make some bread here quickly and get out, or things start getting very ugly soon.

My mind was distracted. The next round saw my chips disappearing into the ethers…into the hands of Brex. I should have known that grinning ape had some trick going. *Why didn't you fold, you stupid fool?*

Konrad now whistled a low note. "Well, looks like you tanked at 2000 in the red, Mr. Jive."

Brex stared balefully at me. "How much money you got stashed elsewhere, Mr. Jive? Cause I hope it's a shit ton. I don't think the bank's going to spot you any more."

I just stared down at my nonexistent chips with despair, almost defiance.

Brex nodded, a thin leer on his lips. "Didn't think so. You got a ship?"

"Yeah, I got a ship." I looked up and held his stare.

He grinned at me soullessly. "Always tell a man with a ship. It's the pride in the eyes, the roughness of the hands, the swagger in the walk. I've been around a lot of men, Jive, and seems to me I know a risk taker and a shit disturber when I see one. Fits you to a T. Seems to me, you might also be having to pay back your debt with this ship of yours. A shame. Well, I usually settle for cash, but I can always use a ship."

The next hand was being dealt. My mind struggled for a way out of this mess, to salvage something from this unpleasant turn.

As far as game plans go, mine had been the practiced deception of the bluffer, the aw-shucks green boy at the table looking as ripe a pigeon as there ever could be. I'd gotten better at the art over the years, managing to take many a sharper down. Though it didn't seem so, considering current affairs.

Deidra picked up her cards and I watched those expressive eyes of hers almost practically change color. Slender fingers fussed with her silky hair. She fanned her flushed cheeks and said something about the heat of this place as I watched those beautiful sea-green eyes blink twice in rapid succession.

As good a cue as any.

"Spot me one more bet, Brex. 5K," I pleaded. "I lose, you can take my ship."

Deidra registered startlement but she contained her dismay upon seeing the set of my jaw and the tense warning in my eyes.

"What and where's this ship of yours?"

"A U56 parked up north and west at Big Nanda's. You can see her for yourself, Brex. Mint condition."

His eyes brooded and bored holes in me. He exhaled a breath. There was curiosity there, mixed with greed and exploitation. After three heartbeats, he nodded. His face relaxed. "Sure." He signaled one of his henchmen who arrived carrying a black case.

After some whispered words, the cashier dealt out three big black stacks of hundreds and pushed them before me.

I smiled and slid all three stacks over to Deidra. "All in. I believe this little lady has the luck of the day."

Alf snorted. "Well, I do believe you're the right stupidest human this side of Vala. This gal's done nothing but lose every hand she's had!"

Brex gave a contemptuous grin. He pushed over 5k to match her bet.

"So, we have a standoff," I said.

"We sure do." Brex cracked his knuckles.

Dominoes fell and cards were dealt. Davish, the mean-eyed dealer inspected Deidra shrewdly and dealt two additional cards to all players. "Let's see what you got."

Deidra lay down her hand. She showed four Roids with two more matching on her dominoes.

She spoke in an innocent voice, "Golly Gee, Alf. Does that mean I won this pot?"

No answer came readily to the table.

Brex clamped his lips and tapped his cards gently on the table.

"It does, dollface," Alf wheezed.

"Yoo hoo!" She spread arms wide and pulled the stash toward her. "Well, that's a surprise. I'm mighty tired, Alf." She faked a yawn. "Seeing how's it getting late, I think I'll be moseying along. Gentlemen, it's been an honor. I'll just switch these here chips into cash yols so I can come back tomorrow and give it a whirl and give them all back to you fellas!"

"How about giving it all back to us now?" Alf said harshly. His hand shot out and grabbed her arm.

"Hey, leggo! That smarts. You're hurting my wrist."

Brex reached over, snatched Alf's fingers. I swore I heard a bone snap. Alf gave a gurgle of agony. He looked up with fear and pain in his eyes. "Brex…no, please."

"Alfy, leave the girl alone. She earned her stash, far as I can see."

"But Brex," moaned Alf. "She just took us for 10C and—"

"Yeah," Davish snapped.

"I said, let her go."

"Fine." Alf withdrew his paw and Davish tipped his stack of chips over in dismay. He cursed.

Alfy grunted and whimpered, massaging his swollen red fingers.

Brex looked over at me. An expression better seen on a crocodile. I kept the same poker face as Deidra. Hard suspicion welled up in those unforgiving, hawk-like eyes as the chivalry he'd exhibited with Alf's hand was replaced with new hatred for me.

Deidra gave a jerky nod of thanks to Brex. She gathered her winnings and tucked them in her leather jacket. She swallowed hard as she tread on light feet toward the ropeway.

Maybe her eyes lingered a tad too long on me, I don't know. It would have worked but for that little tell of recognition, one that Brex saw in a flash. Deidra had revealed it in the slant and flicker of her gaze.

Quick as a hare, Brex caught up to her before she'd taken the last three steps to the rope. He gripped her around the waist, lifted her easily and propelled her back to the table. "Slow and easy, honey bun. Let's see those sleeves."

She struggled but he shook out her wrist. Two fifty chips fell out and then a high-domino of Roids.

"Well, well," Brex murmured. "Alf, you picked a nice one here. Could be we have a sharper."

"Maybe she was just stashing away a couple for a nightcap later on?"

"Then again maybe she was feeding dominoes to this shyster here?" Brex bunted a quick elbow my way. He threw her toward Alf.

Alf nodded in easy acquiescence, though his face had darkened as he caught her in his arms. "Girls will be girls, Brex. We could cut the lady some slack, leave her with me for the night to explain to her the folly of her ways."

"We could, but not this lank-toothed hound." He took a menacing step my way.

Things were going sour. The thickness grew in my throat. We needed to get out of here fast.

I shifted my weight, my hand going to my R1 but Brex was faster. His mallet fist clocked me square in the left ear.

I staggered back, flipping over my chair. I curled in a half crouch, staggered up beside the chair's front legs, shaking the daze out of my head. My hand reached for my sidearm, near got off a shot, but Brex bounded leopard-like in and hoofed me in the solar plexus, lifting me five inches off the ground. Damn the man was strong, and fast. Down I went like a sack of meal.

I looked up through double vision to see the color draining from Deidra's face. For a moment she stood like a deer in the headlamps.

Brex said in a huskier voice, "You and me, pet, are going to tango—" he leered at her. "Forget that bum you've been making eyes at over there. He's no good. Going nowhere fast." I saw him snap out an arm and pull her into his rough embrace. She fought back, struck hard at his thick wads of muscle but he just increased the pressure.

"STOP! You're hurting me, you brute!" She struggled in vain.

Brex dug a fist into her pocket and ripped loose the batch of chips. He sent them spinning on the table. "Divide em up, Konrad."

Konrad nodded vigorously.

I lay on my side groaning, fighting the stars that swirled about the orb of my skull.

Pig-ass Alf hissed and hauled himself up to grab-handle the chips, but he stopped short as if he'd gotten cold feet. "You want to go this fast, Brex? I mean, you could have any of these bimbos in this joint. Casino's full of them. This one's a bobcat. Iron's out there and he's—"

"I don't give a shit about Iron. That arrogant posturing fuck can suck my left nipple."

The mist was still thick in my eyes. I crawled to better vantage.

Brex hoofed me again, a friendly tap in the midriff to keep me down. "Drag this maggot through the back way, up to the chicken coop."

Alf grimaced, but he complied.

I'd been hastily shoveling air back in my lungs and fumbling for my gun. With a sudden heave and lunge, I got my barrel up. A shade slow. My first shot went wide, slid past Alf and nailed Davish in the arm. He gave a mewling howl and sank in his chair, pawing his wrist.

Brex knocked my barrel aside. He made a grab for his own piece but Big Alf fumbled off a shot which nicked my shoulder, sent a world of pain scudding through my upper body. White hot streaks went winging into the table next to us, sending chips and bits of wood flying, frying the nearest guy's thigh. There came howls of rage and pain. A regular stampede. Shouts and pandemonium filled the air.

Sharp agony stabbed at the left tip of my shoulder. Something like razor blades prickling at my flesh. But I couldn't focus on that. I sucked in a mouthful of air and lunged forward.

Deidra was on the move. She'd broken free of Brex's monkey-grip and taken two steps back. The compact R1 was in her hand, but Brex elbowed it away and sent her flying before she could peg anyone or do anything useful.

I leaned to the side, swung out the other leg. Clipped Brex on the side of the head with a boot and a solid round house. Sweat sprayed off his brow. He shook his head. He didn't seem to feel anything, just stood there like a fence post, grinning like a fucking galoot.

Alf heaved his fatty bulk toward me. He was gearing up for another shot with that pop gun of his. A pansy ass R9—and I lifted the table and heaved it at him, sending colored chips flying in his face.

It fouled his shot. But the fat, angry ass was coming at me again, much too trigger happy.

Energy flares careened everywhere from Alf's muzzle. Shit for brains was trying to laser everything that moved in the casino with his messed up fingers.

I scrambled around his gun arm and smacked the weapon out of his hand. Not before the fool squeezed the trigger and sent a white-hot shaft of bright light angling at his left leg. He fell clutching at his shin, bleating like a hog-tied calf.

Play with guns, you get your leg blown off, it's that simple.

Deidra was behind me to my right. I looked through my mist of pain and felt the blood trickle at my shoulder. The pain was heavy now. Gasping, I saw she'd trained the gun at Brex.

"Hold up, cowboy! Nice and slow. Ease back. Get down!"

Brex made a false start to charge her.

It was a bad move.

She loosed fire at his feet and he danced like a medicine man, smoke trailing from his boots.

The steel door burst open from somewhere behind and a pig-faced man with broad shoulders and upturned snout of a nose came running out with four of his mall cops in black suits. He looked like the manager, the one they called Piggy. They trained weapons on us.

"Enough!" came his shrill, gravelly voice. "Stand down, you idgits! Enough bloodshed!"

Alf and Davish lay groaning on the floor and I stumbled on, trying to break through the knot to get to Deidra.

No dice.

My ears were ringing. This mawkish country music kept droning through the speakers of the main hall.

I crouched down, reaching for my weapon, knowing that fighting with fists and feet was as about as useless as drinking muddy river water on a hot day. I got a piece of my R1 and rolled. I got one shot in, taking out one of the black suits, pegging another in the chest as he tried to get to Deidra. Pain bloomed in my left shoulder. The entire front of my body ached like hell.

Deidra backed herself all the way to the ropeway, keeping others at bay. The back of her slim legs touched the swaying rope. I saw she kept backing up past it, weapon trained on the mall cops and at Brex. She kicked a post out of the way and edged her way back into the common area.

Two of the mall cops lumbered after her. One lifted an arm. "Everybody calm down! All's contained. Nothing to see here, folks. No need to panic."

Gunfire and blood is bad for business, you mean. Gets everyone scampering and yelling, instead of feeding money into the machines.

A swish of movement came to my left. Brex came charging at me. I turned and fired. Grazed his ear only. I got another good chop to his face with the muzzle of my gun before he smacked it away and laid me low with a mean hip check that sent me to my knees.

Clutching at his ear, trickling blood, he gave a caustic sneer. "Jive Retro, you're a pain in the ass. Also in a world of trouble." He hoofed me another vicious one in the kidney. I sank back and the world floated merry-go-round-like, a dim haze of dream figures.

The manager and the monitors came hauling me to my feet. They thrust me toward the open steel door at the back and I staggered, swinging with my good arm, cursing. I felt a R1 butt ram into the base of my skull. I was shoved forward sprawling through the door into the dark space beyond.

The door clanged shut, in tune with my throbbing skull. The last two of the mall cops worked me deeper into the interior down a dusky corridor. Only the echoes of their scuffling feet and my grunting and heaving filled my ears.

A dim thought came to my mind: I should be worried about blood loss.

My space leathers were tight enough to contain the blaster wound. But I could see crimson drips on the floor in steady synchrony, and as I was herded on like a pack mule, I thought that maybe I'd pushed my luck too far.

CHAPTER 14

I felt a stupor come over me, a dreamy sense of unreality. Brex boxed my ears as I rounded a corner and was frog-marched down another corridor. We went around another corner, down an ill-lit hallway and into some dark cubbyhole. It was littered with electronic gear, monitors and control panels. Brex's minions were behind me with the pig-faced manager, snuffling at my back.

On the side wall were plastered CCTV screens, the other side was deep in construction, clotted with sawhorses and tools as if it were being gutted to make room for a second command central.

A troop of eight black-suited goons watched the screens in alert unison. One ziplocked my wrists. I was tossed, arms behind my back, on the cold tile floor along the opposite wall. I shook my head groggily, in a state of shame and sluggish rage. Somewhere I'd lost Hoss's sombrero too. Damn.

The pig-faced manager gazed at me with skepticism and black-hearted malice.

For a while he was speaking words, but my mind couldn't register what he was saying as it turtled along in slow motion. I kept thinking that, once the ball rolls down the hill, there is no going back up. Yuk, yuk. Certain facts had been illuminated in stark clarity. That grave acts had been committed and were not retractable. Upon venturing into this casino, I had passed the point of no return in crossing Brex. No mercy could be expected, nor help from the outside.

"Want me to torture this fuck a bit?" a hard-bitten voice rasped from the side. A booted heel landed in my ribs.

I gasped. A hand gripped my hair and tilted my head back and I felt the cold steel of a blade caressing my Adam's Apple.

A heavy hand came up to snatch the young man's wrist before blood was drawn. "No, Jit. We have yet to discover where this huckster has come from…who he was working with."

The dark-eyed hood nodded. Friend Jit had a crop of curly jet-black hair, thick at the sides and cascading down the middle of his back. It thinned at the top despite the fact that he still appeared young.

I say 'young' relatively. He had me beat by at least 15 years. There was a hard-boned meanness that made him dangerous.

His smiley-ass smirk bugged me. It was just begging to be broken in two off his thin, ferret-like face.

"Excuse the mess, but we're undergoing some renovations," Brex said.

I flapped an elbow as it were all one.

Rough hands frisked me: fingers looking for sidearms and other weapons. Several articles were placed on the nearby counter:

One R1, 80 yols, two dog-eared capsules of Myscol and a sealed condom.

"He travels light," some wiseass said.

Another grunt kept pawing at my left leg and pulled out a silver gleaming knife.

"Found this on him. Taped under the sock." He lifted my bowie knife and handed it to Brex.

Brex examined it curiously as it gleamed in the ruddy light. He flicked me a speculative look. "What you need a cleaver like this for, Jive?" He laid it gently on the table before the CCTV screens.

I shrugged in my best possible way in this cramped, trussed position. "Useful for carving pumpkins, I guess."

"Jive, you're a bit of a comic today."

"You know what they say. Good to the last drop."

"And the last one laughing laughs the loudest," Brex added.

"Enough bullshitting!" Piggy swept the articles off the table. They clattered to the floor.

"Take it easy, Pigs." Brex drawled. "You're a bundle of nerves. You need to get laid more often."

"Says the one dripping blood off his ear."

My blurred vision roved around the chamber. Racked computers and other hardware sat to the side. Luminous virtual keypads floated in blue and green light near the monitors.

It was a more effective and monitored setup than I'd guessed.

Twelve wide-angle plasma screens showed various views of the casino. From the craps tables to the gaudy arched entranceway. From the Shiastro lounge to the water maze gambling theater, the wagon wheels, the bar, the bandstand...places where we'd all been not too long ago.

I took some tense moments to study the hired help. Six men and two women with serious demeanors and suspicious faces. Eight sets of beady eyes glued to those screens, looking for any hint that there was suspicious activity progressing on the floor.

I sat there biting back my humiliation and rage as the pain receded a bit from my brain. I was hoping to pull my thoughts together enough to muster a way out of this mess.

"Knew you were a phony, Retro," Brex said.

"Oh yeah, What gave it away?"

"The spiky purple hair?" He gave a mordant laugh. "No, we saw your kung-fu routine, the way you hop-handled Basky boy earlier in order to sneak onto the big tables."

Piggy grunted. "We allowed it, on account of Brex being watchdog at the tables. Though we kept our eyes on you. Not to mention the brassy fishwife you contracted to run interference at the cheapie tables. Our computers pegged you as an operator, and that little episode as a 79% bullshit con. If you were really after a dame, you'd have gone for a younger, much prettier piece of ass than that hound."

I nodded lamely. "Makes sense. I should have known."

"You should have. Life's a bitch and then you marry one."

Brex swaddled in closer. "A tricky act too, Retro...you and Miss

Strawberry Hair." He frowned as if in memory of it. "She's a bundle of joy. Had Alf half up to his ears in jizz."

I gave a toss of my shoulder, with all my ability of a quarter inch. "Maybe a little drink spilling would have been better? A little slap at the—"

"Nah… 'Geronimo' sees through farce like that. In five seconds you'd have been made."

Piggy grinned at my puzzled frown. "Our computer here, Retro. Equipped with the latest AI pattern recognition. Identifies scammers like you, those who like to waltz in and have the gall to try and game the system." He beckoned to where one of his technicians was studying a clip of me casing the joint. The computer had put a wire frame box around my hand, lifted in signal to my ear, then zoomed in on my cheeks, noting the expressional giveaways, the tells. A red upside down triangular alert icon with text caption flashed and highlighted suspicious areas. "See? 98% accuracy. We've cleaned out most of the con artists that way in the last four months." He waved a hand. "Sure, a few have slipped through the cracks, but we caught up with them the next time they came. Gave them a broken limb or two and a few words to relay to others who might try the same."

"A pleasant thought."

"Yes, that is the least you can expect from us, Retro." Piggy gave a husky sigh. "Big Alf doesn't like to be shamed or have his leg shot in front of a crowd. An embarrassment to him. An embarrassment to us." He lifted his shoulders jocularly. "You know how it is."

Sure, I knew how it was. Fat Stuff gets a leg shot out from under him and a VIP game goes to shit. I wasn't going to give this smarmy bastard the satisfaction of seeing me tremble.

A plan started to form, and that's when the pain began.

Piggy made a quiet motion. "Start with the left hand, Jit, then move to the right. If that doesn't do it, try the knees."

Jit gave a smug nod. A sadistic line of anticipation crossed his narrow face.

He smacked a hairy fist into my jaw, first loosening a few teeth. I thrust my elbow up to block the next blow, but he shoved me aside and snatched my middle fingers and near twisted them off. The whole room heard my knuckles snap. I bared my teeth. It was all I could do not to snap out and bite his face. I vowed I would make it my mission to gut this filthy creep.

"Smarts, eh?" he quipped.

"Don't look so smug, Retro," Pig-face intoned. "Things are just starting to ramp up." He sidled over, kicked me in the shins. His hard leathered toe found a sweet spot in my left shin, bringing another bolster of pain to my roster of hurts.

"Jit?" Brex said.

"What?"

"Fetch the other one."

Jit shook out his knuckles and whined, "Why bring that bum when we can gut this—"

"Get him, I said!"

Jit held his tongue. He hopped out of the room to fetch the mystery man.

While I dealt with my pain, I scanned desperately for openings. They were adding a whole new section to this upscale control room. Bringing in racks of equipment. Probably like that Geronimo piece of crud Piggy was bragging about. Carpenters had left a series of sawhorses laden with tools, drills, staple guns, hammers and screwnails. My eyes fixed on them. I wondered how such items could be used to advantage.

Jit returned a minute later, dragging a short muscly figure. After some bangs and slaps, and with the help of a brawny associate, he dropped his victim scuffling and cursing on the floor next to me.

Marty. He sent a glare my way that would freeze a gleer.

They'd roughed him up some. He looked to have a broken nose, maybe a couple of cracked ribs. His left arm was hanging loosely, scraped and bloody. None of which had done anything to improve his looks.

I grinned back at him through my bloody mouth.

"You stupid idgit, Rusco. You and your bullshit promises."

"Rusco?" Brex called. "I thought it was Retro?"

"Don't matter what you call him."

Good ole Mar.

"Caught your friend near butt-fucking our wagon wheels by the slot machines. He's got a busy pecker, that boy."

I gave a small smile.

"You two are quite the pair," Brex remarked. "Hunky and Dory."

Marty rasped, "You motherf—"

I heeled his shin with my boot. Seeing as there was a chance we might come out of this alive, it didn't make sense for bullet-head to tip the scale and foul it up. But that point may have already passed. I shafted him a dark, murderous look.

"Had your bully boy pegged from the start. Clown set off the Myscol detector by the craps tables. Fool was high enough to float off the ceiling. You should hire better help, Retro, or Rusco, whatever your name is."

So that was what that alarm beeping was all about.

"Marty's not that subtle," I explained.

"And you are?"

I scowled. Better to play dumb.

Some further examination of video footage ensued and a decision was made. On another signal from Brex, Jit made his second exit.

He returned moments later, manhandling a tall youth frothing at the mouth. "Couldn't find the dame," Jit croaked. "She bolted, but I got me this angry fish."

He hauled Slapper over by the scruff of the neck, arm twisted behind his back, and forced him down beside us.

"This your little go-to glowbug?" Piggy sneered. He smacked him hard in the face.

Slappy yowled. "You in the habit of mistreating your customers?"

"Only when they're shysters and shitbags like you."

"He's just our valet, Brex," I said. "Leave him alone. Doesn't know a thing."

"Doesn't work like that, Jive. You should know. Any person of suspicion or collaboration is treated with contempt."

The matter seemed out of my hands. I shrugged.

A side door flew open and a giant of a man thrust his square-shouldered bulk through. The monitor staked out at the door was half thrown across the room. He landed in a tangled heap.

The visitor's chest heaved and his eyes were fierce pits. An R1 was clutched in a meaty fist. Two other biker-like figures, Reaper men who I recognized from the casino earlier, were at his side, tucked slightly behind. Muzzles were trained at the figures within the room.

"You'd best let that boy go," the man warned. "Unless you've got a death wish."

"Now, Iron, settle down." Piggy lifted a hand. He placated in his whiny voice, "I don't know how you got back here, but this section's off limits." He licked his lips, not savoring the busted face and tangled limbs of the slumped form at his side.

"Bullshit! You can't hide behind the skirts of your mall cops, Pig Shit. Give me the boy, or your balls are mine. Last warning."

"Can't quite do that, Iron," Brex said. "The boy's caught consorting with the likes of thieves and shitbags." He jerked a thumb toward Marty and me slumped in an undignified sprawl.

Piggy piped up, "These two were caught cheating our A1 members, including Alf and Brex. You know the rules."

"I don't know those bums from Adam." Iron's eyes slid off us like shit from a duck's ass. Slapper'd have nothing to do with these sharpers or any vice, you know that. True, he's no angel, but he's not a con."

"Don't matter, Iron. House rules is house rules," Piggy said matter-of-factly.

Brex stared with displeasure. He motioned an upturned palm at us. "These two are getting their just desserts. By the time we extract the truth out of them, they'll corroborate."

"Consorting don't mean doing."

Brex shrugged. "It's a matter of semantics."

"I'll pay for the boy's involvement," said Iron. "How much do you want? An even thousand? Here, you can have it now." He dug a fist in his waistcoat.

"You can't buy your way out of this," Brex intoned.

"Pound of flesh, eh?" Iron sneered. "Take your blood price then, you maggot." Fast as an adder he leveled his R1 and let loose a round of fire. Brex skipped back and dragged a henchman in front of him. The man spasmed, jerking marionette-like to Iron's blaster fire. Brex jumped away, his right black boot singed. Piggy caught a whiff of hell on his left arm. Suddenly the room was in chaos. R1 fire rainbowed from all corners of the room. Plasma screens exploded. Racks of new computer equipment splintered into pieces.

I ducked in time as a line of golden blaster fire nearly ripped off the top of my skull. Piggy knelt crooning, taking short, hoarse gasps behind some packing boxes. He flexed his left wrist. He cursed, fumbling for his gun which he now held in a shaky hand. "Now, hold on, Iron. We don't want bloodshed or an out-and-out war!" His voice was lost in the chaos of gunfire.

"Too late, Miss Piggy!" Iron shouted. "You already got your war." He scooted over to Slapper, cut his wrist bonds, then struggled to drag him away while loosing shots into the fray. He might have been hit too. He was moving fast, but slower now, in jerky, knee-length hops toward his Reaper buddies. The first black suit he'd wasted lay sprawled with a smoking hole in his chest, eyes and mouth agape. Another was dead before he hit the ground.

I ducked away from the carnage. With frenetic speed I crawled behind the new unpacked computer equipment. I made a frantic effort of trying to loose myself from these tough cords that circled my wrists. Marty was groaning ten feet away, dragging himself to cover in the same direction. I spotted a drill beside one of the sawhorses. I knocked it over and began sawing at the tough plastic tie wrap with the jagged edge of the drill's bit. I felt the cords snap.

I low-crawled over to Marty. I snatched up my knife lying on the floor. I cut loose his bonds and we crawled together away in the smoke and chaos.

A lumbering shape with blood-smeared cheeks saw us. He came angling out of the smoke. The knife was in my hand. It was airborne before I consciously knew it. Whirling like a toy, it came hurtling at the figure, sharp blade catching the ruddy, smoke-blurred light. It was a sloppy throw and only stuck in the tough leathers above the left breast. Brex gurgled out a curse. He hunched, one heavy arm lifting to pluck it out.

I kitty-crawled on the heels of my hand, every moment an exercise in torture. Somewhere along the way the fingers of my good hand snatched up a staple gun. I found a hammer next to it which I stuffed in my jacket pocket, wincing and half puking with the pain. I saw Marty grab a good-sized drill gun. A cadaverous grin was writ on his blood-smeared face.

An iron clop of boots echoed behind us. I heard the squeal of a heavy steel door opening somewhere down the hallway ahead of us. More footfall echoed in the stony dimness. Grunts, shouts, labored breaths.

Trapped!

A couple of casino cops were clambering our way from the back door answering an urgent summons.

The first flew at me and drew his weapon.

I reached up and smashed the nearest light bulb with the hammer. The corridor was plunged in near darkness.

I gave a banshee yell and lunged forward, staple-gunning the guy's face and forehead. His buddy lit a flashlight and I saw his eye purpled as he cried out in agony and gargled fury, spouting blood from his punctured eye.

Marty sent a couple of spikenails into his friend's shin, straight into the bone. He fell back, howling, clutching his leg. Marty eased by, hoofing him in the face. "That'll teach you, fucker."

We snatched up their R1s and kept hobbling on.

I was about to kick open the steel door when more R1 fire came arching through the latch mechanism, blowing the lock out from the outside.

I staggered back, ready to kill.

A familiar figure wrenched open the metal door, sucking in sharp breaths. *Deidra.* "Where were you fools?"

"Decided to stay a little while," I wheezed.

Her eyes were fierce. "Two rent-a-cops were making a beeline inside. Been trying to get to you! Casino's in chaos, mostly cleared now. Best we exit this rodeo show, get to the speeder asap."

I squinted around in the darkness.

We were out in the back of the casino lot. Only three service delivery trucks sat parked at low, concrete loading bays. No human figures. The city lights showed a blue-green halo farther behind us to the west. A single lamp burned high on the brick wall some 40 feet away, screened in a wire cage. We were in near shadow. Lucky for us.

It was an understatement to say we'd made some powerful enemies this evening...

CHAPTER 15

Like wraiths we skirted the wall and shambled round the corner of the building. My fingers were on fire, body aching, but I pushed the pain aside.

Deidra muttered harshly in my ear, "I had the chips in my hands, Rusco. We had it! Then I let it all go, and it was gone."

"Don't sweat it, Dee." I brushed her shoulder with my good hand. "Let's concentrate on surviving this night."

We made it out to the side of the building along a narrow alley flanked by storm fence and tall hedges. I peered around the front of the casino and took in the main lot. About fifty ships were still in residence. Some were lifting off in a heck of a hurry, others parked. A lot of motion and feet moving. People not in easy, relaxed moods. A pair of load lifters and supply trucks blocked the service entry at the right front side, those that had brought the equipment for the renovations. I assumed the three scutzer ships in between us and Hoss's speeder, bearing the stark logo with the bandanna-ed pirate bad boy, were those of Brex's Bratts. They would never let us escape from this hellhole. We were never going to get away in the air speeder, even if Slapper had managed to make it out and we could track him down.

A lot of heavy hurdles.

We needed a diversion. Even to get out of this damn parking lot was going to take some doing.

Two dumpsters sat side by side over at the corner against the east wall.

I motioned to Marty. "Think you can hunker down there and act as sniper?"

"I could but why? I'd get myself shot up."

"It's not a question of why or getting shot up, Mar, but—"

"Forget it, Ruzbo, we should just all of us as a team get the hell out of here."

I looked at him sidelong. "And have three dead rabbits?"

"Sure, fine. If I'm supposed to be the gopher, I'll do it."

"Wait. Better idea, Mar." I nudged him between the shoulder blades. "How hard would it be for you to run over there, fire up that lifter and drop a load on that first ship of Brex's?"

"If I could get it running and if my leg doesn't give out before I get there, not hard." He cast me a cock-eyed stare. "What's with all these fantasies?"

I gave him my usual crooked stare.

"Oh, all right. Somebody has to do the heavy lifting around here."

I felt a bit ashamed. With this shot-up shoulder and busted hand, I was not much use at doing any 'heavy lifting'. I gave Mar another brush on the back and a grim chuckle. "You're a trooper, Mar."

The distraction'd give Deidra and me time to hop that ship of Brex's yonder and get the hell away.

Marty turned back my way, his eyes narrowed in thought. "So, if we do all this, then what?"

"We play it by ear, Mar. Fill in the gaps as we go along."

"That's a bad plan, Rusco."

"You got a better one?"

"No."

"Then let's hop to." I gave him a shove.

Marty cursed under his breath. He shambled off, his new R1 gripped in a clenched paw.

"I'm going with him," Deidra hissed.

I started to object but she was already gone, sprinting like a gazelle into the gloomy night.

Mumbling curses, I crouched low in the shadows. Barrel lifted, I ran interference for Marty, covering him while he and Deidra hotfooted it toward the two-pronged forklift. The pain in my shoulder was getting worse. A deep, throbbing ache. Deidra had broken into the cab now and Marty had climbed up and sent it rolling toward the first ship that bore the Bratts' logo.

I heard a rough voice bellowing behind me.

Six of them must have followed us around the side of the building.

"There he is!" Brex's weapon lifted. "Get that fucking shitbag. He'll sabotage the ships." He emptied sharp blasts into the side of the lifter.

Jit lifted his gun, aiming for Marty. The lifter rocked and trembled to multiple blasts. The frame of the cab had nearly disintegrated. I saw Deidra hop out on the tarmac, landing on the balls of her feet then tuck into a roll while Marty ducked under what was left of the lifter's cowling. More blasts slammed into the forklift, sending tough side plates smoking.

I was sick of that little fucker, Jit. I leaned my barrel out and sighted down its length, balancing the rounded muzzle with my bad arm. I fired off five quick shots.

Jit flew back in a spray of smoke and brains.

Good riddance. Another of the six ratbastards down. How many more to go?

I saw the lifter with its heavy load of cement blocks piled high on its forks plunge on and smack into the side of the Bratts' ship. The load tipped and fell heavily on the port wing.

Marty rolled free before impact. He staggered up to his knees. The left wing was crushed beyond repair and now liquids and lubricants leaked from the side. One spark and the whole thing would go up. That bird was going nowhere.

"Good work, Marty," I muttered under my breath.

A bearded face suddenly came veering up behind me. A black muzzle lifted.

No time to draw. I snatched the first thing available: the staple gun at my hip and fired rounds into the man's face. He cried out, clutching at his eyes.

Another thug was beside him, sighting a long barrel down at my throat.

My life flashed before my eyes.

I caught a flash of movement—from a parked air speeder about 50 yards away. A fire trail whickered out and I glimpsed a small dark head behind that trail. A woman for sure. Deidra? No, she was too far away. The hair style was wrong. The gunman at my side cried out in surprise, the one who would have killed me, the one whose arm was shot off at the wrist.

I swore in bewilderment and snatched at my gun with my good arm. A hot flash whickered out of the muzzle and finished him off. He fell dead in a cloud of smoke and blood.

I stared down at the corpses. Who was that shooter—? The girl from the karaoke? No, it was too ridiculous to consider.

But bright arcs flew my way.

I rolled past the smoking corpses, biting back the foul taste in my mouth.

No time to reminisce. Just keep propelling yourself away from these shitbags, Rusco, like a good little fugitive.

I caught up to Deidra half way down the parking lot and we hunkered in the shadows between a pair of air speeders, not far from Hoss's speeder. Marty was busy scrambling toward safety of his own: the dumpsters on the other side of the lot.

I had missed my opportunity to take out Brex, and I winced with frustration. He and his crew were in the air in that fierce LC1 alligator-nosed locator craft. Its menacing forward cannons were trained down now in our direction.

Another scutzer ship had gained the air to meet them. One with silver hull and diamond-shaped middle. The Star Reaper insignia hung on its starboard flank. It seemed to be the only thing stopping Brex from taking out all the parked ships in our vicinity. Whether it was Iron or one of his lackeys I did not know.

Bright blazes filled the sky, accompanied by the roar of more ships overhead trying to get the hell out of the way.

I did some quick calculations. If Brex got the best of the other ship, he would come after us next, even if he had to torch this entire area to get to us.

Where did that leave us? Nowhere.

And where the hell was Slapper? Could he be on that ship with the Star Reaper emblem? Could we even get the air speeder running? We'd have to break into it and make our getaway fast. Good luck doing that against an armed and deadly LC1. Was there even enough time before we got blown to hell?

We had to act. Think, Rusco, think!

Two husky figures came scrambling for the last of Brex's ships with the Beryl Bratts logo on its side. They were about 40 yards away; Deidra and I waited till they got the side hatch open. I ignored the pain in my shoulder—most of it had gone numb anyway. On my signal, I lunged out of the shadows and hoofed it toward the back of the ship and pegged the lead man in the spine as he was stepping up the ladder.

Deidra was on my heels. She clipped his comrade in the legs. He rolled, grabbing at his knees. The man rocked on the ground in agony. She kicked him in the ribs. We scuttled into the companionway and down the narrow hallway toward the bridge.

I felt lightheaded. Time had slowed; scenes felt like they wrapped around to the beginning. I banged my bleeding shoulder against the curved wall and hissed twice in frustration.

"Your hand, Rusco," Deidra murmured.

"Fly this thing! Never mind me. I'll work weapons." I badgered my way into the shadowy bridge and plopped my sorry weight down in the copilot seat. I familiarized myself with the controls, a smallish grid of simple touch panels and knobs that a child could operate.

Theoretically.

Deidra gained the pilot's chair. We lifted off. We swung about in an airspace lit with fire traces. Brex had already banked away from the Reaper ship, sensing a new enemy in the air. The LC1 was a heavy plate-metal beast with upturned wings. The alligator snout came angling for us and fired off three surface flares at our starboard vanes. Maybe to test our mettle. Iron's ship came hurtling in between us and Brex's, and the Grim Reaper craft looked only slightly less menacing than the LC1.

Deidra worked the main thrusters and pitched us directly over the casino. We blitzed the golden galleon sign which had me squinting in its carnival glare.

I saw that Marty, scrambling below, had earned the wrath of more of Brex's men as they tagged his heels. Bight fire lit the lot.

Damn. Two of Brex's mercs had now pinned Marty down between the dumpsters. They were trying to flush him out. One of Piggy's mall cops had joined the party.

Deidra banked and I laid cover fire, sending two of the mercs sprawling in charred heaps. I momentarily lost my focus. I felt our stern rock to ion surface fire.

A big mean ugly ship bearing the Beryl Bratts logo was bearing down at us. No time to get to Mar. He had his R1. He'd have to fend for himself.

This was getting out of control. What a hare-brained scheme to have come to this accursed place, *The Rip*. So much for a friendly game of Shiastro to rustle up a few g's. *You're a damn walking disaster, Rusco.*

I could only feel albeit a certain pride having survived thus far. Me, a lone shit disturber with no master plan, doing his thing. Through my blood-caked eyes I could see the *pattern*. Just like in the old days—those lost years when I was given the twisted grace to bear the alien artifact...yes, I felt a wash of its eerie light in me now, carving out my destiny even after all these years. This is what I was made for.

Brex was already chiseling his nose into the fray ready to finish us all off. Iron's ship appeared shell-torn. A thin trail of gray wisped from her left vane. His one port cannon only emitted fizzles of fire;

the other was only sporadically spouting blasts.

Not good.

A couple more shots and the Reapers' shields would give out. She'd be toast.

"There! Bank there!" I yelled at Deidra.

She let out a strangled hiss. We came blitzing down at 40 degrees starboard toward Brex's ship. I let a wash of ion fire peel into our prey's broad flank. I pegged her from the side and she wavered. Fire slid from the good gun of the Reaper craft. It tore rivulets into the LC1's other side, finishing the job. Smoke curled from her starboard vane and the sleek hull careened down to slide on its big narrow belly along one of the wide boulevards sending folks skittering in all directions.

No more enemy ships were in sight.

Deidra and I decided to make ourselves scarce.

We banked into the casino lot, ready to abandon the doomed, enemy craft and let the blame for any civilian injuries be pinned on Brex's boys.

We had to get to Marty, then get the hell away from here.

CHAPTER 16

The Star Reaper ship dropped down and landed a safe distance from our bow. We waited a moment, blinking, breaths held, deciding what to do.

A square-shouldered figure emerged from the starboard hatch with a slight limp. A long barreled R1 was gripped in his steady fist. He lifted an arm, hailed us. I flipped on the ship's mic.

"Rusco! Jet Rusco!" he called up at us into the night air. "Get your ass out of that shoebox." His thick, booming voice echoed off the hardtop across the lot.

With a shared grin, Deidra and I came out of the hatch. We approached, weapons on the ready.

Iron took one look at me and his jaw dropped...then a broad, crooked grin twisted his weathered face.

"So, it is you..."

I gave a slow nod. "Yes, me. The one and only."

"Get your hide aboard, Rusco. You've got a deal of explaining to do."

"First, Marty."

"Who the hell's Marty?" he barked.

I yelled into the open air in the direction of the dumpsters. There came a loud retort of blaster fire as a hidden figure pegged the last of Piggy's goons. A moment or two later he came out: a squat figure, limping and ragged. Both hands were gripped warily on his weapon.

I knew our bully boy was not happy with the way things had turned out, judging by the caustic sneer on his pug-ugly face.

"Having all the fun, Rusco?" he said sardonically as he trudged closer. "While I do all the dirty work?"

I shrugged. "What can I say, Mar?"

"We can talk about this later," Iron called, motioning us. "Inside."

We piled into the hatch. No sooner had we gained the narrow companionway than the ship lifted off and took to the sky.

We made our way to the bridge where Iron's crew was piloting the locator. I saw Slapper, white-faced and slumped in a chair, looking subdued and schooled. Two of the Reaper henchmen I remembered from the casino worked the nav. One's arm was set in a bloody sling.

"Clyde, what's our status?" asked Iron.

"Starboard plates sheared. Left cannon fried. Shields at 60%. Could be worse."

Iron nodded. "We'll swing back to Tylas for repairs when the heat's died down. Hold our course due west."

Deidra rasped in my ear, "I hope you know what you're doing?"

I gave a crooked smile.

I did a quick inventory, assessing ourselves for damage. Me, a broken rib, two broken fingers and a scorched and dislocated shoulder. Marty, an ugly scalp wound, broken nose and pronounced limp. Deidra escaped fairly unscathed but for a gash above the left eyebrow and some red marks and bruises on her arm. Slapper seemed more scared than anything. His pale tongue flicked out from time to time from a slack-jawed mouth to wet his lips.

"You okay, Slappy?" Iron asked in a voice as near to tenderness as a father's might be.

"Yeah, just a little shell-shocked is all." His beardless jaw drooped. He stared out the viewport at nothing in particular.

We ran on a wide western course away from the city.

I was pleased about that. I eased back in my seat, squelching a groan. "We need to get back to our ship." I let my busted fingers fall in my lap. "How much of that regen we have on *Trident*, Marty?"

"Not much, maybe two more doses. Slim pickings though." His

voice was like gravel, rattling down a rusty chute.

"No worries, we have some aboard," Iron grumbled. He heaved himself up from the captain's chair and rummaged through the utility compartment under the weapons' console. He tossed me a small white-blue salve tin before settling himself back in his seat.

I nodded my thanks. I smeared some of the poppy-red goo under my leathered shoulder, wincing with every dab; the rest I slathered on the twisted fingers of my left hand, even though it hurt like hell to wiggle them the smallest bit. Marty cupped a gob on his left leg and his lower ribs then smeared some on his face.

Iron grunted and assessed the sorry condition of us with a distasteful frown. He smoothed his heavy droopy mustache. "When you boys are sufficiently recovered, I'd like to add you to my employee list."

"You would, would you?" I said a touch sarcastically.

"We Reapers can always use more able-bodied men."

"What about Brex? He's going to be objecting to that proposal mighty strongly, gunning for us every moment of the day." I stroked my tender jaw.

Iron wheezed out a conciliatory note. "Brex's got other troubles on his mind. I'll fix it between us."

"How're you gonna fix it?" Marty crowed. "Him and Piggy's gonna—"

"Piggy ain't going to be doing nothing much special. Got a lot of pondering to do, seeing as he's going to be in a wheelchair for the better part of this year."

I wondered what that boded. These casino moguls had long reaches. They were a mean pack of sons of bitches—shanghai anyone who crossed them, let alone assisted in their demise.

"You have a ship?" Iron barked.

"We do."

"Well, what and where's this ship of yours?"

"Parked over at Big Nanda's. Busted warp coil. Her name's *Trident* and she is one tough bird. We owe 5k for her overhauling, if you're thinking of commissioning her."

"*Trident?*" Iron blinked and his eyes gleamed. "You mean you're the lone rogues who Barrel Ox said busted up those goons back on Trito?"

"We are." I allowed myself a thin smile.

"Well, more to you than meets the eye, Mr. Jive, or should I say, Rusco? Slapper here's been telling me a bit about you. Though I can't hardly believe a quarter of it." He took off his tall stetson and smoothed the thinning brown hair underneath. His face split in a wide grin. "Jive Retro, I shoulda known by that fake name that you were a player."

"How big's your enterprise, if you don't mind me asking?"

"600 scutzers. We're the Reapers. Loyal men and women. Working in twos and threes in all their own ships."

I arched my brows, impressed. "That's quite a fleet."

"'Tis." He paused, his gray-flecked brows narrowing. "I see something special in you, Rusco. I'm going to take a chance. I know that you saved my man Ox out there and his ship from rustlers and helped me deal with Brex this time round—up there in those night skies over that shit-for-brains casino. Means something to me. Crestar's commissioning me to watch over more of these out-of-way installations. I need more personnel hunting down new lodes. What I'm saying is, I'll back you the cash to get your ship repaired. But your first claims come out of your pay, you hear? You stiff me and you're a dead man."

I considered. "What about the pay?"

"Commission based. The more you work, the more you earn. Some of my guys are earning thousands every month, living quite well."

The idea had appeal.

"Five big companies I contract mostly with. Crestar being the largest. If we sign over ownership rights of a roid with significant spoils of beryllium, begrium or even gold, then the scutzers, that's us, reap a percentage of the rewards. We can milk it forever."

"How much percentage we talking about?"

"As high as 1%."

Marty toyed with his thumbs. "You know the old saying, 1% of nothing is still nothing."

"Not if its beryl."

"How much is out there?" I asked.

"Lots. Or there wouldn't be the abundance of drifters and gold diggers and badasses out there as it is."

"How much do you rake off?"

"5% off the top of all collected from my scutzers. It's a good deal for my protection given my clout with the mining companies."

"What's to stop locators from going solo?"

"Nothing. There are a few who try it, but they don't last long. It's a cruel and depraved world out there, Mr. Rusco."

I considered it. The scheme sounded solid. But I didn't want to get down and dirty out in the depths of space doing a lot of hard labor scouring the hinterlands for nothing.

Who would? But then again, what else did we have?

I gave a crisp nod. It only took me a moment to decide. "Deal."

Deidra threw her shoulders back and shot up from her seat angrily. "Don't I get a say in this?"

"No."

"What do you mean, no? Aren't there other options here? I mean, you go off deciding this, that and the other thing—"

"See here, Missy—" the Reaper in the sling working the nav rumbled "—you can join the Gravediggers if you think you can find yourself a better deal. You could also try your hand with some Skurgs."

Deidra slumped back, biting back her annoyance.

Iron stared hard. "Once again, do not sidewind me, Rusco. You do, and I'll catch you and you'll wish Brex'd ripped out your lungs first before I did."

I gave a grave nod, not doubting the man for his word.

"There're many a space rogue in this corner of the galaxy. Men who'll sell their grandmothers at the slave block for a chance at the big score." He downed the drink at his side. He wet his lips. "Still can't believe that was you back at the table, you lying, deceiving varmint."

"It was, sadly, yes."

"Shoulda known." He shook his head gamely. "Slappy, what do you have to say about all this?"

The young man dropped his gaze. "Not much, Iron. Seeing as I brought him to you, then this all happened, I—"

"Don't beat yourself up." He laid a hand on the youth's shoulder. "You go with them, Slapper, show them the ropes, see that they don't get into trouble."

Slapper stirred, blinking with sudden interest.

"And don't you be putting any funny ideas in their heads, you hear, being back in a ship. You owe me fifteen hundred, if I recall."

"I know, sir...I mean, no, sir, I won't."

The husky nav operator waved his good hand in Iron's direction. "I still think we should have killed that bastard back there."

"And what, Sydney? Create a full out war between the Reapers and the Bratts? Already done enough damage as it is." He gave a tired sigh. "I've invested too much in this venture. We'd have the casinos and the mining companies at our throats. Maybe even the whole damn town."

"But we just blew Brex's ship out of—"

"If death-dealing's done out in space, fine, Syd, but not on home turf. Too many yes men around this pissass town. We'd have the whole place gunning for us, if we up and slaughtered Brex in plain sight."

"What makes you think he's not already dead?" I asked. "Lot of sparks flying in that crash back there."

"Ha! Take more than a shallow dive to kill that crafty bastard." Iron gusted out a weary breath. "Man's tough as nails. Lives up to his name. Ah well, to business. Our work is out in the Muridon Belt. Ever wonder why it's called that, Rusco?"

"Nope. Why, should I?"

"The Muridon Belt's a joke among the scutzers, as far back as the pioneer days, when brave souls went out to scutz space rock for a living. Space rock there was as thick as mouse droppings. So they called it the *Murid*-on Belt. Get it? Murid as in a rodent."

Marty gave a forced laugh.

"It's not supposed to be funny, boy." He scowled sidelong at him. "It's a risky business, dangerous as all shit. More dangerous than a nest of rattlesnakes. But I think you boys are up for it. The Belt is unique in its being close to the inner planets. It's a killer of many a spacer. Once you get in that maze of rock, you're in. You'll be dogfighting your way all the way out if you get into trouble. You ain't going to be hypering your way out in a desperado rush in some of the denser areas, unless you want to smash head on into a mountain of solid rock. End of ship." He narrowed his eyes on me slyly. "Just in case you get cold feet about this venture, Rusco, I'm telling you now so you can't say I didn't warn you."

I said nothing, just looked him in the eye.

"Right. Didn't think you were the timid types. You've got a bit of the dog-fighter in you, Rusco." He clapped me on the shoulder, causing me to wince. His face broke into another wide grin.

Slapper had gone to the loo. He returned, opted to retire, claiming he wasn't feeling well.

I could feel the regen doing its work. I felt a warm tingling sensation moving all along the nerve ends and the bones of my broken fingers. I could actually move them now without the fierce throbbing pain. I knew within half a day everything'd be back to normal, touch wood. I reached for the tin and smeared some more paste on my shoulder.

Marty applied some more to his busted ribs. "What's this goop made of anyway?"

I shrugged. "Some wonder plant they found on the frontier world, Gangko. Started harvesting it. Apparently the local anteaters were gobbling the stuff up by the shovel-full. Some scientists noticed they lived to more than 100 years. The biologists started to mix it in with some nanobot agents, and you have what you have."

"So what are the side effects?"

"Better not think of that, Mar. Just sit back and relax. Think of it as some kind of super-duper stem-cell steroids that work wonders. Be thankful we're not cripples."

Marty muttered. He shot me a dark look.

Iron interrupted, "One more thing. That boy Slapper, you ought to know. He's fragile. Keep an eye on him. He's had a bad spell out on Nyus Rock. Nearly caused the ruin of many men and some ships. Had to bring him out to Hoss's to dry out. He's a good kid, just a little…headstrong. Don't let him have his head. Keep a firm watch on him, Rusco. He'll be fine."

I nodded as if in half understanding. His peculiar affection for Slapper had surfaced again. Considering Slapper was just a lowly grunt doing dog patrol over at an oil derrick out in the middle of nowhere, Iron's concern seemed incongruous. A part of me wanted to press him for the details but I decided against it, seeing the sad sharpness in his eye.

I wondered exactly what we were being hired for. Noodling with the regen tin, I decided to come at it from around the side. "Do you Reapers guard the outposts or just hunt for spoils and ore?"

"Mostly scutzing. A bit of both though, truthfully. Big outfits like Crestar'll pay significant monies to team leaders like me to take care of their installations for them. Rather than bring in their own infrastructure and hire militia. It's cost effective. Even if it means they lose the odd rig.

"Seems to me it's not just the odd rig they lose."

"It isn't, you're right. But to a big outfit like Damocles, they don't give a shit. They treat it as chump change."

I gave a quick nod. Things were starting to make sense. I believed we'd landed a solution to our 'problem'—to get as far away from the likes of Sharki and shitbags like Brex as possible—also landed a job, hopefully one that would cover our expenses and pave the way for a brighter new future.

CHAPTER 17

A week passed and we got our ship back from Nanda's, forking over cash that Iron'd loaned us. Slappy wrapped up his watchman job back at the derrick and hopped a ride to Tylas to return Hoss his speeder. I bought Hoss a new hat. We made our farewells.

We were pretty much healed up from our ordeal at Brex's dog yard. At least as far as raw injuries were concerned. Only a few more background aches and pains to add to those I'd accumulated over the years. My sneaking suspicion was that regen didn't repair everything perfectly.

Slapper became part of our ensemble. We boarded on a sunny mid-summer morning back at Hoss's ranch. The U56 was big enough to accommodate 6-8 persons. Double that if we doubled up in the crew's quarters. We loaded the hold with all kinds of gear that we got from one of Iron's depots south of Tylas—drills, drill bits, sample kits, storage bins, scanners, space suits, thermal wear, guns... We even secured a weird-ass, high-wheeled kind of space buggy for traversing rough terrain. For longer excursions away from the ship, I guessed. Slapper knew all the accessories by name and exuded the air of confidence of a man who knew how to operate them.

My bloodstained jacket was due for an overhaul. Some industry garb was tacked to the depot's wall and was calling my name, reminding me that I could use a replacement.

I grabbed me one off the wall: an off-brown trenchcoat, with grim, Reaper-like figure and pickaxe emblazoned on the back. A bit too baggy around the shoulders maybe, but no harm. I wore it loose, open-fronted, trailing down past my hips just above the knee with a nice flair. Marty selected a matching, blue-gray outfit, also slightly oversize, making him look like a grumpy dwarf. Deidra preferred her own outfit for which I couldn't blame her.

Slapper lifted the hood of the excursion buggy and proudly showcased the interior. "80 horse electric engine. Spare 200-kilowatt-hour battery. Grav pack. Extra oxygen tanks." He stepped to the side and put a proprietary hand on the heavy-duty cross bar. "This baby's equipped with magno track and state-of-the-art grav stabilizers. Keeps us grounded while we go gallivanting for ore samples. Go too fast, we could launch ourselves into space at the slightest bump."

"Fun," I remarked idly. "How do you know so much about this stuff?" I smoothed out the rumples from my new jacket.

"Did a stint for a year out in Delta quadrant. With Capra and Bhoi. Reapers from Iron's outfit."

"Sounds messy."

Marty's easy manner had given way to a sneer. "Why're you running babysitter on a derrick out in the middle of nowhere then?"

Slapper's face reddened. "It's a long story. Something I'd rather not talk about."

"Fair enough." I shrugged. "Everyone's got his secrets. But you better know how to use all this stuff, Slappy, so we don't end up roiding it out there a pack of dead space tinkers."

"No problem, Rusco. I do."

Of course he did. Why would Iron have foisted him on us then?

Marty wouldn't let it alone. "Still doesn't explain how you ended up at Hoss's. Seems to me derricks run on their own, without need of a babysitter."

"It was an old rig," Slappers said defensively. "Needed monitoring. Gauges on the front were not working. Central relays in town couldn't get an alarm if something went wrong. Iron told me to watch the place against saboteurs. Other shitbags had taken a swipe at it. Almost succeeded. Probably Brex's boys out wanting to get hooks in Iron. I put the night eye hidden infrared cameras up before I left, watched them from Hoss's place at night. Daytime I had my trusty shotgun." He tapped his thigh with pride, as if his trusty weapon were still at his side, and I wondered if such an antiquated thing was match for anyone with a modern blaster.

"You don't need to explain, Slapper, it's alright." I knew from the tick in his left eye that there was a lot he wasn't telling and that he knew Iron'd just given him a make work project.

Maybe he was a nephew to Iron, or some relative or such. He'd screwed up under Iron's watch and instead of shanghaiing him, Iron'd put him to work out here, as punishment for his misdeeds. That, or at least to keep him on the payroll and out of trouble. Maybe he was giving Slappy a second chance, partnering him with us.

We'd find out soon enough.

Our paperwork came through the wire and we were officially licensed as locators: to secure mining rights on asteroids in the Vala system. Any licensed operator who could plant his flag on an otherwise worthless hunk of rock, could claim ownership, provided he had filed the proper paperwork at the office in Tylas—along with the specifics of the lode, the coordinates and orbital parameters of the space rock, and an estimate of the lode quantity—all with the Public Records Mineral Ownership Database (PRMOD for short) in accordance with the Vala Galactic Charter.

Of the handful of competing mining behemoths—Mivilex, Dancor, Apogee and Damocles—Crestar was the one that took most of Iron's commissions. The others split contracts among the scutzer gangs, the bulk of which went to Brex's Bratts.

The companies contracted the local scutzers to hunt down ore and lucrative deposits for them. Scutzers belonged to either the Gravediggers, Beryl Bratts, Mongers, Scags, or the Star Reapers, our outfit.

Our first port of call was the virgin asteroid field in the Veta Sector past Terminus where drifted a dense zone of what looked like undisturbed, fresh roids. All waiting to be surveyed. At least, according to Iron's calculation.

"Plenty of pickings here." Slapper planted a palm enthusiastically on the display scanner.

"We'll see." I twirled my finger somewhat more doubtfully. I looked at the motley crew of space rock revolving to port ever so slowly in the blackness of space. It looked like a dog's breakfast. I wondered what pots of gold lay out there.

Two of the space rocks in our immediate vicinity looked like sizable chunks that had a decent chance of good finds. Neither looked very aesthetic: prune-shaped uglies with small craters and pock marks on their surfaces. Both were smoothed by eons of time. Because of their mass and proximity, they seemed to be orbiting each other slowly while still tracing their long slow elliptical paths around Vala.

A fact which Newt corroborated with pedantic detail as he suddenly appeared on the bridge and hovered a few feet over my shoulder. Having spent the bulk of the week in the utility bay— avoiding the servicing personnel, with no one to offer advice to—he was in a petulant mood today, wasting no time offering useful orbital statistics and advice on approach vectors to the two roids.

"...Yes, Jet Rusco, it's true the roids orbit each other, at a period of 3.21 weeks."

Slapper blinked in surprise. "What the heck is this tin can?"

"I am a Mark 6, generation 4 device," Newt said peevishly. "It should be apparent from my rearboard antennae and transelectric shell, pure titanium. I am equipped to handle informatory downloads and advanced computation to ship personnel, versed in all aspects of engineering, maintenance and ship function."

Slapper smoothed the stubble on his chin. "Very interesting."

Newt bypassed the remark. His glistening outerbody swiveled to take in Slappy at a better angle. "Ship capacity is 8 persons, Jet Rusco. Should you wish to incorporate new crew members, I suggest you review article TC52-1 which is located in the owner's manual in utility box A9 above the—"

"It's alright, Newt," I said, raising a hand. "It's all taken care of."

A short pause. "Very well. I see you are studying class C Roids. Allow me to state the important facts concerning them. The first is of B spectral type, formed *in the early part of the solar system when cosmic dust and gases were—"*

"Again, Newt. All under control. Why don't you make yourself truly useful by cleaning the air ducts or tidying up the utility bay? You seem to be quite familiar with it by now."

"That is clearly outside the range of my functionality," Newt said crankily.

"Exactly. Precisely why I made the request." I turned my back on the chattering bot. "Let's focus on those roids," I grunted. I motioned to the visual with an expert's confidence.

"Sure, Rus, whatever you say." Marty flicked Deidra a wink.

"You want to pick a rock, wise guy?"

"No."

"Then ease up on the sarcasm, please."

Slapper gave a quick nod to confirm that my guesses had potential. "The scanner says there are denser metals in their subsurfaces. Could be molybdenum or scandium. Could pay to take a look."

Newt hitched in to make an erudite disclosure but I headed him off. "Good, Slapper. Do we have everything we need?"

"Ready to debark, Jet, whenever you are."

With some nods, we set about the preparations.

We made our descent to the roid. We had all the proper gear stowed—scope, drill bit, column, lode scanner, analyzer. Slapper was in high spirits. He was happy to be done with his dull routine minding the oil derrick back at Hoss's. Even if his experience with space mining was perhaps a little new, he was a positive influence on our group. A regular adventurer. Despite his big talk, he seemed to have a more romantic idea of space mining than anything else.

He launched himself into the approach to secure ourselves on the roid with zeal. He seemed to be a keener when it came to procedure, as we were to find out. Deidra handed over the nav to him with a flourish and a hint of a complacent mirth.

I helped Slapper direct *Trident* to a place which showed the most promising reading from the display scanner.

Hard, dry, bare gray rock loomed closer on the viewport.

The landing studs made contact with firm rock. Though we were on a 20 degree cant on what was a relatively flat area, our thrusters kept us flush to the roid.

We christened this Orphan Annie, 'Ithica A-333', for lack of a better name. We all wondered what her inaugural survey would yield. The three of us, Slapper, Marty and me, trooped to the hold where we all donned our beagle-brown suits, boots, helms and headlamps. I strapped on my air pak then grav pak—while Deidra remained up on the bridge to watch the ship and monitor our progress.

Marty carried the stake kit—a pear-shaped bundle the size of a breadbox— complete with extendable rod, drill and flag.

Slapper and I took probes; Slapper's was equipped with a backup analyzer and sample kit.

Slapper secured the rod-like scope and lode analyzer in the bundle he carried and motioned for me to carry a backup drill in case we needed to take an ore sample. We did a last minute check. We tuned our coms to make sure we could talk to one other, and that we could hear Deidra too.

I punched a button on the wall. The cargo hold door swung open. Immediately the space within the hold was reduced to a vacuum. The ramp slid out to touch the gray rock below. We trudged down to plant feet on the roid. There, fortunately, the small square artificial-grav units on the back of our suits kicked in to keep our feet in contact with the surface. Otherwise, without such units, we would be airborne in free space, once outside the ship's 50 yard artificial grav range.

Marty and I had packed blasters at our hip. Why would we need them? To fry some space aliens? I suppressed a laugh. A sudden urge for humor had me visualizing target practice at some roid rodents. There was nothing and nobody out there. A spacer's caution though pinged in my brain to bring weaponry just in case.

I carefully catfooted my way behind Slapper, following his lead. We trudged to a place about 60 yards away from the ship. Our short steps took us across the primordial surface. To a place which had showed some promise on the ship's sensors. The needle on the rod-like device Slapper held didn't seem to rise much into the green zone. Despite Slapper's show of enthusiasm, my suspicion was, he was more excited about this first roid walk in a long time than anything.

No harm.

Surface temperature was absolute zero. Our night side was away from Vala for the first hour of rotation so Deidra directed the ship's spot lamps to train on an area directly ahead of us to provide additional light. My headlamp cut a good swath in front of us, showing smoothed, porous, bronze-colored rock at our feet.

I felt a strange, but mild sense of vertigo as the stars swung overhead. Much too quickly for my tastes. I felt oddly disoriented here, to have so much space around me without the protection of a foot of solid metal of a ship. The stars wheeled in synchrony to the slow spin of the roid. The Milky Way gleamed radiantly, high off to the left, a luminous band of countless stars and bright-lit gases. Far away, Vala shone as a distant yellow globe. Some brighter specks included Terminus and Vagella, luminous beacons far off on the horizon.

With every buoyant step I took, I could feel the compact grav pack tugging down at my back, anchoring me to the roid.

I'd done space walks before, but I wasn't crazy about them. Neither was I afraid.

"The spin is tolerable here," Slapper remarked. His voice sounded odd and rusty through the com as he watched me miss a step. "Gets too fast and locators miss even a potential prospect. That, or suffer from roid sickness."

I inclined my head. "For several thousand yols in royalties, I'd be tempted to take the risk."

"Some loners risk it and in the end, end up dead. Can't get back to the ship."

"Slappy, that's some cheerful information," Marty muttered.

"Just telling you what I know."

"Well, if we wanted the info maybe we could have brought along Newt."

I snickered.

My step felt light, as if air was pushing me up into the blackness. If I were to apply too much pressure on the next step I might just drift off into space.

This roid was 10-15 miles across at its widest point, with spin I guessed about once every few hours.

That said, I'd hate to have my a-grav crap out.

We pushed another 80 yards from *Trident* when the needle on the scanner suddenly twitched. Slapper cocked his head. As I learned from his excited explanations, we used a 'modulator' to hone in on beryl or other metals.

The rod he held was a radialis device. Used in conjunction with the modulator for locating ores. The instrument was equipped with a modulator-frequency filter to help isolate certain substances. I saw Marty gazing at it with some awe and suspicion. "How does that thing work anyway, Rusco?" His scratchy voice echoed through the com.

"You point it at the rock, like a divining rod," Slapper explained. "The hypertilized metal's a good conductor and sends vibrations down through the surface. Picks up the reflected wave. Allows the circuit on top to identify what metals, minerals or goodies lie below."

"Nice, but how can it do that?"

I gave an impatient wave. "How can they bounce radio signals through the hyperdrive, Mar? How does brown paste regenerate flesh? How do bees mate? These miracles and modern tech gizmos are like magic. The eggheads have it all figured out."

"Sure." Marty scowled at me and became sullen. Couldn't blame him. He was surely not comfortable out here in the black emptiness of zero g. Nor was he the quintessential space miner.

While Slapper tinkered about with the radialis, deciding where we should head next, Marty peered about, grumbling to himself. He started humming an out-of-key tune.

On the verge of boredom, he sprang to his left, hefting his bulk a good five feet off the ground.

He floated down like a pixie, an ugly thug-faced dwarf in a space suit. I scowled. "Really?"

"Come on, Rusco, Lighten up."

Slapper, not to be outdone, mimicked Marty's movement, adding an extra foot to Marty's height. He wore a dog-like grin behind his tinted faceplate.

"You're next, Rusco," Marty crooned, slapping a heavy glove on my shoulder.

Deidra's voice rasped through the com, "You guys having fun?"

"Bet you wish you were down here."

"You guys find anything?"

"No."

"Okay, enough clowning around, folks." I said. "Deidra's getting antsy."

Slapper turned and saluted up toward *Trident's* bridge. "Sure thing, Cap'n."

We took readings, checked out another location a hundred yards away in a small crater-like depression.

Nothing.

Slapper took his hand off the analyzer. The rod-shaped unit just hung in midair to the tune of his silly grin. Whether he was showing off or not, I could not tell. I did the same with my gear, letting it hang at waist height, and caught the drill kit at the last moment before it drifted sideways out of reach.

"Quit playing around, Rusco," Marty mimicked, as he strode past me.

Slapper motioned to the gauge. "Look, scandium's down there. About 300 yards. Not a whole hell of a lot to report. Let's move on."

After an hour of more messing around, we finally gave up, deciding that this location was a waste of time. We'd taken many readings, and trudged here and there many hundreds of yards, invariably around the perimeter of our ship. Quasi sunrise greeted us as we made our slow way back to the ship. The faint glow of Vala spilled over the roid's sawtooth horizon.

Sunrise on Ithica. A thing to behold. The roid's slow rotation brought distant Vala in view…a bright star promising to bring feeble warmth. We were still plunged in a kind of maroon twilight gloom, but it was magical.

CHAPTER 18

The second roid, the smaller briquette-shaped one, proved more promising a venture.

Our second test site had us striking pay dirt. 200 tons of beryl, as indicated on the scope. The lode, 187 yards down, was too deep to get a physical sample, but we snapshotted the sensor readings—a page of data—which we transmitted to the claim office along with the location.

Marty had the stake kit ready and we rolled out a flag with the Reaper insignia on it. Slapper drilled a hole wide enough to fit the flagpole. I inserted the extendable rod in the hole while Marty raised the flag. Up it went to a height of 4 feet: the stiff fabric held outstretched by a thin metal rod running along its top. We stood back, admiring our handiwork. I was not sure what I felt about the hooded Reaper that stared back so cynically at me with its dim, gimlet eyes. The eerie thing had a way of casting a dark energy over the place.

I tipped my helmet and murmured under my breath, "One small step for man…a great leap for mankind."

"What you babbling about, Rusco?" Marty grunted.

"About small steps and great leaps."

"Turning into a poet?"

"No, just dredging up some doggerel I remember from the ancient past."

"Yeah, from who?"

"The alleged first man to step foot on Earth's moon, if memory serves."

"Why alleged?" Slapper asked, pausing from his work.

"Come on, Slappy, that first moon landing was a pure con job. To convince the masses they were 'winning the race'." I shook my head. "The CGI was so bad they had to purge the archaic web some time later of all media clips showing the supposed 'space capsule' blasting off from the moon and meeting the 'alleged' lunar orbiter high above. The graphics were so abysmal it'd make some of the cheesy scifi flicks that came out around then look like avant-garde holo wizardry."

Slapper blinked.

"Yeah, NASA was a real card back then."

"NASA? Who's that?"

"You mean, 'what'. National Aeronautics Space Administration. An institution back in the 20th century of the superpowers at the time. In charge of space exploration and the drive for the space race." I paused, nursing a grin. "Back in the day when space travel and exploration needed to be faked... For political reasons. Global control via a cold war. Give people the sense that they were winning 'the war'."

"Seems you have some strong opinions of past history."

"Not really." I sighed. "Just some opinions about some dubious institutions, like the CIA, NASA, the NSA."

Slapper bristled. "Just because there was some bad video of the moon landings doesn't mean they're fa—"

"Slapper...let me tell you a story about space drive. It was ion drive that revolutionized space travel. There was none of that back then when they faked the moon landings. Only rocket propellants and multistage rockets. You need an atmosphere in which to push against to create lift. You could blast off from earth but you weren't going to be blasting off from the moon or any atmosphere-less world.

"Let's review: the capsule blasts off from the moon defying all laws of physics and contemporary tech and then it rendezvous with the 'space orbiter' *Columbia* in lunar orbit. Problem is, no way could it take them back to earth, for the simple reason of thrust and lift that I mentioned. There's no atmosphere. No way you can slingshot around the moon either to create velocity. You need thrust in order to escape the gravity. So if such a craft was in orbit, it's there to stay."

Marty broke in, "I thought they used tanks of gas to jet the ship around and make small adjustments to its course?"

"Yeah, like the 'supposed' nitrogen gas jets on the lunar lander? No. You might be able to generate some small thrust using the laws of momentum—mass times velocity—but you would need a hell of lot of mass. Certainly not enough force or mass of propellant necessary to get a ship up to the speeds necessary to get back to earth in 3 days."

Marty shrugged.

"Let's do a little math here for some fun. It's a voyage that takes them 3 days, according to NASA. 240K miles from Moon to Earth. That's 80k miles per day, or beetling about 3500 mph. No way. How are you accelerating to these speeds in a vacuum with no atmosphere to push against? You can't. Not to mention the whole thing of trying to stop yourself once you get to your destination. Park yourself on the moon? Ain't going to happen. You'll be in 3500 mph orbit around the moon at best. Good luck landing some small capsule using a few little nitrogen gas jets. Pretty hard for 3 people to shit and piss too in zero g for seven days. At least if you want to keep it real. Must I go on?"

"Okay, so it's a hoax," Slappy finally hissed. "But not all the early explorations and projects are—"

"Trust me. They are."

I knew that Voyager and Viking and lesser known projects like Osiris-Rex—a 2 year mapping of the Bennu asteroid—and Orion and Artemis Moon Stations and many, many more projects were fake. A great hijack and theft of trillions of public tax monies over the years to create propaganda and a space mythology that didn't exist. Amazing they got away with it. For almost two centuries. Wasn't sure if I wanted to hit Slappy with that. He looked as if he were ready to slug someone, what with his eyes bulging out of their sockets.

Marty was okay, he could handle the bugfuckery, but in the end he could give a rat's ass about it all. Maybe he was the smartest of our lot.

Deidra's voice came over the com. "Okay, professor, how's this ion drive work?"

"From what I understand, by making huge mass and velocity, then applying the law of conservation of momentum."

Marty shook his head. "You lost us."

"Let's suppose you are in a toy train on metal wheels—wheels that roll easily on a railway track. Someone gives you a shove from behind. You coast forward on your track then stop somewhere down the line. Suppose you are stationary and you chuck a metal ball out behind you. You chuck it with enough force and you notice the train rolls in the opposite direction. The harder you throw, the faster you go. The weightier the ball, the faster you go. Imagine creating a huge mass of 'propellant', ion propellant, with the help of artificial grav-tech, and shooting this heavy mass of molecular particles behind you at enormous speed. You put the two together and you have mega thrust."

"Okay, that makes sense," Slapper conceded with a jerky nod, "but doesn't account for the trickery." Teeth gritted, he looked like the proverbial dog with a bone in his mouth, daring anyone to pry it out.

"Doesn't to a lot of people. Until you take in the whole of space history. How many people you think are doing that?"

"Doesn't make the moon landings fake and other pioneer expeditions fake."

"To skeptics it does. You don't fake one thing without faking a bunch of others. One lie breeds ten more. The whole foundation stinks."

"But why?"

"It's a reasonable question," I said. "Your first clue was that no such Voyager or deep space exploratory craft were ever found by starships on the coming of the varwol space drive. The images and video of the Apollo mission were very obviously filmed on Earth in studio lighting. They unfortunately got the shadows wrong too, sloppy bastards."

Slapper paused. "So they must have—" He was not sure what to say.

"There's an iconic black-and-white video that was broadcast to everyone on Earth. Showing the two astronauts in their baggy white spacesuits putting up the 'flag'. When they raise it, it bristles in the wind, fully outstretched. Except there's no wind on the moon. No air. So how does that work? If you listen to the conversation between the astronauts and Houston back on Earth during the raising of that flag, there are points where the question-answer dialogue happens seamlessly. Like a second in between responses. Except it takes 3 seconds for a radio signal to travel from the earth to moon and back, making it physically impossible for the conversation to have taken place. Unless it was pre-recorded on Earth. A couple of little oversights the propaganda team had forgotten about."

Newt's voice broke over the com, *"It takes 2.42 seconds at perigee, Jet Rusco, not 3...otherwise everything else you said is true."*

Slapper's face hardened.

"NASA had to sell the lie of space exploration. The CIA and the cartel of intelligence agencies were the glue that kept it all together. Puppeted at a distance by the banksters. Back in the day when the superpowers vied for control over the earth."

I laughed. Even the superpowers themselves were a joke—a front for the real ruling class, the very few who controlled the movements of trillions in wealth.

"NASA was itself superseded by NAVO (New Avionic Vanguard Order). It went the wayside some few centuries ago, made obsolete in the days of full-on terraforming and space travel to the common man."

"That's quite the world view," Slapper said.

"It is."

"And you know this how?"

"I'm a little older than you, Slappy. Been in a lot of bad, dark places. Kept my eyes and ears open. Had the grace to hear some of the testimonials right from the head honchos themselves—" Here I could only think of the detestable Gy-ar and his brood of space ghouls who ran the Temple of the Moon. I would never forget Gy-ar's chilling recounting of humanity being choreographed from the get-go, from the time of the Great Pyramids and before. Fake histories, usury, orchestrated revolutions, endless takeovers, hostile mergers, armies of top-down-controlled institutions, barrels of pseudoscience, propaganda, lies, controlled opposition. The list went on and on.

"Once when I was in a Skurg camp, my friend and fellow prisoner Skel would talk about this when the Skurgs weren't watchdogging us. We had deep discussions. I learned a lot. He was a knowledgeable fellow. Opened my eyes to many things I hadn't considered before."

"What happened to him?"

"He was murdered. By a space thug like Brex. I killed that bastard with my bare hands." I looked away and it was all I could do to squint back the tears, remembering the brutal way Skel had died.

"He had a father, a space archaeologist who traveled to countless worlds and knew a lot of what I'm telling you. Skel got much wisdom from him. They shared a lot of what I'm telling you in their joint discoveries, and from his own travels, even though we were about the same age. We were young...Younger than young."

Slapper dipped his head. "I'm sorry about your friend."

"Yeah, well, me too. Those days are past." I firmed my jaw. "Makes you wonder what psyops they got going these days. At least people can hyper out to these places now and refute a lot of the space myths and pseudoscience created back in the old days. Probably why those agencies became mostly obsolete."

"Yeah, maybe."

"Makes you wonder too…how, with that primitive technology, they could even receive and send signals from billions of miles across space…as far as Pluto. Communicating with these Voyager and deep-space craft, at a time they needed to put up radio towers every few miles on Earth to send cellular signals."

"Different technologies," Slapper said. "Not a fair comparison."

"I know, but you get my point."

Marty gestured. "Didn't they have some big ass radio dishes to pick up signals from far space?"

"Maybe good for radio astronomy and studying large masses like quasars or distant galaxies but not good for tiny probes, giving off a few watts of signal across billion-mile gulfs. You forget there is also such a thing as the earth spinning on its axis and rotation around the sun. Tracking such fly-drop signals'd be a bitch."

Slapper shook his head. "There's some flaw in your argument, I just can't see it."

"Fooled you. That's why they had some fancy motor control adjusting the dish's direction to follow the path of moving objects. The dish is not stationary, remember?"

"Yeah," chimed in Deidra, "I think they figured out how to amplify signals way up the ladder too."

"You're talking so many orders of magnitude, Dee, it'd be like trying to get a count of grains of sands on the beach. Not enough amplification to explain how they could pick up a signal of a few watts over billions of miles."

Newt spoke again. *"A supplementary point. There is evidence to support the fact that many of these large radio dishes weren't even real. Just pictures and elaborate videos posted on web sites, making grandiose claims about space communication. Like this one I see, in what was Barstow, California, designed to give the illusion that NASA had the means to communicate with deep space craft and robotic probes. Hmmn. Further references have been curiously purged from darkweb sources. Odd. I must look into this more."*

I could only grin. I think my little audience had reached their limit. When I tried to explain how it wasn't until 200 years later that humans started to really venture out in space with the discovery of the early varwol, Slapper grunted in defeat. "Enough history lessons, Rusco. Let's head back. We're batting zero over here." He studied the gauge with disappointment.

"Okay."

We space-walked our way back to the hold, dumped our gear and got the ramp lifted. We sealed the 6-inch thick steel door and re-pressurized the area and de-suited, pleased at securing our find. We climbed the companionway on sea legs made such by the lighter artificial grav. Back on the bridge, we filed our claim. I learned that each locator was encouraged to submit a digital Time and Location Stamp, a DTLS, showing proof of discovery. Some locators even offered a DTLS video time stamp. Slapper was somewhat versed in the process; we didn't omit any paperwork or delay the process.

The PRMOD office was more than happy to take our claim. An official response came back and our claim would be sent in due time to the mining companies that would bid for purchase if they deemed it worthwhile. We would take the highest offer. Somewhere in the process, Iron would negotiate the deal since we were licensed, working locators operating under him. Of course, he'd take a percentage of the cut.

Slick and sleek. A good operation as far as operations went, if not a tad slow...and contingent on the mining corps' interest and a large amount of luck. But I could see that experience gained in this field could net one some significant cash, particularly in divining what rocks to check out and what to ignore.

Deidra was content to work the bridge. She had no real urge to get down on the surface and engage in the boring work of locating. Could I blame her? Even Marty seemed a bit of a third wheel in the process. Slapper and I could easily handle the basic operations. In some of the later surveys, I'd taken turns with Marty to assist Slapper.

I noticed Slapper always checked the ship's long range radar before we set foot on any particular roid. "You jumpy, Slappy? Expecting somebody?"

"No, but can never be too careful."

"Claim Jumpers?"

He stared at me, poker-faced.

I nodded. "We'll keep an eye out for ruffians…like Brex."

CHRIS TURNER

CHAPTER 19

Some weeks had gone by and we were scoring some lucrative finds. We hadn't got any pay yet but we'd filed 8 claims. Slapper was confident we'd see some yols in the next few days.

This was to my liking. For a while I was thinking that we'd given our enemies the slip.

I couldn't have been more wrong.

It was on our 19th scutz mission when Slapper, Marty and I were down on Roid AC-34 that Deidra's voice suddenly sounded in my helmet.

"We got company."

"Who?"

"Look to two o'clock. Who do you think?"

I peered over my shoulder. I saw a lone ship—an inverted T with a sickle-shaped stern and blunt, adder-shaped nose. It was circling down to our vicinity in no hurry. A rather small, but fast, souped-up locator craft. Even from this vantage I swore I could make out the extra metal plates and armor she'd been equipped with. No doubt she'd had her shields up and her weapons trained on our U56.

Slapper cringed. "Scavengers. From Brex's Bratts, I guess." He licked his lips. "Sometimes these weasels tail loners like us out of range of our scanners, then beetle up when they see a locator spending significant time on a space rock. They assume there's been a find, that someone's about to make a claim, then they hightail it out to steal the lode before you can register it."

"Must have been monitoring our channel," I mused. "Impressed maybe with our recovery rate."

"They wire ahead to the PRMOD office making a bogus claim, thus beating you to the mark. There's a lot of that going on these days, Rusco. Nothing much you can do."

Great. Thugs from our favorite rival clan itching to claim our space rock. "We'll make sure that doesn't happen," I rasped, scanning the sky for others. Marty'd come over to peer up with me.

The ship eased down and landed about two hundred yards away, twice the distance from us to the U56. A couple of explorers in suits not dissimilar to ours but of grayish color came ambling out of the stern hold. They padded toward us with ease. I didn't like the fact that they hadn't hailed us, or tried to contact *Trident*. It smacked of skulduggery.

"I'm coming over to pick you up," Deidra hissed.

"No," I said harshly into the com. "Take the ship back out. Pretend to give us up. Leave us here."

"No way, Rusco!"

"Double back," I hissed at her. "Pick us up later. If we're still around."

I just hoped they couldn't hear me on this scrambled channel.

Marty and I shared glances, our hands not far from our blasters.

The first suited figure was now only a few dozen yards away. His motions were practiced, the mark of a competent spacer. His white-booted feet were moving at an impressive rate.

"Need some help there, fella?" he said at last through the com. The strident voice brushed at the back of my head like a cold glove.

"No thanks."

I sized up the other skulker in a glance. How the hell they'd closed that gap in so quick a time still amazed me.

The first was all smiles and chuckles, busy with his hands that held a beat-up, but serviceable radialis, his face overly round and his eyes unnaturally glassy. The other was thin, beetle-like with darting eyes and steady grip on his blaster. Both packing significant muscle and oozing stressless confidence.

"Locating's a dangerous job out here in the boonies," the first one said. "Lonely. Easy for some unscrupulous shit-bag to jump you and rob you blind, eh Gilo?" The man laughed. "Me and Gilo here, we saw you land just an hour ago. Just wanted to check in and lend a hand. Protect our fellow scutzers. Decided it'd be on our conscience if something bad happened and we allowed anyone to scam you out of your claim, or stave in your skulls."

"Yeah, sure," I said dryly. "Just good samaritans passing through. The models of civility."

"Right." His head swiveled to his comrade, trading an oily grin. "The man catches on quick."

I'd been at this game too long to be sidewinded by a couple of yobos. I motioned. "If you could help me with this radialis…Seems to be out of whack." I gave it a sharp shake.

"Sure, Chief." The first one stepped forward. "Gilo? Git your buns over there and help this fine gentleman out."

Gilo smiled and obliged.

As Gilo was reaching for my rod, I kneed his weapon aside. His shot went wide while Marty plowed helmet first into the other, smashing his ribs. R1 blasts careened wildly around the landscape off into the maroon gloom.

I ripped the grav pack off the first thug's back. He went spinning away from the roid, screaming obscenities. I knelt, trained my R1 and ravaged fire at the other with a full blast in his side. His suit imploded.

The T-shaped ship moved alongside to confront *Trident*, but Deidra had swung round and trained cannons at her. Bolts streamed out, tickling the enemy vessel's shields.

Long bolts of ion fire came smashing at our feet, chopping rocks and chipping fragments at us. A weird floaty cloud of debris spiraled all around. Slapper crumpled to his knees. His gloved hand came hard against a place on his left shin.

Damn! His suit had been hit, a micro puncture. He was losing air fast.

I cursed and space-hobbled toward him.

I saw by the size of the perforation that it was a pinhole breach. But Slapper's gloved hand was not doing a good job in sealing it. I cursed, kicking myself for not packing a proper suit repair kit.

I could see fire streaks careening left and right in the sky above us. The U56 and the enemy ship exchanged debilitating fire. *Trident* took some hard hits but her shields held. Her starboard and port cannons gave back more than she was receiving.

The battered locator craft was not faring as well.

She took a cruel bite of ion fire to her stern; now she dropped, nose first toward the roid—a place not far from our position. Down she came, angling faster and faster.

Marty and I dragged Slappy as far as we could away from a certain collision course.

The ship blitzed overhead, then crashed not 80 yards from us.

"Deidra, get down here!" I hissed at her, my voice nothing more than a hoarse rasp.

The giant oblong dark shadow of *Trident* passed over us and landed a few dozen yards away. We bent down to gather up Slapper. The hold door auto opened. The ramp snaked out and Marty and I dragged him in as quickly as we could. I ran to the side and smacked the hold door mechanism and started the auto-pressurize sequence, breathing curses.

The wait seemed interminable. Even though maybe only a few dozen seconds had passed, Slapper was white as a ghost. His lips seemed peeled back from his face, his eyes wobbly. The moment the green light came on, we shucked off his suit and lay him there flat on the floor. I chaffed his skin.

"Slapper, Slapper, you okay?"

He was chilled, ashen, shaking uncontrollably.

He managed to croak out a garbled response.

We pulled a couple of heavy thermo sweaters over him and got him to the bridge. We settled him into the copilot's chair. He was going to be okay, just in shock, shaken by this brush of death.

After a while he stirred and looked down through the viewport at the broken ship and cold duskiness, eyes narrowed at the dead man lying crumpled on the surface. The other was long gone spinning away through space. "Brex's Bratts," he murmured hoarsely. "What do we do with them?"

"Leave 'em," Marty growled. "But we ain't leaving the equipment."

"No," I agreed.

We went back to fetch the radialis and the analyzer.

I paused at the sight of the ravaged body. Sure enough, a couple of Brex's Boys. I could see the burned-out, half crumpled logo of the cartoonish grinning pirate on the side. They'd come to ambush us. Probably greedy with the promise of reward for our heads. I looked toward the crumpled hull of their ship and thought of trying to salvage some gear. No. The hold door was tilted and twisted. Not worth wasting our blaster fire to try carving a way in.

Marty just kicked at the body and sent an extra bolt of R1 fire into his brains before we left him there in that forsaken place.

We got back to the *Trident* and reported as much to Deidra and Slapper.

Marty had some shrewd ideas about filing our claim and cashing in on the spoils, but I advised against it. "We're already in the bad with the Bratts. Should we be traced to the murder of Brex's men, it'd only bode worse for us. Better we just get the hell out of here."

"Just leave the claim?" Marty protested. "There's thousands in beryl here for us."

I shrugged.

Slapper shifted weakly in his chair. "I reckon he's right. As much as I hate to admit it."

"I wouldn't be surprised if Brex put a bounty on our heads," I grumbled. "Any scutzer just happen to bring us in, or our heads as proof, gets a large sum of yols and moves up the ladder."

"Who wants to bet," Deidra said, a small quaver in her voice, "the pilot got off a message to Brex, relaying our location before he crashed?"

"Why stop there?" Marty said. "Why just the Bratts? Could be the word's out to all the gangs."

The thought hung in the air and left a pall of gloom over our company. We impulsed away from that miserable roid and took up in Pradus sector far away. Needless to say, we watched our backs with ever more vigilance.

But even such vigilance is never enough.

CHAPTER 20

None of us was sad to leave the dead bodies and the grounded ship far behind. We set a course for the Naigon Zone-A4, diametrically opposite the place on the Belt's ring where we were. Fastest way to get there was to impulse up on a right angle till we cleared the roid disc, then hyper the rest of the way to the ring's fringe on the other side of the Vala system.

If Brex had put the word out for a hit, I'm not sure how any place in the Muridon Belt would ever be safe. But then what part of this galaxy ever was?

None of these deductions left me with any warm, cozy feelings.

Slapper, sufficiently recovered after a day of rest, took comfort in busy work at the nav, concentrating on trying to find our next survey site. "Computer says this Class B egg-shaped roid is uncharted."

I grunted as I made a wide turn around the light side of the roid. My eye caught the glint of something unusual. Three or four ships huddled in a narrow gully on the surface. Why would so many ships be clustered on an unknown roid?

Slapper frowned. "Readings are showing no sign of beryl or anything too lucrative. Scant traces of selenium and magnetite, but nothing to merit staking claims."

Newt inserted himself between the visual and nav. *"98% probability of criminal activity transpiring below, Jet Rusco. I suggest we report this to the APC authorities—"*

"And I say we don't, Newt. Why draw attention to ourselves?"

Deidra squinted to get a better look at the ships. "Shouldn't we be moving away from them?"

"How close do you think we can move in without them detecting us?" I asked.

Marty shrugged. "Maybe a few miles if we stay below radar. It'd be nip and tuck. Why you so desperate to get a peekaboo?"

"Those ships—" I murmured. "There's something familiar about them. The shingled armor, the upturned bows. I've seen those type before. They're not scutzers."

Slapper nodded. "No, they're not."

"Curiosity killed the cat," Marty said glibly.

"Lack of intel killed many more."

I steered us on a wide sweep around the back side of the roid while Marty activated our limited cloaker system. I set her on dead slow...and skimmed yards above the surface. We practically hugged the ground. Then I slowed down to crawl behind a low ridge, relying on visual. Through a gap in stubby crags, I saw a curious sight.

Six ships nestled in a small indentation sheltered by the rocky bumps of the ridge—the same behind which we hid. Seems as if our quarry had visitors; judging by the way the four with upturned prows were cramped together. They'd created a kind of club house. An ugly squat, square-shaped tin structure with a low roof. A gathering place for illicit dealings? Some kind of scutzing station? No. Couldn't be. I saw white steam rising from a pair of vertical pipes at the side.

What could be going on down there?

"That's a Scag ship," Slapper reported. His voice sounded hollow. "See the beetle insignia?" He zoomed in using the viewport magnifier. "There's another one too."

"Scags? What the hell are scutzers doing here?" Deidra asked.

"Yes. Scags for sure." He zoomed in another notch. "Look at the armor on them. The raised turrets, the tapered side cannons."

I frowned, bit my lip. "Doesn't make sense. Unless—"

"What?"

"They're in league with the Skurgs. Those others sure as hell are Skurgs.

Slapper gave a wild laugh. "How? Why?"

I jerked my head toward the visual. "There's your answer, Slappy. That's how Brex and these others must have found us. They must be making side deals with them. Maybe using them for recon. Makes me wonder about Iron too."

Deidra cast a dark look at me.

There was no proof of any of this, so I dismissed the conjecture with a toss of my head. Suspicion though, had a way of gnawing at the roots, eating its way into the brain and eroding one's faith.

Turned out our so-called 'stealth' turned out to be a joke. The first Skurg vessel had sighted us easily. Lights flared up on her prow and she lifted her upturned nose to veer up in our direction.

"Damn, Marty! I thought you said we were cloaked and out of radar range?"

"So I was wrong. Spank me."

I gave my head a frustrated shake.

Your shit show, Rusco. Blame yourself. You should have known better.

My eyes wandered back to the cross-visual. I saw two sets of dark-suited figures scurrying from the 'clubhouse' across the stark landscape and aiming for the tightly-parked vessels. They were not human. Much too tall and thick around the waist and chest. No, these were Skurgs. No doubt about it.

"Seems as if they're pissed at us for discovering them," Marty observed.

"Enough to eliminate the witnesses?" Deidra's hand moved to the weapons' grid.

"I reckon. What do you think, Slap?"

He was blinking, jaw agape, engrossed with zooming in on the ships. "I don't get these damn Scags."

"My guess, some rogues gone over to the dark side."

"My guess too. We're thinking on the same channels, Rus."

The weird humanoid figures had gained the hatches of the remaining snub-nosed vessels. Now the stern jets of three of them flared to blue life and the ungainly craft rocketed up to meet us.

"Let's gear up for a hoe down, people," I called. "Battle stations! Get ready to fire!"

The easiest thing to do would be to hyper the hell out of here. But it was risky, with all these roids floating about. My gut told me it would be better to play fugitive on ¾ impulse. The worst thing that could happen was we'd have to fight off these bastards.

Our shields were not the strongest part of our defense though. Nor were our odds. Right now, one of the Scag vessels, a long barrel-shaped craft with wedge-shaped prow, had lifted its bulk in the air to join the Skurgs. I glared hard at the cylindrical hull, wondering, like Slappy, what went on in the scutzer pilot's head.

Deidra rapped out blasts from the starboard guns. Slapper kept his eyes glued to the nav.

While Deidra laid down cover fire, Marty sighted on the first Skurg vessel.

"Danger, Jet Rusco!" Newt hovered nearby, cramping my world. *"You are not strapped in—"*

"Get lost and shut the fuck up," I swatted him away. "Marty, deal with this pest."

"You deal with him. I got other more important things to do."

The first Skurg bombs hit us hard—at stern and midships and sent *Trident* fishtailing and our bodies knocking hard against one other.

Marty was lifting himself off the floor, shaking his head groggily.

"Marty! Get the hell back to the weapons' console!"

He snatched himself back to his command seat and gripped the controls. He rattled out fire at the ships that had crept up on us.

Trident's port cannon flared. The lead Skurg was knocked out of formation. One of the wingmen closed up to take the lead.

I grinned. "Nice hit, Mar! We got three bogies still coming in. What say we give them the old 'pin the tail on the donkey'?"

Marty gave a vindictive smile.

It was an old routine we'd perfected that had saved our asses many a time. We bank far out, lure them in. Then flip hard over and hit them with maximum fire. "You and Dee nail the wing man farthest out. He'll be least expecting it. Shields are at 70%. We have room to spare…"

Newt interjected, *"Shields are at 68.3%, Jet Rusco. Estimated 4 days, 3 hours, 2 minutes to recharge cells to 100%. It is not a wise course engaging so many foes with more maneuverability, firepower and updated hardware."*

"Marty?"

Marty loosed a low growl and leaped up from his seat to swat at the annoying bot with the butt of his R1.

Newt went flying across the bridge. His gleaming shell spun wide. He recovered and hunkered down sullenly under the auxiliary weapon's console.

The hull rocked to more Skurg fire. If we were to die here, it wouldn't be to the tune of Newt's useless chatter.

We clamped on our shoulder harnesses. More not so friendly fire lashed us broadside. The hull shuddered and I rocked in my seat as *Trident* stabilized. I kept her on a zigzag course away from the roid. Megawatt blasts had pounded our forward vane, threatening to breach our hull.

I wondered why these cretins hadn't finished us off. Then the horrifying realization struck me. If they could run us to ground, they could capture us and eat us alive.

"I don't know about you," I hissed, "but these pricks are starting to annoy me."

"So what are we going to do about it, Rus?"

"Give them a taste of their own medicine." I turned to the nav. "Slapper! Find me a roid. Any roid. So long as it has a significant dark side."

Slapper tapped on the nav's keypad. He pulled up roid charts and schematics. "This one…here! Pegasus 221. Coordinates 03.34.67. Registered and named, but no claims."

"Good. It'll have to do!"

I punched an escape vector using the quoted number and charted a quick course toward the barbell-shaped roid, a haunting shape on the horizon.

"Roid's big enough to launch an attack!" I blared. "If we can make it around the other side, we might be able to play cat and mouse, set up an ambush. Still too dense with roids this side of the Belt to hyper out safely."

"How much shield damage can we withstand?" Deidra cried. She let loose a scathing barrage of ion fire at the lead Skurg vessel.

"Not much! Keep smacking these bastards' flanks. Something's got to give."

I was worried about our shields. Newt was right. In the weak solar radiation of Vala, it could take days if not a few weeks to get shields back to full strength.

The roid grew larger and I swung the hauler around toward its dark side. I angled down on a steep cant toward the pock-marked surface, trying to lure the birds of prey into its shadow. We blitzed the largest crater and I roared forward at near max speed over the stark terrain. A blip on the radar appeared. I decelerated, pulled up on the wheel. I frowned down upon a flag and some odd crumpled metal hulks that loomed up as we zoomed over. The twisted wrecks of two locator ships. They had passed under us several hundred yards away from the claim site. No mining expedition had yet come to this forsaken place. Yet a claim had been made. Another mishap? No. If it had been lucrative enough to yield ore, why had not some mining corp set up shop, machines been installed? Where were all the telebractors?

Something pinged in my brain. Something untoward tainted this whole region of space. My mind could only wander upon the darker, sinister overtones.

I did not want to become another of those casualties below.

I spat scathing curses at the three Skurg ships that pursued us. All the fearsome legends of their kind came back to me in haunting, lurid color. Cannibalistic bounty hunters—a mutant race of subhumans who hunted and terrorized the known worlds for sport and profit. Mercenary slavers. Monsters for hire who made humans disappear.

I remembered the bit of history Skel'd told me that had chilled my marrow. A race that created alliances with whoever or whatever would have them, whether good or evil. They were rumored to be the mongrel breed of human and alien spawned in the Netara System. A criminal mastermind and mineral prospector, Krung, had fled there, or rather been exiled to the earth-like planet, Hru, in the Netara System. He and his score of associates had bred with the violent, indigenous quasi-hominid female species and whelped the first generation of Skurgs. Centuries had passed. Now their race had spread like a cancer throughout the galaxy.

I snapped out of my grim reverie. "Marty, I'm going to loop over them in a sudden crazy arc. Then you and Deidra're going to take out that lead vessel."

Marty gave a somber nod. "Copy that."

"Not getting a good feeling about this," Deidra said with a brisk click of her tongue.

The Scag ship had fallen behind, maybe losing interest in the chase. But the Skurg trio kept dogging us.

"On the count of three," I said.

I pulled up on the controls and *Trident* did a fierce loop de loop. She rocketed up in a tight ferris wheel turn, end over end.

While we were upside down, Marty poured max fire into the turrets of the lead ship's hull. Ion-flare lashed the tough metal. Her shields burst. The fiery hulk nova-ed in a livid flare. The remnants of red-hot twisted steel smacked into the roid's surface, ripping a crater dozens of feet wide.

Deidra raked a steady stream of fire out at the other's bow close in behind. I saw bright flashes curl around her fluted metalwork armor and I knew she was done. Her shields must have been vaporized. She fell behind on quarter impulse and I knew she was crippled.

I beetled *Trident* out on a sharp tangent: max thrust at right angles to the roids. On this course, we'd clear the belt in just under 10 minutes.

It did not surprise me that the remaining Skurg did not follow. We couldn't have been worth much to them. Not with one of them down and the others crippled.

I took a trip to the scullery and came back with three bottles of Old Sunrise arrack. We celebrated our victory in style. Slapper drank, his lips peeled back, his cheeks glowing red, accepting the praise I slathered on him for finding the coordinates of the decoy roid. I complimented him with slaps on the back. Marty drained his drink in one gulp. Deidra declined a second glass. Her eyes gleamed, but tiny sweat droplets beaded her forehead and she said little.

We toasted our success at surviving two bouts of skulduggery. But I sensed tension among our company, an uneasiness edged with forced cheer which was not good for any crew.

CHAPTER 21

We dogged it for two days on a mixed bag of uncharted roids. Without success. The good news was, some of the mining corps had picked up our charters and paid out. Crestar and Apogee. We'd created a group credit account in Tylas at the First Holo Credit Union over ship's radio. We were now officially money-making scutzers. 4k in the good…minus the 6k we still owed Iron. Three-quarters of our earnings went to Marty, Deidra and me, a quarter to Slappy.

I felt good about our enterprise. I had a bad feeling about the future. Peril lurked around every corner. I could feel it in my bones. Between Skurgs, Brex's vigilantes, random space disaster and the threat of Sharki, there was plenty to be worried about.

The question was, how far could we push this caper?

I vowed: after we'd secured our first 50k, we'd get the hell out of Dodge, make a new start in some star system far away from Vala and these wretched roids.

It happened unexpectedly and with welcoming arms, as these things tend to go.

In *Trident's* narrow corridor on the way to the mess hall—a sudden brushing of my shoulder against hers as she passed me. Maybe it was the stress of the last harrowing encounters, or our mutual sexual awareness of each other, a need that had been building and was now at an apex. Deidra paused and there was a moment of tautness between us, an expectancy in the carriage and lean of her body of which I was in absolute admiration.

I grabbed her and pulled her in toward me. Her mouth was yielding, full, ripe. Her lips parted, cheeks flushed, green eyes gleaming—eyes which held that dreamy black hole one could fall into, so hypnotizing they were. Both of us were almost drugged with anticipation.

She made no sound, just beckoned me with a little head motion toward her bunk, a sudden mutual understanding.

I gave my head a little shake and directed her back to my private quarters at the end of the hall with the larger bunk. Our clothes were off before we could both take six breaths between us.

I wondered if I were dreaming or in some weird half reverie. This was moving very fast. I'd never taken lightly the hell Sharki had put her through and had made the conscious decision to maintain an arms' length relationship, no matter how drawn I was to her.

Now, to my thrill and surprise, she seemed to be open and willing and not one for foreplay.

She quickly assumed an authoritative position on top, straddling me at the waist, her back erect, hands gripped on my shoulders.

She began a gentle rocking motion: sensual enough to bring me to the edge. But I wasn't in the mood for delicious moments as these to be over so soon. I pulled her in tight toward me. She hummed a warm seductress's breath in my ear as she leaned in ever closer, amused at my heroic attempt to draw out the moment, to squelch any telling sound of pleasure. She dragged her nails the length of my neck, her shoulders back, her skin glistening with sweat, as if to say, 'How long can you last, Mr. Rusco?'

Not long if you keep this up, Miss Dee. I squelched back another heady groan.

"I'd guess I'd better stop then," she murmured huskily.

"That's not what I had in mind."

I flipped her on her back and we started anew.

She shivered in pleasure, took in short sucking gasps, a tigerish growl in her throat.

Back arched, breasts and loins pulsing against mine with a fierce heat, our mouths and tongues sought and quested each other.

The play went on, each teasing the other, testing each other's limits, always on the edge, but not tumbling over. A period that lasted what seemed forever.

When our congress was over and we lay in each other's arms, basking in our combined warmth, Deidra nuzzled against my throat, her eyes dreamy slits.

I awoke with a start some time later. Her eyes fluttered open. I felt a buoyancy and lightness I had not for a long time. She gave an animal purr and trailed her finger seductively along the curve of my shoulder and up my back.

"Rusco, why don't we pack up and fly free from this hell? We have a ship. Let's scram. From Brex, Sharki, everything. We don't owe anybody anything."

I blinked, my mind still slow in taking in her words.

"You mean cross Iron? I still owe him 2k for this ship."

"Screw Iron. He's got a bunch of grunts doing his dirty work for him. He's a millionaire. What's a few k to him anyways? We saved his ass. I'm thinking that's worth 2k yols."

"Maybe, but it's not how I handle things, Dee. If it were Brex, I'd say yes in a flash. Not Iron."

She bridled. "Like you're the golden boy with a halo over your head. Honest and true, Jet Rusco. A regular boy scout. Gives to the poor and robs from the rich. Running cons and scams up and down the galaxy."

"Your words, not mine, Dee."

"You and me, we could do stuff, go places," she said fiercely.

"Yeah, what about Marty?"

"What about that bullet-head?"

"He's not just going to go away, sulk in a corner."

"Bullet-head's got his own problems to deal with. I'm thinking, you and me, we have a future." A conspiratorial gleam flickered in her eye. "Three's a crowd. You know, the third wheel, all that. You married to the guy?"

Marty and I were tight. I could not just abandon him, as tempting as it might be to be free of his bullshit from time to time, to be solo with this energetic vixen of bountiful talents and tricks.

"No, Dee. We finish this job," I said. "We decide what to do from there."

There was more to it. I doubted that Iron'd give us leave so easily. He'd transformed us into assets. He'd not take kindly to us cutting out. When we did split from him, it would have to be done with tact and stealth.

Deidra shrugged her slim shoulders. She rolled away, lips pursed. I could see that my blunt reply had stung.

She leaned back. "Sometimes you have to take a chance, Rusco, because you reach for it too late, then tough luck, it's gone."

She got up and dressed quickly. Back to business as usual. She packed up and left.

Me, I lingered, stroking my chin, gazing at the wall, left to my thoughts and my restless desires. Had I been too hasty in my decision?

Our next roid was Beta-Cygnus 1, a large, vaguely ovoid Class B dinosaur with irregular features and rugged, upthrust ridge lines radiating out like the curved spines of prehistoric saurians. Not a roid looking easy or inviting to survey; indeed, shaped more like a lopsided rhomboid now that I had a closer look at it. The roid was about 100 miles long on its longest edge, 70 on its shorter. Not pretty to look at from the air, but the readings showed promise, possibly large beryl deposits.

Slapper frowned down at the scanner as he studied the contours. He recommended we take the buggy on this excursion, because the points of interest seemed spread out over a distance of eight miles— through rugged terrain, and there'd be many such stops. We'd waste more time hopping in and out of the ship for short jaunts to check test sites than just buggying it from one place to the other. The terrain in between ridges seemed flat enough to warrant no serious mishap. Relatively. All the same, we would have to steer clear of rifts and gaps that pocked the surface.

We had a few hours of faint 'daylight' left—nothing to cheer about, no more than pre-dusk—in which to survey the eerie place while away from the ship's powerful flood lamps.

Slapper seemed enthused to be out on the sporty excursion vehicle. Reminded him of his atv-rollicking days back at Hoss's, I imagined. I'd been on enough sport vehicles throughout my lifetime not to get caught up in the spell of the small vehicle obsession.

I'd gotten in the habit of also allowing Newt to come down with us the odd time. As annoying as the bot was, the hours were long down on the desolate surfaces and sometimes the bot's chatter was welcome, especially if he could advise us on technical details or help diagnose problems faster than our combined brains could, or than Deidra could extract from the ship's computer.

We parked the U56 in a relatively flat area flanked by low, winding spine-backed ridges. One to the east, or what the computer designated as east, one to the west. Low was perhaps not the right word. The ridges were 3 to 4 yards high at the most.

Even though Marty's presence was entirely unnecessary on this venture, he opted to suit up and come down with us, bored of hanging around the ship. He was not keen on buggies—the thing was crowded with three—and Slapper suggested he take his radialis and check out the ridge to the east. With a limp shrug he agreed and moon-trudged on.

Slappy drove west toward the other long ridge while I sat in the back behind him watching the gear. Newt magno-clamped himself to the rear crossbar on the back frame and we bumped along with speed. Three figures in a surreal landscape. We followed the lee of a gully, all gray and dun-brown.

To say I was only mildly distracted would be disingenuous. The memory of Deidra's warm body snugged against mine occupied the bulk of my thoughts. I was tantalized by the prospect of a future meetup.

When we stopped to take readings at the third site, I felt the radialis slip out of my hand. It floated in the near-zero gravity.

Slapper caught me daydreaming and his voice crackled over the com. "Shape up, Jet, or please go back to the ship. We can get Marty to take your place."

"No worry, Slappy, I got this covered." I gave him a sullen glance. Not that I had an excuse, as I had to admit he was right.

My mind fell to wandering again. I had the bright idea ten minutes later that our troupe'd cut out when we bagged 20k. Screw the 50k plan. Yes, the moment we got that much coin in our pockets, we were out of here. The risk of Skurgs and Brex wasn't worth it…and Deidra well, she was worth saving one's ass for.

My reverie was interrupted by Slapper's excited cry. The radialis needle'd shot up well past the green. Seems we'd scored a big one this time. A sizable lode of beryl about 80 feet down.

We were in the midst of planting our flag to mark our find when Newt let out a thin squeal of alarm. *"Jet Rusco! Danger! Danger!"*

"What?"

"Intruders! At 120 degrees."

I jerked my head around and saw a shiny triangular speeding toward us. Another vessel appeared at its side, both come out of nowhere. They shot closer and I felt a cold lump bead in the pit of my stomach.

"Mother fuck."

"Rusco, Marty! Get the fuck back here." Deidra's voice echoed tinnily in my helmet.

How the hell had those ships gotten past our radar? Cloakers maybe?

We were in trouble. A half mile or more we'd come from *Trident*. If they were who I thought they were, we were screwed.

But no. These ships looked more polished, and different from Brex's vessels. I did not like the cruel look of their cannons or the shape of their triangular hulls. Skurgs? No. I had a dull, achy feeling of deja-vu when I scrutinized those triangular hulls. Brex's thugs would have been a more welcome sight.

CHAPTER 22

Slapper and I hopped on the buggy. The knot only hardened in my stomach as we turned her nose back toward *Trident*.

Oddly, the two ships did not come after us. They surrounded *Trident* along east and west points of a compass; I saw the thin red flash of a peculiar beam emanating from a shiny panel below the bow of the first enemy ship.

"Deidra, get the hell out of there! It's a trap!"

Too late.

She'd taken to the air, gained about 200 feet of height, but the crimson beam of energy smacked her broadside and held her immobilized.

Some kind of tractor beam. *Trident's* shields were up, her weapons still operational, but her drive was now useless.

I saw *Trident's* starboard cannon flare. The shots ripped hell in the second ship's shields.

I could picture her now twisting in her seat, cursing and trying to work both sets of controls: nav and weapons. While we were stranded here, hapless victims of their weaponry, the raiders would board *Trident* and come for us at their leisure. Likely, when our air supply was gone.

The first ship held the tractor beam while the second ship did a slow loop over *Trident's* low-turreted top. She headed on toward us, landed at a leisurely distance in the faint shadow of the gully, cutting us off from *Trident* or any help she could offer. Marty was nowhere in sight.

I saw the cargo hold door drop down and two black buggies

speed out. Five figures in gray suits, two in one vehicle, three in the other, came bouncing toward us. They were sturdy vehicles outmatching us in size and speed. With the sinking dread of a sailor on a scuppered vessel, I watched the enemy ship rise slowly and follow us in lazy pursuit.

Slapper turned the buggy about and took her farther down into the gully. We followed the line of the shallow bank.

I peered to either side. I saw only some small rises and humps to the right and long, slanting shadows to the left. Barreling on seemed futile. No use just sitting here either. Waiting for them to pounce on us and blow us to shit was about as smart as quaffing rotgut whiskey to stave off a hangover. No word of communication from the mystery ship.

"Slappy," I hissed at him, "make for that cross-canyon there."

He nodded, his throat working as he tooled the buggy along, swung the wheel, steered into the darker shadow of the gully. I caught a glimpse of his eyes bulging with what looked like fear.

The buggy bounced forward, taking us further away from the flag we'd planted. The big balloon tires rolled roughly over the uneven ground.

I snatched a look back behind me. I did not like the two gleaming triangular ships arched menacingly at low altitude, one heading our way, nose first, forward ion cannon sighted on us, the other keeping *Trident* in tractor.

"What do they want?" Slapper croaked. "What's their game?"

"Whatever it is, Slappy, it's not good. Ride, friend, ride!"

"To where?" he wailed.

"Anywhere but here!"

I gripped the safety bars. Newt sped after us, trying to catch up, bleating inanities. The bot finally managed to electromag onto the rack next to me.

All the while the enemy buggies kept gaining on us and the hovering craft maintained a close watch, keeping slightly back and above our trail. I could feel the knots in my joints tighten.

I saw lights on Newt's spherical front change from red to green. *"Jet Rusco! Please take care your R1 does not clink against my side. It affects my magno-sensors."*

"Newt, please shut it." I let my R1 rap against his shiny outerbody for emphasis.

The foremost ship drew lower. It tailed us, as menacing and annoying a presence as could be.

Slapper shot a harried look back at me. "What gives? Why are they toying with us?" His voice cracked, edged with desperation.

Damn! I wish he'd put a lid on it. True, they could have blasted us to shit, but they didn't. They just followed us like a hungry vulture. I could see the ominous, eagle-like shadow pass alongside us. Sometimes overtop us, sometimes switching, passing from left to right.

The ground got rougher and we had to slow down or risk wiping out.

Slapper did not slow down. Nor did I encourage him as blaster fire ripped by our side rack and half shredded it with Newt nearly along with it. Slapper wheeled the other way, barely missing a hump of rock which would have set us airborne.

The lead buggy was now less than 50 yards behind and I saw R1s lifting.

I grunted, slung my own R1 over my shoulder to pick them off.

The bastards were ducking low under the dash and the steering wheel as they weaved back and forth, making it hard to hit. I aimed for a place dead center on the front cowling. I knew the grav stabilizer housed itself there.

My first bright ray ripped a black gash in the hood, unseating the driver.

The pursuing buggy lurched. Must have upset the stabilizer because the front wheels lifted and the vehicle went airborne as it jounced over a hump. The vehicle tipped, dumping the back rider. The front wheels spun in midair. The entire frame fell as the grav kicked in again and the left front tire bit at the rock and spun out, tossing the driver a good ten feet.

I gave a crow of satisfaction. Serve the fuckers right.

But my glee was shortlived. Blaster fire licked our way from the other vehicle and blew out our back tires. We were thrown sideways and our buggy fishtailed and rolled—even though we were only doing maybe 25 mph. We were pitched flying.

I lay dazed on the hard rock, my vision grainy. The overturned buggy lay to my side. Left back wheel rotated slowly. An underwater whine hissed in my ears. Slappy sprawled unconscious face down about 12 feet away. One arm was tucked under his beagle-brown suit, another gloved hand was flung to his side.

A figure came plodding toward us, black blaster aimed.

Another jumped out of the buggy parked a stone's throw away and followed him. There was something familiar about his stilted swagger but I could not quite put my finger on it. The cocky, arrogant gait sent cold chills up my spine.

Words came through the general channel. "Keep them pinned down, Blythe." With one hand he beckoned another figure to approach from the side. "No sudden moves or violence yet."

The unsettling figure approached within a dozen paces and stopped, assessing Slappy and me for several moments.

There was a cruel undertone in that familiar voice. Though he was wearing a helmet with darkened faceplate, I glimpsed the hints of a gangsterish face, sizzled and burned from the left ear to the bottom right lip. One eye was bulging out of its orbit like an elephant man. The eye glared with an oleaginous fervor that shocked me as it stared madly out of true with the other.

Sharki! My nemesis.

I don't know if his bounty hunters had gotten wind of us by fluke or when we'd crossed to the other side of the Belt. But I guessed it must have been sometime after we'd taken Slapper on board.

Quick as an adder he lessened the gap between us in a headlong rush. I tried to snatch at my weapon and get up and sight on the bastard but he knocked the legs out from under me. My R1 lay loosely gripped in a palm. Before I could react, he had his long-barreled R1 pointed at my head.

"Down!"

He kicked the R1 out of my grasp. He scrunched down on his haunches, shaking his head with an odd sadness. "Life, JR—it's a slow squeeze. Nothing but a series of little lessons, each more painful than the last, ones that each of us must learn and yet hardly appreciate until the end draws near." He clicked his tongue. "Wisdom comes much too late. Like this little episode here. Wouldn't you say?" He flicked me a contemptuous grin, his face writ with gratification. I could only think of the black widow spider ogling an insect it had trapped.

"I hope you're appreciating the value of this insight?"

"Very much, Sharki. How did you find us? Tarot cards? Ouija board?" My mind was racing. I had to keep the bastard talking. The improbability of this 'little episode' in this remote location seemed absurdly over the top.

He shook his head with sad amusement. "Rusco, always the inquisitive one. Up for a gag, even when the chips are down. When some bitch you cheated on has your balls in a knot, there's JR cracking a gag."

I shrugged. "Nothing much to do about that." With what little dignity I could, I raised myself to a crouch.

"Unh, uh." He shoved the muzzle of his gun at my faceplate, unbalancing me. "Stay down, Rusco. Don't get up."

I glanced over to where Slapper was slowly stirring. The other gunman sauntered over to level his barrel down at Slapper's head.

Sharki's other man came over to examine the wreck of the black buggy. He gave his head a grave shake.

"Bo's dead," he said. "Suit punctured. The rover's toast."

Sharki stared, his scarred lips pursed in a thin line. "Another pound of flesh to come out of your hide, Rusco." He rounded on me. "You're probably wondering what happened to my face."

"I can guess."

"I'm sure you can. *Thetis 3*. You remember that place? The explosion. The destruction of a multi-billion yol enterprise. The end of an era. The one you helped bring about?"

I did not answer that question right away.

"Let's get these shitwits back to the ship, Gredis. Mr. Rusco and I have a rendezvous to keep and a lot of talk to catch up on, don't we, Mr. Rusco? Truth be told, I don't like parleying in these subzero wastes."

"Sure thing, Sharki," Gredis said.

Blythe hauled Slapper to his feet and the two herded me and Slapper at blaster point to the intact buggy.

In a sudden flash of movement, Newt unlatched himself from the crumpled, overturned buggy and made a blitz for the open sky.

Sharki's head whipped around and faster than a striking serpent his draw arm came up and whipped off a shot. The light trail grazed the metallic outerbody and sent the bot spinning aside dizzily.

"What the fuck's that?" Gredis called.

Sharki's henchman in the baggier gray suit stared up at Newt now tracing a jerky sinusoidal path of retreat. "Dunno. Some spy device, I guess."

"Do we need to worry about it?" Sharki growled.

"Reckon not, Shark."

"Then let's pull out. Don't want to be stuck here while our air runs out."

While Newt had gone to hide somewhere in the rocks, we piled into the buggy. It was a rugged rough-and-tumble model, one and a half times larger than ours and more durable. Sharki sat at my side, R1 barrel jammed in my side. Slapper was kitty-corned up front between the driver and the other lean rogue called Gredis. On a sad day on Beta-Cygnus roid, we were taxied glumly to Sharki's waiting ship.

Sharki stared balefully at me from his ruined face. His look egged me to make one false move. He said nothing on the whole trip and offered nothing in response to my queries. Slapper remained subdued, his lips trembling. My eyes flicked upward. *Trident* hung as before in limbo a few hundred feet up, still caught in the tractor beam and I wondered what Deidra was thinking. Maybe she had some plan in motion. The girl had a devious mind.

But my hope was flimsy at best.

CHAPTER 23

Sharki's buggy came to a halt ten feet short of our claim flag. His ship sat parked another few stones' throw away. I noted her tapered nose was angled away from us, her broad white-washed flanks spread bluntly like a manta-ray. Brazen lettering etched in crimson on her side read, 'Tristar'.

Sharki shoved me roughly out the side. The other goon elbowed Slapper to the ground.

Gun trained on me, Sharki kicked at the ugly flag we'd raised, wearing a venomous grin. "Might be inclined to run your little claim in, Rusco. Help pay for some of my expenses out here."

I did not feel inclined to reply.

"I'm not of mind dicking around with chump change though. So I'll let you have your little claim."

I scanned the featureless plane. Marty was nowhere to be seen. Where the hell was he? Not a lot of places to hide on this dead rock. Though there were a few in some of the upthrust rock formations to my left. Farther apace too in the spine-backed, low ridge.

The ridge was more like an ancient pressure crack lifted by unknown forces from some time in the past. It stretched about a mile in either direction. Lurking like the jaws of a waiting beast.

I racked my brains desperately. Marty had an R1. If he could set up an ambush, get off a shot, anything…

My thought was interrupted by Sharki's hard knee in my side. "Pay attention, Rusco, when I'm talking to you. Get down on the ground."

He glared at Slappy who had fixed sullen eyes on him, as if he'd like no better than jam a knife in his ribs. "Who are you?" Sharki demanded.

"Slapper. Who're you? You ain't no scutzer. No Bratt man or Monger. All I can say is you're gonna wish you'd never been born when Iron gets word of this."

Sharki stared at him with the malignant look of a sun-baked viper. "Slappy? I'm going slap your ass from here to Betelgeuse if you don't shut the fuck up. Do yourself a favor and answer only when I rattle my zipper."

I stepped up and sneered, "Didn't know you had it in for boys, Shark. Slapping asses? Rattling zippers? Little midlife crisis, or a new fad? Leave the kid out of it."

"You're a witty one today, Rusco, I'll give you that. Maybe I'll be slapping two asses from here to Betelgeuse."

"Knock yourself out."

"Always the wisecracker. Let me ask, how many men've you killed, Rusco?"

"Why? You cruising for a record?"

"No, really. A dozen? Maybe 20? I bet you raise less than two fingers answering the question."

I shrugged, stared back at him, my guts curdled with contempt. My tally had been one too many killings for my tastes. Every one of those deaths still haunted my dreams.

He sensed my hesitation and thought to discern weakness. "You get squeamish about killing, Rusco? Just asking."

"It's not a pissing match, you freak!"

"You're damn right it is. Not until you can stare an enemy in the face, shove a knife in his guts and watch his life force ooze out of him before he dies, that you can call yourself a man. No one lords over you. No feeling of guilt or shame. The ends justifies the means. You understand what I'm saying?"

"No, but hurrah, Shark, you're a real man's man. A model among killers. If I could have an idol, it'd be you."

"You got a mouth on you, and a death wish, Rusco." He

punched the muzzle of his weapon at my faceplate, aiming between the eyes.

"Listen, you swine. Because I can feel, and don't take lives wantonly, is the reason I'm human—nothing I can say about you. Feeling's the only thing one can do to survive in this cruel world without going insane."

He tilted back his head and laughed. "Rusco, you've been listening to too many damn soap operas and pansy asses. They all puff up hotter than air balloons before they get their throats ripped out by the sharks and wolves. People like me. The meek shall inherit the earth. No, the strong shall conquer all."

"Again, congratulations, Sharki. Maybe you could write a book on it."

He blinked, seeming to like that. "Maybe I will."

I motioned to his scarred face. "I see you've gone for a makeover. It suits you."

For a moment the prideful affability vanished. His teeth bared and glinted puke yellow against the blackness of his burns. But he contained it. His eyes turned distant and cold. "I was blinded with half my face charred off. I could barely grope my way around refinery level 6."

"Sorry for your loss."

He didn't hear me, or chose not to, his eyes staring far off on the horizon, somewhere in the direction of Terminus. "Sargoff half dragged me to the last intact ship. Four of us escaped from the bonfire of Thetis on ships before that. Those who you see here—" he motioned to his henchmen "—minus the one you killed just now. 180 men crisped like fries in that bonfire on Thetis, Rusco. Ten billion yols of infrastructure down the tubes. State-of the-art solar gun, specialized ships and equipment. You proud of your achievement? Your bloodbath, you son of a bitch?"

"Don't twist it around, Sharki. You created your own hell over there, under your direction. The whole operation was evil waiting to explode, and you know it. I was just a catalyst."

"You keep on believing that, Rusco. You're so caught up in love with your own lies, you even believe them yourself as you jerk off every night to fairy tales. The honorable Jet Rusco. The death-stalker of bad guys and the righter of wrongs in the universe. He who can do no harm. The avenging angel. What a crock of shit. You're nothing but a two bit thief, out for himself like all of us, claiming to be morally superior to everyone else."

"You seem to have me confused with someone else. I'm just a guy, an everyman, trying to survive in this messed-up universe."

"We got company, Shark," grumbled Blythe.

Sharki gazed skyward. "Who the hell's that?" A speck grew to a bright light in the sky, coming closer. "You a popular man around here, Rusco?"

"Seems so."

Sharki's man, Gredis, gave an impatient grunt. "Looks like scutzers."

"Well, let 'em come. The more the merrier. We're just seeing to our claim, aren't we, boys?"

"Right, Shark." Gredis laughed.

The mystery ship hovered, then landed not a few hundred yards away from *Tristar*, her nose pointed away.

"That's a very odd thing to do." Sharki frowned then radioed up to his scout ship. "Red alert. Shields up. Sargoff—did they make any contact?"

The response came back garbled. Sharki cursed. I deduced the answer to that to be a negative. We had missed something...we all had, so absorbed were we with our mystery vehicle.

The shot came from somewhere far away, along the eerie, blue-black shadow of the ridge.

The blast hit Sharki's man, Blythe, in the leg and he toppled like a log. Howling bloody murder, he palsied as the vacuum of space filled his suit. The air departed in a millisecond's fugitive gush.

I sprang for cover out of Sharki's reach. Slapper scrambled the other way, aiming for the buggy. What the hell had taken Marty so long?

Two more scutzer ships appeared on the horizon. Now another came into view, blitzing close to Sharki's ship in the air. Brex's ships. There was no doubt about it. The alligator snout of *Gator* stood out like a sore thumb.

Somewhere the Bratts had tracked us. Or maybe Sharki himself had led them here, who knew? Now there was going to be one hell of a free-for-all.

Bright fire pelted down and clipped Sharki's parked craft before the crew could retaliate.

I bounded in a half crouch toward the shadow cover of gray rock—still too far away.

Sharki grunted a bewildered yell. "What the fuck's going on here? Gredis! Watch these jerkoffs! Otto! Flush out that bastard who shot at us. He's to your right!"

The tall, rangy man, Otto, raked off a shot. The beam went wide, shattering rock where Marty had been. I recognized that bobbing head that had popped up over the humpbacked ridge. He'd dipped back to his hiding place, weasel-quick.

Gator landed 180 degrees opposite us—in line with the other parked ship, Brex's decoy, about 100 yards away. Three blue-suited figures jumped out of *Gator's* side hatch. They broke into a brisk trot toward us.

Bright fire licked out at us, skidded by, some landing at our feet. Flakes of rock kicked up and hung in the zero g.

Gredis dropped to one knee and returned fire. He yelled at us to stay back.

I looked up at the sky. At the same time, ion fire belched out from the new arrivals, slamming Sharki's goon who piloted the ship holding *Trident* in stasis. Everything was chaos. Things were happening too fast.

Sharki mounted his buggy and barreled forth at the figures coming from *Gator*. Tires chewed at the rock. While I contemplated making a run for the ridge, Slapper made a crouching lunge for

Blythe's gun. Sharki ducked low in his seat, R1 spitting fire at the intruders.

Gredis was lying belly-flat, spraying a wild volley of shots into the oncoming figures. One dropped, clutching at his leg. Gredis gave a wild shriek and jerked marionette-like as return fire peppered his defenseless body. His helm split in two and grav pack floated up, his left side ravaged to all hell. A thin ribbon of blood jetted above his head, floating fairy-tale in the zero-g atmosphere like ink-jets in a tropical sea.

Just as Otto's head exploded into fire at the same time, I cranked back the grav dial on my pack. I ran in floating hops toward the ridge.

I could hear the blood thumping in my ears. I took half running bounds toward the shadow cover.

All Sharki's men were down. There was nowhere to run. I was caught between the ridge and two sets of foes.

CHAPTER 24

Sharki had ridden down one of the raiders and was wheeling his space buggy around for another pass. His R1 blistered out rainbow fire.

The lead figure of Brex's raiders, whoever he was, knelt and pegged off a shot. The left tire of Sharki's buggy blew out while the other caught in a rut and sent Sharki flying over the dash.

The blue-suited shooter came running up and kicked Sharki's weapon out of his grip before he could use it. He kicked him in the chest and rolled him a couple of times till he lay still.

Warily he approached. He nudged Sharki with a boot. Sharki twitched. He waved him to his feet. Then herded his prisoner over toward the flag, the landmark I was desperately trying to put as much distance from as possible.

Captor and prisoner came slouching over, long barrel of R1 with wide mouth stuck at Sharki's back.

Sharki spat, hurling sullen curses.

The hulking leader caught a glimpse of me when I turned to look back. His round cheeks flushed in malice while the stony gray-brown eyes glinted a most wrathful promise of unfinished business.

I picked up my feet, booted it hard for the ridge. Fire blossomed from the place where Marty'd been, covering me while I ran. Volleys of shots sprayed back in return, shattering the humped rock to shit where Marty'd huddled.

I couldn't get far. Without a weapon I was a sitting duck. One of the gunmen lay fire at my feet.

I stopped short, grunting curses. Too far to make it to the ridge. I shook my head in defeat as the gunman approached and herded me back toward the flag, barrel pointed at my back.

A team from the first decoy ship had snuck around the back of the ridge trying to flush out Marty. I watched in dismay, but with a fierce hope that my bullet-headed friend could elude them.

Two of the figures pushed Slapper forward at gunpoint and thrust him before the brawny leader who captured Sharki. Five grim figures now surrounded Slapper and me in a loose semicircle, blasters pointed at our skulls.

The lead figure nodded. At last I recognized the brute, from the thick black beard and the hard line of the jaw.

He motioned a hand toward Slappy. "Take this foolish boy to the ship. I'll decide what to do with him when I've dealt with Rusco."

"Done, Brex."

The general stared at me for some time before he huffed out a malicious breath and I could see no forgiveness in that black look. No doubt about it, the memory of the knife I'd plunged into his shoulder and the other hurts I'd afflicted burned hot in the man. Not to mention the ship I'd downed on the streets of Tylas.

Two armed henchmen prodded Slapper off. Brex, at the last minute, halted them. "Just more baggage for us to deal with. Bring the muppet back. We'll get rid of them all at once."

Slapper wailed out in protest. Brex clubbed him down with the muzzle of his R1. "Any more lip out of you, son, and I'll gut you here. Don't care if you're Iron's godson or grandson."

Slapper spat up at him. "Iron's going to fry your balls in acid when he finds out about this."

Brex trooped closer and aimed his gun at Slapper's head. I turned away.

"I remember now...you're Slapper, the dumbfuck who okayed the hopper cart while drunk on the job. When it was spewing all those raw beryl chips and all those men died out at Nyus 6 some time back."

Slapper's head drooped. But his eyes burned. His mouth was

pinched in a grimace of perilous anger.

"Some of those men were mine, boy," Brex rasped. "Back in days when Iron and me saw eye to eye, when we did the odd venture together."

Brex shifted his uncomfortable gaze onto me. He hitched closer to better assess my previously 'mangled' hand. He stared at its relative intactness. "You mend quickly, Rusco."

I lifted an arm. "You know how it is, the wonders of modern technology."

He nodded. "I bet. Feeling lucky again?"

"Sure." I spread my palms. "I see you got your ship back. *Gator*, isn't it?"

He smiled, a forced grimace. The topic was a sensitive one and he inclined his chin toward *Trident* which hung in the air like a captured moth in a spiderweb. With Sharki's vanguard ship now blown to smithereens, *Trident* was still caught in yet another tractor beam and surrounded by Bratts' vessels.

Brex wheezed out a chuckle. "You got yourself a real hellcat of a lady out there, Rusco. The language on her. My god. Hogging her for yourself?"

Sharki started forward, a murderous snarl on his lips. "She's mine, not this twit's."

Brex laughed. "Well, well, a little dogfight between paramours. Amusing. A filly like that should be spread around. Whether it's you, me or this lank-toothed hound who calls himself Jive Retro, don't matter."

Deidra's wail came over the com: an angry, mournful, defeated sound.

A chill hit my solar plexus. Hatred and vengeance warred in my guts. I clenched my fists, edged a step closer. What could I do here with a broken buggy and no weapons? Two more steps and I could wrench the R1 from Brex's hand—

Brex hefted his weapon sharply. "I don't think so, Rusco." He twirled the barrel toward Sharki. "Looks like you got your hands full dealing with this hound sniffing up your butt." He gave a coarse laugh. "I think I'll keep that chicklet you got stashed up there for myself. A souvenir to commemorate this happy reunion." He trooped over to yank the flag out of the ground. "Straight into the coffers of the Beryl Bratts, Rusco. I thank you for your generous contribution." He motioned for his man to plant their own flag, with the Bratts' pirate emblem.

I growled, "You can thank me after I skull fuck you and rip off your balls."

Deidra's voice spat over the com. "You can go jerk yourself, Brex. Rusco, do me a favor and kill those subhuman creatures—"

Brex called back in an angry voice, "And you can shut up, you whiny bitch. You'll be grateful enough I don't leave you to the likes of this bloodsucking, licentious pig, Sharki."

Sharki bridled. "Who you calling a pig, you mongrel?"

Brex shook his head and clicked his tongue. "Sharki, Sharki. Tall tales of you range up and down the Vala system. The pillagings, the black-hearted bloodbaths, the rapes, the murders, the massacres. The competing cartels smashed. Dreams shattered. Blameless souls ruined. Innocent victims' lives lost, lying with their guts streaming out on the floors of their ships."

Sharki acknowledged the tribute with a sober nod. "So, what's your point?"

"My point is, that by my reckoning, there's only one spare oxygen tank here. Not a lot to share while time ticks on." His eyes roamed over to the defunct buggy with its spare tank, and the crippled *Tristar* looming a few hundred yards off. "You boys can fight over it. Best man lives—or at least lives for a few more hours. Maybe cursing his luck he didn't die two hours ago."

"Mighty generous of you, Brex," I said. "You should be written up in the 'who's who' of philanthropy."

Brex laughed and tipped back his head.

He gave word to *Gator.* "Aim for the stern thrusters. Without drive they'll be grounded."

Gator's cannons swiveled, spat out red bursts and blasted Sharki's ion drive to molten shreds.

"Just in case you mutts get any ideas." He paused. "Breach the hull too. No sense giving them an extra week of life support."

Another blast arched from skyward and took out the bridge, and with it our last chances of survival on this desolate world.

I watched bleakly as the other triangular ship of Sharki's, a burned-out hulk, was floating away freely in space.

Brex's eyes turned skyward to *Trident*. "Yeah, she'll hold out till the end. She looks capable, your bitch up there, or is it Sharki's bitch?" He laughed. "Word's come down that dame gets around. I'll give her that." He gave his head an admiring shake. "I reckon when I get her beneath me, I'll be taming myself one supple young shrew and sex kitten."

I bit back a curse.

Sharki didn't flinch. Not at the destruction of his ship or mention of Deidra. He just met Brex's stare with a cold-blooded one of his own. "Think you're a big man, General Brex? Well guess what. Beating a dead man doesn't prove nothing. I was already dead long ago, so what happens to me now is irrelevant. But you? You're clinging to life like a flea does on a dog's back. A dirty dog deciding to go jump into the river to rid himself of a problem. Others'll be catching up with you, Brex. The fires of doom'll be coming on your heels soon. Don't doubt it. If I was you, I'd watch my back." He let that ominous thought hang heavily in the air.

I saw Brex's throat work as he struggled for a response but just couldn't quite manage it.

"Only one ride out of here, Shark," he said hoarsely, "and it's mine." His voice was thick with gravel and rocks.

After some lip-licking and shifting from foot to foot, Brex gained a bit more confidence. "Heard about your bad luck at Thetis. That's a tough break. All the power and wealth snatched away from you in a few seconds... A man can't give himself a makeover fast enough—judging from that new face of yours. That's tragic."

The team of two thugs who had gone off to flush out Marty returned, looking sullen and grim. Men with beady eyes, muscled arms and long sober faces.

Brex rasped out a curse. "What you doing back so soon? Where's Layo?"

The first looked away, gestured idly back to the ridge. "Got himself pegged back there. We couldn't save the bastard. Suit was shredded."

"You bloody fools! What of the other one—the bullet head, the monkey midget?"

"Got himself hid."

Brex stared, lancing daggers. "And you didn't think to flush the weasel out?"

"We tried." The other gritted his teeth. "Little fucker was waiting in ambush to hole us in the back. Past that first gully is a jumble of crevices and humps of rock. Ideal weasel's ground for ambush. That's how he pegged Layo. These damn blue suits put a target on our backs. Maybe good for spotting lost locators but bad for hunting down rogues like him." He peered up at the sallow, maroon glow in the sky. The distant globe of Vala was slipping fast toward the horizon. "Night's coming on, Brex. Another half hour and we'll be in full gloom. Best we get out of here, by my reckoning."

Brex considered. His face tightened in indecision. He vacillated, about to order the two back to search out Marty but stopped in mid-sentence. "Leave the little brat. His air'll run out in a few hours or less."

The two nodded, somewhat relieved. I saw the briefest flicker of satisfaction in their hard soulless eyes.

"What about these fucks?" The first man said, waving his gun at us.

Brex toyed idly with his own gun. "We're in no rush. I'm of mind to make these clowns suffer a bit. I've already decided what to do."

He motioned them and the others on and they tramped back to *Gator.* One of them kept a gun trained back at us, in case we tried anything fancy. They left the corpses where they lay, but the gunman gathered up all the blasters.

The ugly, alligator-snout of *Gator* rose into the sky.

I watched, glum-faced as the ships formed a convoy—*Trident* in the middle, *Gator* in front and two scutzer ships behind. They impulsed off and became specks dwindling in the sky.

Deidra's voice crackled over the com. "Rusco…remember—" her voice started to fade "—hunt down all these dumb fucks."

Brex's laugh came over the com. "Yeah, you get right on that, Mr. Rusco. Wow, how these sentimental farewells get me all choked up."

A bleak feeling washed over me as I stood there in that group of broken, beleaguered men. A feeling like a tsunami hit me, then washed away like surf as if it had never been.

CHAPTER 25

Sharki was not as spellstruck as I was. He hotfooted it over to the overturned buggy and wrenched a three-foot piece of bar free from the rack. He came at me, all Halloween-faced and spitting rage.

I ducked his first blow, but got bashed in the knee and nearly doubled over. If not for the padding of the suit, he might have cracked my kneecap.

I hobbled out of range before the pipe could smash down on my helmet, ending me there.

I did not want to fight this lunatic on the open ground, especially one with a metal pipe in his hand. He was superhumanly strong. His psychotic need for revenge had eclipsed all forms of reason.

"Grab a brain, you stupid fool! We need to pool our resources if we want to get off this rock alive."

"Ain't nobody getting off this rock," he croaked. "Ain't enough air. I'll have the satisfaction of ripping out your throat before I die."

He came charging at me again, bar coming up to swipe at my faceplate. Slapper got a moment of courage and smacked into Sharki's side, head first. His helmet bull-headed him square on the hip.

Sharki twisted around and bitch-slapped him on the legs with the pipe, sending him howling and clutching at his knees.

Slapper was rocking on the ground. I regrouped and hobbled a few steps out of range of his baseball-bat swings. Sharki couldn't give a rat's ass about Slapper. He came straight at me, just left the boy there.

I was unable to help Slapper or get a purchase on Sharki's

weapon. Without an R1 or some chunk of metal of my own to brain him with, I was screwed.

Where the fuck was Marty? How far away had he hid? Had he been hit? I don't remember Brex's rogues reporting they'd tagged him back in that ridiculous melee.

Slapper gained his feet, hobbled off at a dogtrot toward the ridge. Hoping for the protection of the rocks and Marty with his gun.

That was where I should be going. But I was on the other side of Sharki and his wretched pipe.

About 150 yards off, I saw a squat figure in a beagle-brown suit frog-hop down from a jut of rock. *Marty*. Sharp fire licked out from his weapon and lay a glitzy trail at Sharki's feet.

The gangster paused.

For some odd reason, Marty's blasts ceased. I looked back to see him toss aside his blaster with an attitude of disgust. What the hell? Had his R1 died? He was too far away to tell. Our young cowboy, Slapper, didn't look like he was up for much more, given that gimp.

Sharki gave a sawtoothed grin and came loping after me with renewed vigor.

Smoke rose from Sharki's ship about 100 yards ahead of me. I winced. The idea of holing up there brought a queasiness to my gut. Still, not many options at this juncture, nor did I want to be playing ring around the rosy with friend Sharki till my air gave out.

I put on a burst of speed toward *Tristar*. Her bow viewport was blown out, pyroglass shattered. Gray smoke wisped from her fire-blackened metal. I snuck a look back. Sharki's halloween face peered at me with sinister clarity through the faceplate. His blackened lips, mashed nose and chilling leer dared me to fight him on open ground. His thirst for justice was as bright and fiery as the day he'd taken it in his head to kill me. He was just crazy enough to chase me full around this miserable roid.

I made it to within spitting distance of the triangular hull, my lungs exploding. Sharki was no more than 30 yards behind. The bridge viewport was just a black gap of shattered glass and metal. It was too high for me to jump up into that gap, let alone climb the sleek blackened steel. The hull was too sheer. On a quick impulse, I adjusted the grav pack and dialed it to its lowest setting. Stepping back about five feet, I catleaped up on the balls of my feet. I floated up on an angle, along the port side of the triangular prow, knowing should I miss that narrow perch, I might be floating out in space, a free satellite, something unsurvivable. Nor did I relish turning the dial back and breaking my ankles on the sheer fall down.

As I floated up I reached out along the sleek line of *Tristar's* bow and strained my back until my fingers caught the rim of the shattered viewpane. I pulled myself in, careful not to rip my suit on the jagged edges.

I got inside, peered down over the lip, saw Sharki looking up at me with black malice in his eyes. He darted glances around, contemplating a similar acrobatic feat. I admit, it had been a clever maneuver that might buy me a few more minutes of life but I didn't need someone to explain to me that Sharki'd try his own space leap before long.

I scanned the bridge for a means of defense. A lot of blackened walls and consoles and equipment. A charred lump in a chair that might have been Sharki's erstwhile pilot. No weapons anywhere that I could see. A single door at the back led to a companionway, or hallway to the crew's quarters. I booted it through and passed the crew's quarters, bunks and commode, a few cross corridors with steel bulkheads and a mess hall. The rest of the ship outside of the bridge seemed intact.

I came to an air lock at midships. I could hole up in the stern and surprise Sharki if he tried to come at me with his club. Hopefully Slapper and Marty would have by then rallied together.

A tiny light was still on the activation panel to the right of the heavy door. I fisted the switch and with a poof of released air, the metal slab slid aside. I peered over my shoulder. I caught a glimpse of his jerky bulky shape limned in the pale light of Vala as he pulled himself over the rim. He climbed through the hole in the shattered glass and then onto the bridge.

I got the door closed and made it through the second barrier, another heavy steel door with thick circular glass pane. I activated the switch. I got the door closed tight, cranked the captain's wheel at waist height just below the window pane.

I was in the hold.

The space was roughly square, about 30 by 40 feet. A dim emergency light shone from the ceiling above, casting an eerie glow around the interior. Equipment crates of all kinds were piled around the edges, casting long amber snaky shadows. Space suits, repair kits, various tools like power drills and sensors were strapped on the walls.

I cranked the air lock's circular wheel counterclockwise another half turn for good measure, to a 'sealed' position. An airtight chamber. I could find no lock from this side. Only the crew from the bridge could actually lock the hold. It made sense but it boded poorly for me. If Sharki got it in his head to seal me in, he could do it. But I didn't think he would.

Movement came at the wheel.

I saw the familiar figure through the oval of glass. Hunched gamely, I scrambled to my right, looking for any place to hide. I wedged myself deep between two supply crates. I had no clue what was in them.

The door slid heavily aside. The menacing figure stomped in, a suited wraith silhouetted in the submarine light. I could hear his heavy breathing over the open channel.

"Know you're in here, you yellow-bellied coward. Come out and fight like a man."

I stayed quiet, hid behind the crates wedged to the side. I was waiting for Sharki to miscalculate, make some crucial mistake. One moment of inattentiveness and I'd pounce on him, rip the brutal weapon out of his grasp and brain him for good.

My eyes caught a series of long vertical shapes hanging dimly in the shadows. R1s racked up on the far wall. *Shit.* Three of them. I cursed myself. If I'd only seen them sooner, maybe this would be all over by now.

Sharki cranked shut the door, as if sensing my thoughts. He rasped out an evil chuckle.

"No, you ain't going anywhere, Rusco—not till we've done our little dance. And no, I see you didn't get one of them guns. Too bad."

Could I make a dash and grab the first R1 off the rack? No, the bastard'd cut me down in a trice. He had already circled and cut me off from the gun rack.

In his mad confidence, Sharki didn't even go for the blasters. He just stalked around the perimeter searching for me. As a wildcat would his prey.

He said with slow pleasure, "Just like in the cave man days. Two brutes clubbing each other to death. Picture it, Rusco, back in the dusks of time, when the saber-toothed tiger howled into the night and ate the little monkeys."

Sure, I thought, when you're the one with the club, all peachy creamy.

I ducked lower, waiting for the psycho to pass my way.

CHAPTER 26

He came six feet from where I crouched, then winced, clutching at his throat piece. He staggered slightly and hit a diamond-shaped button on the nearby wall, flooding the chamber with oxygen. I could feel the pressure change with the slight outward billowing of my own suit. I watched the gauge on my wrist rise to a safe level. Sharki unlatched his helmet and I could see his mouth open and close in a relaxed, confident manner. Something must have gotten messed up with his air intake. Maybe back when we had our last tango, or perhaps Slapper had done some damage when he'd crashed into him.

My air was getting low too. I debated taking my own helmet off. I was having trouble thinking. Thoughts were coming in slow streams. Like I was dreaming, or suffering from slow oxygen deprivation.

With slow care I released the catch at my helmet. There came a tiny, elf-like click.

Sharki's head whirled around, his cat-like ears detecting the sound. He came leaping at me, pipe raised to smash the hell out of me.

I vaulted up out of my hidey-hole and met him half way. Ducking a strike, I twisted, but on the upswing he smashed my arm, sending a jolt of stinging pain up my elbow. My left arm hung limp.

With my good hand, I managed to grab his wrist, stopping the pipe from smashing my brains. We wrestled for tense seconds. He was strong and he swung in his hip and bunted me aside before throwing me to the ground. I felt my back crack. He was unnaturally strong. I would need every trick to stay alive. With lungs heaving, I gained my feet, bunched my fist and lifted elbow to deflect another stinging blow to my left side.

Damn this bastard. He was a pain in the ass! Where the fuck was Marty? Having a siesta out on the beach?

The bulkiness of our suits was not helping. We grunted and heaved and circled round each other like cave men, trading blows. Life had seeped back into my arm but my body felt sluggish and bruised all over. So far I'd sustained grazing blows but on the first direct hit with that pipe, a broken bone or similar, and it was all over.

I darted left, avoiding a crushing swipe to my jaw. But he tripped me and I went rolling like a cub, barely eluding him as he alternately smashed pipe down and tried to heel stomp me, intent on either braining me or crushing my windpipe. I felt my back edged against a crate now. I scrambled to my feet and took a jerky run, crashed into his side as the pipe cracked against my thigh. Another shaft of pain shivered up my side.

But he had not anticipated the move. I rolled on top of him, pinned his weapon arm, pummeled him with my gloved hands. I lay blows to shoulders, ribs, face.

He ripped and tore at my gloves.

I went for his ruined face, and got some grunts from his blackened lips. Then his eyes, his ears, his charred wasteland of a nose.

His cheeks were budding red with blood where my mitted hands had broken the skin. My own blood dripped now from my face onto his suit where his bar had swung and nicked my cheek and nose.

On the dozenth or so blow, at the mere touch of his sadistic pent up rage-revenge, a strange dizzy sensation came over me and images started to flash in my mind. Not the images I wanted to see. Dark, dismal ones. Something that had nothing to do with me. As if I were possessed by another body. I was seeing into a strange world: of dark, heavy oily drips in a dank tunnel of dark, coppery rock. The drip of sulfurous water echoed tinnily in what looked like a mine shaft, above my head, the looking glass of my mind, which showed a high, gaping cross-shaft from where a lift had jammed and trembled on its thick, rotten cable. It swayed. As it poised maybe a 100 feet above, it gave a shuddering creak as if its ponderous weight would crash down on my skull.

But it didn't.

I shook my head, wondering where I was. Was I mad, or had I slipped into some death dream? But no, I sensed Sharki was there raining blows as he grunted and exerted near superhuman strength to end my life. I knew it was no dream, that I was still alive and conscious, not hallucinating.

I suddenly realized the source of what had prompted this weird vision. That last hit where my bare knuckles had broken through a rent in my glove had touched his bare skin. The power of the *weave* required physical touch to activate.

A little of the artifact's essence still remained in me.

I remembered the times in the past when it had resurfaced, inevitably at inopportune times. It gave me unusual glimpses into the future or past, glimpses into corridors of something inaccessible to but a chosen few humans. Such was the artifact's alien power even after all these years. But it was smoke and ghosts, inscrutable, full of poignant memories and disturbing images.

In the blink of seconds, I had a vision of Sharki as a young boy in the mines, a scrapping rat of a youth with a mane of disheveled tawny hair and copper-toned muscles. His garments were rags, muddy and oil-spattered. He hauled an unknown kid into some human-sized, narrow crevice in the rock, told him to scrunch up and be quiet, not to breathe a word. While he distracted the guards, the savvy rodent of a youth who was Sharki drew away, waving his arms. I saw him draw the night monitors in the opposite direction, down the far end of the shaft into the shadows. Gave the younger boy time to slip out of his hiding spot and escape the other way. When the night watch caught up with young Sharki, they beat him within an inch of his life. The pummeling was too horrible to watch. His face, neck and arms were bruised pulp. I jerked out of the vision, scrunched up my eyes and gave an agitated moan. "You were beaten! You were there, Sharki!

Hold up!" I squirmed away from his fist that threatened to break my nose. "You were good once. You helped a boy, that boy. When the slavers came down on you in the shaft, you saved his life, even though the cost—" the image brought a strangled shiver in me "—That twisted arm of yours, the stilted walk, its because, because—"

Sharki screeched, "How the hell—did you—"

"Never mind. You were good once. You became bad. Embittered, hateful."

"Shut up!" Sharki's gloved fist came down to smash at my face.

I bunted the fist aside and rasped, "You kill me now, we all die. Do the right thing. None of us gets closure in this. You want that lug Brex to get away with this?"

"Fuck no."

"Then help me escape here. You need all of us—Marty, Slapper."

Sharki wasn't listening. My words, or whatever I'd told him, seemed only to upset him more, to spur him to new heights of rage. He crabbed back, snatching up the pipe. He flew at me, clubbing with all his might, cursing. He was a demon, beyond reason. He went full out, trying to bludgeon me. He swung the metal bar like a madman, wielding it like a baseball bat.

But he was also flailing wildly and it was not so hard for me to dodge his swings.

I jerked back, nearly tripping over my heels once as the bar swung hairs'-breadths from my face. The bar caught the edge of my grav pack and the next blow threatened to smash it. Without ground or sky I'd be a goner if I stepped outside the ship. In a desperate purchase for life, I wrenched the bar out of his grip and smacked him off balance, sweeping his legs out from under him. I raised the pipe, looming over him, ready to send it down on his skull, and end his life then and there.

But something stayed my hand.

Sharki's words wracked the dead weight of silence between us. "I never saw him again! For three months I wallowed in the bottom level of that cursed mine. We'd been searching for food, stolen the keycodes to the locks."

Silence. Only the gasp of our lungs laboring.

"What mine?" I croaked at last.

"The dwellers of the damned. A prison-pen for the deviants. One of the occupants happened to be a medic, some healer, a misfit who mended my fractured bones. Why the slavers kept us alive, I don't know. They had every reason to kill me, slit my throat. But every second of that torture fueled my spirit. To survive. To seek revenge."

I stared at him for several moments. "He lives still."

"Who?"

"That boy you saved."

"How do you know this, Rusco? If this is some trick—"

"It's no trick."

"Cadvil. His name was Cadvil."

"*Is* Cadvil, not was."

Sharki looked at me with a quivering mouth, lips twisted in bitter snarl of memory, of times long ago. His gray eyes were portals into a ghost realm. I saw his throat swallow, his lips peel back from his gummy teeth as he wiped blood from his face. "That kid was my brother."

My eyes widened. It all made sense. Why else would this hardened career criminal risk his life for some no name kid? He had, and that was what mattered. The key to whether we lived or died on this forsaken roid lay in this moment. If there was still some good left in Sharki, perhaps we could make use of it. I remembered the cruel treatments, the blood-soaked bodies and blaster-fire back on Tyrone and how he'd nearly killed Marty and me in the scrapyard.

Every cell in my body was screaming to waste this fucker and be done with it. But I controlled my vengeance. Another voice spoke, deeper than words. *Waste Sharki and you'll never see Deidra again.*

There was no logic to it, only lunacy. But I was wise enough to pay heed to such voices.

I let the pipe slip from my fingers. My arm dropped to my side and I looked away with an empty, sick feeling.

"What's wrong with you, Rusco," Sharki snapped. "You turning into a yellow-bellied pussy?"

"Sick of death, Sharki. All my life, only killing and destruction. When does it end?"

"It doesn't, you dumbfuck. Get over it. Get one of the guns. Point it and aim between my eyes. I don't want to have to listen to your sniveling."

I grabbed a gun from the rack. I sat down on my haunches and leveled it loosely at him with a carefree hand. "Something tells me that's not the right play, Sharki. There's more to this story than what's been written."

"A philosopher?"

"Call it what you will." I motioned to his blood-grimed face. "Tell me what happened back there on Thetis."

He shrugged, growled a thin note of hate. "I was on plant refinery level D6, doing a spot check. Overseeing Beryl processing. Ready to take off on my ship *Starhopper* to Tyrone. To get new equipment, upgraded hardware to replace some of our antiquated stuff, secure some deals and new trade shipment schedules. You know, that type of thing."

"Sure."

"All of a sudden this explosion. I found myself flying 15 feet through the air, face smacked into a hot pipe, a gas line or something. Half my face was seared off, my fingers burned. I managed to half drag myself across the loading platform to a ship, the nearest ship.

"Blythe was burned too. Gredis and Otto were okay. Half blind, I clawed my way into the hold and Sargoff dragged me the rest of the way. Five of us escaped with fire leaping at our asses before we engaged the hyperdrive. I watched *Thetis 3* burn up like a fireball before the heat wave tore at our stern. For every moment since, I vowed to punish you for that deed, if it was the last thing I did. And here we are."

"A nice story."

"Kind of funny how it's worked out, Rusco. It isn't like I thought it would be."

"It never is."

"And you?"

"Same deal. Maybe not as harrowing, but we got out in time. Me, Marty and Deidra. Pure and simple luck."

He gurgled out a sad laugh as he licked blood from his lip. "Can't blame you, Rusco. I'd probably have done the same thing if I were in your shoes."

"You think? How'd you find us?"

"I figured from the tangent of the U-56's flight path that you'd gone to the Muridon Belt. I'd installed trackers aboard all my ships, which you probably didn't know about. I sent spies out to find you."

"It figures."

"I hit pay dirt pretty quick. Told my guys to keep a watch out for a couple of scumbags. In Tylas, my man, Gyra, spotted you. A trio of no-goods in the casino matching your description. It didn't take much effort after that. Here I am. A bloodhound on the scent of fresh meat."

"Nice." My mouth twisted in a cryptic grin.

CHAPTER 27

There came clinking and movement at the air lock. Through the glass pane I saw two figures had already passed through the first stage. Marty, Slapper. I hustled over to make sure they didn't bust in and blow out our air. I peered quickly through the glass, kept my gun trained on Sharki.

But there was a moment of inattention and Sharki capitalized on it.

He made a frog-hopping leap, hands wrenching for my gun. The bastard was ready to lance ion fire through my brain.

I whipped the barrel back and slapped it down hard on his side. I veered away just as Marty burst through the air lock and clubbed Sharki down. He rolled back clutching at his knee. I came within a hair's-breadth of wasting the brute. But I held back, again.

The air lock pressurized and Slapper scrambled through.

I trained the gun at Sharki, lungs pumping. "Here's the deal," I half spat through clenched teeth. "We work together. We survive. If possible we get off this shithole roid. You're either in or out! Decide!" I leveled the muzzle at his brow.

Sharki's chest heaved. As much as the bastard had ranted on about his being a 'dead man' before Brex and his goons, he scrubbed his lips with the back of his glove and grimaced. He did not seem to want to die. At least not yet. He glared at me for many seconds before huffing out a grunt of capitulation.

Marty tore off his helmet and sucked in a breath. "You going to trust this sack of shit?"

"There's a bigger picture in all of this, Marty."

"What bigger picture? All's I see is a dirty murderer. An eye for an eye, spade for a spade."

By the glint in Sharki's blackened, pus-ridden eye, I think he too was in agreement.

Who knew if we could trust the bastard. We'd have to watch him like a hawk. Wasting him was the logical plan. But my intuition was strong that we had to keep him alive.

Sharki staggered to his feet. "On one condition, Rusco," he wheezed.

"Yeah?"

"You let me kill Brex if we get off this rock."

I gave a dismissive wave. "You can have that crapster. He's not worth my time."

Sharki huffed, satisfied with that.

Marty inclined his head. "Nice crib you got here, Rusco. You been busy?"

"A little."

"Out there we got three dead bodies, two smashed-up buggies and one dead ship, *Tristar,* with stern drives blown to shit."

"It's not much," I agreed.

"It's all we got."

"So let's go out and salvage what we can, Marty, before it gets pitch black and our air runs out."

He grunted an acknowledgment. He slapped his helmet back on and we pulled down the rifles. While I quickly de-suited and grabbed one of the spare gray-toned suits off the wall, Marty held Sharki at gunpoint, allowing the gangster to clumsily follow my lead. Both mine and Sharki's suits were toast. His air intake was botched; the liner of mine was ripped at the mitts. Slapper regarded Sharki askance. Marty tossed Slapper an R1. "Watch this fuck."

Slapper nodded. I donned the spare suit I'd snatched from the wall—the same light-gray color that Sharki's crew'd worn. Sharki did the same.

I tuned my radio to Marty's. We were all on the general channel.

"We can salvage the batteries from the buggies," I said, "in case we need juice. For what I don't know. For food, there must be some packaged jerky or some crap in this rig of Sharki's. We can hole up here when our air gets low."

Marty gave a grim nod. He was already through the air lock. I took up the rear; Slapper and Sharki ahead of me.

I stared in renewed dismay at the ruin of the bridge. No radar, no port, starboard cannon, no sensors, no impulse, no hyperdrive. Everything was toast. I shuddered to think by what miracle the air lock mechanism and oxygen dispersal system had remained intact.

Brex's boys'd torched everything; they'd compromised the bridge and the crew's quarters, but they'd neglected the hold. It was a safe haven for us!

The only place we could hang out was in that small hold. We had scant few hours of air left in our suits. We wanted to preserve the precious resource in case we needed to go out for some emergency duty. There was nothing out there anyway, except rock, space dust, a cold, absolute-zero vacuum and maybe a fortune in beryl. But we would gather what we could.

I touched Marty's shoulder. "First priority, let's scavenge the bodies for their air tanks."

He thrust aside his disgust at the state of the bridge and was already moon-hopping down to collect the tanks and bring them over to *Tristar*.

Slapper and I tagged at his heels. Slapper gave a hoarse sigh, "We're cooked, Rusco, once that air runs out."

I knew it as well as he. I stood and gazed about bleakly. I did not like having matching suits with Sharki either, but it was the least of our troubles. Funny how the mind focuses on trivial things when death is staring one in the face.

All of us peered around glumly. From left to right, a desolate wasteland. A low rise of blasted, ridged rock where Marty'd held out against Brex's thugs. A massive shallow crater to the east. Mini-gullies elsewhere. Everywhere silence and emptiness. Just the eerie glow continuing to fall lower and lower like a pall of doom. This haunted roid hardly rotated, so I guessed the night would be long, very long. A night that would have been our deaths, had not the life support systems aboard Sharki's ship miraculously materialized.

Newt had unfastened himself from his place of concealment under the buggy and floated over to us now and inserted himself in our conversation.

"Jet Rusco! I detect a minimum of three dead bodies in the near vicinity. Please report this to the APC! As soon as possible. Withal, your life support systems are tenuous. I predict a maximum of 8 days, 5 hours and 3 minutes before suffocation becomes—"

"How be you shut your tinny little loudmouth up?" Sharki grated. He edged forward with his fists.

"Newt, please heed this man's advice. Help us salvage supplies."

The bot reluctantly descended a notch lower, out of Sharki's face. The shiny outerbody dipped on a sulky angle, front lights flickering yellow, green then red to the tune of small beeps.

I did not want to be working in the pitch black when our headlamps failed, so I hastened to catch up to Marty.

He was already picking at one of the three bodies not far from the forlorn flag. The blue-suited figure of Brex's man was sprawled on the rock surface, legs twisted under him like a spider. A black burn mark showed across his middle where his suit'd been tagged with blaster fire.

Marty kicked at it. A weak moan came through the man's com. How he'd still stayed alive was a miracle. It was not until I crouched lower that I saw that he'd somehow managed to jerry-rig a kevlar patch over the burn mark and contain the breach with some suit goo in the repair kit he'd been carrying. Smart lad. He was barely hanging on.

Sharki bent low to the dying figure, his breath wheezing, his expression horrible to look at—half grin, half rictus. "Well, well, flyboy. Your lucky day." His hand shot out ready to smash the helmed head against the rock.

I dove in faster and shoved Sharki aside. "Where'd Brex go?" I yelled at the near corpse. I shook him like a dog. "Where'd the bastard take her?"

The bleak, unshaven face looked back at me with ashen-white torpor. His eyes fluttered open. I knew he had not much time left. Maybe he knew he could be spared a long agonizing death if he said the right words.

"*T-terminus,*" he rasped and I saw blood drip from the corner of his mouth and stain the inside of his helmet.

Sharki growled and swore. He stomped on the man's throat, putting him out of his misery.

"*Terminus,*" I muttered. I vowed if I ever survived this rock, that'd be the first place I'd visit.

The stars wheeled overhead on this small, dead roid. My dry, red-streaked eyes looked helplessly across the stark landscape and the wan light that was rapidly disappearing into night shadow.

We gathered what we could. Three extra air tanks from the last bodies, two spare batteries from the ruined buggies. We hauled them up to the crippled insect that was *Tristar*.

I looked up at the ship: our home for the next days before we died. The life support system on her was a godsend. A dwindling resource that only extended our lease on life for at best a few fistfuls of hours.

In spite of this bleak predicament, my mind cast a beacon of hope out to Deidra. I wondered where she was. Was she at this *Terminus*? Was she in the sweaty clutches of that brute Brex?

It made my blood boil.

CHAPTER 28

For five days we were holed up in that stinking, cramped hold. Cabin fever struck us hard, like an anvil, particularly Slapper: he was going ape shit, pacing the hold back and forth. I started to despair and think forlornly we would be spending our last days in the company of my most hated enemy.

Marty was on the edge, having run out of Myscol long ago. The direness of our situation had kept his nerves sharp, his energies moderately occupied. He'd come to blows with Sharki at least three times; the last time Sharki'd almost bit it when Marty'd come close to taking him out with that piece of pipe.

Fortunately the grav stabilizers had not given out on *Tristar*, otherwise we'd be up shit creek. The crapper or commode was useless. We settled on the old fashioned way. Stoop, shit in a discarded food package and chuck it out in zero g. As undignified as it was, it worked. Kept our environment quasi-hygienic.

The crew's quarters were not accessible either, being on the other side of the air lock so we could not hang out there and escape our own miserable company. No, we were stuck with one other. One big happy family.

We moved some of the equipment aside and piled some of the lighter crates on top of each other. All to make room for us.

Even the lighter crates seemed as heavy as sin.

I grunted with the effort, sweating. "What the fuck you got in these babies, Sharki?"

Marty yanked off a lid and gave a low whistle.

I turned in closer to squint inside. A stack of IPGs—Ion

Propelled Grenades, some standard stock grenades, R1s and some body armor.

"Planning for a war?" I stared at our friend Sharki.

He lifted a hand in disinterested fashion. "Picked them up in Tyrone. A small detour. Can never be too careful out in space."

"Bet you wished you'd bagged these before you tangoed with that bastard Brex."

"Yeah, that's a clever observation."

"Nah, it was just little old Jet Rusco and his band of cowpokes to deal with. Nothing that a few R1s and some pansy ass buggy drivers couldn't deal with, right Shark?"

He muttered an expletive but made no comment. Marty smirked as the beaten-down gangster went back to his listless brooding. I'd caught him making sidelong glances at me more than once. Perhaps wondering how I knew about his brother.

We paced the cramped quarters, verbally sparring, fighting often, trying to conjure a way out of this mess. But with the communications system fried, there was no hope.

We munched on packaged dried beef jerky, some mashed potato-turkey protein mix and frozen bread and whatever else we could find from the depleted food-dispersal unit. We rationed the last of our fresh water, trying to spread it all out for as long as possible. We'd already run out of food a day ago and hunger was now a serious issue starting to gnaw at the edges of our sanity.

I started to think that yes, we would in fact be spending our last hours in the company of Sharki.

Slappy, restless and edgy, sick of our bickering and bad energy, suited up to dump his pot of piss. He came back in a flutter of arms and legs, yapping on about two bright shapes he'd seen coming out of the sky at 320 degrees.

I jerked up out of my lazy sprawl and grabbed for my suit. Marty and Sharki suited up likewise. We hustled to the bridge where we gazed out of the jagged black gap.

Two ships. They were veering closer. No doubt they'd spotted us and'd be here in a matter of minutes. Whether they were friend nor foe, we had no idea. But we had nothing to lose.

The vessels flew in formation and descended lower... Just eyeballing them, there seemed something familiar about the one on the left with the funny upturned snout.

Sharki glanced at me sharply. I think he was divining where I was going with this and muttered, "What do you see?"

"I know those bastards."

He growled. "How? That's a Skurg vessel. A Scag too, if I'm not mistaken. What are those fuckers doing tag-teamed up like hound dog and bitch in heat?"

"You tell me." My grim smile made him frown.

"They could just blow us sky high from the air."

"They could, but they'll not do that. If they catch up with us though, we'll wish we were dead."

Whether they were the same Skurgs from the uncharted roid we'd blitzed some days ago, I did not know. But I had a feeling they were. I was positive it was the same Scag ship for sure. Its long, angular look and slightly blue-tinted wings were too much of a coincidence.

An idea popped in my head. "Quick! We don't have much time. Marty, you and me'll go out and play dead. This could be our last chance. If we do this right, we may have a chance to live."

"How?"

"No time to explain. If we catch them unawares, maybe we can hijack their ship. I know it's a longshot but I'm getting the feeling they're drunk for spoils. Likely on a mission to end us. Remember, we caught them consorting with each other?"

"Yeah, but—"

"Listen. Shut up. Sharki, you and Slappy stay here. Get the IPGs trained on them and whatever weapons you can rustle up."

"Hell no," Sharki growled. "I'm going out with you."

I paused for a second. "Okay, it's your ass. Slapper, you stay back with Newt. Man the IPG at the bridge. Train it on the ships. Fire when they least expect it. If all goes to shit, do what you have to. Do not fuck this up."

Slapper bobbed his head like a pecking rooster.

"Good, let's go." I tossed Sharki an R1. "You'll need this."

Marty and I grabbed our own. I saw Slapper crouching to wield one of the big, bazooka-like IPGs from the crate. I nodded with approval. I'd scanned the weapon previously, both its scope and firing mechanism were easy to operate, well within Slapper's capability.

Sharki reached for one himself.

I pushed his arm away. "No, they'll see that. Too big. Take this." I shoved a grenade in his palm. I pushed two more in the front pouch of my own suit, passed one to Marty.

Sharki grunted, "Rusco, you're a fucking risk taker. Ballsy though, I'll give you that."

"Focus on the Scag ship. It's our only ticket out of here." I had no time to say more.

We opened the hold a crack and the three of us slipped out with our weapons. I hoped to hell they hadn't seen that movement or it would be game over already.

The ships were in no hurry. We were hidden from sight of their visuals; the ship's bow between us and them. On my instruction we lay sprawled at oblique angles with our weapons hidden underneath us. We were trying to look as torn apart as possible, the victims of a blaster battle. If they sent a landing party, which I'm sure they would, we could purchase a few moments of time that just might save our lives. Just a few seconds to get us within proximity of one of those ships...

The first one, the Skurg vessel, landed about 120 yards away. Perpendicular with us and the Bratts' proud flag. The other, the Scag, stayed 80 feet in the air.

I peeked out the corner of my helm. I had about a 20 degree field of vision. So far all was quiet.

· As I expected, the Skurg hatch opened and three hulking brutes emerged in dark, gray-mottled suits, armed with what looked like long, green-glowing staves.

They approached stiffly, jerkily, as if on wooden legs, with only a cursory wariness to their step.

Not wary enough. It looked like a done deal to them. A dead, gutted ship. A sprawl of fresh human corpses ready for cannibalistic feasts somewhere off in their hinterland hidey-holes on some faraway world. There were three of them. Three of us. A fair fight by most standards. Except they were Skurgs.

I peered through narrowed lids, making sure I made not the slightest movement. The element of surprise was critical to this operation or we would be dead. The brutes were all seven and half feet tall if they were an inch. Their hideous faces, with the pig snouts, high brows and pocked cheeks, were barely visible through the tinted glass of their faceplates. Mean, ruthless animals with no mercy or compassion for human life or life of any form.

I caught the glint of fang-like incisors through the faceplates as the first figure drew near. I saw lips moving in a sinuous gurgle of motion of speech, relaying some command to a comrade.

They held their hideous electric goads loosely in their hands as if not expecting anything untoward. Why would they?

Such weapons were not to be underestimated. The merest touch of goad could pump hundreds of deadly volts into a victim as easily as stun him at low power. They preferred the latter. Live humans were worth more to them than dead ones. The weapons served as skewers and quarterstaffs too for close-in fighting.

And now I felt the first tremors of real alarm. For fuck's sake, why did there have to be three of them?

CHAPTER 29

They had come around the front of the ship and were now staring up at the blackened hulk of our bridge and the smashed viewport. The Scag ship had landed farther away—about 80 yards or so past the flag. The Skurgs were dialoguing among themselves. Two were about to move closer, but the lead figure stopped short and barked something to the others as if suddenly getting an odd feeling about this situation. A feeling of skulduggery?

What the hell? Had one of Marty or Sharki moved?

No time for deep analysis. I burst up out of my faked death pose, snatched up my blaster and whipped off a shot before I launched myself straight at them.

It caught the wing man on the hip somewhere in the ribs, ripping a smoking, gaping hole in his suit. He clawed at his side. The protective liner was torn; he began a macabre dance like a big straw man on fire.

Marty aimed for the lead figure. He missed only by a hair, but was now in full flight, cursing and angling for the shadow side of the ship to avoid getting goaded down.

I'd mistimed this badly.

I glanced to my left. Sharki had jumped into action and now ran at the third Skurg, his weapon belching fire. But it fizzled out and I heard his sneer loud over the com. The wing man now came running at him with goad whirling like a quarterstaff. Sharki must have forgotten about his grenade for I just saw him pile into the Skurg hulk's legs, but not before taking an electric shock for his trouble. The two rolled and rolled out of sight behind the ship and I feared the muscled Skurg would get the upper hand.

They were too far away for me to join the fray. All I could hear were Sharki's grunts and gasps and howls over the com before they cut out.

A flash of light came arching above my head from the bridge. Slapper. Bright fire licked out across the plain. The first ion propelled grenade lashed heavily into the Skurg's starboard flank.

Good old Slapper.

No time to screw around. I went straight for the lead Skurg, who was trying to flush out Marty, now pinned down behind the wreck of the ship's thrusters. I launched a grenade at him. It sent the hulk flying eight feet backward. I got to Marty and gathered him up. "Quick!" I yelled at him hoarsely. "This is our window of opportunity. Forget those knuckle-eaters. We have to get to the Scag ship."

Marty nodded vigorously, growling an acknowledgment. We raced across the desolate plain toward the Scag ship before she had time to take off. I saw the faded black insignia and lettering on her side. *Ghostblade*.

Right on cue, Slapper sent a barrage of fire at the Scag vessel. It smacked midships back of the Y-wing, pushing down her shields and keeping her grounded for a few important moments.

The lead Skurg, now realizing how cunningly he had been suckered into ambush, had spidered off and was sidling his way on long legs back to their ship. I caught a sick glimpse of yet another Skurg who'd come out of the hold and was now dragging Sharki by a back leg back toward the Skurg vessel. Sharki was kicking and bucking but he was weaponless and his strength waning from injuries and lack of food.

Another bright flash. I saw a glowing missile lick across the roid's surface. The figure dragging Sharki stumbled, clutching at his throat. He fell to the ground. But the lead Skurg doubled back and snatched up Sharki, ignoring his fallen comrade.

Return fire peppered back from the Skurg vessel and rained hell on *Tristar's* bridge. I saw smoke and fire rim the viewport. *Tristar* seemed to jump and shake with multiple impacts.

Slapper? Did he have a chance?

I could almost not bear to look. But I caught the flutter of a beagle-brown suit roll out of the hold before the ship was completely engulfed in flames.

Only seconds had passed. Marty and I booted it the last thirty feet to the Scag ship. The hull had not lifted yet. In the fire and confusion that followed, she was slow to pull away.

Slapper's IPG had hammered her shields down significantly—or maybe they were already low? We stood there panting five feet from the cargo bay door.

Precious seconds were passing. In desperation, I fisted one of the grenades. I thought to chuck it at the cargo door but then I desisted at the last second. It could backfire on us.

I motioned Marty and we blasted it in tandem with our R1s but the rays bounded back and almost fried us..

"Shit!" I leaped back, my life flashing before me.

Newt had caught up with us and whizzed past—he must have exited with Slappy.

"Jet Rusco, stand back."

The bot extended some odd, retractable rod-like proboscis and twirled it into the lock mechanism. There came a fizzle and a blast of electricity that arced across the gap… nearly taking out our intrepid Newt. But for some reason the force field momentarily went offline. I could see the yellow light on the hexagonal panel flicker. Marty and I sprang up and aimed our R1s and rained full fire at the lock mechanism. The door blew out. We hustled through the smoking gap into her cargo bay. Her shields were down.

We piled into the dark space beyond. I looked back to catch a glimpse of *Tristar* on fire. Slapper was somewhere behind that wall of flames, the only thing separating him from the wrath of the Skurg guns and cannons. We could do nothing for him. We turned and flicked on our headlamps, plunging forward.

At the far end of the hold was a double decompression chamber similar to *Tristar's* that buffered passage to the interior of the ship. We did not want to breach this vessel on the small chance we could escape this roid.

We wasted no time. We scrambled into the booth-like compartment, sealed the door, then got the decompression sequence started up.

10 seconds, 9, 8, 7... If the crew locked the inner portal... No matter, we'd be forced to blow it. I just hoped it would not come to that. We could not afford to ruin this decompression chamber, at least if we wanted to get off this roid alive. The Skurg ship was sure not going to be an escape vehicle for us.

The moment the green light came on, I shouldered my way through the inner door. Marty and Newt were fast on my heels.

The ship lurched and tugged into motion. Marty fell sideways and nearly knocked me off my feet. We scrambled down the hallway past the crew's quarters and the captain's chambers, our shoulders buffeted against the walls. We paid no heed. Marty blasted the door to the bridge, sending smoke and debris every which way.

Two figures sat hunched at the controls, caught by surprise. The nearest lifted his bulk, a horse-faced brute with lank stringy hair and buck teeth. I pegged him between the eyes. He went down, his skull split in two. Blood pooled underneath him. The other just stared, his mouth working noiseless syllables.

I thumbed my wrist panel and activated the external speaker on my suit. "Hands off the nav!" I barked. "Now, or die!"

"What the hell? God damn, you! You wasted Darmy."

"You're next, bitch!" Marty scrambled forward to pistol-whip him. "Get away from those controls."

He lifted fingers of both hands off the console. Marty swept in and smacked the R1 hard on his skull, sending him flying to the floor. He hoofed him in the ribs.

I raced to the controls, got a visual on the plain below.

We were surging upward on a sharp angle. I gained the pilot seat and aimed the Y-Wing back around. I squinted through the viewport, trying to make sense of what I saw on the ground below.

The smoke had cleared. The Skurg ship had ceased firing. Oddly it had not lifted off. Was it damaged? *Tristar* was a blackened hulk 150 yards away. Her superstructure was still extant. I could see no sign of Slappy. My worst fear, the youth had been vaporized in the attack.

"Jet Rusco. We must save Slapper if we can. I suggest we—"

But I was not listening any more. My mind was faraway and yet racing.

Slappy's air would be running low if he was alive. Sharki was still missing. I assumed the worst for him too—he'd been fried, or they'd dragged him into that cursed ship. The thought sent a chill down my spine. The Skurg vessel was parked where it had always been, a predatory presence, with hosts inside waiting to feast on whatever cadavers were still left behind.

I bit my lip and scowled. The ship must have been damaged or why wouldn't they have just blasted off to shoot us down?

That there was no more ship fire worried me too. Were they just playing cat and mouse?

Marty rooted around in the utility compartment looking for something to bind our prisoner with.

I peered back at the Skurg ship. A funny T-bone shape with wicked curled lines at its upturned bow. Three cannons, fore, aft and side. A sleek death machine.

Nonetheless, they were easy prey for our guns if they were in fact, stranded. We could rack her shields to nothing. But was it the right play?

Marty bound cord around the lank-haired pilot's wrists and ankles and muttered some foul words about scumbags, before thrusting him in a corner.

The prisoner squirmed and struggled. "Hey, watch it, buddy. Seems to me you flyboys are egging for a bruising. Once the Scag brothers find out I've been kidnapped and a ship's missing—"

"Shut up." Marty pistol-whipped him in the head. He ripped off some of the man's soiled jacket and stuffed it in his mouth. "Rusco, why don't we just call it a day and get the fuck out of here? We don't owe anybody anything."

"What about Slapper?"

"Probably dead. He and Iron knew the score when he enlisted aboard. We go down there and we'll have the Skurgs open fire on us."

"We could destroy their ship first."

"We could. But how does that help Slapper?"

I chewed my lip. It would also waste Sharki if he were, in fact, aboard that ship.

My mind was already made up.

We banked the Y-Wing around for another pass, hoping to see another clue that would make my choice somewhat easier.

There was none. No life from the Skurg ship. No movement from the blackened *Tristar*. She looked as forlorn and abandoned as a war-torn derelict. Try as I might to distance myself from Sharki, I could not just leave the bastard to those ghouls. And yet, blasting him to shit seemed cold-blooded too, considering the sacrifice he'd made. He had unwittingly created a diversion that had landed us this ship.

I needed some answers quickly but there were none there. I whirled around, ripped the gag out of the prisoner's mouth. "Talk, you scum. What the fuck are you doing here?"

"You're going the wrong way, brother." He laughed through an oily, gap-toothed grin.

"Shut up." I knocked the butt of my gun against his skull. "Answer the questions, or eat the barrel of my R1."

"Sure, cowboy, what's on your mind?"

"I repeat, what the fuck are you doing here with these Skurgs?"

He spat a gob of phlegm on the metal grate floor beside me. "That'd take a month of Sundays to explain."

"Marty?"

Marty leaped up and smacked our wiseass hard in the face. Blood dripped from his near shattered nose.

"Alright already. Calm down." He spat. "Beefeater shafted us. Cut us short. Shortchanged me and Darmy and Teer and a few others on some ore claims and work ventures."

"Who the fuck's Beefeater?" Marty growled.

He stared sweetly. "General of the Scags. Where you been, bully boy? Shooting pop guns out your ass?"

"Out hunting down and blowing away bastards like you. What are you doing cozying up with Skurgs?"

"Oh, we decided to do some side ventures. We don't owe Beefeater nothing." He spat out more blood.

"What side deals?"

"Nothing to concern you."

I rapped the R1 on his skull. "I think it does. What side deals?""

His mouth puckered in a sullen sneer. "Skurgs're useful scouts. Good at sniffing out beryl and selenium."

"Taking up with cannibals and slavers, you mean?"

"I don't care if those mutants're butthole-eating, dick-fucking catamites. They help us find ores and that means claims. What of it? Pays the bills, yields double fare. You'd do the same."

"In return for what? Party favors?" I jeered.

"No," said Marty, "this pasty pansy ass just likes a big rod up his ass."

The Scag ran his tongue along his lower lip, as if knowing he had nothing to lose. "Maybe your fantasy, not mine, chief. Let's just say that some of the scutzers go missing. They meet with unfortunate accidents out in space. Ain't entirely by mishap, you see."

"Meaning what?"

His head did a little bob. "Suppose a couple of ships disappear. A few men go with it. Maybe somebody tipped somebody off. Skurgies happen to show up. They do what they do best, eating and carousing. They take what's theirs, anything they can."

It took me a moment to grasp what the scum was saying before I began to see red everywhere.

"You miserable fucking toadster."

He laughed. "Skurgy boys like to take ships for salvage. They take a couple of humans, like live mice and use them in their rituals. No harm, it all works out."

I knew what rituals he was talking about. I'd escaped two camps of cannibalism and gladiator games fought to the death. Violent, horrible rituals on remote planets. I had no wish to ever return there again. Or see anyone suffer such a gruesome fate.

I cocked my weapon and blew the miserable shitbag's brains all over the wall.

Marty drew back with a cursing grimace. "Shit, Rusco, who's going to clean up all this mess?"

"I could give a rat's ass."

"Tone it down, bud. Not that I had any love for this sack of shit but we could have used him later."

"Yeah, maybe, but you don't know the Skurgs like I do, Marty. This cretin deserved his death ten times over."

Marty shrugged, his expression showing mild distaste at the moist, gleaming pieces of flesh and bone and fried brain sliding down the wall. Death was neither pretty nor glorious, and this death was about as inglorious as it got.

Now that I knew what the end game was, I had extra reason to do what needed done. Direct the full force of my fury at the Skurg ship.

"Let's go down there, Marty. We take them by surprise."

"You crazy, Rusco?" He shook his head with slow understanding. "What drug're you on?"

"I've always been crazier than a coot, Mar, you know that, and I'm still alive."

"Yeah, well, one day your nine lives are going to desert you."

I gave a devil-may-care grin. We came in a low sweep, hard and fast, in case the Skurg guns decided to sight on us before we landed.

They didn't.

We set down on the other side of *Tristar* using its blackened, gutted hulk as a shield. Her fires had long fizzled out; she was cold as a tomb. My guts growled with hunger and I felt the first tremors of fatigue. Adrenaline was starting to burn down. We checked our suits and ventured out with cautious steps to find Slapper.

CHAPTER 30

I saw a whisper of movement and the ghost of steam curling from behind the ruined stern thruster. The steam was discharged from what must have been a space suit.

Turned out the occupant was huddled in a crevice of twisted metal on the hull's side away from the Skurg ship, not far from where Marty had holed up. His blaster was gripped in both hands, shaking uncontrollably. Poor bastard was scared shitless that we'd left him here.

But Slapper was okay, smoke-grimed, dark patches on his suit, his eyes flitting about like nervous swallows. His com had blinked out during the blast. I hauled him up out of his cubbyhole and patted him on the back. I gave his smoke-stained helmet a couple of raps and it seemed to come back to life.

"Jeezuz! Rusco, Marty! For shit's sake, am I glad to see you!"

"Good work with the gunning, kid. You got us a ship. We're going to be okay, Slap, we're going to get off this roid."

He nodded. His ashen face was sweat-slicked, his pale eyes gleaming. There were beads of tears in them.

"Sharki?" I asked.

Slapper shook his head, motioned toward the Skurg ship. "Those ghouls took him. A pair of mutants. Came out of the hold and dragged him into the cargo bay before I could do anything. All while you were in the air." His gun arm trembled.

Two blasts raked out from the Skurg's starboard port and ripped against *Tristar's* bow.

We fell flat on our bellies and rolled for cover. More return fire followed, a pair of coordinated blasts that ripped off half of *Tristar's* left wing.

So, the bastards had been playing possum…

I peered back at the hated vessel.

Don't do it. This is stupid, Rusco.

But I knew I had to. There were other reasons. I needed to know if Sharki was dead or alive. I did not want to spend the rest of my days looking over my shoulder with the remote fear that he might be alive and come back to haunt me, stick a knife in my back. If he survived this, and I knew he just might, given past experience—he would come after me with all the vengeance of the universe behind him.

"Okay." I nodded somberly. "This is what we're going to do. You go stay in the Scag ship with Newt, Slappy. Keep the cannons trained on the Skurgs. Any sign of trouble you blast the shit out of them. Marty and I are going to pay them a social call. If things go sour—" I trailed off. "I suggest you lift off and get your ass the hell out of here while you have a chance. You got it?"

He nodded, his face pained.

Marty shook his head in dismay. "This is insane, Rusco. Stupid and insane."

I let Marty have his say and when he'd finished, and Slapper had safely low-crawled around the stern and boarded the Scag ship, we scooted out around the side of blackened *Tristar*. We kept crouching low, keeping our guns in front of us, knowing this was a do or die mission and our moment of vulnerability was now. We scurried past the two grisly Skurg bodies, trying not to look at their fried guts and grizzled faces. One of the husks floated free at about waist height, bent leg hooked under him, a grotesque face carved in a rictus. Just another ghostly corpse on an uncharted roid.

We approached the ship from the rear, away from their cannons and fire ports. They hadn't sent out a greeting party yet and that was a good thing. My breath came in short gasps. My heart pumped with adrenaline. Odd, no fire raking our exposed figures. Saving their fire power, or did they have some other trick in mind?

I peered around the side of the ship and caught a glimpse at her bow of metal spikes fanning out like spokes of a wheel. As if to spear game? I thought humorously. More ornamental deep Skurg humor here.

I saw that Slapper's IPG blasts had done some extensive damage to her hull. Dark scorch marks showed below her port vane, also an ugly, wedge-shaped gap. Maybe ruptured a power line to the drive? Maybe her shields were ultra low too. Grounded her when she was not expecting an attack. I smiled. A power line out might mean her shields were kaput. Which meant—

I gave Marty a signal and we crept around to the side hatch and opened fire. We blasted the hatch with the gleeful relish of kids burning a Halloween scarecrow. We ducked inside, weapons held in front of us.

We flicked on our head lamps.

Nothing. Only shadows and darkness. No movement or sign of life. No heavy equipment or tools. Or desiccated bodies. Just some spare tanks and five monstrous space suits strapped on the far wall.

We bypassed these and went through an open air lock and wended our way stealthily down a wide, ten-foot high hallway. We came to a massive, oval-shaped door, riddled with cryptic symbols: odd, angular-shaped ships, glyphs and script. I shot a look back to see the air lock behind me snap shut. I grimaced. So, they knew we were here. Why allow us to infiltrate this far? To lure us aboard? We were trapped now in this sinister corridor. Marty and I clenched teeth and opened fire on the metal door, reducing it to molten shards. With grim zeal I pushed my way through the smoke and Marty crowded in on my heels.

They'd holed up in the bridge. Two baddies, hunched there like rats. They glared back at us with goads gripped in their greasy, mitted hands. They were crouched before the weapons' console, enjoying the fruits of their labors. Sharki was hunched in a corner, his blue-white suit half torn off, shaking, no helmet, his black matted hair hanging to shoulders, arms tucked at his middle. A blood trail ran down his side to his leg.

It took me a while to register the horror of his situation before I could react. These animals probably figured they were toast anyway, so they wanted to conserve their strength, get some fresh meat in them and hole up here till the very end, till their air and food ran out. They took pride in their work, carve a little here, a little there, maybe they could last for weeks in this hell crib before some brethren took interest to come look for them. They'd started with Sharki's arm, carved off half way from the elbow down. The foremost Skurg's eyes pulsed with malevolent, gluttonous need, his lips and snouty chin dripping red of the flesh they'd recently devoured.

"Jesus!" A bile-like phlegm floated up from my throat. I resisted the urge to puke.

"Fucking ghouls sawed off my arm," I heard Sharki moan. "Ate it raw, like it was a drumstick." He grimaced, wracked with anguish and revulsion. His skewed eyes bulged like a horse's running through a lightning storm.

I had no time to process my horror. The two came at me, leaping like wild beasts. Goads were in their hands, whirling like staffs.

I brought up my blaster with vengeance, lips peeled back in a snarl.

The nearest leaped at me, faster than a vampire, teeth snapping. Goad, six feet long, whipped out and sent electrical arcs spinning at my head. The arcs blinded me. I fell back, staggering. My first shot clipped his way but went wide. Arcs of light went skidding around the cramped control room. Blaster fire and goad flare licked every which way. Marty was crouched, short barrel spitting blasts into the ghouls. A long rangy arm hooked out and knocked my barrel aside. Marty tagged the first husky shape in the shoulder, but the other nightmarish fiend, behind him, did a flying leap and zapped Marty with his goad, wrestling him to the ground.

I regained my feet, shaking the fog out of my skull. Stars spun before my eyes. I sprayed fire at anything that moved. Some must have caught what vaguely seemed the Skurg's back. The monster mutant's arms flung wide as my fire must have clipped the back of his neck. Marty bucked the hulk off. I sent more shots thunking into his skull. Others careened out and away around the space. I did not care what I hit and what I didn't. It is a scary thing to be half-blinded, with monsters of flesh-eating rapacity ready to clamp teeth in you and chew you to pieces. I discerned the second Skurg coming in at my left. Did the mutant bastard not die?

I shot at him, but he would not die.

The hulk loomed on my periphery, a colossus of death. He dwarfed me and I had no doubt who was the stronger should it come to a one-on-one. The blue-black kevlar-like body armor they wore seemed immune to blaster fire. Only a head shot would finish them off and good luck doing that with my wonky vision.

Sharki launched himself up from his anguished crouch and kneed the Skurg low in the thigh as he was coming for me. The thing tripped and reeled sideways. Sharki, white-faced, a livid curse in his throat, let stomp a boot into the mutant's face, crushing its nose, vampire teeth, jaw in one fell swoop. The Skurg spasmed and choked on his own blood before it gushed out its last dying breaths and lay still.

Sharki swayed on his feet. He slumped against the wall.

I caught him before he collapsed. I saw him clutching his left stump, pulled tight into his middle. The Skurgs'd cauterized the wound half way up to the elbow with some primitive method, the likes of which I saw in the form of a long heat rod tucked to the side.

"Get to the Scag ship, Marty! See if there's a spare suit and first aid kit."

Marty shook the haze out of his skull. He hunched forward and put ion fire into both of the Skurg's heads. He stumbled back gamely through the sawtoothed door and vanished into a mist of smoke and blood, not uttering a word.

My vision was still double, everything a vague blur, but not as much as before. I staggered forward, both hands gripping my blaster, doing quick sweeps in case some other jack-in-the-box jumped out at me from a darkened corner.

Some time later Marty returned, carrying a spare suit in hand. He grumbled something about how in his old age he resented being an errand boy.

Newt was with him, hovering at his side, offering statistics, condolences for our ill state.

These we ignored.

We suited up Sharki and frog-hopped him back to the Scag ship. Slapper had found a first aid kit. We sterilized the wound with alcohol and re-cauterized it with a heat ring thingy from the kit while Slapper held him down. Sharki hurled howls and curses into the air, but it was for his own good.

I could only think of the sacrifice he'd made slowing down the Skurgs, offering distraction, without which we would not be on this ship right now with our lives and our freedom.

There was no regen—to Sharki's loss. He'd have to suffer through the worse of it.

Newt hovered close to the console where we worked. *"Aiding and abetting criminals is a breach contrary to Vala federative law, Jet Rusco. My recommendation is to turn yourself in and plead—"*

"You've got a mouthy pipsqueak of a bot," Sharki growled hoarsely, clenching the fingers of his good hand.

"You think?" I squinted at Sharki, his face still partly blurry, trying to grasp the part he played in this new twist in the *weave*. "I'd say you have as many angels looking over you as Slapper here." The youth was staring hollow-eyed through a dirt-grimed face across the lifeless landscape, looking out the viewport like a lost soul. "How the hell did you survive that Skurg blast back there?"

"I saw them swiveling cannons on me. I knew the gig was up...so I hotfooted it fast as I could to the stern. Rolled out before the ship was torched. Saved my ass."

I gave a sober nod. "Good call."

I heard Marty rustling about at the pilot's seat, grunting and flipping dials. The Scag ship lifted off. Beyond the viewport, I saw the ruined hulks of ships pass below.

I was not sad to see the last of that murdersome roid...

CHAPTER 31

I jolted upright, awakened from a hideous dream. Sharki was chasing me with a pickaxe, the stump of his other hand jetting blood.

Cold sweat clung to the back of my neck. The sheets were rumpled. The narrow bunk where I crouched was too hard. A sour taste lingered in my mouth—the aftermath of the mud-like, synthetic paste I'd ingested from the ship's stores before I'd lain down to crash.

How long had I slept? My vision had returned somewhat, only a slight joggle in the left eye when I squinted at the nearby wall of the crew's quarters.

Cold memory returned. We'd survived and yet had no right to survive. We had a ship. Did we deserve that either? Our thirst for revenge was as potent as ever. But I felt a dull throb in my heart, knowing that Deidra was not at my side. That we were not sharing each other's bodily warmth.

I made my way to the bridge in a fog and saw that my companions were already up and about. Slapper gave me the briefest of acknowledgments; all were in tense moods.

The place smelled of blood. Marty had done a hasty job of cleaning up the blood spatter from the corpses of our erstwhile Scag marauders, and jettisoned the bodies.

He'd already set a course for Terminus. Slapper sat by him at the nav, chewing away at some of the same green goop I'd eaten last night. He was stomaching it with a flat-lipped grimace. Sharki stood peering through the viewport, a baleful scowl on his face. A fiery energy exuded from his hunched body. He clutched at his stub, as if dreaming of all the malevolent things he would do to Brex.

Somewhere the bridge felt empty without Deidra...

I was not going to lie...the loss of her was like a stab to my heart. The chance of ever getting her back seemed slim. I looked hollowly at my companions, such a hardened group of misfit space bullies, and wondered if such resources were enough to pull it off: a midget bully boy with a hair-triggered temper, a scrappy ranch hand barely out of puberty, an aging murdering scumbag with one arm.

Not the stuff of heroes.

It was no good to dwell on this or much else at the moment. Nor deny that I was attached to her. She had a chip on her shoulder and was sometimes impossible to be with, but these foibles paled next to the excitement and passion we shared when we were in each other's arms.

I vowed I would get her back, or die trying.

If Sharki showed any depression from his loss of arm, I did not see it. If anything, it only stoked the man's fervor for vengeance. Perhaps it was another echo of the man's spirit. Battered and half starved, pulped with bloody bruises as a youth in the mines... Nothing much changed. I shuddered to think of what he could have become, had he not walked the path he did.

I paced the bridge, brooded on the next course of action. Sharki joined me and spoke in a low whisper, "If you're thinking the same as me, Rusco, some people are going to be paying some high prices in blood. Sargoff, dead. Blythe, Gredis, and Otto, killed. They nuked my ships, took away the last things I had, and for that they'll pay."

I refrained from making a blithe comment about what that made me.

He turned and slowly inspected me, as if somehow reading my thoughts. "I will never forgive you for what you did back at *Thetis*. Yes, we'll raise hell on *Terminus*. We'll make this Brex bastard wish he were never born. But after that you and me are going to tango. All pacts are off. We meet up again, you can bet your ass there's going to be blood flying—" His good first clenched and made a cutting motion across his neck.

"Whatever yanks your crank, Sharki. Let's just call it even and take it one step at a time."

He shouldered me aside as he made for the head.

"Cap'n Hook looks like he's got it in for you," Marty muttered.

"Yeah, well let's not underestimate our Cap'n Hook. We need to keep a close eye on him, Marty."

"Aye, aye, Skipper." He gave me a satiric salute.

We hypered on through the gulfs of space—to Terminus—on the other side of the belt. ETA, well, who the fuck cared? Did it matter? It was close enough in terms of relative space-time.

But it was one thing to plot a course, another to dredge up a plan.

"Let's put our heads together," I said. "How're we going to get Deidra back and my ship? Not to mention in broad daylight, under Brex's nose?"

Marty spread his arms in haphazard fashion. "Well, since we don't know anything about this Terminus, all we can do is show up and do a bit of reconnaissance."

"I've been there," Slapper piped up.

Sharki'd returned with a face not much more pleasant than the one he'd left with. He guffawed. "What are you going to do, kid, show us where the playground is?"

"Lay off him, Sharki," I said. "He's just trying to help."

"Yeah, well…" Sharki shook his head and knuckled his eyes.

"First things first," I said. "We can't do any snooping around there going in as we are. Brex's put a price on our heads. It's still fresh in people's minds."

"Let's disguise ourselves then," Slapper suggested.

It was not a bad plan. We raided the utility stores, digging around for props. We found some, in the way of clothes and weapons.

We tied bandannas over our heads. An eye patch felt good over my left eye. I dyed my skin an ocher tint using iodine and salve from the first aid kit. Marty wore a loose brown spacer's outfit. It was too big for him, rolled up at the knees. Slapper donned a tuque he'd scavenged from Darmy's utility trunk.

All in all, crude accessories, but better than no disguises at all.

Sharki opted for no such gimmicks. With his ruined face, it seemed unlikely anyone would recognize him or venture too close. He shoved a knife in his suit. I caught only the briefest flicker of black fabric he stuffed in his other pocket.

Crap, but we looked an ill breed of space pirates.

"This'll either work or it won't," I muttered.

"That's very helpful, Rus." Marty looked away, his voice terse and impatient.

Sharki paused in midstep. He took me aside. "About that little trick of yours, back there on *Tristar*... talking about Cadvil."

"It's nothing, Sharki." I shrugged. "Forget it. A little insight maybe some gypsies gave me a long time ago."

He gave a curt scowl, knowing he'd get no more.

I pulled him away from the others. "Listen, we could put a call in for Iron and the Reapers—"

He swatted my arm away. "No! This is between me, you and Brex. It's gotten personal, Rusco, and as I mentioned, I want Brex for myself."

"Suit yourself. But I take Deidra. You agree to help get her back."

He gave a hissing breath, but followed up with a grudging nod.

There were plenty of holes in this plan and things could go very wrong. But the essence of it was sound. It all hinged on the fact that Deidra was holed up on *Terminus* as Brex's goon on the roid had told us before he'd died.

We came out of hyperdrive and swung in slow orbit about 10k miles above *Terminus*, the Ghost Planet. It did not look like much. A gray-brown disc, slightly misshapen at the equator and flattened at the poles. I thought maybe if the forces of nature had been kinder, she could have been a planet. But no, she was just some leftover droppings of the primordial soup.

I turned to Slappy. "How many times've you been to this place?"

"Once or twice. On duty leave. Once or twice is two times too many. They have brutal competitions at the drome, a massive dome where the scutzers, pretending to be warriors of old, do battle on some kind of mini war-like speeders. A kind of demolition derby. Sometimes they work in teams. Awesome to behold, hellish to participate in."

Sharki nodded, the briefest flicker of interest in his eyes. "I've heard of these games, kid. Never witnessed one. After dealing with Brex, maybe we can all join in on the fun."

"Maybe we can," I grunted. "This place seems not lacking in kicks or entertainment." I frowned, lost in thought. "Weird to do sports on a wannabe planet without an atmosphere."

"'Weird' is *Terminus's* second name," Slapper muttered. "It's a planetoid waiting to be become a roid. Just a few hits by some massive wandering asteroids and I think she'll split in two."

Mar gave his head a mocking shake. "I don't know what fantasy you're living in, Slappy, but—"

"No, look—" I jerked a thumb at the ship's display. Zooming in on the magnifier, I saw a huge gap widen at the equator, a black gash bisecting her in the middle, dropping nearly a quarter of the way to her core.

"You see…it could happen," Slapper said defensively.

"But likely won't," Marty intoned.

The big question was how were we going to get down to the settlers' town and set a trap for Brex without attracting attention?

A good question.

The good news was that the Bratts were on civil terms with the Scags, unlike the Reapers and the Bratts. We could potentially sneak in on this Scag vessel. But something about the idea bothered me. If they found out it was a stolen ship of a murdered crew, we were in for a world of pain.

Nothing was carved in stone though. Along the way we could improvise, forced as we were to take some risks.

There'd be plenty of that where we were going.

CHAPTER 32

I took *Ghostblade* down on an oblique angle and we made our approach over the outskirts of Terminus Town.

Large, heavy machines and drilling equipment passed underneath us. At the steel gate of the barbed wire fence surrounding the mining compound, an impressive placard of 'Dancor' was lifted high.

A steady stream of ships flew over the barren terrain, hauling ores out from the many mining sites and on to city centers and refineries around the galaxy.

All the major mining corps had laid claims on this stark world, doing extensive drilling and harvesting of lodes—from beryl to gold.

According to the ship's database, there had been much talk of terraforming the planetoid and making it a major mining mecca and habitable region. But the gravity was too low. Modern technology had not yet figured out a way to normalize the gravity of an entire world. At least not yet. The CEOs and bigwigs thought it better just to scavenge the place as much as possible for profit without investing too much.

A scutzing community had struck up overnight and stretched in a mean, ugly sprawl across the desolate landscape: between the two major stations of Dancor and Damocles—earning the notorious, if not minimalist title of 'Terminus Town'.

We moved along the spine of the settlement and came to a massive chasm we'd seen from space. It was like a monstrous chunk had been bit out of the planetoid. To say it was daunting, even awe-inspiring, would be a euphemism. An abyss of infinite blue-black darkness tumbled down, endlessly down, to fuel children's nightmares for years after. The rift stretched for as far as the eye could see, a jagged crack across the planetoid's face. Opposite the town, the rift's width was only 5 miles, the narrowest span. Elsewhere the gap ranged up to 50 miles.

I could see why this cleft made Terminus a mining corp's dream. Their machines had free vertical access to about 200 hundred miles of exposed crust to extract ores and metals of unfathomable wealth. Normally it would be impossible to reach such depths using conventional methods, or even supra-modern techniques like telebracting.

I wondered what forces had been at work in shaping this weird world some billions of years ago. It was a black trench that dropped endlessly down to unfathomable depths.

As we traveled over the rift I could see the lights of futuristic machinery working far below like tiny insects, digging and hewing at the rock. The far face of the cliff was draped in blue-black darkness as the shadow of the nearby wall fell sharply.

How many more excavations and machines were on levels far below?

Marty mused, "They got enough operations to keep them busy into the next century."

Three battleships roved and patrolled the gap. Another loomed closer to the town where the mining operations were the densest, where the many drilling machines clustered about the rim like archaeologists burrowing for lost treasures.

All of the battleships were big bruisers even at this distance. Intimidating shapes with cryptic 'Damocles' logos on their sides. Long, black submarine hulls with curious, massive metal arms for lifting heavy machinery aboard. My guess, they were deployment platforms for mining machinery, also working as part terraformers when needed.

"What the fuck're those monsters doing here?" Marty grumbled.

"Protect the corps' interests, what do you think?" Sharki wagged his stump. "I assume most of the infrastructure here is Damocles'.

Probably prey to a bunch of rogues too, I'd guess, not to mention uprisings. I'd do the same—deploy battleships."

I was on the same page as Sharki. "We'll steer clear of them. Maybe it's more posturing than anything. To keep the locals in line. We'll give them a wide berth." But I had a disheartening feeling that would be too much to hope for.

I steered *Ghostblade* away from the battleships and toward the teeming, more primitive colony of Terminus situated at the edge of the narrowest point across the chasm.

It had been probably a tiny outpost at one time, but when the goliaths moved in with their billions, she grew to her present size and infamy.

Aye, she was a rough town, where only the rule of the blaster prevailed. From what Slappy had said, worse than Tylas, making our little casino town look like an angels' hangout.

Newt, having overcome his wariness of Sharki, came buzzing over to plaster us with details, *"Terminus is a unique place! A wonderfully curious anomaly of contemporary colonization and mining effort. A wellspring of mystery. Culturally diverse. A geologic conundrum as you can tell from her massive trench. The town is half terraformed by private means. The scutzers funded the first outpost out of their own pockets. They called it 'New Terminus', making charters by which they could keep 100% of all ores. The mining companies, particularly Damocles, took up the slack and bought up the rest. Did you know this small, airless planetoid comprises about 1/12 of all the mining efforts in the Muridon Belt?"*

"Didn't know that, Newt. And not much interested." I quickly quashed his prolonged monologue lest we become old men by the time he finished.

We could see for ourselves what Terminus was. A sprawling hovel of tent-like domes, a near tent city, a ghetto of down-and-out scutzers scratching out an existence on their patch of land. Yet alongside them were the more well-to-do locators with their larger quasi-domes beside their rigs and ships, wearing rings on their fingers.

A network of crude roads crisscrossed the settlement, along which rovers and buggies and speeders ran. Grav units had been installed at the traders' depot and center town and Terminus Square so that people could enjoy normal, Earth-like gravity. But the rest of the planetoid was a free-for-all of 1/30 Earth gravity.

A small group of kids had hopped a low fence and were playing hopball in a utility yard that adjoined the water tower: a bulbous pale-green tank raised 50 feet in the air on metal legs. A wide-diameter storm-drain-like pipe ran from its bottom edge to various parts of the shanty town.

As I swung *Ghostblade* down, the youngest in his space suit hoofed the white ball and it drifted like a leaf in the wind toward the others who space-hopped in the lower gravity after it. All five turned and gave us high fives.

I did a little showoffing and buzzed them from above, did a low, slow roll.

They cheered and clapped and gamboled about. A couple fist-pumped.

Kids. What was this world without them? The good old days...

Enjoy the times now, kiddos, while you can, cause you are on borrowed time.

Not far away a mix of miners, locators, layabouts and their families teemed, setting up camp on the edges of the town and its mining operations. All on the cheap. No charge, not relying on terraforming infrastructure. It seemed any hard-of-luck locator with no skill or stamina could hole up on Terminus and do his prospecting here.

As we swung up and over the last telebractor, Sharki grumbled and summed it up in his rough, crude way, "Bunch of snakes and wolves—hissing and howling and killing each over a few nuggets of ore on patches of land where they've made claims. Not much different than elsewhere in this sad universe. Easy to kill a man, take his wealth and make your own fortune—easier than pull your own weight or share the booty with your partners. If you got the head for it, ain't nothing you could ever lack for here."

I listened to his words sadly as the group of kids disappeared behind us. Steam rose from pipes in the nearby cinderblock utility building.

Elsewhere loomed a water generation plant and several low concrete buildings, perhaps admin buildings, and an ugly brown, cube-like complex with transformers and thick electrical wires that I guessed must have been the local nuclear generator power plant, supplying energy to the settlement...and the nearby mining equipment and operations.

Smack in the town center loomed an imposing U-shaped dome. As Slapper had said, this was the drome where the scutzers played their barbaric demolition derby.

Here was Terminus, an improbable town on the edge of an even more improbable abyss.

A mile and half distant from the drome sprawled a giant space yard, filled with ships.

I guessed it at maybe 2 miles square. Center left of the town rose another impressive building where folks in spacesuits were milling about, ships were parked and many mining machines were ready to be hauled to local sites.

The sector was surrounded by grav generators every 100 yards. Figures in suits walked and went about their business without grav packs on their backs.

I stroked my chin. "How hard would it be to turn one of those grav generators up or down?"

Marty shrugged. "Probably not hard, Rusco. But why?"

"I wonder what would happen if one of those grav boxes were to just up and shut off?"

"There'd be a hell of mess, Rusco, what do you think? A lot of squalling, bawling and bitching."

I blinked and raised my brows in a sweet grin.

"You're not thinking—?"

I slapped him on the back. "You're officially elected First

Saboteur of the Reapers. Sharki and Slappy are your Deputies."

"You've got a vivid imagination, friend."

I tipped my head in a bow.

Ghostblade passed over the shipyard of parked vessels. My lips curled in a vindictive grin. "Well, what have we here? Is that *Gator* down there? Or am I seeing alligator snouts on every ship?"

Marty gave a laughing snort. "Yeah, that's her all right, so what?"

"It means we're on the right track."

Marty's frown turned to a look of suspicion. "You're not suggesting we go and—"

"Why not? We could use another ship in this caper."

"As in 'nothing ventured, nothing gained'?"

"That's why I like you, Marty. You figure things out quick." I gave him another slap on the back.

"There'll be guards…screens, alarms."

"Nothing a couple of veterans like you and Sharki can't handle." I could see the gears working in Slapper's head too. "Look, I can see Slappy's grin already. I'd have to say you guys are perfect for the job."

"I don't see *Trident* in that mess of ships—"

"Why would you? They're not going to park it in plain sight. It's one of Sharki's craft, remember?"

"I don't give a shit about that old clunker," Sharki growled, his voice terse and bitter. "I just want Brex."

"That's why you three are going down to run interference for me. I'll find out what I can. You find out what you can."

"No way, Rusco," Marty objected. "Sounds like one of your fly-by-night schemes."

Newt interjected, *"I must concur with Marty. Just another highly irregular and risky—"*

"Take Newt with you," I rasped.

"I object, Jet Rusco. Newt's place is on a starship, not gallivanting out in zero gravity or near zero g conditions. It is taxing to my grav stabilizers."

"Take him," I rasped louder.

Marty smiled and rolled his shoulders. "What're you going to do?"

"Somebody's got to take care of this junker, find out where Deidra and *Trident* are. This Scag vessel is a good decoy for you guys."

A wide-hulled, turreted scout was nosing up to our starboard vane. Damn. I could see the Bratts' logo inscribed on her flank and a yellow pulsing light on her low turret. Must be one of the yard monitors watching the place, judging from the busybody look of her and the brazen way she dogged our heels.

Nosy bastard. We'd have to deal with her. Or maybe we'd been already made?

Sharki narrowed his eyes. "Time's a wasting." He clenched his fist and scowled at the ship through the viewport. "We have to do something. Drop us off at the docking posts, Rusco! We either do something now or fly back to that cursed roid and roll over and die."

"Best place is at that terminal there." Slapper stabbed a finger at the high-faced, cinder-block building.

"What is that place?" Sharki asked.

"Local hang out, called the 'Depot'. A traders' surplus where all news is shared and supplies are had. There's gossip galore."

"Good." I nodded. "Follow Slapper's lead. He'll show you the town. He seems to know the ropes."

Newt buzzed in beside me, a flurry of beeps and flashing lights, *"I must highly object—"*

"Get on the ground," I hissed. I'll let you all off at those docking posts. Merge into the crowd, make your way to this 'depot'. Find out what you can. Board Brex's ship or fuck it up if you can. I'll nip back, pick you up later when possible."

Marty opened his mouth to argue but I silenced him with a chop of my hand. "No time, Mar. Snoop Dog's almost on our ass."

Marty peered and glared at the turreted bird dog behind us. I made a quick head motion at him toward the hold. I banked the ship out of the scout's way near the cement pylons at the loading gate, a stone's throw from the cinder-block terminal.

"Quick, get off," I ordered. "I'll steer them away— Remember our agreement," I hissed back at Sharki.

He was first through the ruined bridge door. "And you, remember yours. After traitor Deidra's back and Brex is toast, our business is done."

I scowled at his mulish belligerence. I could not stop the curse quick on my breath.

Marty stayed back. "You're going to have to kill him, you know."

"A deal's a deal, Marty."

"It's your head."

"Yours too."

Marty glowered. "See, that's what I don't like about this. Loose ends that can come back and bite us in the ass."

"Everything about this caper is loose and messed up. Hunting down claims to pay our debts. Getting shanghaied on roids. Our job is to end this rodeo once and for all."

"And how we going to do that?"

"First, Deidra. Then we go from there."

"Fine." Marty stomped away, his neck red. Glancing over my shoulder, I saw him and Slapper slipping into their suits then gathering at the air lock with Sharki to gain the hold. Once they were through, I imagined bullet-head buckling his blaster and warring with friend Sharki over who was going to take command of this little commando unit.

I could not be critical of the scenario. I turned my attention back to the console.

CHAPTER 33

The left panel showed a light blinking, indicating that the air lock had closed. Marty, Sharki and Slapper hopped out of the jagged ruin of the hatch and merged into the scores of figures milling about.

I took off, steering clear of our monitor. He seemed to be losing interest now that our craft had decided to lift off. It had been a wise move. Just another random ship dropping off a load of passengers and getting on with her business.

I took the Y-Wing high, away from the town, down along the crooked rim of the chasm. I hovered well above and waited, pretending interest in the deep mining operations far below on the other cliffside. After a while I came drifting back to check on the mysterious ship yard.

Something about the place seemed to be the key to what we were looking for.

Sure, *Gator* sat parked, a definite clue, but there was something more.

Sharki and Slapper hadn't seemed to mind being dropped off in unfriendly territory. I had to give them credit. Slapper just wanted to feel useful, as would any faithful dog gaze in hound-like devotion, panting and slobbering at its master.

Sharki, the gangster, was all gung ho, eager as a gorilla to kick ass and break some heads. You could see it in his twisted features. Put the man in the fires of hell and he would have his nostrils flared, inhaling the fumes.

I gave a fledgling smile. We needed such fanatic energy in our group. We were already faced with such insurmountable odds that the only ones who could pull it off were lunatics like Sharki.

I didn't see any of them now—no figures around *Gator*—so they must have entered the terminal. Maybe to get a lay of the land? Or maybe to play video games. What did I know? I was just flying by the seat of my pants.

I darted glances left and right—raked my eyes over the parked ships. Now where would you hide a hauler as big as *Trident*? Not here in open sight, with these little buggy scutzers and mobiles parked every which way, said the little piggie to the big piggie…

I buzzed about the yard, like a hound sniffing out a hare.

There was an open hangar far down at the back of the yard. A repair shop or refitting place? It was set in a direction away from the town. I buzzed closer, keeping her at dead slow, as if looking for a space to land. I squinted in the ship's visual and grinned at what I saw on the magnifier. *Trident* was inside, almost lost in the blue-lit shadow to the immediate right. Five suited figures were working on her. Two other locator craft were being serviced too. The technicians were applying a new coat of pale green paint to *Trident*, making her look ugly as fuck, covering her old red lettering, the proud 'Trident', with gaudy gold characters reading 'Lodestar'. They'd outfitted her with extra cannons too, fore and aft. Brex's new little workhorse.

I wish I hadn't dropped off Marty and Sharki so hastily. Extra bodies and blaster hands would come in handy now.

No matter.

I'd lingered too long.

A general hail came over the com. A stiff, perfunctory voice with a face to match flashed up. "What are you loitering around here for? Landing bay's on the other side. Identify yourself, Y-Wing." I saw a helmeted face staring hard at me through a glass faceplate with smalt blue eyes.

The only gambit that could possibly work was to stall him. "Some freight to deliver to Hangar dock 2A. Couple of sensor scopes and manifold cowlings."

The man paused and frowned. "We have no such record on file,

Ghostblade. You sure you got the right outfit?"

I squinted hard at the supposed manifest on my console. "Order #321A from Damocles Station. For a hauler named *Trident.* Do I have it right?"

"That craft's being re-classified, decommissioned. She's over there being overhauled."

"Oh." I frowned into my console as if scanning the fictitious order. "Must be a mix up. I'll just scoot back to command post, tell them what I think of their damn accounting."

"Not so fast. We're going to have to run a security check. You realize this is a yellow zone restricted area?"

I drummed up a thin, artless look. "Sure, boss, just let me suit up. I'll come down and talk to you fellas."

"No, that won't be necessary. We'll come up, if you don't mind. I see your hatch is blown. We'll meet you at the air lock."

"Okay, if you insist." I hesitated, scratched at my eyebrow, made my shrug casual.

Damn, this was definitely not working out as planned.

Think, Rusco, think, you fucking muppet! I racked my brains for a solution. Could I just fly this rig out of here, lose these bozos and regroup?

No…Marty and the others'd be left hanging. No chance I'd be able to get the Scag ship down here again without half the bloody security forces of Team Terminus on me.

I knuckled my fist. With a sour curse, I flung on my suit, strapped blaster to my hip and got through the air lock. I hoofed it to the midships' hatch, my breath short and pulse hammering in my ear. I waited just long enough out of sight before I thought the sods might muscle their way aboard.

Then I put on my most innocent face and stepped out. I got past them before they could climb in.

"What's the problem here, fellas? Some kind of Fort Knox security you running here?"

"No." The head security guy looked at me critically from a round face with large, hound-like eyes, a man no more than 5 foot 5. His eyes squinted up past the burn marks by the logo on *Ghostblade's* side. "A Scag ship? What's a Scag vessel doing making deliveries?"

I shrugged. "You'd have to ask the authorities at Damocles. I'm just an errand boy. This's the ship they gave me."

"And the blown hatch?"

"A little explosion on board last week. Supposed to drop her by repair and get it fixed up."

He grunted. "What's with the plain Jane gray suit? You don't look like no Scag. "

"Jacket and clothes don't make the man."

"Good one." He jerked a thumb at his associate who'd come running. "Darby, this man thinks he's clever. Let's see your sigil, wiseass, the little one you wear round your neck, identifies you as a scutzer."

"Lost it," I said.

"What else you lose? Your sense of direction?" I saw his comrade smirk and his hand drop to the R1 strapped at his belt.

This was going sour.

My eyes strayed back to the hangar. My hand dipped to my own blaster. Not 100 paces away was the 'new and improved' *Trident,* her cargo bay door yawning open just waiting to be boarded.

I silently swore. So close and yet so far.

The motion of my hand to my waist the security guy took as a sign of aggression. He drew his R1. "Sir, please step aside. We're going to have to take you in for questioning."

He came to apprehend me but I dropped back a step. I shifted, lightning quick, shoved the man against his assistant, putting him in between me and his gun.

He twisted away but I ducked and made two quick blasts, frying the underling. The other had dropped to his knees. He was swearing and aiming his gun. I booted it behind *Ghostblade* just as shots winged off her side.

I crouched, panting.

Shit! This was going to hell. What now?

The main security guy'd crab-crawled away from the ship, R1 in front of him, looking for cover. He seemed to be under no illusion that he was as much of a target as me. I saw his hand go up, beckoning reinforcements his way. Neither of us wanted to get pegged by stray sniper fire.

I took the opportunity to make a risky run for the open hangar and the open cargo bay of *Trident*.

I skidded up the ramp, crouched and turned. Breath rasping, I laid fire at the two security agents careening toward me. I hadn't made two shots when some knucklefuck in the shadows tackled me. A busybody little mechanic. I hadn't seen him. He knocked my barrel aside and I fell to my stomach, cursing. I felt the wind knocked out of me.

The security guys were on me before I could aim. They hauled me to my feet, tore the weapon out of my hand.

"Well, flyboy," the lead man panted. "You got some dirty tricks, as I suspected." Weapon trained, he signaled to one of his three subordinates. "Take him to detention. Gorn, call security. Brex'll want to hear about this."

"But...I think he's at the derby."

"I don't care if he's shagging the Queen of Sheba at the Royal Baths. He told me to watch over this hangar and report any suspicious movements, and that's what I'm doing."

"Sure." The other gave a sullen grunt.

He stared hard and shook his head at me. "Fella, I would not want to be in your shoes."

"What about his ship?" his other henchman demanded as he flung a hand toward *Ghostblade*.

"How the hell should I know? Haul it into the shop. Another one of the gofers'll refurbish it. Or chop it before long."

The assistant gave a crisp nod. He went off to climb in the hatch and blast the airlock to *Ghostblade* if need be.

Darby and his buddy shuttled me into an air-speeder, and we

took off toward the dome they called the 'drome'.

I slapped a palm at my helmet. Damn. Radio was dead. No chance of contacting Marty.

I contemplated several gambits of taking these chipsters down by force. Each was more suicidal than the last.

Better to wait it out.

The drome rose to my left: a looming monstrosity of steel girders and plate-metal forming a long, wide-bellied inverted U. We passed under its shadow and came to a halt at an adjoining squarish building.

I'd gambled on this one and lost. Forfeited the only ship we had and our ride out of here.

I'd at least gotten one step closer to Brex and hopefully Deidra.

I frowned. It was a low hanging fruit better to have been left behind.

I shook my head in bitter reproach. I just hoped Marty, Sharki and Slappy were making better progress than me.

We got out of the speeder and halted before the soaring entranceway. I was thrust forward into an automatic air lock. The silver-steel door closed behind us while the one ahead of us slid open. The guards removed their helmets. I kept mine on.

Tall metal doors swung open and admitted us into the drome's main foyer. The lights were bright in this place. The guards flashed a special pass and we went in. They prodded me past two monitors who flanked the chambers to a special holding area, for special 'guests'.

No more than ten minutes passed. Darby and his grinning monkey returned to prod me to another bare-walled room. Here, a familiar hulking figure was already present, shifting from foot to foot in a foul mood. He was wearing dark blue leathers with silver rings on the arms.

"This better be good, dragging me away from my sport time."

The guard smacked me down. "Kneel before General Brex."

I stood up and faced my enemy, eyeing him with cool rancor.

When he saw who it was, a flash of recognition glistened in his steely eyes and for a while he stared, his lips parted in menace.

"Back from the dead, eh, Rusco? For crap's sake, you're a hard bastard to kill. Do you have angels hovering up your ass? Where's Sharki?"

"Fool's dead."

He nodded. "That doesn't surprise me. How'd you get a ship?"

"Some raider Scags stalked us. Paid us a little surprise visit. Didn't go well for them."

He nodded again. "That's just about plausible. Or as farfetched a piece of horseshit I've ever heard."

I shrugged. "You can take it or leave it. I'm here."

"That you are. And now you're going to wish that you weren't. Jimpix!" he bawled at the man hovering behind Darby. "Take this hillbilly to the bully pit. He's about to be the next flyboy up for sport, in about—" he glanced at his wrist monitor, "I'd say in a half hour. I might personally attend to our friend's humbling demise."

"Yes, as you wish, General Brex."

They hauled me off with an air of the sinister carved on their bearded faces.

CHAPTER 34

I was thrust into another holding area, wincing at a wall of iron bars that looked out over the vast arena of the drome.

The space was a 300 by 100 foot expanse of sand…stained crimson in many parts. Bits of wreckage were strewn about—plate metal, windshield glass, odds and ends. A few blackened metal hulks had been dragged off to the sides.

Three to four hundred spectators sat in the stands—with about 25 tiers of seats rising to the curved edges of the dome.

Not a bad turnout. Gaunt-faced men, some drunken and bearded louts, mostly down-and-out scutzers and ne'er-do-wells coming out of the woodwork for a bit of afternoon entertainment. As long as they could pay their 2 yol fare. They'd taken their helmets off—having just come from outside, laughing and joking. They still wore their space suits.

My heart skipped a beat.

Deidra sat in a carved, high-backed chair like a throne in the lower stands under a bright purple canopy. Back erect, face sullen, like a frozen ghost. She wore no suit. Her hair was brushed to perfection, a golden red, not a hair out of place. Her skin glowed, but her face bore the look of ice.

Brex sat beside her, proprietary arm on her thigh like a trophy. He played the role of king in a kingdom, on a larger throne neon-lit on all sides, with a supercilious grin plastered on his rough, chisel-jawed face. It made the back of my neck burn to see the two of them together, seated side by side.

Another man sat on the other side of Deidra. His expression was as smug as Brex's, a walrus mustache drooping low from his sagging jowls, eyes staring out of deep-set raccoony sockets. The crowd cheered the pair.

All hail, Brex! All hail, Beefeater!

So...this was the infamous Beefeater. The short-changing, cheating General of the Scags.

The two self-professed avatars stared down over the long, oval-shaped grounds of the drome with avuncular authority. The lights flaring down from above made it look like a gladiator spectacle—which I suppose it was.

Impressive. I wouldn't be surprised if Brex owned or co-owned this place with his throne-buddy.

A set of stone stairs descended to the sand-packed arena to the left of the thrones. To the right, a small darkened entranceway allowed easy access of vehicles and personnel. All this—100 feet opposite from where I peered out with clenched teeth from behind the bars.

Beefeater thought to get casual with Deidra and let a hand trail amiably over her left wrist. Her fingers were clenched like claws.

It turned out to be a mistake. Brex caught the hand and slammed his fist down hard on the offending fingers, eliciting a grunt of pain from his comrade-in-arms.

The briefest hint of a grin touched Deidra's bloodless lips.

I whistled out a bitter curse. I'd gotten my wish. I'd found *Trident*, found Brex and found Deidra.

One must be careful what he wishes for.

I turned my attention back to my gloomy prison. Two other men shared the rectangular space with me. One with gray scraggly curls, hanging shoulder-length, the other, taller, younger and thinner with a square cut mane of lank black hair.

"First time in the bully pit?" Gray Beard asked, lifting a hand.

I did not answer.

He leered, an oval gap of broken and yellow teeth. "You're going to like it here, friend. Enjoy the show. When it's your turn to drive the bender, you'll need to be relaxed."

I swung my gaze back to the arena where another monitor was already flying out an odd, armored tank-like speeder. One of the 'benders', I assumed.

"What you in for?"

I shrugged.

"That bad?"

I gave a morose nod. "You?"

"Killed a man. A no-good scutzer trying to horn in on my tent-dome down in shantytown. Turns out the scumster was Brex's third cousin. Imagine that."

I nodded, as if it didn't surprise me.

"Friend, you're just a bucket of cheer today. Lighten up. Life's too short."

The first elfin curl of a smile touched my lips. I liked this old guy. He had a sweet way of putting things.

I was about to pump him for information when there came a clank of billy club at the bars. I stepped back, as a surly, horse-faced man, the one who'd thrown me in, opened the iron gate and prodded the Gray Beard out with an electric billy stick he was carrying.

Gray Beard winked at me and our cellmate. "Well, looks like I'm up, boys. Wish me luck." He gave me a mock salute. "Catch you in the next life, friend."

I did not like the ominous sound of that jaunty farewell.

The attendant herded Gray Beard toward the beat-up speeder that had just been flown out. Speeder was not quite the word. It was the size of an air-speeder, but with the souped-up halftrack-like quality of a war machine. Built to survive the bunts and collisions and impacts that the crowd craved. I saw scrapes, gouges and dents on its side.

Gray Beard opened the side door with ceremony. He tipped his head and did a little pirouette which I thought was amusing, considering the occasion. He settled himself in his seat, strapped himself in and slowly the vehicle rose about three feet off the ground.

I glanced quickly at the yardie who'd come back to shove another prisoner in with us. A haggard, unkempt character with squinty eyes and a foul tongue. How hard would it be to rip that electro-billystick from the yardie's hand and grab his R1?

Yardie must have divined my intentions. He scowled, and with a flick of wrist, his baton clipped out to jab me in the gut. I fell back cursing and clutching my stomach.

"Liking it, you fucking mudrat? Back the hell off next time. No one gets past Elra."

I wheezed through my teeth, "Nice chaperons you have here." I jerked my chin at my cell-mate.

"Ah, don't mind the yardies," he said. "Full of piss and vinegar. Brex don't pay 'em enough. Ain't that right, Elra?" he jeered.

"Welcome to the Terminus jail, friend," the other said.

After the yardie had locked up and left, I rubbed my gut. "Ever try to fight them?" I stretched my back to proper height, groaning.

"And get plugged in the head? No thanks."

"Maybe better than sitting here, waiting—"

He gave a sour smile. "Old Askal, the gray beard you saw, gets a little theatrical at times. He'll be back for another round, methinks. Had a few bouts already."

Yeah, we would see. I hobbled over to grip the bars and look out upon the sand.

The current champion of the arena had entered on the far side of the stadium. A middle-aged bruiser in blue leather vest with silver spikes on his shoulders. He had a bald head and dark black ruffs of hair flared from his ears. He swaggered over to his vehicle that'd been brought out—a souped up crimson cruiser with two-foot spikes on its sides. Big chromium pipes curled snake-like from cockpit to hood. A skull and crossbones was painted on the side with the skeletal script, 'Bonecrusher' writ in blood red just below.

There was a great hoopla as he strapped on his helmetish skull-cap. A rousing cheer rattled from their lips as the few hundred or so spectators in the stands rose in their seats to hail their hero.

"Kybar! Kybar!"

My lips curled in heavy irony. They were fans of this sport, I'd give them that. Their little joy cars, these benders, were something else. Built for abuse. The blue-black vehicle Gray Beard was consigned to was missing some plate armor and had blood on its bumper. Not as much as on his contender's. I caught bits of bone and gristle flecked on its side and bumper.

I bit back a grimace, trailed a tongue over my lower lip. Looked as if it could get pretty western here.

I studied the width and breadth of the bender as the champion veered his craft forward. He passed twenty feet from the prison bars, hovering about 6 feet off the ground. They did look like tanks from the old days, but squashed down at their tops to a more credible height. A single local ion turbo engine glowed blue at the rear. Bumpers were heavy-duty bars of steel. Sides were reinforced with spiked rods. Windshields small, tapered on shallow angles to reduce impact and shatter on collision. No mounted guns or cannons. Just brute force speed and well timed hits. The first one to incapacitate the other vehicle won. No other rules that I could see.

At first glance this seemed like a simple enough objective. But I'd learned that surprises awaited the unwary.

Brex piked a fist in the air. His voice boomed over the speakers. "Begin!"

A heady song, like a miner's rowdy anthem, played over the PA. The monitor sprinted out to the center of the arena, flourished a bright crimson flag then quickly sped back to the exit by the thrones.

I watched as the combatants rose into the air, hovered there as the crowd cheered, then they turned to face each other.

CHAPTER 35

To his credit, Gray Beard started off well. He gunned his gray bender straight at Crimson and managed to get a few good hits into Hero-Boy's side and back bumper. But these hits were merely token annoyances as it became obvious that Crimson was just toying with him, messing with his brain, scouting out his weaknesses. When Gray Beard tried a second round of smash and retreat, I had to turn my head. Crimson gunned around in a heavy burst of speed and smacked into Gray Beard's right side, sending him in a spin to the sand.

Gray Beard revved up and tried to bank left, desperately seeking to get out of the way of being rammed to oblivion, but was too slow. Crimson smacked him hard again, this time just a bit beyond the driver's door—an impact that sent a thunderous crack echoing across the stadium—and one that saw Gray Beard's back end fishtailing.

Movement by the thrones had my eyes wandering for a second. I saw Brex reach for Deidra. The lug was enjoying himself, his other fist pumped and lips curled in a loud guffaw. Deidra watched, stony-eyed. When I looked back, Crimson had bumpered Gray Beard over, crushing his hood, driving his bender hard into the sand. The vehicle skidded along, digging a wide trench before it rolled.

The vehicle came to a creaking halt and lay upside down on its flattened top. I saw through the rectangle of glass Gray Beard's head loll…before he slumped motionless.

There came a series of raucous cheers from the cheap seats. A group of them had hopped on their mates' shoulders for a better view, drunken and rowdy, laughing as their mates did a twirl, horsing around. Audiences, I saw, loved blood.

I ground my teeth. Why? The cruel bastard had messed him up, maybe put him in a coma.

Brex gazed my way in satisfaction, like the benevolent circus master, patron of the games. An arrogant smile was etched on his face.

How I so wished to wipe that pasty smirk off the bastard's face. But I was trapped here—a prisoner in a cage, waiting my turn to next join the victims.

The bender smoked. Twisted metal creaked. A black cloud rose over the bender and stained the air. I must not fall for such tactics when it came my turn to play.

There came no motion from the vehicle. Gray Beard was down and it looked as if he was not getting up.

A trio of teens in red vests ran out to check on him. I saw that between rounds their job was to gopher about the yard to pick up flotsam and small pieces of wreckage that had smacked off benders in violent collisions.

The first youth who did a peek-a-boo through the windshield, backed off with a grimace. He held up his hand, thumb and finger turned down.

The yardie sidled by. He did a quick inventory and motioned two derby attendants over with stretcher and straps. They tugged softly on the crumpled metal and dragged out the body. Gray Beard sprawled in an undignified pose on the sand. Crimson liquid pooled under his ear. They trotted him off, left the crumpled craft where it was. So much for cleanup.

The yard gopher came jolting into our holding cell, sticking his electric billy stick at me. "Git going, cowboy! You're next."

I minced my way out on the sand, a soft curse on my breath, keeping clear of the man's cattle prod.

Only a few muttered words I heard from Brex as the crimson craft of the champion floated slowly over her kill. Her ugly helmeted driver pushed a bull head through a half-opened window and raised a fist to the crowd. Brex resumed his seat on his throne beside Deidra.

I sneered.

There were no cheers—just jeers as I was dogtrotted toward a much less-armored craft. Dog-eared, battered, slimmer, and much lighter on the metal department than Crimson's gaudy ride. "Here's your airboat, buckaroo," the yardie called. "Like it or lump it. I'd be wishing ya good luck against Mr. Bonecrusher there, but I know it'd mean jack shit."

I tipped him a salute and jerked open the metal door. I slouched into the front seat. Familiarizing myself with the controls was not too hard. Stick shift to the right. Foot pedal for acceleration, brake beside it. Steering wheel front and center, tucked into the belly like the old race cars from 20th century ancient Earth.

Primitive as she was, this baby was equipped with voice-activation control. I strapped myself in, slapped on the headset and grunted some test words into the mic, "Up left. 20 mph". The bender responded, albeit jerkily. Up she rose.

"20 degrees to port." She swiveled and faced the bars of the holding area, threatening to drive her bumper into the bars. I yanked the wheel left and her nose missed by two feet.

What a crock!

Screw that. With a snarl, I ripped off the headset and stuck the shifter into second and pumped down hard on the accelerator. I cruised up and away toward the far side of the arena where a few stragglers sat. My way was driving the old-fashioned way, with the sticks and the pedals.

I turned her around, bumper aimed toward the thrones.

Crimson and I faced off at opposite ends of the arena, a distance of 200 feet.

The music started…the derby attendant's flag came down in a flamboyant flourish.

Champion's engine revved high and I shot forward to meet him. He came lurching straight at me, hell bent for leather, as if trying to play chicken. I gunned my engine and came flying at him, watching the distance close fast.

I did not know what was the best approach here. Truthfully, I was a bit out of my element at this sport, if 'sport' were the proper word for it.

I banked sideways at the last second. Up close I saw the black skull and crossbones and skeletal script 'Bonecrusher' whizzing by as she flew past.

Champion looped around and the hardened maverick he was, tried to bumper me down to ground.

The wicked front prods clamped on my hood and drove my front end into the sand. My bender spun dizzily, stirring up clouds of dust.

I sat dazed, strapped in my seat. Sharp pain dug at my side, a dull throb building behind my temples. The shifter had bent and dug into my thigh when I had been bounced around upon impact.

I peered goggle-eyed through the windshield. I saw the curved metal plates of *Bonecrusher* loom overhead. The rogue was banking around to drive in for the kill.

What the hell? He'd won—no question there, so why was the bastard—

I braced myself; a ear-splitting crack came loud in my ears, nearly jarring my brain from its sockets and bones from their fleshy housing.

My senses swam. I shook my head, fought dizziness, caught a blurry, starry look out the thick tempered glass.

Deidra was on her feet. I could see a strangled cry forming on her lips as she mouthed words. Brex pulled her down, a jealous, belligerent shout on his lips.

I swore, gave my head another shake. I had to get out of this tin box or I'd be crushed. I loosened my strap, kicked open the door and tumbled out. Sand filled my mouth. I spat it out, tottered to a half crouch.

Bonecrusher loomed above me, a specter of doom. My blurred vision could just barely make out the man's chip-rock grin as his skull-cap tipped my way and his fist piked through the open window.

I scrambled to my knees, crab-crawled round the back bumper.

Just as the crimson horror slammed full into the driver side door, I sprang backward, feeling the air shudder as the bender flipped over on its side. If I'd been a second late, I would have been crushed under that rolling mass of a few tons of steel.

A small gurgle forced its way out of my throat. I made a crouching hobble for the lone vehicle parked by the holding cell: a nice puke-yellow job ready for her next victim. I'd gotten my legs back. Instead of running around the monitor, I shoulder-smacked hard into his chest as he cursed and snatched at his electric stick.

I could make out Deidra gnashing her teeth. She was trying desperately to free herself from the cord that bound her wrist to the throne's arm.

A high-pitched whine droned in my ear. The cruel laughs and jeers of the crowd echoed in a kind of underwater blur.

I wrenched violently at the bender's door and pushed my aching body into the low-riding craft. I fired her up. I was in the air.

I was blood mad and ready to crush heads.

So, you like to play rough, you little motherfucker?

This time it would be different. Mr. Crimson Assbanger was in for some rude surprises.

I swung back round and barreled full speed at the bastard, daring him to play chicken with me this time.

His engine whined and he came at me, bumper on, but I did not give an inch. He pulled up, rattled, missing my hood by bare inches.

So, a little pansy-ass pussy coward! What's a little death to you today, eh, you motherfucker?

The mob seemed dissatisfied with their champion's cowardly display on that last maneuver and rocked in their seats. Lips formed boos and derogatory insults.

I choked on a laugh. The small victory gave me courage. I rose and banked around and came barreling at Crimson again, angling for his ridiculous chrome-piped hood.

The maneuver caught him by surprise.

For a death-defying moment he wheeled back round in a tight

circle. He was trying to give himself room, but he was caught flat-footed, knowing not whether to play offense or defense.

Life's a bitch when doubt creeps in.

I revved full up and came in at top speed. I dipped. I clipped him on the port side and sent him spinning down to the sand.

No mercy. I banked around and flying upside down over his hood, I cranked hard on the wheel and bumpered the hell out of him into the blood-flecked ground.

He tried to pull up, to correct his fall, but his back end was dragging on the sand. It pulled him sideways. His engine was cooked. He could only fishtail in an uncontrollable spin. With vindictive fury, I smashed hard into his middle.

Bonecrusher stalled out in a smoky heap. Her driver sat unmoving, unconscious. Blood pooled from his neck, maybe broken.

There was a stunned silence from the stands. The crowd's eyes bugged out. It was all over quickly.

I hovered in the air, ready to take on another foe, but none came forward.

The lead yardie skipped over to pry open Crimson's door. He leaned in to check for a pulse. I could see blood. Lots of blood. The yardie ducked out, licking his lips. He looked up at Brex, shaking his head.

Brex blinked and glared. In a fit of rage, he vaulted from his seat. He came stomping down the cement stairs onto the sand. Fisting a belligerent signal to his yardie, he stomped forward. His champion was dead; he meant to settle scores himself. I thought I could read the angry words on his lips. Perhaps 'Rusco, you're a dead man' or 'Rusco, your ass is mine'. But I could not be sure.

Upon his signal, another bender was aired in. Bright electric blue with polished chrome up front. Fresh metal plates riveted to her wide flanks. Her bumper was angled V-style, razor-sharp, like a plow. Spiked steel horns curved on her front hood. Long knife-like steel rods flared out on her rear. An instrument of death. All her barbarous accessories gleamed like white bone under the dome's cold light.

In the space of an instant, I wondered if I could zoom down and take Brex out before he got in that bender. But then I saw R1s pointed up at me. Two arena deputies had stepped out of the deployment area beside the thrones. They trained long barrels up at my windshield.

With a last, malicious flourish, Brex plunked his bulk in the driver's seat. His blue craft revved up and took to the air, her horn-pointed hood turned to face me.

So…a duel.

Bring it on!

CHAPTER 36

Brex's next move was unexpected. Underscored by cowardice, he shot a brawny arm out of the window and stuck a bullhorn to the top of his bender. There was a crackle and pop as his voice blared over the megaphone, "We have an upstart among us! One who killed Bonecrusher. Are the scutzers of Terminus going to stand for this?"

No! came the unanimous roar from the audience.

"Then what shall we do? Shall we crush him? Shall we break his bones? Who will tag-team with me to deliver justice?"

There came a scattering of roars.

"Come! Come any and all!"

There was a flurry and shuffle of men and low, vengeful shouts as a dozen or so figures trudged down the stairs to the landing area.

A stocky but quick-footed spectator in a black hoodie and mask trooped faster. He pushed his bulk past them all and shouldered the lead man aside. There came some more pushing and shoving, grumbles and curses, but such was the aura of menace of the masked man that the others did not try to push their luck with him. One arm was tucked in his space suit seemingly clutching a blaster should anyone cross him.

The yardie shrugged and peered up at Brex in the bender.

Brex gave a gruff but satisfied nod. "We have ourselves a recruit! A man wishing, it seems, to remain anonymous. Let us call him 'Our Masked Avenger'."

There came hoots and catcalls from the crowd.

I shook my head in confusion. Odd way to play this out, but this was Terminus.

The mystery man was escorted with little ceremony over toward a green airboat that had been brought forth from the main landing area. A pearly, puke-green bender with curled fenders and a deadly rack of sharp jabber-daggers piked on its front bumper. A wicked looking rod trailed from its back bumper like a sting ray.

I shook my head again. Only on Terminus.

So, Brex was another coward who would not risk facing me alone. He'd have a stooge do the heavy lifting for him, perhaps get himself killed in the process.

So be it.

I turned to glower at the masked driver and study the green ship. He puzzled me. I had a vague feeling I'd met this fellow before, something about his swagger and belligerence. But where? It eluded me. At this distance it was hard to conclude anything.

I swung my gaze back to Brex as he was revving up the engine, champing at the bit to send me to oblivion.

I was not naive enough to think that the bastard hadn't skill at this game.

No. He'd watched my driving patterns and already probably compiled a cunning plan to undermine me.

Brex's fist came down and the music started up. Our benders shot forward to confront each other.

He drove me upward with the help of his partner, cutting me off from looping back round. My guess had been correct. He came underneath me, forcing me to rise higher and higher, up to the peak of the dome. I was running out of room. My head jerked back as Brex's dagger-toothed bumper smacked my back end. His bender dropped and shot forward, came suddenly smashing up at my underbelly. Sneaky bastard. The top of my airboat skidded off the dome. The rest of the frame with it, rebounding off like a hot potato with a hard electrical snap.

Sparks went flying off the yellow-sheened metal as my bender lurched and lost altitude and came dropping down on an angle toward the spectators.

Some instinctively ducked, but others held their ground. They laughed, enjoying the moment. My bender dropped like a stone. The engine seemed to cough in mid breath, threatening to crush heads of those seated opposite Brex and Deidra.

I banged hard against some invisible force field, bounced off like a rubber ball with enough force to jar me out of my wits. The rebound set a bright arc spraying across the air with an electric zing.

I realized then why this arena had been enclosed in a dome. To prevent benders from flying off and escaping. To act as a shield too with a secondary invisible barrier that angled back over the spectators to protect them from collisions—accidental or deliberate.

The engineers had figured it all out. Probably a few glitches along the way before they ironed out all the wrinkles. Clever.

Brex's blue bender came roaring down to finish me off. The green mystery-mobile trailed at his heels.

I recovered from my spin and got back up to a safer height.

We circled, tracking like wolves. I was on the defensive, forced into a passive role in this two-against-one fight. So far, I'd always been on the run. With an angry hiss, I gunned out of this circling escapade of stupidity and got a clean hit side on with Brex's craft. The move had him cursing over the megaphone which brought a boyish smile to my lips.

I couldn't get one hit on the green mobile though.

Whoever he was, he was good. He could have taken me out during that last bit of impulsivity, but he hadn't.

It seemed odd and I frowned. But then, the longer these brutes drew out the roguish games, the better. Better for business, better for entertainment. It was all Brex's show. The fucker seemed to be enjoying his handiwork.

Cold sweat beaded my neck now. My brow, armpits flowed like rivers. I felt my life line getting shorter.

I jammed the shifter into third, then fourth and had the engine whining at top rpms. Do or die. Now or never. The risk taker in me had not died yet.

I aimed for Brex's bumper but he anticipated the move and swerved, swung up and flipped upside down over my tail end for a split second. He was behind me and cracked me hard in the ass. I felt my head whip back, my brain practically knocked out of my skull. I couldn't see where I was going. Stars flooded my vision. I pulled hard on the wheel. It was like moving lead. I was flying blind. I was going down.

Down, down, Jet Rusco. Aren't you used to this by now?

The bender dug a trench in the sand as it struck at a low angle then came to a grinding halt.

Mist filled my world.

An underwater roar droned in my ears.

A long time passed. But maybe it was only a few seconds.

Some instinctual sense had me jolting sideways and crawling out of that crippled vehicle, through the mangled, hanging door. My faceplate was shattered. When my head had hit the dash, the helmet had saved me. I wrenched the lopsided thing off. I sucked in a breath. The air had a dry, antiseptic flavor. It hurt slightly to fill my lungs to full capacity. I crawled on my hands and knees free of the wreck. I vaguely registered a roar of human voices. Above me, many clown faces with beards and yellow teeth, ragged hair-dos, pointing and leering at me, laughing at my busted craft from some distant place on the stands. A fair maiden looked on from afar. She had risen slowly to her feet. A girl I seemed to know. Who was she? Why was her face so distorted and distressed?

I clawed my way across the sand, managed to get to my knees. I saw the blue bender loom over me like a squat tank.

In a split of a second I knew where I was, that I had little time left—only seconds to live.

I ducked and threw myself to the side. The blue bender hurtled at me and nearly tore off my leg. I kept crawling on. The bender kept going, rose, then banked and barreled back my way. Oddly it landed twenty feet away from where I gathered in a crouch. Brex hopped out like a mad dog, some commando tin soldier. A knife was in his hand, a long, shiny knife not dissimilar to the bowie I used to have and that had clipped him on the shoulder so long ago. He approached on steady feet, a cold gleam in his eyes. My eyes focused on that knife. I knew fear.

The green airboat swooped down toward us. The door kicked open and the driver hurled out a knife at my feet. The blade stuck in the sand inches from my boot. The bender hurtled on as the green avenger went to deal with another thrill seeker who'd fired up a bender and was out for glory.

Like an automaton I crouched and picked up the blade. I began to back away, my fractured mind reviewing and rejecting unsound gambits. A knife fighter I was not. Less so in this shaky condition. I could only assume Brex was handy with the knife.

The brutish figure loomed closer, his shadow arching my way like a heavy curse.

"Rusco, I'm going to stick you like a pig. You're like a bad weed that keeps turning up. You pull out one from the turnip patch, toss it aside, and it comes up the next day after a light rain. Only way to kill such a weed is to snip off its roots. Understand?" He flicked up his knife, casting me an evil grin.

I gave a jerky nod, mouth dry. I kept my steady gaze on that knife and his movements. A blaster was strapped at his hip. I did not want to encourage the fuck to do anything rash. With those bloodshot eyes he looked like one of Hoss's mad gleers on the brink of an explosive charge. It was one of those rare moments where I did not feel compelled to insert a witty rejoinder.

He gestured his knife airily. "Yeah, I could blast your ass, but more satisfying this way, as I seem to recall a small hurt you did to my shoulder." He clapped his left shoulder. "I'm a man that believes in the law of equivalence. Know what that means, Rusco? It means Karma. As in capital K for Karma. K for killing. Means that I owe you a slice of the pie, and you can bet your ass it's going to be a lot more hurtful than the one you gave me."

I looked on, my expression deadpan.

He came at me in a rush. I twisted aside, his wicked knife slashing my suit, the tip digging into my thigh. I grimaced. Felt the blood trickle down my leg.

Figured this was how it would play out. I was in for a few more nicks before it was all over.

I crabbed back, feigned nonchalance. Smirked as if the pain were but a pleasure.

"Tough man, eh, Rusco?" He laughed. "Good. That's what I like—a fighting spirit."

This time he came in faster and more carelessly. I held back, lashed out with my own blade when he was within two feet. Sharp steel caught him across the cheek. It sliced down dangerously close to his neck.

He drew back with a foul curse, wiping a wisp of blood from his face. Now he seemed to have lost all sense of jocularity.

He came vaulting at me again, a bull roar thick in his throat. My vision was clear but my head was still pounding. I sidled around to his left, swung the knife, slashed at his ribs, but he roundhoused me with a kick, catching at my wrist, knocking the blade out of my hand. He came bounding in all animal strength and I ducked, rolled to keep away from that vicious blade. But was it enough?

CHAPTER 37

I'd gone to that faraway place within myself. A place of slow motion, of quiet of mind. Events were happening too fast around me for rational functions to process. Now everything deep inside had stilled. The noise had diminished. In the back of mind, I registered the cheers and wild hoots of the crowd, the ignoramuses and the wise, as a mere background chirping of birds. Men standing in their seats slapped fists in palms, piked fists in the air and uttered such foolish vapidities as "Stick the pig!", "Gut the traitor!" and "Get the bastard, avenge Kybar!"

These were just random snippets of noise that were irrelevant to the current situation at hand: staying alive for the next few seconds.

The masked man in the green airboat had taken care of the pretender who'd come into the arena hellbent on being the first vigilante to end my life. Vehicle and occupant were now strewn on the sand, joining the graveyard of wrecks that were tilted and smashed on the sand. The broken man looked as if he wished he'd never entertained such a foolish notion.

While I was on my back, Brex's knee pinned my chest and his knife hand was now plunging down to rip open my throat. I saw the green bender come hurtling at us a few feet off the ground. It zigged and zagged and at last swung in and the door flew open and a grunting, cursing figure came leaping out like some crazed chimpanzee. The figure landed on Brex's back. Brex was dragged down. The riderless vehicle kept going on to smash into the invisible field protecting the thrones and rebound back with a sizzle of electricity.

I shook the stars out of my skull. I rolled away. I came up limping to my feet but nearly toppled over. Blood pounded in my ears. Somewhere I registered multiple hurts to my body: whiplash, knife wound to thigh, bruised forehead and torso, aching arms.

I watched like a dream figure as the masked man was up on his feet, stalking Brex.

Was this his would-be ally? Or was he a nemesis? Brex had come drunkenly to his feet, crouched low, cursing in confusion. He'd lost his knife—his eyes searched for it—only to find it lying about ten feet away, glistening like a lost treasure.

"Who the fuck are you?" he rasped at the masked man.

"Told you I was coming for you, Brex. That the fires of doom were on your heels, General," the figure crooned.

Brex hissed an expletive. "You got a death wish, you fucking nimrod. Like dickhead Rusco here?" He lurched forward and got his fingers into the mask and ripped it off.

Brex's mouth sagged when he saw the burned, twisted face. "You!" he bawled.

I nearly could cry with amazement.

Sharki gave a pleasant nod and a mock salute with his stub as he jerked out of range of Brex's fist.

"I'm gonna fuck you up."

It was the last thing Brex said.

Sharki twisted back out of the way of the sweep of Brex's fist. Brex reached for the R1 at his hip. Sharki's boot landed there first, breaking fingers. There came another scissor kick. Boot bashed hard in the face, sending a spray of Brex's teeth to the sand.

Brex fell to his knees, shaking the blood out of his mouth. Sharki crouched, snatched up the knife lying in the sand and ripped it across Brex's throat in a single, savage motion. Larynx and windpipe were opened clear to the bone at the back of his throat.

Brex's eyes bulged. He did a little jerk, tried to stand. He lifted a hand to his throat. That awful mouth gaped, making fish-like sounds from bloody lips. His mangled fingers tried to stop the gush of

294

blood, but somewhere he knew that when one's throat was ripped out, loss of blood was kind of superfluous.

He did a last twitch and fell face first in the sand, back legs kicking up.

A stunned silence fell over the audience.

Sharki stood erect, chest heaving. He smiled at the crowd that had stood up to roar and boo. He laughed and did a little bow.

He stalked over my way and spat at my feet. "Now Rusco, I think you and me are going to be mighty unpopular in these parts at this moment. Nothing to get your panties in a knot, relax. I have a little plan."

I gaped.

Casually, he strolled over to Brex's downed bender—the blue vehicle, now a crumpled mess. He bent, examined the half cracked bullhorn. He tapped it a few times, eliciting feedback loops and a range of hisses and crackles that hurt our ears. He leaned in past the dangling door, snatched up the receiver on the dash.

"Now listen up, everyone!" he bawled. "By the law of this drome, and the law of the Scutzers, I claim Brex's legacy. All his belongings—ship, holdings and men—are mine. You're looking at the new General of the Beryl Bratts!"

Dead silence fell over the stadium.

A rogue yelled from the stands, "He's right! Anyone who bests a general and kills him in a fair fight on land or air, wins his post. He takes his wealth, and his followers."

Sharki blared out a noise of gratification, "Truer words were never spoken. Now anyone who wishes to contend that can come down and face me in combat. Anybody? No? Beefeater? I thought so. You're just a little slinking coward. That's right. I can drive a ship better than any of you pissants, even with one hand."

Grumbles and shouts rained down at him, many leaping to their feet and gripping blasters. But there were many who murmured agreement, and who could see the lay of the land. There rose a slow cheer from the audience. "Sharki! Hail, Sharki!"

The chant grew louder.

Sharki beamed and nodded. His face was carved in a gruesome smile. "Well, well, fellow scutzers. Fellow Bratts, fellow Scags. That's what I like to hear!"

I blinked. Since when was Sharki ever a scutzer? Was this some scene out of a crazy holo flick?

"He's a fraud!" someone yelled. "An upstart!"

Beefeater leaped to his feet. He pointed with fury down at us and drew his R1.

The general's hoarse cries were drowned out as the chant rose.

Sharki ignored the posturer, but stared coldly at Deidra who was standing behind him and I could see her face blanch under his scrutiny.

Sharki hissed at me. "As I'm a man of my word, Rusco, you may take your leave. Take your little piece of fluff with you. Go! And go quickly! Before I change my mind."

I swallowed hard, gripping the knife in my crow-clawed fingers. I made slow steps toward the glitzy throne where Beefeater held firm with Deidra at his side.

"Wait!" Sharki flicked me a gesture made more gruesome by his distended eyes bulging from his elephant man-like face. "A life for a life, Rusco. As of now, we call it even. Okay?" He kicked Brex's gun dropped from the nerveless hand my way.

I snatched up the weapon, hesitated in light of the dark shadow of his meteoric rise to power. Beefeater glared at me from above. For a moment there hung in the air an unspoken spark of rebellion. He looked ready to try something, but hesitated.

"Hail Sharki! Hail Sharki!" the crowed continued to chant.

Sharki gave a low laugh. He held up his arms—one now just a stump—and circled slowly.

"That's right, Bratts! Holler it again!"

"Hail Sharki!"

"Louder!" he cried.

"Hail Sharki!!" The thunderous roar was such to take down the

roof.

Beefeater, gnashing teeth, sensed an opportunity. Knowing the balance of power was swinging like a pendulum, he rose and made his play. "Kill them all! My friends! Brothers! These are usurpers and outsiders! They must die!"

There came yells and unanimous shouts. The patter now of men's boots sounded on stone as they swarmed down from the stands to storm us. How fickle the flow and ebb of power was! Blaster fire ripped at the sand around us. A score or more men came scrambling, packing weapons, hatred in their eyes.

Beefeater laughed, satisfied at having stirred up such turmoil along with a brood of minions to do his dirty work for him. He turned his lascivious attention to Deidra. Seeing the girl and knowing what a prize she was, he grabbed her wrist as she tried to fend him off.

My heart hammered in my chest. I had to get that bastard!

For a moment he held her tight and they were locked in a teetery dance of embraces and thrusts. Her back was to me. I could not open fire and take him out without risk of killing her too.

Her right arm flailed out. The cord at her wrist pulled tight, exposing the leather like a tautened garrote. I whipped off a shot. The bright flare snapped the cord. Deidra gave a triumphant cry. She twisted out of Beefeater's grip and with a joyful scream smashed her elbow into his teeth. He fell back and she clocked him square in the face with her other fist. His arm came up to shield his broken nose as she ran down the steps into the arena.

Bright blaster fire rang at my feet. More bolts whizzed past Sharki's head and his lean flanks.

I flung myself on my belly, aimed a torrent of fire at the stands, covering Deidra as she bolted toward me across the sand.

One of the arena deputies came running my way shooting wild. I pegged him and he went flying back in a spray of blood.

Sharki grunted and fled to the cover of Brex's overturned bender.

This was suicide. We were too exposed. Any one of our defensive moves was doomed to fail. We could be shot down any second.

Deidra plunked down belly-flat at my side, her bosom heaving. In a frantic purchase for life, we low-crawled toward Sharki's green airboat.

Fire licked around her rear flank, threatening to fry us. I hoped to hell this bender was still rideable.

Fights were breaking out between scutzers. It was hard to tell who was the good guy, who was the bad.

We were sitting ducks. All I could see was death. I could only count the seconds before we died in pools of our own blood.

All of a sudden the top of the dome exploded in a flash of bright light. A ship appeared through the gap of the pale light beyond.

There was no mistaking it, that alligator snout—*Gator?*

How the hell—?

The air pressure was dropping fast. I could feel a sudden fierce, squeezing pressure against my skull as the air escaped through the rupture and the vacuum threatened to freeze and suffocate us all.

No time to think. I grabbed at Deidra's arm. We scrambled for the bender's door. Heedless of the thinning air, I jerked it open and clambered inside. I pulled her down on my lap. I fired up the vehicle. She sat there, tense and afraid, but a joy to behold. I thought I'd never hold her again.

The warm feel of her nestled against me, the scent of her, it was like a narcotic. I wanted to grab her and kiss her and—

"Ride, Rusco, ride! What the fuck are you doing?"

I was hallucinating. Too many hits to the head, too many hurts.

I whipped out of my reverie. "Right!" I grit my teeth and floored the bender, just as the yardie who'd zapped me earlier with his billy-stick came stumbling around the hood, firing roughshod at our windshield. Deidra grabbed my gun and aimed it out the window. The left corner of the bumper caught his shin and sent him skidding back like a ragdoll, his leg snapped like a rotten twig. We rose up and away, R1 fire pinging against our metallic underbody. Deidra got the window closed. She helped steer our bender up toward the dome's breach.

Gator? It could only mean…

Marty…and Slapper. The sly bastards! Somehow they'd hot-wired her.

My elation was shortlived. This bender was not air-equipped—I had no helmet, Deidra wore no suit—we had precious little air left before we would all suffocate. Which meant—

I turned a glance through the cracked windshield. *Gator* was banking off and flying away in the direction of the tent community. She must have gotten visual confirmation of us.

Scutzers below grabbed for their helmets strapped at their backs.

Suited figures were running everywhere in panic. There were cries, chaos, pandemonium. The smart ones were stampeding for the main gate to get to their speeders as fast as they could.

Sharki was landing blows on a yardie in the middle of the yard, fighting over who would get into the last bender. At last Sharki shouldered him aside, leveled his blaster and blew his brains out. How the hell that rogue could have driven that bender and survived this ordeal was beyond me, but then I remembered he had voice control over the craft.

I flipped the airboat in high gear. The small tank-like bender burst through the jagged gap and angled up toward the black shape of *Gator*.

Below loomed the pitiful sprawl of tent-like domes to the west. Shadowed by the cold soaring metal of the mantis-like telebractors, it looked like a slave colony. Beyond, to the north, the haunting chasm of the void and its tiny strip of mining machinery huddled at its brink.

Deidra stared unblinking at the panorama and the fleeing ship. She hadn't said much of anything. Shock, I guessed. But she was alive, and with me.

I realized then why I had not wasted Sharki back there on that roid. I'd be dead now if I had. There would've been no rescue of her. That was what the *weave* had been trying to tell me all the time…*fuck*, that root hog scrabble back on the roid—a nightmare. I thrust the chilling thought from my mind.

CHAPTER 38

I turned my attention back to *Gator* and waved to Marty through the glass as he looped over to our side. He jerked back a thumb.

Deidra tuned the bender's radio to a general frequency. His voice croaked over the com, "You piece of shit, Rusco. Do I always have to bail your ass out of a jam?"

"Good morning to you, Marty."

"Hope you're happy," he griped. "We hopped Brex's ride."

"Yeah, I see that. I'm happier than a clam in water. You happy?"

"No."

"How'd you know to find us here?"

"Sharki. The grump tipped us off. Saw you being shuttled off to the drome. We assumed the worst, that our Scag vessel had been hijacked and we knew we needed a ship more than ever. Sharki went out to look for you. He was getting in the way anyways. Why the hell didn't you respond—"

"Radio died."

"You have Deidra with you? She's okay?"

"Right here beside me."

"Where's Brex?"

"Speaking with his angels."

"Good. Follow us to ground. We'll get you on this ship."

"No, better we try to get *Trident*."

"You found our hauler?"

"Yep, holed up in a small hangar off the ship yard where we dropped you at. She's being refurbished."

"You mean go back there? That depot? The place is crawling

with—"

"It's risky…but—"

"What?"

"We're dead meat flying *Gator*, Marty. Every scutzer in the universe'll be gunning for us. They'll come and blow us to hell and back."

"Okay." Marty sighed. "Lead on."

I took the bender down on an angle as fast as she could go, to the place where I remembered *Trident* was cached.

Gator trailed in our wake.

I did not like the look of the enormous battleship that loomed to the north over the cleft. She'd turned and showed the breadth of her nightmarish hull and was making for us, all 300 feet of her submarine sleekness.

"You see that L19, Marty?"

"Yeah, means we have to work fast."

We swooped low over the rows of parked craft and swept out toward the hangar, me leading.

The hangar doors were still open.

"That pale green hulk to the right," I said.

"That?" croaked Marty. "Holy hell, did they bastardize her?"

"Never mind. Focus. Cover us as we fly in and board her."

He gave a throaty guffaw. "Good luck."

I took the bender straight past the double doors and flew into *Trident's* cargo bay. I astonished a couple of techies in gray suits who hunched at the side working on her hull. There was the problem of how to get the hold door closed now and pressurize the chamber. None of us had suits or remote control to activate the switch. In the nail-biting moments that passed, I figured it out. Hovering in the gloom, I eased the bender nose first to the wall. Her bumper touched the triangular button that activated the ramp. The hold hatch started to lift. The decompression process fired up.

There came quick blasts through the open bay as the ramp lifted slowly to seal the chamber. In those few murderous seconds, we ducked in our cramped cockpit to avoid getting our heads blown off as bright blaster trails whipped off our plate metal and rainbowed about the shadowy confines.

I put the bender down none too gently in the corner. We crashed with a jolt, her nose flush to the hold's innermost wall. The cargo door had closed tight and the chamber was almost fully pressurized. I motioned to Deidra and the R1 she clutched. "Cover me if we have any trouble."

The green light on the wall came on and I dropped out of the bender and half-hobbled over to the air lock.

I got through to the bridge.

I winced. How long before they blew the hold?

I plunked my tired ass in the pilot's chair. I raised *Trident's* shields and fired up her cannons. Her systems were online.

Trident's ion jets flared. The craft moved like a slow leviathan toward the open hangar door. The double doors were closing: two sets of sliding moving slabs of metal soon to meet in the middle, and cut us off and trap us here like rats.

Deidra swore and plopped herself down beside me at the weapons' console. Her face was flushed. Pent-up energy radiated from her every move. She trained both starboard and port cannons at the closing doors. Bright flashes spat from the newly-installed barrels. Metal sheared in fiery fury. An open smoking gap appeared before us. I set *Trident* at half impulse. We squeezed through the smoke and metal and met Marty up in the air. Her cannons were raining fire down at the small force of patrol ships that had come to harass us. Blasts pinged off our shields. One of the turreted defenders blew into fiery shards as Marty swung broadside over us and loosed fire.

"Hot damn!... Rusco, you're slower than dogshit today, what's wrong with you?"

"It's called logistics, Marty. It takes time to get hold doors closed, re-pressurize air locks, win past mall cops, yadda yadda."

"I suggest we get the fuck out of here then."

"Roger that."

Another blast tagged our port vanes. I watched the needle dip lower on our shields. I needed no prompting to know we had a very limited window here.

We hurtled into the pale sky and banked off away from Terminus. The remaining two patrol craft spat fire at our heels. I saw the L19 battleship advancing. Another destroyer had joined the party from farther out across the chasm. Long submarine shapes with red con towers, racked with 50-foot long cannons. Equipped with extended range and firepower. One hit from those missiles and it would be game over with these low shields.

Marty's growl shattered my reverie. "The bastards must think we're a security threat to their precious mines!"

"Aren't we?" I sneered.

They'll blast us to shit, Rusco."

"We have to get away from this cockroach of a roid, Marty. Hyper out of this wasps' nest, ASAP."

"Only way to hyper out of this shithole is to clear Terminus. We need a 1000 mile window of safety for that, if I recall. Even in this puny gravity."

"Slapper!" I cried, "Pick a roid, any roid!"

There was a pause as I heard a clacking of keys in the background. "Vyrna 4. Mariner Sector!" he said.

"Okay, it's done! We'll meet there!" I punched the coordinates into the autonav.

"Roger." Marty grunted and signed off.

I aimed *Trident* up and away from the enemy ships at full impulse. Marty spiraled and corkscrewed behind our stern vanes drawing the bogies away. People can say bad things about Marty but he was a hell of a good pilot. He showed it now. Eeling away from their slanting fire like a small snake in slicked oil. He pulled off some impressive maneuvers, drawing attention away from our slower vessel. Slapper and Deidra reamed fire at the pursuing ships.

The first L19 missiles came arching across the black gulfs. Round golden globes that came with heat-seeking hunger at our metallic hide. We were 720 miles from Terminus. The ghost planetoid was receding fast below us—sinking now to a gray-yellow disc.

800 miles... 900...

Gator'd already swung ahead and hypered out to our destination...in her wake a long light trail stretched as far as the eye could see toward Perseus.

With mounting dread, I realized we would not make it in time.

Uttering a foul oath, I peered at Deidra. We shared a mutual pang of regret. For times never to be and moments squandered. I jammed the hyperdrive to 'engage'. It was either do or die.

There came a horrid creak of grinding metal and an unnatural hum of grav boosters pushed to their edge as distant stars bent and light trails sheared in our viewport.

We'd activated the light drive 50 miles short of the recommended safety window. The first death globes had not reached our hull...we'd escaped, but god only knew what our disrespect for physics would bring down on us.

CHAPTER 39

The ship came thunking out of hyperdrive in a long tail of light trails. A field of roids swarmed before us almost touching our starboard vanes. I clapped hard at the impulse slider, trying to clear us up and away.

Too late.

A space boulder, the size of a bender, disintegrated against our hull.

The ship went rocking and we slipped sideways out of our seats.

"Where the hell are we?" I cursed. I peered at Deidra, disoriented, my voice hoarse.

"Probably not Vyrna 4." She shook her head in a similar daze.

I pulled myself up, cursing myself for not harnessing my shoulder strap. I hunched over the nav. What's this? "Neta Sector? Five points off our trajectory. A million miles away from our destination."

She stared glumly, massaging her bruised hip as she tottered back to her seat.

I palmed the directional wheel and veered *Trident* away from the litter of small roids. I just avoided another space rock that would have hammered our port and compromised our failing shields.

Whether the varwol had been damaged permanently, I did not know. The thought was worrisome.

We strapped ourselves in and I set out a hail for Marty, a curse humming in my throat.

We may or may not be out of range, depending on where he was. I hoped he hadn't met with some disaster...

While we waited for a reply, I scanned the ship's radar for

anomalies, unable to shake the bad feeling that was knifing my guts.

I reached for the utility compartment under the weapons' console. What I wanted more than anything was the last of that regen. Every tooth in my head felt loose in its socket and my joints creaked.

With a close eye on roids, I stripped out of my blood-soiled suit, wincing. I smeared the poppy-red goo on the open cut at my left thigh and the rest on the wounds here and there. The headache would not be fixed. Regen was no good for that. Only a good rest or a cuddle with Deidra would help and it didn't look like much of that would be happening too soon.

I heard Marty's voice rattle over the com. "Where the hell are you?"

"Neta sector. You'd better come out here, Mar. We can't trust this drive. Gone cockeyed. Coordinates are 65.32.54."

"Over."

We stayed put while *Gator* seemed to be taking her time to arrive. I gazed at Deidra. Her face was pale, fingers clenched; she was as listless as ever.

Marty came out of hyperdrive a safe distance from the roid cluster then impulsed the rest of the way over, avoiding the scatter of random space rocks. I saw the black alligator snout heading our way. I felt some relief.

We communicated over radio on an encrypted channel.

I heard Newt's voice ring like a bell before Marty could even put two words in, *"Trident can get her shields back to 40% in 24 hours, Jet Rusco. That is, if you don't go gallivanting out on the dark side of a roid. Keep her solar panels in direct line with Vala."*

"Thanks, Newt. I'll keep that in mind. Please put Marty on."

"That ship was sound, Rusco," Marty bawled, "then you get your mitts on her and—"

"Settle down, Mar. When you have missiles up your ass, you count your life in breaths. There's bound to be some screwups somewhere along the way. Nothing we can't deal with."

"This caper sucks, Rusco." I heard his fist slam on the console. "We should have hypered the hell out of Vala way back before Tylas was a dot on the map."

I felt his pain. "Agreed. But all hindsight, Mar. It's useless to get all worked up about it."

"Sure, says the man who has angels looking out for him. What's our plan then?"

"I say we hyper the hell out of here," Deidra mumbled.

"With your wonky light drive?" Marty gave a sour little laugh. "Even if we make it to some safe port, what then? We have no dough."

It was a quandary. If we ditched *Trident*, we took our chances with a red hot ship that was ripe for getting missiled. If we ditched *Gator* though, we'd leave ourselves prey to a dodgy drive unable to get us to safety if we needed it. I chewed my lip.

"I think we should leave *Gator*," I said at last. "Maybe here on a roid. We can always come back, get her if we need to."

"And have only one ship?" Marty protested.

"We can always come back and get her after we secure some claims. With *Trident* we don't have to worry about Sharki. His little onboard trackers only work when we're docked at a port of call, not out in the boonies like this."

"Good to know."

"We got 3 options, Mar. We take both ships. Or we ditch one or the other."

We debated long and hard over whether we should keep *Gator*, trade her in or sell her at some distant port. All roads seemed destined for disaster. The longer we held on to *Gator*, the more chance we'd be targets for some pissass vengeful scutzer. We'd always be targets.

"What about a chop shop?" Marty suggested.

I mulled it over. "It's a long way to Vega for a black market parts shop, only to get a few k yols. Not worth it, Mar. Easier to scout out a few more claims on these wretched roids than peddle her for peanuts. We could make 10 gs or more out here on claims."

Marty seemed to hem and haw.

"Speaking of which, why don't we do just that?"

He still seemed reluctant. "Yeah, well, you know we're spending way more time skittering around dodging rogues and murderers than making claims."

"And whining about it isn't going to help. Let's make it work, Marty! One more claim—a measly 5k—then we're out."

He shrugged then offered a defeated grumble. "Sure. Might as well look around these miserable outlands while we're here."

"Atta spirit."

I watched Deidra shake her head and slump back in her seat.

So, we picked the nearest roid to rendezvous at. We transferred the scutzer equipment from *Gator's* hold to *Trident's*—along with two buggies. We left *Gator* down there, a lonely derelict in the middle of a gray wasteland.

We assembled on *Trident*, put our heads together, trying to decide on where to start looking for some easy yols...

CHAPTER 40

The once battle-ready Deidra grew quieter and more reserved than ever. There was a somber, almost penitent cast to her mouth, and I could guess why.

The jaunty cock of her head, the pantherish prance to her step, the leopardish twinkle in her eye—all had changed. She was not quite herself.

My unspoken intuition warned me that her experiences on Terminus had set her back two notches. That Brex, strapping a leash on her wrist as if to subdue a wild dog, had crossed a boundary and taken her to a place of no return. That such things were not to be borne lightly by a proud, vixenish beauty as her without lasting consequences.

I tried to work around the edges, even joke about her captivity with her, get her to open up, but she flew at me all nails and claws.

"Whoa, settle down," I said. I grabbed her wrists and met her fierce glare.

"I've always had trouble with men trying to possess me!" Her cheeks burned, her breath was sharp, bitter.

"Can't imagine why," I said dryly.

"Not because of your charming personality," Marty added.

"Bug off, Bullet-head!"

"Dial it back, Marty," I warned him.

He turned back to the nav and when he saw my baleful look, he dropped his gaze, pretending to fiddle with the dials.

I took Deidra out in the hallway then slowly steered her toward my chamber for some privacy. She didn't seem to resist.

I caught a brief look at her sullen face as she sank down heavily on the farthest corner of the bed. I moved away with a sigh, glimpsed myself in the small mirror on the wall. The tense hunch of the shoulders, the gray patches under the eyes, the cuts and bruises on the battered cheeks.

There was a hard and craggy lift of cheekbone there that I'd not seen before. The rough and tumble jetting about was starting to take its toll. *It's giving you gray hairs and taking a pound of flesh, Rusco. For trying to save your skin and those of others, you're paying the sandman a hefty price.*

Did I like what I saw? No. Did it matter? Probably not.

The weathered face had changed over the years: from the youthful, striking, happy-go-lucky, somewhat carefree flyboy named Kip Rees, to the chiseled, hawk-cheeked, jaded outlaw, rawboned and cynical, who was Jet Rusco.

I looked back at Deidra. How old was she—maybe 25? With a fire and rebel spirit of a woman far older. It set off a pang in my solar plexus, to see that fire sizzling out, her spirit broken by that lout, Brex, and what had gone down at Terminus.

I took a deep breath. I saw the angry flush of shame darkening her face. I didn't have to guess what was eating at her. If Brex had taken her by force, or messed with her in any way, it would be a hard road back to normalcy. From her desolate expression and red-rimmed eyes she was an open book to read.

It shamed me too to admit that her sullying changed my perspective of her. Now she bore the look of the archetypal tainted flower. The soiled virgin. I could not look at her in the same way. It was an age-old conditioned response, working in the back of my mind, completely unfounded in reality. If I could have turned back time, I would've. Made different decisions to prevent what'd gone down. But life is full of harsh turns and deep chasms that deal us cruel fates. Deidra'd stumbled down one of those dark ones that has plagued humans from time immemorial, left people gnawing their knuckles with angst and looking over their shoulders for a lifetime, expecting the worst.

Her lower lip trembled and her eyes wavered…then slid away as tears stung her eyes.

A rift had come between us—the passion we had shared, the moments of magic had flared out. They were somewhere far away, maybe not to be regained ever or at least with the same wild abandon or spontaneous combustion that had happened some time back. I bit back my loss, knowing she could read me as easily as I could read her.

"Talk to me," she murmured.

I clumped down on the bed beside her. "Brex's dead. He'll never be able to touch you or lay a hand on you again."

"I know."

"And Sharki's not a problem either. The tyrant's moved on. He has bigger fish to fry. It means you're free."

"I know that too."

"Then, what is it?"

"You know what it's like feeling used, soiled?" she said in a dead voice.

"You want to live in a broken, fractured place?"

"No, who does?"

"Then why—"

"Listen! It doesn't just heal overnight!" she cried.

I could understand that. I let out a weary sigh. How many broken places had I crawled out from over the years? For her, maybe it was different being a woman. Always being targeted, always ogled by lechers and having to watch her back at every step.

Suddenly I felt very awkward. My throat felt dry as the *weave* wound its way through me. I wished I hadn't opened this can of worms. Maybe better to have let her process this on her own. But events were in motion, and I could not stop them.

"As crazy as it sounds," she said, "a part of me knew you hadn't given up on me, Jet—that you'd never give up, that you'd come back and get me, or die trying." The corners of her lips turned down in a hurtful grimace. "Even though I knew that was impossible, you being marooned on that unforgiving roid with no air, no ship. But the belief gave me hope. Another part of me laughed at such a ridiculous idea. What if I'm stuck here, to be slave to that brute forever? Being hauled forth like some prize to watch his silly games and sit at his side like a well-polished trophy. Hours of the senseless violence, slaughter, the jeers. While those creeps craved for more. *'Hail, Brex! Hail, Beefeater! Hail, Kybar!'* What a bunch of murdering scum."

"I hear you, but—"

"When I was at my darkest hour, when he toted me back to his fancy, rich-man's dome to share his bed with him like a whore, I had this—sudden realization—that no matter how strong I was or how hard I fought back, I had to rely on protectors like you to save me. And that was what hurt and crushed me the most. Because I knew you were dead." Her eyes blurred with tears.

I reached out a hand to her shoulder.

"I thought I would kill myself, Jet. I almost did once. His knife was on the dresser in that—that cage. But I hadn't the courage." She knuckled the tears out of her eyes.

I leaned in to gently put my arms around her. She was rigid like a board at first, but her voice broke and slow sobs rocked her shoulders. Like a lotus flower she opened up and revealed her true feelings for me.

I felt an ease come over my tired bones, which soothed the thudding pulse of my blood and the urgency of my pent-up passion. I whispered in her ear, "Deidra, I think we can make this work—I just—"

"No words. Sh." She pushed a finger to my lips then clutched me tighter. She guided me down to the bed then slipped under the covers. "For once, I'd like to be with a man, without being intimate."

We lay under the thin sheets and drank in each other's warmth. Her left arm was draped around my shoulder, her nose snugged comfortably into the hollow of my throat, the silk of her fine hair wisped against my neck and jaw. My arms encircled her narrow waist, my fingers brushed at her spine, reaching under the fabric, massaging the small of her back. Her inner fire was burning stronger now. I could feel the heat of her. Hopefully she could feel mine too. I sent out a wish that time would heal this wound. But how much time it would take was not for me to guess.

After we'd slept for many hours cuddled in each other's arms, we both stirred to each other's movement.

She shifted onto her side, one arm propped under her cheek, meeting my gaze through even green eyes. Her lips met mine. She withdrew. I could see her tongue trail along her upper lip, the familiar twinkle back in her eye.

"Let me tell you a story, Jet, since you never cared to ask. I grew up on Tyrone on the outskirts, what they call the Ramblers' district. Practically raised in a garage. My father was a mechanic. My mom left him early one summer morning—I don't know why, I was too young—and he got into the habit of bringing me to the shop. I had nothing to do there but watch him work on his motors and engines and machine parts. He'd lay on his back in coveralls, fussing over manifolds and assemblies, all greasy and hair out of place. He used to listen to an old grungy shit-can radio, pumping out newfangled country. Used to drive me crazy. Explained why I was never into karaoke. I got good pretty fast at understanding engines and how they worked and how to fix them.

"I had a step sister. Marcela. We used to fight a lot. A prissy bitch, all dolled up and always trying to talk snooty lingo to me all day. She used to call me a tomboy, make fun of me, call me a butch, and it used to bug the hell out of me…she and all her perfumes and scented lotions and frizzed up hair. I wanted none of that. I cared little for it. I had to put her in her place a few times. Walloped her good. Whooped her ass a few times in front of her friends. The laugh was, Rusco, I ended up being ten times prettier than Marcela and all the guys wanted me over her. They'd choose me in a flash… I had no idea what a curse that'd be."

I gave a guarded chuckle. "I can bet."

"A couple of years went by. My dad used to service some of

Sharki's equipment: air-speeders, lode railers, floating grav docks. One day he came to the shop. He saw me working away on an engine block. He gazed at me for some time with that twisted stalker-like look of his. You know it—the kind of creepy show of teeth along with those stalker eyes. He couldn't take his peepers off me. He liked what he saw, he liked what I did. More than what I did, I suppose, when I look back on it.

"He offered me a job—out on his rig at Thetis. I was thrilled. Hungry for the chance to get out of our poky little town and make some decent yols. My dad—he was reluctant at first, but I bugged him so much, he finally capitulated. 'Don't tell me I didn't warn you,' he'd said."

"Well, that went in one ear and out the other.

"I started piloting Sharki's heavy commercial vehicles for him. Haulers, ore-drivers, scout craft. When I showed enough aptitude, he moved me up to a junior position as part of his security detail. I was naive, I was young, Rusco. I did not know how much of a scoundrel he was. But I learned, and when I found out, it was too late. I couldn't get away from him."

I gave a slow nod. My brain kept working to connect the dots as I absorbed her words. "You have any kids?"

"No. Well, almost."

I let that pass. Tears were starting to well in her eyes again. I let it go. I'd pried a lot out of her already with my gallant Jet Rusco persona.

After we'd cleaned up, combed out our bedheads, we returned to the bridge, both of us keeping a chill and lid on our conversation, pretending as if nothing'd happened.

I had a very heavy feeling in my heart. As if this was the last time I would be this physically close to her.

Ridiculous. We were on a road to brighter pastures! A few more k yols and we'd be able to start up fresh far away from here. Brex was dead. Sharki had his hands full, rallying his Bratts; he had no time to bother us.

I thrust the rogue fear from my mind. And yet, as the feeling gnawed at me, I stared defiantly at the field of roids that barred us from the expanses beyond. I went over to the nav to plop myself at Marty's side and plot our next course.

CHAPTER 41

Our first searches drew us deep into the remote belt and its cluster of small, odd-shaped roids. We discovered a likely prospect, an oblong hunk of rock, spinning slowly, roughly 15 miles in diameter. It had potential for scandium, but our scanners picked up a more curious anomaly deeper within the cluster—a large metallic mass drifting some 250 miles away. Odd. It seemed to be the center of a maze of metal fragments floating around its perimeter—of some 20 to 50 miles.

Weird, if not intriguing.

We decided to check it out before we committed ourselves to toiling on smaller finds on the roids.

Our long range visual showed the mass in the cluster to be an enormous ring-shaped construction.

We impulsed closer, and while it took us some time to pick our way through the sprawl of micro roids and space debris, we halted short, spellbound—at the brink of a jaw dropping sight.

A distant ring shape, tilted 30 degrees to the ecliptic, dominated the scene. There must have been thousands of twisted hulks floating about the ring. Ships? Probes? Random space debris? The trail extended for miles.

"It's not space rock. It's metal," I mused. "Which likely means human space expansion effort."

"What? There're miles of it, 50 or more," Deidra exclaimed unhappily.

"We've struck something." Slapper gazed reverently at the mysterious ring.

"What, like space junk? You loony, Slappy? Catalog all this?" Marty waved a fist. "It would take years, a century."

No, there would be no cataloging all this garbage anytime soon. A massive space battle had taken place here. But when? The ring shape looked ancient. Somehow I felt the details we'd never know.

We impulsed closer and using the magnifier, I zoomed in on the wreckage. My suspicions were confirmed. Blackened hulks of space ships torn and twisted by tremendous firepower—derelicts, all spinning slowly in eerie synchrony with the silent roids and the massive ring shape in the center. The unidentified mass was huge, beyond imagining. Five miles across, if I guessed an inch.

A Ring Station? Cold black metal curved in a massive doughnut shape. Its smooth surface was dull and unbroken but for the odd radio antenna dish or control tower or octagonal turret. It seemed uncannily mysterious and alien. The only menace seemed to be those turrets, which may or may not have been weapons' dispersal systems.

Four long cylindrical, spindly cross corridors spanned the empty space in the middle of the ring like cross girders or the spokes of a giant wheel. The four braces linked one side of the massive craft with the other. Where they met in an X rose a bulbous black node at the center, like the all-seeing eye of a gigantic spider.

"That looks like the bridge," I said in a hollow voice.

"A ship that big?" Deidra crowed. "Looks like nothing I've ever seen before."

"It's a god-damned goldmine," Slapper hissed excitedly. He slapped the console with a palm. "A freaking cash cow!"

I could only marvel at the vastness of this derelict, the far-reaching implications of the *weave* to have brought us here. What twisted set of events had put this wonder before our path?

"Boil, boil, toil and trouble," I murmured.

"What're you mumbling now, Rusco?"

"Nothing, Mar. Just another old verse you'd probably hate."

Slapper frowned. He pushed forward a weak smile. "Sensors detect some weak gravity emanating from the ship. Must have stabilizers. It's generating some grav field of its own. The hulk's still online."

"Shields?"

"None that I can detect."

"The ship is unregistered," came Newt's silky voice, breaking the uncomfortable silence. *"Upward of 93% probable alien origin. I'm afraid I am failing to find a match for it or any meaningful information on such a craft. Most peculiar. The bulk of any reputable cataloging, including imaging of such craft, is classified..."*

For once, the bot had nothing more to say.

I thought I'd seen everything, but still I stood somewhat awed.

Slapper did a happy pirouette. "I hereby claim this find," he said in a high-spirited voice.

Marty blinked with mistrust. "Do you think anything is still alive on board?"

"No, anything'd be long dead." I picked at my teeth, nursing a frown. "Though I wouldn't want to be quoted on it."

"We're explorers, guys!" Slapper cried, all smiles and chuckles. "Like the space pioneers of old on Earth!"

"You mean like the fake Voyager and Mars missions and moon landings we talked about, Slappy? To boldly go where no man goes before? You been listening to too many space opera tales."

"Yeah, sure, Rus, you and your theories."

Now I'd heard of a lot of stories and conspiracy theories of Old Earth, like non-existent weapons of mass destruction, climate alarm hoaxes, fake histories, fake aliens, quirks and quarks, lofty big bang theories, that kind of thing. Even seen some of them in action through my favorite asshole Gy-ar and his friendly neighborhood ghouls from the Moon Temple. Pushing their agendas and herding people into underwater cities by manufacturing natural disasters like planetary wildfires. But nothing like this. Not like a mammoth station out of a nightmare fantasy. No conspiracy theory here.

"Deidra," I said, "send word to Tylas. File a preliminary claim with the PRMOD office."

"Roger." She sent on a few close-up photographs of the derelict hanging in space. I saw they preserved the perspective and tilt on its axis.

"What now?"she asked.

"We wait."

Yes, we waited for a while, spellbound by the eerie majesty of the drifting derelict and its entourage of soundless wreckage, but no confirmation was received from Tylas.

Odd. Never had it taken so long. Especially for something this big.

But then maybe not so odd. Wouldn't this phenomenon cause a sensation?

Alarm bells began to chime in my ear.

"Deidra... Send word to Iron. Get him and the Reapers out here as quickly as possible. There's going to be a shitstorm, when word gets out."

"How's word going to get out?" Marty cried.

Deidra scowled at him. "Beefeater and his goons'll hear about it soon enough. The other generals too, once it hits the claim office..." She trailed off.

Marty scratched at his chin, looking schooled.

I clambered to my feet and paced the bridge. I stared at the roids and the wrecks surrounding the eerie ring shape. I could hear Marty's voice grumbling in the background, "...we never shoulda abandoned *Gator*. With scavengers out there ready to creep up on us, our varwol on the fritz—"

"The varwol works, Marty, it's just not reliable. Like spinning a roulette wheel."

"Great, that's very comforting, Rusco. Makes me feel a whole lot better."

"No one's going to be hypering out of this soup too soon, Mar. Not with all this space junk floating around. Don't get all pouty on me."

But his worry was also mine. Somewhere we'd miscalculated. Or better put, I'd miscalculated.

Iron's voice boomed over the com. "What's all this I hear about derelicts? You people spooked about some boogie man? Haven't made a claim in well on two weeks, Rusco. What are you doing out there, sitting on your asses?"

I snatched the com from Deidra. "Iron, we have a problem. Some good news and some bad. The good is, we've landed the claim of the century. The bad, well—" I filled him in on the details of the claim office not acknowledging our find.

His face popped up on the vidcom. "Send me video."

Deidra transferred a vid-link showing a view onto the alien ship.

When he saw it, his eyes nearly popped out of his head. "Jesus, how big is that thing? What have you stumbled on? PRMOD hasn't responded, you say?"

"No."

"Damn. Some bastards must have stalled the process. But why?" He chewed his lip. I saw his brow furrowed in thought. "Maybe the mining companies. Maybe someone up the chain. We're going to have to do this the old fashioned way. I need you to plant our flag, Rusco. You'll have to go down there and pin some Reaper emblem on the hull."

"Wha—How?"

"With your hands, what you think?"

"You think we're—"

"You heard me. Take a kit, one of the flag beacons. We can lay proof of claim manually and skip the bureaucracy. Otherwise some shyster'll claim jump us. It's the only way."

"That's a tall order, Iron."

"Do it now! Before it's too late. Or you're all going to have every damn rustler and claim jumper in the galaxy on your ass in less time it takes a pig to shit!"

I bit down grimly on my lip. "Okay."

I took *Trident* in closer, first for reconnaissance, then for...well, I didn't know yet... While Slapper zoomed in on the ring's curved hull nearest us, Marty's fingers remained clamped on the port cannon control. Deidra watched the console like a wary tiger, as if waiting for something to spring.

I stabbed a finger down on the display as Slapper scrolled along the hull. "There! Looks like a deployment bay, or some landing depot. See the cracks outlining that massive door? I don't fancy going all the way out to that fancy belvedere or bridge smack in the center. The place I got my finger's on is as good a place as any."

Marty grinned. "It's your life."

I eyed the gargantuan ship and the black gulfs of space with growing wonder. I forced a smile on my face. "Well, here's looking at ya. Wish me luck."

"Newt, go with him," Deidra called out.

Newt bridled, *"My systems are not programmed to withstand such—"*

"Go with him!" She rose in one fell rush, gun in hand.

"Very well…" The bot's red lights flashed on his shell. He hovered a step back from the wrath of Deidra's raised blaster. *"Jet Rusco, at the very least I suggest you pack an extra weapon. Maybe take this young lady's?"*

Somehow I had the feeling blasters wouldn't be helping us much where we were going.

I made my way to the hold. Marty trooped with me. Newt trailed above our shoulders. Together we gathered gear. I suited up in one of the fresh Reaper suits strapped to the wall. I clipped on one of the jet packs around my waist, just below the grav pak. No lie, I did not wish to be doing a space walk out there near that goliath.

"Rusco, you look a little pale." Marty smiled and pointed to the bender. "Maybe take that shitbox. It'll get you faster and closer to the hull."

I clamped on my helmet. "Good plan, Marty. What would I do without you?"

I tuned my wrist monitor to a private, encrypted channel so our conversations couldn't be tracked. I threw the scutzer claim kit and beacon in the front seat of the bender and hopped in. Newt settled in beside me by the stick shift. I turned the bender around to face the cargo ramp where I would be heading out soon. Marty threw me a salute. He withdrew through the air lock and I watched the cargo ramp slowly open up as Deidra activated the hold door from the bridge.

The blackness of space yawned before me and I impulsed the bender forward through the open bay. I could hear my breath whistling as I reflected on this improbable scenario. Never in a million years would I have imagined climbing back in this piece of crap again.

CHAPTER 42

The monstrous ship grew even more monstrous as I impulsed toward her cyclopean sweep of hull, nearing that place I'd scouted on the ship's display.

What looked liked twin doors stood out as a rhomboid section of steel that looked slightly grayer than the uniform jet black of the massive hull. *Trident* trailed me at a safe distance. She shone her powerful flood lamps down on the hull.

I checked my wrist monitor's gauges. Oxygen level 95%. Air pressure 0.3 atm. Temperature 72 degrees.

There'd be a tense moment where I'd have to go and magnetically clamp the beacon on the hull and jet back to the bender. No big deal.

Theoretically.

Once the deed was done, everything'd be forgotten. Iron'd be off my back, we would collect our yols as reward for bagging this prize and we'd fly the hell out of here, enjoy our freedom, our spoils—

A disturbing crackle bristled through the com. "Company! Four o'clock, Rusco!" Deidra's hiss had my stomach churning.

I jerked my head around to peer up through the windshield and saw the sleek curve of a war-ship with triangular turret and four cannons and Bratts' logo come impulsing down at us out of nowhere. She came at significant speed, heedless of space debris or roids. All this before Iron or any of the Reaper ships could get here.

A familiar voice trumpeted over the general channel, "Well, if it isn't our favorite hauler, *Trident.* And our friendly gang of scutzers. Remember, Rusco, what I told you about those trackers on board.

No? Not that I even needed them when you so conveniently sent the coordinates down to head office. So easy to bribe a few people down on Tylas and get the scoop whenever something big comes in. I'm learning this General business pretty quick, wouldn't you say?"

Deidra's voice lashed back angrily. "Back off, you bastard. You've no business here, Sharki. This is not your claim."

"Well, well, mighty saucy tongue on you, Dee. You covering for that flyboy Rusco? Get him on the line. Maybe he's sleeping off his stupor, his hurts from the games. Didn't plan on seeing you folks so soon, but what of it? You remember my promise to you, Rus? My capacity for compassion is mighty low."

I called up through the com. "No need to remind us, Sharki. Iron's going to be here any minute. You can duke it out with him—leave us out of it."

"Maybe I will, maybe I won't. Good timing then. Look—here comes trouble."

I squinted up at 11 o'clock and saw a starfish cluster of bright traces flare from beyond the roid belt. Two score of Bratts' ships had come out of light drive. Now they impulsed in to join the party.

I tooled the bender closer to the alien hull, champing at the bit to plant this beacon and get the hell out of here.

I caught a blip of another ship materializing on the horizon. It impulsed toward us and I recognized this ship. With silvery hull and diamond-shaped middle. She banked our way and swept over Sharki's twin turret cannons and poised herself between me and *Trident*.

My lips curled in a grin. *Iron*.

Sharki's warship positioned herself at the head of the cluster of Bratts' ships and swiveled her bow to face the newcomer. More Reaper ships appeared on the horizon and advanced to form a loose line alongside Iron's ship.

Iron's voice clipped over the general frequency, "So, you're the new general of the Bratts? The one called Sharki who killed Brex? Congratulations, boy! I would have killed that bastard myself, had it come to it, but I guess you beat me to it."

"Nice to meet you too, old man." Sharki offered a non-committal grunt. "Seems we have a little problem of jurisdiction here. By my standards, your claim is loose. I'm claiming Squatters' Rights."

"I think you can shove off, Sharkbait. We have video timestamped proof of discovery."

"Don't mean nothing to me out here in the billies of space. Who's going enforce it? You, Iron boy? No claim's been made—at least from what I hear on Tylas."

"It hasn't, but it will—My man's down there. Shit, who's that now?"

I turned sharply in my seat and looked up through the windshield. Another vessel was angling our way. A spaceboat different than the rest. Not a scutzer ship. More like a space yacht, a fancy space-cutter with upswinging middle and curved prow and stylish lines at midships. It had a pleasingly-ornate bow in the shape of a swan's beak. I'd seen ships like this before, but that had been many years ago, and the chill of the memory brought a fresh prickle over my skin.

The message from the ship was one that sent more chills down my back. "Gentlemen…this is the Cruiser *VoldeVoid*—" The voice, calmly placed, was carefully controlled and enunciated with perfect diction, "It seems your little jurisdictional problems are of no concern. Take your fingers off your cannons—I shall claim the Ring Station and spare you the trouble, gentlemen."

"Who the hell're you?" Iron blurted out.

"I am Dy-ar, Prime Ascendant of the Moon Temple."

"And I'm Iron," he laughed. "General of the Star Reapers. If it's a pissing match you're looking for, then let's square off."

A covey of fifty ships impulsed in toward us, having just come out of light drive. Dodging space wrecks, they halted a safe distance away from the space yacht. Reaper men, with the hooded, Grim Reaper logo with pickaxe over his shoulder.

Sharki called out in an irritable voice, "What's your stake in this,

Reverend? A rosary to put on our ship with a blessing?"

"Nothing so vapid, my cynical reaver," said Dy-ar. "I am simply laying claim to this archaeological treasure. So I shall spare you fools the trouble of squabbling over it. Go home. That is my advice. Pretend you never saw it."

Iron's voice swept over the com in a contemptuous bellow, "By my reckoning, the first one to plant his flag, claims the prize. At least, according to salvage laws of Vala—and that's my man, Jet Rusco, down there."

"Ah, Jet Rusco—an outlaw wanted by the Brothers of the Temple of the Moon as well as many other factions."

"Stand down, little man!" Iron called. "I don't care who the fuck you are. Ain't nobody steps between me and my scutzers. I gave the pledge of my protection to them and by hell, I'll uphold it."

"Very noble of you," Dy-ar grunted.

I was proud to be a Reaper then. Iron was all balls and bravery. But did he know what he was taking on? The Moon Temple people were merciless. Killers. Architects of chaos. I remembered the Prime Ascendant of old, Gy-ar's single-minded drive to dispose of anyone or anything who interfered with his messianic agendas. The ruthlessness he exhibited in hunting me down, his attempt to break me, even if it meant snatching my soul.

Iron gave a sour curse. "This is a turf war. Stay where you are, Jet Rusco. Sharki, you stand down too! Rusco has already filed the claim."

I called up through the com. "I'm in position to plant the beacon, Iron. 22.66.89, the coordinates. Let me know if you need me to—"

"Oh, you're down there, are you?" Sharki bawled.

No sooner had the man spoken than fire lashed out at the hood of my bender. A streak grazed her nose and sent me spinning away.

"Shit!" A flood of panic poured over me as I struggled to regain control. I watched pieces of her metal armor float off in space. Damned if I was going to die down here or let this golden nugget, the Ring Station, get stolen out from under me.

Newt clipped out in a soft voice, *"Jet Rusco, perhaps I could plant the beacon for you and—"*

"Shut up! No one's going out there—unless he wants to get his ass fried. Deidra! Fire on that damn hull! Open her up so I can get inside. I'm gonna plant this beacon whether they like it or not, if it's the last thing I do!"

"It's not worth it, Rusco! They'll swarm in and kill you!"

"We're all walking corpses. Do it!"

I saw *Trident's* cannons swivel. At the same time Sharki's swung on me. A gush of bright light opened up a gap in the great ship's hull not 300 yards from where I hovered. I shot forward, hoping to gain the gap, but I knew I'd be too slow. I braced myself for death but *Trident* winged in to shield me from ship fire. Bright blasts careened off *Trident's* broad flanks. Her shields held and she escorted me toward the smoking gap.

I shot toward the jagged fissure before Sharki's fire could fry me.

Looking back, I saw that now the last of the captains had arrived. Beefeater and the Mongers' and Gravediggers' generals with their ships were surrounding the station.

Beefeater spoke in a nasal, weaselly voice—likely a result of his broken nose, "We have you surrounded, Moon Ghoul. Retreat your fancy ship! This is a scutzer claim."

"Impossible! I have received confirmation from PRMOD office that a full claim of the vessel has been awarded to Moon Temple stewardship. Do you wish to violate interspacial law?"

Iron gave a caustic sneer. "Your 'interspacial law' means nothing out here! That, and your jerry-rigged claims. You're outnumbered and outgunned, Pastor. We'll make mincemeat of you. Push off, if you know what's good for you."

"While you jackals tear out each other's throats over the scraps and gut the ship? Never."

Fire from Sharki's Bratts lashed out at the space yacht. Her shields held. Oddly, she made no move to retaliate. More blasts lanced down from Sharki's war craft, hammering *Trident* and the place where I hovered by the Ring Station. If not for her shields, I would have been space dust.

Marty's sneer came over the private channel, "You should have killed that bastard when you had the chance."

"With Sharki pitted against Dy-ar, it could work in our favor," I hissed.

"Another enemy to betray us. Dumbest thing you ever did was to trust that snake, Rusco."

I gave a moody nod. Marty was right. I wished he was wrong.

I pinched my eyes shut. Too many signals. Too many variables. Too much noise. I had to think. What a convoluted mess.

I jammed my foot down on the accelerator and impulsed through the jagged gap into the ship before any stray fire could blow me to bits.

CHAPTER 43

I'd come into a cavernous landing bay and the speeder's light shone dead ahead into the gloom. Four aphid-like ships sat parked about 100 feet ahead against a high inner wall. The eeriness of centuries hung over those vehicles, like metal bugs watching for centuries.

Why was I in this mausoleum of oddities? What was I hoping to achieve? Some place to cache this beacon that sat in my pouch?

I floated closer and discerned thick dust carpeting the curved fuselages of those ships. The place was large enough to hold a small fleet, but looked like only a few of the craft remained. Black mantis-shaped prows stared back at me. Flared insectoid wings, fluted hulls sitting on stilted legs like those of a grasshopper's. They looked as if they had not been used for centuries.

To the far left emanated a glow of faint blue light. What looked to be an entrance somewhere into the heart of the ship.

I parked the speeder behind the creepy aphid ships, caching it in the shadows of a sunken pit behind the last vessel's stern. I had to make this quick. I gathered my resolve and dismounted, my feet touching hard metal.

First contact with the alien ship.

I approached the leftmost wall and halted. Newt trailed a good two feet back over my shoulder. Two horizontal bands of blue light crossed the barrier…something of an upside down U-shaped portal, a few yards wide. An air lock? Maybe some kind of force field that prevented intruders from going in or out. Cryptic symbols were writ on either side of the portal: two upside down L's with circles above, like the small dots of an 'i'.

The glow, like the presence of the grav generators, suggested the ship still retained some power. Power yes…but maybe her defensive systems were offline? I tipped my R1's barrel through the blue beams. The first inch passed right through, unscathed. I withdrew it. No heat, no marks. No visible damage that I could detect.

My trance was broken as Deidra's voice hissed over the com. "Rusco! Things are looking bad out here. Have a look."

She flashed me a video and I cursed as I peered down at my suit's wrist monitor. The feed showed Iron's ship sweeping in to block the gap I'd entered. Her hull was instantly wracked by ship fire from three directions. Another blast smote her bow, sending her tipping sideways. She caught more rays and slewed sideways, slammed into the Ring Station. I saw a flash of light enter the gap and felt the reverberating thud of impact vibrate through the ship. Iron's ship went up in a balloon of flame, the wreckage skidding off the sheer side out into space.

Sharki's warship flew by in triumphant glee.

I heard Slapper's heart-wrenching wail echo over the com.

Fuck.

"Deidra, talk to me!" I yelled.

"Iron's ship is down!" she rasped. "The Reapers are going mental. Dozens of ships're opening fire on Sharki's Bratts. Vessels are going down. All hell's breaking loose. Slapper's bawling his eyes out, beating the console with his fists."

I pinched my eyes shut, trying to visualize the scene…trying not to dread too much what was coming our way. "Okay…"

I hailed Sharki on a private channel. "You fucking bastard! You killed a good man. Why? We could have worked this out."

"All's fair in love and war, kid," Sharki jeered. "Of all people, you should know that."

"Shut the fuck up. You're a psycho."

"Come on, now, Jet baby. No need to get all testy. We go back a long ways. Come up out of that rat hole and we can talk like men.

What say you, a temporary truce. I'll give you a ship, a 10k bonus. You and your mouthy little blonde bitch and that monkey man can enjoy a little holiday. On the house. One big happy family."

I rasped and cursed through my teeth, "I'm going to destroy this beacon, Sharki. You'll never get the ship. You'll have to come down here and plant your own beacon. You can fight it out with those treacherous Scags. Come plant your flag if you dare."

"You son of a bitch! I'll see you in hell." He cut the channel and suddenly I wished I hadn't egged him on.

I flipped back to the private channel. "Deidra, talk to me!"

"Sharki's explorer capsule has launched. He's coming in to get you."

I heard Dy-ar's cool voice speak in strained tones over the general channel. "General Sharki—I hope I have the name right— This is your last warning—Move away from the Ring Station. We claim ownership of the vessel. Repeat, this is your last warning."

Sharki spat over the com, "You don't claim shit, Reverend Dy-fuck! I've deep-sixed that blowhard, Iron, so I'm now Master of the Reapers. This boy who claimed the vessel is working for me now, which means the rig's mine. So push the hell off, you fucking dipstick."

A pause came over the com. A deadly silence of ages, of unspoken, lingering malevolence.

"You don't own anything, you worm. You are a flea, an insect, a speck of dirt. If you have any respect for the lives of the men you command, you will back off, take your puny scutzer forces with you and never come back to this sector again."

"Says who, you? In a pansy-ass spaceboat with no backup?" Sharki jeered.

The Prime Ascendant's voice was one that would chill the dead. "You have no concept of the power we wield." He cut the channel.

My heart sank when I squinted at my wrist monitor and saw the traces of many ships sweeping across the roid field. Skurg ships. A hundred or more of them. An entire fleet.

And now a battleship had materialized on the far edge of the horizon, dropping out of hyperdrive.

Things were about to get very ugly very fast.

It was either now or never. With a miserable shake of my head, I turned my burning attention back to the portal.

I put a toe underneath the luminous band. Nothing happened. The boot remained unblemished.

Throwing caution to the wind, I ducked full under the luminous bars. I pushed my way through. Newt followed.

Blaster fire ripped from across the landing bay as a ship landed and men poured out.

Sharki's men. A team streaming from the newly-landed capsule. The men had not wasted time. So long as my beacon was alive, the alien vessel was technically mine. Or his, now that he claimed General-ship over the Reapers. But he'd have to come and get me or it.

So be it.

I had gotten through the airlock but I was now trapped on its other side.

I turned and peered down the wide, octagonal, coal-black corridor that ran deeper into the ship. What lay moldering down there? The possibilities left a chill over my soul.

I peered back through the air lock. More figures were running from the capsule. Another ream of blaster fire ripped into the portal's flank and some made it through the U-shaped gap and almost took off my head. I crabbed back, chest heaving. Shit! How many rogues had he jammed into that piece of crap?

I murmured into the com, "Deidra, they've pinned me down. I can't—"

"We're coming in, Rusco. Hang tight. We can take them out."

"No, no! Stay put!" My voice was a hoarse rasp. "It's a suicide mission down here. This is a death crib. I have the bender. I'll make my way out."

"No you won't, Rusco. There're too many of the bastards."

"Stay the hell away, I say—"

But she'd cut the channel and I spat out an oath. Pigheaded fools! We were all going to end up dead down here.

In a moment of clarity I realized that I had but one option. To hide this beacon deep in the ship and save my skin. It wouldn't take Sharki's goons long to realize there was no danger here at the airlock—that they could just waltz through without injury. Hell, I'd go over to the Scags or Mongers before I'd let that bastard have it. I had to stop them somehow.

Blaster fire ripped past my ribs and down the illimitable corridor where it struck and rebounded off the black walls. I swore and ducked deeper down the dark corridor, shuddering at the faraway curve of the outer ring. Newt trailed behind me. I was afraid to light my headlamp lest those ghouls have an easy trail to follow me.

I activated the small pen lamp on my wrist monitor and used it to guide me as I half stumbled down the eerie, octagonal-shaped corridor, blaster gripped in hand. I turned every ten seconds or so to jerkily open fire on anything that might have been a pursuer.

After a time, I halted and turned down a cross-corridor to the right. My breath rasped harshly in my ear. I turned left and headed down another main corridor, slipping deeper into the ship, following the curve of the ring. My hope was to lose those wolves, plant the beacon, double back to the air lock. A flimsy, if not ridiculous plan.

But a plan at least.

The ship had the feel of a tomb. A place where shadows crept and nightmares bred. Shadows that had lived long in a place long ago, and now they crept back to life again with the fugitive light of my headlamp. The thin beam paved minuscule paths through the unreachable gloom—the ever curving, ever slightly bending corridor that ran on forever, bulkhead after bulkhead. I could feel the pulse and beat of my own heart pounding under the layers of thermal suit, pumping in sync with the steady throb of blood in my ears. I cursed myself that I had not taken that extra hit of Myscol that Marty'd stashed in the utility bin with the regen. It would've helped my nerves at this time. Down, down the wormhole of this crypt-like ship I wandered. Rusco, you're getting too old for this shit.

The ship was somehow alive. I had no evidence of it though I could feel it. I had no idea how old the leviathan was—but I had the feeling it was older than centuries. The idea staggered me.

The floor was built of metal grate with inch-wide octagonal holes cut in it like some hurricane chain link fence titled sideways. It allowed me to see through to the corridor beneath that ran parallel. The one too that had a metal grating floor under which ran another corridor and another. For a good five levels down. Maybe six? I glared in bewilderment and dismay, thinking my eyes were playing tricks on me. The metal was of some dark-tinted bronze material. Iron, steel, titanium, copper?

At intervals I passed narrow stairwells that seemed to provide access to hallways and corridors above and below. My curiosity wanted to explore those corridors, but it was too easy to get lost.

Stay on the main level, keep it simple. Hide your golden egg then get out of here.

I'd lost Sharki—thanks to luck—but I was getting disoriented myself.

I turned to Newt ever slinking over my left shoulder. "You keeping track of these twists and turns, Newt?"

"All is recorded, Jet Rusco."

"Any word from *Trident?*" I banged my wrist monitor against my thigh. "Seem to have lost the vid feed."

"They are temporarily offline. Not sure what the problem is. I will alert you when I receive more information."

I peered up at Newt. The bot seemed uncharacteristically distracted. "What?"

"My data analyzers have been working on this problem of ID-ing the ship. I have discovered a match: to an obscure sighting of a similar craft long ago. One much smaller. An explorer vessel, the Gideon Gamma 5, sent 3 centuries ago to the Dendara System, discovered a Mentera ship of similar configuration. It

crashlanded on a planetoid, X13. Purported to be the vessel of an ancient insectoid alien race. Four foot high creatures. Resembling locusts that stood on their hind legs—at least according to skeletons found at the site. No other details are listed. The data has been carefully redacted, the link well hidden, seemingly buried and consigned to the murky area of conspiracy theories."

"I don't doubt that, Newt, and no conspiracy theory here either, would you agree?"

"I would have to agree. I think that we—"

"Shh. Let us go a bit further."

I began to realize that something unexpected and awful had happened on this ancient ship. Where were the crew members? A film of cold sweat had budded on the back of my neck. I felt a chill as never before as the enormity of the implications of this derelict ship and its alien science hit home. Who had built it? These insectoid aliens? For what purpose? Why was it out here in the middle of a roid field amid all this space junk? That there'd been a massive space war seemed plausible enough, but why had this vessel alone survived?

Questions…questions. That maybe would have no answers.

It was like a big honeycomb within a honeycomb, bulkhead after bulkhead, with all its slightly curving corridors and side branches and heavy slabs of riveted metal looming overhead. The ceilings were high, about 12 feet. Almost as if these smallish aliens had deliberately built such cathedral-like corridors to feel like kings flitting around their castle.

It was a silly notion and I dismissed it at once, brought upon by the silly unreality of my being here.

My mind was wandering—on an eye-goggling journey through a place of dense silence and mystery.

I came to another blue-lit air lock and pushed my way through. I nearly stumbled over a diamond-shaped power box at its base. I was running on fumes, feeling light-headed. Maybe the effects of this weird ship?—no, more likely just simple exhaustion. When had I last eaten? How much more could my battered body take?

Just a little farther, Rusco—the scutzers'll never find the beacon where you're going. What's a little jaunt on an alien ship anyway?

I buzzed Marty over our private channel. No response. Where the hell was he? Was he still trying to bust me out of here? They had no idea where the hell I was. How could they bust me out? I didn't want to communicate over the general channel, what with Sharki and the others so close. Why give that bastard any clues as to my location?

Guess you're going solo, Rusco. Hop to it.

CHAPTER 44

Just beyond the third air lock, I paused to examine a disturbing shape in the middle of the corridor: the desiccated hump of what might have been one of the crew members. More humps appeared up ahead and I did not pause to examine them too closely. Although such forms were unrecognizable, I thought to recognize, thanks to Newt's testimonial, the blackened carapaces of insect-like creatures and the curled hook of sharp pincers or claws.

We left the corpses behind.

Off the wide, gloomy corridor, I passed a darkened chamber on whose walls I glimpsed metal brackets and manacles. I saw shelves teetering, stacked with curious conical-shaped receptacles or jars that may have contained the withered organs of some unfortunate creatures. Most disturbing of all were the panels of circuitry clinging to the walls—boxes and nodes intermittently poised between the manacles. These could only be designed for some sinister purpose.

I shivered. The sight brought a dryness to my mouth and I stumbled quickly on, wondering how much farther I must go before I planted my cargo and quit this creepy ship.

"Jet Rusco, the technology of this ship—it is singular, beyond anything of known record. We must halt and regroup, figure a way—"

"Sh, Newt. Silence is golden."

I fingered the beacon in my pouch, contemplating again the rabbit hole I had plunged myself down.

I looked back at the dwindling blue light of the last air lock I'd passed, wondering how many more would bring us to new sections of the ship, like segments of a giant centipede.

More humps dotted the floor—the droppings of which looked like those of a wild animal. My wrist monitor flashed. Odd, it was registering some thin atmosphere down in this sector. Barely breathable, but still some oxygen nonetheless.

Jeez. Maybe I should take off my helmet, test it out?

I shook my head, realizing I was hallucinating.

I came at last to an impasse and halted, my breath coming in shallow gasps. To the left, which I assumed was toward the outer wall of the ring, I saw a U-shaped portal open onto a sizable chamber. A faint green glow. More cryptic, inverted L's and dots of i's were imprinted to the side.

I felt the crunch of rubble under my boots. I stopped short again and shone my light in.

A trail of debris led from where I stood to the nearest slightly concave wall. Glass? Before me lay what looked like tempered glass, or the broken shards of some hard brittle material—like the remnants of some large tank. A long flexible black cable ran from its base, about an inch in diameter in a snaking coil for many yards to a nondescript lump—another of the withered husks of an alien skeleton that lay disintegrated. This was definitely insectoid. About four feet long with a curious oversize skull, like a grasshopper out of a nightmare. A heavy mandible jutted out unnaturally from the head. Quasi-human? Pincers for fore limbs? Though the creature looked as if it might have stood upright on its hind feet from which depended claws.

I tried to picture such an animal walking with skin or carapace or organs enclosed, and how it might move around, but could not quite manage it.

Deeper within, five telephone booth-sized tanks were arranged along the points of a wide pentagon. The tanks were at least 4 feet wide by 9 feet tall. They all had open circular tops. Another larger tank stood two feet taller and wider in the center of the five around the pentagon. This one brought an eerie shiver to my spine. I did not know what these tanks were, but two on the outer rim of the pentagon were smashed. Their desiccated contents lay partially disintegrated and sprawled on the metal grate floor. What those black humps could have been at one time I did not know. Only conjured up in the depths of some madman's vividest nightmare, I guessed.

A luminous green glow exuded from the liquid that filled the intact tanks to the brim, as if the waters themselves were somehow phosphorescent. They bathed the chamber in a preternatural radiance…and revealed in greater clarity, the macabre contents of those tanks before my eyes.

Something had gone very wrong on this ship.

The centermost tank was the one that held my gaze the longest. It contained a bone-chilling occupant: a squid-like life form—perhaps a cephalopod, but was not. Six tentacles hung suspended at its sides, submerged but floating in the green-glowing brine. The pocked suckers at their ends showed gray-mottled orifices.

The oddest thing was the plant wrapped around the squid's middle—fused and entwined with the tentacles, almost as if in some obscene embrace.

The plant resembled an aloe vera hybrid. But it looked alive— with sprawling, pale-violet stalk-like fronds that grew out in a fan, drooping of leaves with occasional orange-white blossoms.

The discovery left me speechless; or better put, shivering in revulsion. For a long time I stared and the moments passed as if I were peering in a dream through a looking glass.

Yes, something had gone terribly wrong on this ship.

The other intact tanks contained weird alien life forms too— some squid, some hominid, some jammed with multiple hybrids of each. What was this obscene menagerie? Did the guardians of the ship keep some museum aboard for their personal amusement? As ornamentation?

No, there were black tubes linked from base to base; some tubes arched down into the floor even. Evidence suggesting there was some practical use for these vessels. Maybe a water purification system? Some kind of experimental apparatus or life support system?

No, Rusco. These are all nonsensical surmises.

But the more I thought about it, the more confused I became. A primordial fear began to envelope me, along with the familiar clench of stomach…as grips the forest animal that crosses the path of some menace or incongruous sight it has never before encountered or wishes to encounter again.

I sensed a flutter of movement to my left. I ducked back as suited figures entered the chamber from the place I had come.

I scuttled deeper into the pentagon, dipped behind the base of the tank farthest away lying smashed in the shadows.

I gripped my blaster and aimed it out with a shaky fist.

Carefully, very carefully, I reached in my pouch and withdrew my beacon. I planted it at the base of the shattered tank flush to the floor should I have no other opportunity. I activated it and saw the tiny white light flicker on its side. I could not help but notice the sprawl of strange electronics containing solenoid crystal and capacitor-like components long spilled out from the ruined metal.

I tore my gaze back to the newcomers and I peeked behind my shadowy tank.

Six figures advanced in dark suits. They plodded with slow purpose and stood stone-faced before the menagerie. The leader was tiny compared to those hulking brutes behind him: brutish shapes which I instantly recognized as Skurgs. My heart skipped a beat in the hollow of my chest, plummeting me to new lows. The Skurgs all carried goads. Not surprising. All dressed in peculiar, metallic-blue suits. The leader, who appeared to be a human, seemed sure enough of his bodyguard that he stepped forward without a weapon. Everything about this scenario felt spooky and wrong.

I blinked in new dismay. Newt, who had not cowered at my side as expected, floated out past the pentagon and hovered in the path of the intruders.

What the hell was he doing?

"Newt!" I called out hoarsely through the private channel. "Get your ass back here. Are you insane?"

He mulishly held his ground. *"No, Jet Rusco, there is a moral issue at stake here and I will not stand for it."* He floated over to face the intruders, his lights blinking angrily on his outerbody.

I stared bug-eyed.

The group of six figures halted. The five Skurgs lifted their goads.

Newt addressed them in belligerent tones, *"Sirs! I must instantly object. This is not your claim. It's an intrusion highly irregular. The APC will hear about this when—"*

The Skurg closest to him swung out his goad. The glowing tip connected with metal and Newt fell in a hissing, smoking heap.

I peered on in dismay. Newt lay cracked in two, electrical arcs zinging from one half to the other. Smoke poured out from his innards.

I bit my lip. End of Eye of Newt.

You knew what was coming, didn't you, little one?

I heard a voice speak over the general frequency, "I had to see it with my own eyes to be certain, Sroek." It was a voice I recognized. The lips of the leader moved in synchrony with the words. He walked slack-jawed into the strange pentagon and moved to within a few feet of the centermost tank. He traced a gloved finger slowly across its surface—outlining the cephalopod's quasi face. Then he gazed from pale gray eyes with as much awe as I had.

"Quickly! We must take this specimen, Sroek. It deserves further study." He patted at his conical space helmet. From the hesitant expression on his Skurg bodyguard's face, the statement needed to be qualified. "Yes, we may damage some of the linkage the creature may have with this extraordinary ship, but the risk is worth it. A unique treasure like this cannot go wasted in this gloomy tomb any longer."

The Skurg lifted a goad with jerky reluctance.

The small man flapped a brisk hand. He spoke with an imperial harshness through the com, "Make the arrangements, Sroek. Now!"

The Skurg bowed. He pulled out an octagonal communicator from his pouch and tapped the luminous screen.

I stared with renewed awe as the team of Skurgs poked and prodded at the macabre tank, took measurements, sensory readings while the resentment and discomfit of the bizarre creature suspended in the brine grew. It had begun to twitch, as if miraculously alive.

I took a quick glance to the side, shuddered at the green-glowing tank next to me, not 7 yards away. Three squid-like horrors were jammed in the brine-like waters, glaring back at me with gimlet blue-black eyes. They were baleful, black-skinned creatures with rubbery tentacles intertwined. Each harbored a deformed melon-like head. I tore my gaze back to the newcomers.

The diminutive figure of the leader suddenly spun on the obeisant Skurg. "You say you tracked the scutzer's beacon to here?"

The Skurg nodded. He must have learned the human language somewhere.

The leader pinched his lips in a frown. "Then good. Jet Rusco," he called out, "I know you are in here…Come out wherever you are. Let us talk. No harm will come to you…"

I cringed as my eyes took in the smoking remains of Newt.

On a certain hunch the man began a wide circle of the room. He halted and beamed as his pale, slate-chill eyes caught sight of an unconcealed patch of my suit. "No need to play hide and seek. Come out, Jet Rusco."

"Back off!" I sent a streak of ion fire at his feet.

The man moved back and held up his hands. "Come now, it is only prudent that we—"

"I said, back the fuck off! I'll stay where I am."

"Very well. Have it your way. Must we parley here like outlaws at a distance with weapons at hand?"

I held my blaster firm. "In your universe, maybe." I crouched behind the metal base and felt naked with only three to four feet of shattered metal and glass to protect me. I tipped the barrel around the rim of rough metal. I had enough mass to cover me should those Skurgs try to storm me all at once. They would only get buckets of ion fire. But I too would be pulled down and killed. No other options remained. I was deep in the chamber. There were no other exits or entrances but the one by which I'd entered.

This little man, his Skurg enforcers and I were at an impasse.

The leader spoke, "I must thank you for blasting that hole in the Ring Station. It saved us some time entering this museum."

I waved the tip of my blaster at the five hulking brutes. "You like having an entourage of cannibals with you?"

"They are priests of the Order."

"Like I'm the overlord of Jupiter."

"You have a sharp-edged tongue, Jet Rusco. I would have thought you'd be pleased to see me."

"Why's that?"

"For presenting myself as an ally. You have many powerful enemies on your tail. No good can come of it. It is not a game that ends well, I can assure you. I can protect you from all that."

I snorted. "How are you going to do that, Mr. Prime Ascendant?" Yes, it was Dy-ar, there was no doubt about. Very bold of the bastard to come down here with only a handful of Skurgs. But then, he was Prime Ascendant, he who could walk on water, if he so wished.

"Very easily I can do so. You still have no inkling of the power I wield—the power of our order."

"I do, but I just don't go in for playing the sycophant. Or grovelling at the feet of power mongers and demons."

He gave a humorless little laugh. "You begin to understand something of us, and yet you still know nothing. The Devil, Satan, the wars of the iconic Good vs Evil... It is all noise of the ignorant, and old school rhetoric. We have transcended those barriers and labels long ago. And yet to you, this all appears as some holy war."

"I have no idea what the hell you are talking about."

"Of course you don't. Case in point." He gave a sad smile. He toed one of the dry dark remains. "Where did the bodies of the crew go? I assume these desiccated lumps and those scattered about the corridors must be the remains of the crew. Were they these very same gruesome cephalopods we see in the tanks? No, I don't think so. They bear little resemblance. But then my eye for aliens is not the best."

"Get on with it, Dy-ar. What's your angle here?" I prodded my blaster out at them, daring them to try something impulsive, knowing that many would die. For now, Dy-ar did not seem keen on such a rash move.

"Ah, yes. It is a bad habit of mine—musing idly and sharing my thoughts with those who lack the interest. You don't know how lonely it is being Prime Ascendant."

I gave him a cynical look.

He peered at his minion Sroek as I snatched a glance at the helpless creature in the tank. "What will you do with it?" I demanded. "Where will it go?"

"To science. For curiosity."

"Who else will see it?"

"No one will see it," he replied tersely.

"So, you will sell it?"

He shrugged, seemingly non-committal. "If we must. Why do you care so much about the creature?"

"Because you cannot just go and—"

He lifted a gloved hand and through his faceplate his eyes gleamed with intense fervor. "Say what you must say quickly, Jet Rusco. Perhaps there is a brain behind that skull of yours?"

"Meaning?"

"You were given a chance—the one my uncle gave you, but you squandered it. You desire to know the secrets of the universe. But you cannot have them. Not without paying the dues. You must pay the membership fee to access such networks. I control that network. You do not advance without me. And here we are again. The wheel comes full circle."

I could not help but shudder, for I had heard such words before. Uttered by an older man, Gy-ar, Dy-ar's forebear. I'd tried to shut out those voices from my head. This scion of long dead Gy-ar had triggered the worst of my nightmares.

I could see the family resemblance now—the moony face, the cold, facetious, but treacherous eyes, the sag of chin and jowl. Such things as his diminutive stature were only superficial impositions and did not highlight the threat.

This scion was different. Where Gy-ar, his uncle, had been more direct, methodical, perhaps wiser, I sensed this younger successor to be more impulsive, devious, impetuous of mood. A dangerous figure to deal with in this stark, horror-filled chamber.

I peered sideways at the U-shaped metal contraption standing by the wall. What was it? It was like something out of a space-horror holo-flick. It stood waist high, some portal to nowhere. Not like the air locks and the blue-lit bands. There was no blue glow here, but it exuded a menace which chilled my blood.

While the five Skurgs stood immobile, goads crossed at their chests like ancient mummies, Dy-ar wandered back to the central tank and passed a strange star-shaped device over the glass surface. He nodded and muttered something unintelligible. "There is much mystery here that needs be investigated. The light drive system of this ship—the tanks with their curious occupants—" He cocked his head as if in wonder and decision. "No, these are not for the eyes of the common man."

"Who are you to decide?"

He gazed at me through heavy lidded eyes. There was the faintest hint of superiority in the jutting jaw and the patronizing air of loose fatty jowls. He had a soft, effeminate look and mannerisms. Perhaps it ran in the family.

He shrugged. A look of sly condescension crimped his lips. It was that dry smugness that made my blood seethe—the ultimate knowledge that nobody could do anything to thwart him—an arrogance mixed with false pride and benevolence.

"We cannot have the unwitting masses of humanity that are sprawled across the worlds glimpsing such horrors or such mysteries, Jet Rusco. It would upset the fabric of order, send a warp cascading through the brains of lesser intellects."

"You mean, 'keep the knowledge to yourself'."

He shook his head wearily. "96% of the humans colonizing the galaxy still to this day believe dinosaurs inhabited the Earth. Can you believe it? Fake fossils, bones, stories, grandiose names, scientists and shill paleontologists spewing ridiculous theories. We seeded that lie. You see, we have to give the masses a mythology. The new god was scientism and dinos helped us make the shift. As will we create a mythology out of this ship—but one much modified from the reality. We can't have people getting glimpses of the deeper, darker origins of the cosmos…of worlds like this—" he spread his arms and took in the rich scene and its pall of grotesque horror.

"You mean it throws a monkey wrench in your tentacles of power?"

He deigned no comment.

I went on. "You mean to use this ship—" I waved the end of my blaster at the tank "—whatever this is—to advance your agendas."

A grin quirked his jaw. "You have a devious mind. Are you sure you are not one of us?"

"That borders on an insult."

He scowled. "Enough. We can spar here forever, trading glib jests and pet peeves, but there are things to be done."

He swiveled his head to a movement from back in the corridor. I squinted past him in the eerie light where I saw moving shadows, figures advancing.

CHAPTER 45

There were four of them. Approaching in gray suits with blasters held at the ready.

The figure at the head halted and gave a twisted grin. I could see the glint of eyes through the ruins of a charred face. "Well, looks like we hit the mother lode, boys." The jaunty voice reached through the air-waves like a club.

He squinted and saw me crouched behind the shattered tank. "Ah, there you are, Rusco. On the run again? I see you got some new friends." He waved his blaster at Dy-ar as he moved in with his three thuggish henchmen.

Dy-ar skipped aside. His Skurgs fanned out around him with their green-glowing goads. They followed his movements to a T, as if offering seamless protection.

The maneuver seemed to amuse Sharki. "So you're this Dy-ar bitch?" he huffed. "The lizard from the temple?"

He did not reply.

"Saw you skulking around the creepy corridors with your Skurgy buddies not long ago. Must have beat us to the party." His eyes took in the panorama with a contempt bordering on amusement. He gave a catcall of a whistle. "Well, I'll be damned. A circus exhibit. Never been a religious man, Your Highness, but this is something to make a man start going to church."

"Damn you insolent, heretical—"

"Russy, you sly dog." Sharki lifted his barrel, opened his mouth in a half yawn. "You sure know how to find them. I'd planned to nip in, nip out, just plant my beacon then skedaddle. But it got so damn interesting down here I thought to stay a little while. And look what I find—a little Barnum and Bailey spectacle.

"You know what brought this on?" he continued with a jeer. "I take one look at that Ring Station, a ripe old alien ship, all polished, spic and span and vulnerable out in space, and then I says to myself, 'Hell, if that bastard Iron can lay claim to such a beast, why not old Sharki? To hell with the Hierarch of the Moon Goblins. What are these fucks to me?'"

"Enough of this blasphemy!" Dy-ar bellowed.

"Blasphemy, friend? We're just getting started here. Now get yourselves over by that wall, lest some bad things happen. Me and my hound dogs ain't afraid of a few green-tipped little cattle goads." He twirled his barrel. The lead Skurg tensed. "Unh-Uh, Skurgy pie. Lest you and your dog-wipes are planning on having a terrible time eating caramel pudding with your bellies torn out."

The coldest of grins surfaced on Dy-ar's thin lips. "I see why you and Jet Rusco are a pair. Put together in the *weave* to bring this little pantomime to its lively conclusion. You both have—the same lip, the same reckless impulsiveness and disrespect for authority and the marvel and majesty of—"

"Weave? Marvel? You're speaking gibberish, priest-man. You're a little bantam rooster bobbing about on too much Myscol."

"He's talking," I intoned angrily, "about the *weave* which gave you that stump, Sharki…the same force which made you come back for your brother all those years ago in the mines."

Sharki spat out a curse. "Don't be talking about him or trying to mess with my head. Or you'll be eating my barrel."

Dy-ar moved a step away to snatch for something at his side but Sharki pegged off a shot. The Skurg minion at Dy-ar's side hopped in front and absorbed the blast on his blue-metal chest.

Sharki shuffled back and clipped off another shot. It bounced harmlessly off the Skurg's chest to similar effect. "What the—"

Dy-ar waved a small, reproachful finger. "And you thought I was defenseless."

Sharki hesitated. It seemed he'd not thought of the Skurgs wearing weird, blaster-proof body armor.

Dy-ar, wearing a confident grin at having rattled Sharki, moved his entourage five steps closer to the main tank. "What do I care about a pack of petty little gangsters like you and their feuds? One transcall and my network'll have you all tucking tails between legs, whimpering like curs. The only reason we allow you the latitude of freedom we do, is because you further accomplish our goals. Fomenting chaos out of order. While we bring order out of the chaos. But all this is irrelevant to the matter at hand." He turned his brooding gaze back to me and flashed me a patronizing smile.

He studied the tank and wiped the glass with loving care. "It seems these receptacles, or whatever they are, were built to hold specimens. But I wonder, is there more to it than that? What do you think, gangster Sharki? Jet Rusco concurs that they are singular, and should be preserved, but is at odds with me that they must be protected from human eyes." He stared now with a faraway look at the purple fronds and sucker pods and twined tentacles. "This hybrid creature, for example—it seems manufactured, almost engineered, as if for some insidious purpose. Such a peculiar specimen! Half plant and animal, as if both were not good enough as they were. Some symbiotic parasite. The thing half grows, half gestates like a rock crystal in a chemical solution. And here, so close to the power source of the ship? It doesn't make sense. Do these aliens enjoy having floating museums in their ships' engineering rooms and labs? What would happen if we just upended another creature into the mix?"

On his quick signal, Sroek, the lead Skurg, lanced his goad and its green tip struck Sharki square in the faceplate. Sharki's glass shattered. He spun, trying to get off a shot.

Another Skurg grabbed his arms as he was spinning and with superhuman strength, hurled him up and over into the big tank.

Plop. Splash. Sharki thrashed about the pale liquid, gurgling, desperately trying to clamber out of that noisome water.

But there came a strange whipping and writhing within the tank as tentacles and petal leaves wrapped about the struggling figure. He was pulled under and his yells were stifled as bubbles floated from his lips.

Sharki's henchmen keeled back in horror. They loosed fire. Two died on the spot as Skurgs swept goads at them like quarterstaffs. Only one of the thugs escaped, staggering back into the corridor.

Sharki kicked and struggled in vain. The greenish water entered his cracked helmet and the eerie water flooded his suit. His mouth gaped wide, eyes starting from his head. He gazed glassily back at us as would a bewildered frog being slowly boiled. He drowned swiftly, jerking once, twice, then floated upright like a trussed corpse whose legs had been weighted by iron. His boots floated two feet off the bottom of the tank.

His eyes blinked once, as if he had come back to life, though his movements of neck and hand were slower and less jerky.

I could not witness such an obscenity and turned away.

But before I did, I caught a flutter of movement as the plant unfurled its pale violet fronds and twined them round Sharki's face. The fronds moved caressingly…they unwound slightly from the squid and entwined its new occupant, some fronds working to peel off Sharki's suit.

The ship gave a sudden brief lurch.

I peered around in bewilderment.

The tremor receded as quickly as it had come.

Dy-ar, disconcerted by the inexplicable joggle himself, stepped closer to the tank. He did his best to extend an amiable grin. "Mr. Sharki, it appears as if things are not as cozy as they were before. Are you having a little trouble breathing? Since you are effectively dead…and to quote your own words regarding your rival general—I do believe I am the owner of the Bratts and the Reapers now, which means Jet Rusco's claim is mine. This has all worked out quite splendidly. I am pleased and amazed at how ironic the spin of the *weave* plays itself out."

I watched Sharki's one-armed body slowly rotate. Only to sink inch by inch in the pale green fluid. His mouth gaped. Fluid moved within and a tiny bubble popped out. Horror gripped me as his lips parted in a grouper-like grimace, his moony eyes unblinking.

In helpless frustration I gripped my R1. Part of me wanted to open fire on that tank, blast it to shreds, put Sharki out of his misery, but the other, just to let him sit there in the throes of his cosmic destiny, in that drowning posture in an alien tank aboard an alien vessel.

Dy-ar paused to study the bobbing figure nestled in the grip of the squid-like tentacles for several moments. "I begin to see why the masters of the ships created these odd receptacles. It forms an amusing backdrop to what otherwise would have been dull hours in space, wouldn't you agree, Jet Rusco?"

"Go fuck yourself, you sick bastard."

"No, no, I am not sick, merely amused." He threw his head back and gave a high-pitched laugh like a whinnying horse. "And to think, it was the explosion of a semi-important refinery on the edge of this remote star system that alerted me to the likes of you. It attracted the attention of our prestigious organization. When I investigated further, I tracked the events and questioned the survivors of Thetis, those who had witnessed the blast, unbeknownst to Sharki. When I discovered the nature and identity of the instigators, namely you, Jet Rusco, I knew it was time to resume our cosmic chase. For many years you had eluded us. Knowing my uncle's obsession with you— his wrath after you desecrated our Moon Temple on Riga—I took up his mission to pursue you to the ends of the universe. And in return, I have this fabulous ship and its wonders." He lifted an arm in dramatic triumph.

The *weave* had been working all this time, getting me to a place of deeper understanding of the power structure that ran this universe. I felt silent gears working in my brain, cogs turning as doors and pathways of understanding opened while others closed.

Sure, I'd known of secret societies, cults and networks running in the background of worlds far and wide of whose existence we generally had no clue about. But that these people had such massive, pervasive control over the worlds for so long…? It dismayed me.

They were lowlifes, these lizards, all of them: Gy-ar, Dy-ar, his progeny and forebears and all those to come. Gy-ar had demonstrated that adequately enough. Creating ironic inversions, like peace before war, gifts to the masses before sacrifice, false pledges of transparency with aim to muddle the minds of the masses. To fake enough narratives and create enough cognitive dissonance to gull them into buying into their poisonous agendas. While at the same time giving cryptic warning to the ones who might be semi alert to the reality. To the tune of some twisted 'code of honor' or unwritten rule of transparency. What bullshit! A joke, of course—inscrutable and chilling—to increase the level of obscurity of their shadowy organization.

Even Dy-ar's coming down here with such a small force and arriving on such a small spaceboat was another inversion.

Those in power, or those who appeared to be in power, were not really the ones in power. It was all a show, to obscure the real overlords. Like smoke in the mirror, gray mist rising from the lake, or the stone god rising from the machine—it was all a trick by an invisible magician. Whenever we thought we had pinpointed the head of the snake, there were always others who ruled realms far vaster, lying in the shadows, ready to snap off the necks of those who would expose them.

"I see you pondering there, Jet Rusco. Tell me what is on your mind. I too have something of the *weave* in me, or I would not be in the position I am. I can see by the look on your face—the anger, the bewilderment—that you wonder how we can manage all this, get people to comply with our wishes and accept our programs."

I made no effort to respond, just blew out a disgusted breath.

He echoed my own weariness. "Unlimited wealth creates unlimited reach, even if it is light years away. As easy as stealing candy from a baby. Only the highest up the food chain need be subverted. The ones below follow the orders of the ones above. To bribe, to corrupt, to coax the higher-ups to do one's bidding, to send them in the right direction—it is a skill and an art. When bribery fails, throw some pleasurable flesh at them, see how they jump and conform. Slap 'em with women, men, young boys, young girls, it does not matter. When we catch them with their pants down, we give them the fireside chat, show them the damning video then give them the terms. They'll do anything we tell them. And when that fails, nothing beats the good old jack-boot."

"You're a bunch of parasites, Dy-ar. Like your twisted uncle and the rest of your cultish brood."

He pursed his lips and pretended to overlook the slur. "That is a harsh summation."

"You're all a bunch of scumbuckets, liars and stagers."

He sighed. "Stagers, yes. Like this ship will be a stage that will ensure many decades of people running down the rabbit hole."

"Like you've done for centuries. As far back as the perfidious NASA and the CIA?"

"Ah, you mean the Mars rovers, the endless missions, Jupiter landings and miles of fake scripts and footage of planets and asteroids and whatever else we fed the masses for so many years? Yes, Jet Rusco. But this pastiche of the Ring Station will trump all."

I croaked out a laugh. Slapper would have loved to hear that. "The CIA then—"

"Nothing but banker-bought gangsters. Agents of fraud, deception and domestic terror. Working in our employ, of course, like all the other agents from the various intelligence agencies around Old Earth. Who would have guessed that they all worked for us?"

"You did not call yourself the Moon Temple then."

"We have operated under many names over the years. Is it not obvious?"

I ground my teeth in helpless frustration. As I sank into a pit of despair, a warmth suffused my solar plexus then moved upwards. Then it hit me, the significance of this time and place, these tanks and the derelict ship. The stir of the *weave* moved in my body once more—and it frightened me. There was a flaw in their modus operandi. A force ruled this universe that could not be controlled. It was beyond their reach, their agendas, beyond everything. They so wanted to control everything, but they could not; it was only the most superficial layers of the material universe that were within their grasp. The *weave* was far stronger, much more powerful than they were. It was that which could not be controlled.

I saw all this in a flash, and as I blinked, I caught my breath and smiled and nearly laughed out loud.

For thousands of years these manipulators had always planned, always schemed behind the scenes but hid in plain sight. But where could they go from here? Conjuring up ever more elaborate schemes to control the worlds? More advanced forms of deception? Amassing mountains more wealth, more influence, more dominance, infiltrating every organization and faction that stood in their path? But there would always be a cap, like the speed of a silicon computer, or the amount of yols one could amass, the influence of kingpins and agents, the amounts of joy that could be extracted from food or pleasurable objects. Only so much joy could be experienced from eating two dozen slices of chocolate cake.

They had reached their cap. They had seduced nature and humankind and fomented chaos. But chaos had come to them. They had come to cannibalize the Ring Station. When I felt that next tremor in the hull in sync with the twitching movements of Sharki in his brine, I knew that the Ring Station had stepped up to foil them. As had Gy-ar been foiled in the past before him.

A sinister rumble shook the hull as the workings of some unguessable technology came to life.

A heavy shudder ran up my back. I looked over at the haunted figure of Sharki entwined with the horrific squid tentacles and the invasive aloe vera fronds. There was a greenish tinge to his complexion. Dy-ar saw it too.

He turned to me and rasped in a voice lacking all cordiality, "So, Jet Rusco...I will ask you once again, as did my uncle. Will you join us, or die?"

I hissed through my teeth. "I will never join you. I will burn in hell first."

He nodded. "So be it." He lifted a swift finger and the Skurgs sprang at me from all sides.

CHAPTER 46

I loosed fire into their bulky torsos, slowing them down. The lead Skurg, Sroek, vaulted to the side. He shrieked some sounds at his henchmen, then clasped Dy-ar on the shoulder.

"What is it?" The Prime Ascendant shrugged off the bearish grip. The others had halted in midstep.

The Skurg motioned cryptically to his helmet.

Dy-ar's eyes blinked. He put a hand to his helmet then fussed with his wrist monitor, frowning in concentration as he listened to some private communication from across the gulfs.

"Fools!" he cried. His fingers knotted and he spoke shrilly over the com. "Go home, scutzers! Your generals are dead. Sharki is with me now, staring out from a glass tank. I am your master now by rights. Go home!"

More transmissions were exchanged. Dy-ar's lips pinched and his teeth glinted. "Do not enter the Ring Station! Do not fire on her hull!"

I jabbed at my wrist monitor and scrolled through the various options to navigate to the vid feed. I caught a glimpse of the view from space from *Trident* which was back online.

The scutzers, furious and feeling betrayed, swooped and dove down upon the ring ship, heedless of the Skurg warships targeting them. It seemed they had decided that if they could not have the precious treasure of the Ring Station, then nobody would.

In a forced union, they had all banded as one and swarmed the massive hull, taking pot shots and destroying radio towers, communication antennae, ripping into the station's shield-less mass.

I could feel the tiny impacts even under the feet-thick sheets of metal.

"Fools!" Dy-ar bellowed. "They will destroy the greatest artifact ever discovered in history." He radioed up to his forces. "Damocles L19 Destroyer! Are you online?"

"We are, sir. Armed and ready. Give us the word."

"You may take the appropriate action. Destroy any who resist!"

"Roger."

I darted eyes around my dismal surroundings. This was turning into a perilous situation. Images of doom and blood filled my mind. I could see no way out of it or how to gain leverage.

I called out to Dy-ar in an attempt to gain time. "More of your friends?"

"The destroyers are ours. Friendly to our needs. Damocles has been ever faithful to our cause. Crestar, Dancor...they have come around more slowly." He flicked a careless hand and I saw through the vid feed the formidable battleships blasting their way through roids and any ships in their way as they rounded on the Ring Station. "Our agents control them now. All the major companies in this star system to be precise. Every one on the settled worlds in the galaxy. We have for a long time. As on Earth, before the space age, before the industrial revolution. But I suppose my uncle Gy-ar has told you something of this already."

He had. Plain and simple. The arrogant cockroaches that they were, fingers in every pie, had bought up everything. They who showed up at the most opportune times to wreak havoc and take anything and everything that they wanted. *"It is in our power to destroy empires as easily as we create them..."* I remembered Gy-ar's smug words from long ago. When would the galaxy ever be rid of these parasites? Not until people became aware of their pernicious influence and stopped listening to their lies and being victims of their agendas.

Dy-ar turned to his Skurg priests with vengeance. "Deal with this pest! He is starting to become an annoying gnat. Show no mercy."

As one, the five swept out like greased eels.

I lunged out from behind my base as they flew at me. I ducked the first swipe of goad which would have shorted out my helmet. I plugged fire into the first Skurg, but it did little against his invulnerable shielding. Far off to my right a stocky figure came bounding from the direction of the hallway.

Marty!

A stream of blaster fire came raining into the pentagon ring.

I dove sideways. Just as the irritating Skurg was pummeled back by bright arcing R1 fire ripping across his protected middle.

I wrenched the goad from his huge gloves and jammed the end into his face. Something fried. He clutched at his helmet, his pug face twisting, lips peeled back in agony. I crouch-crawled over to Marty.

"Where's Deidra?" I hissed at him.

He looked back toward the shadows of the hallway. "She was here a moment ago." He flicked a finger on his wrist monitor, tried to contact her. "Deidra, Deidra!" Nothing.

"You left Slapper up there in the ship?" I said incredulously.

"You have to understand, Rusco, she wouldn't listen. She was like a crazed panther. She had to come down here with me."

I grimaced all too knowingly. Deidra was a stubborn, driven force of nature. "So where—" No time to trade stories. Skurgs had flanked us. They were charging us like gleers.

We were hemmed within the pentagon of tanks, cut off from the escape corridor. Four goad-wielding masses of muscle came bearing down on us.

Marty and I stood back to back, raining fire at them. Marty plugged shots, knees bent, yelling like a banshee. Three of them broke through the screen and were on us. I felt the electrical sting of the first goad arcing through my suit.

Bastard! I nearly doubled over in agony as he chopped at my neck.

Bright blaster fire sprayed suddenly from behind the wall of Skurgs. I caught a glimpse of a familiar slim figure standing behind them, R1 leveled. She was raining fire at their backs. They whirled as a team, confused by the new menace.

Deidra!

She came toward us on a crouching run, pelting them with hellish fury.

I could have cried out for joy.

But I saw one of the tanks had smashed under the hail of her blaster fire. Now a thin pool was seeping toward my boots.

I jerked my attention back to Deidra. Another sinister figure was sidling behind her like a carnal animal.

"Behind you!" I yelled.

She whirled, trained her R1 on the approaching figure. She gazed with sudden wonder and contempt. "Don't think so, Sister," she rasped. "Back the fuck off!"

Sister? What the hell was she talking about—?

I saw the expression on the intruder's face as she glanced at Deidra curiously sidelong, as one would regard a dumb animal.

I didn't register the connection immediately, or the improbability of the situation. My cry of warning came too late. "Get the fuck away from her, Deidra!"

The figure did some fantastic leap, grappled Deidra, smacked her weapon aside. There came a snap of neck. Deidra fell like a sack of meal.

That instant was frozen in my brain. I saw the striking face curling into a satisfied grin, the long olive features, the slanting eyes, the tanned skin, all through the faceplate too late—no doubt about it—

The girl from the karaoke bar. The one back on Tylas…

No! The words screamed in my mind.

I swung my blaster up in a single motion and let loose, caught the bitch square in the face, blew off her faceplate and helmet. She fell skidding backwards, clutching at her throat.

Dy-ar stared in shocked silence as the figure twitched then died, suffocating in the airless chamber. He grimaced with outrage then disappointment. He started forward, gave a brisk signal to his Skurgs and they scurried along with him, formed a wall between me and

Deidra.

He strode over to his felled agent behind the protection of his Skurg, Sroek. He sighed with something of a singsong quality. "Ah, Kara, you served me well in this lifetime. It is only fitting, I suppose—your girl for mine, eh Jet Rusco? Even in death she is beautiful, wouldn't you agree?"

"She is charming," I said in a half choked sob. I glared through blurred tears at Deidra's slumped form. "You people have a fucking fetish for hiring beguiling young agents to do your dirty work, don't you?"

Dy-ar waved a perfunctory hand. "It is a tradition, if not a certain weakness among our officials."

I turned to another deadly movement. To my left the tank nearest had burst and a weird creature had crawled free. A squid-like alien that sprang up from the slimy greenish brine pooling on the floor and whipped out its six flexible tentacles. They wrapped about the nearest Skurg and there came a popping of joints, a whipping of muscly flesh, a horrible gurgle of agony and a cracking of bone, as bulk and suit were all crushed to pulp.

I drew back, appalled. The barrel of my R1 sighted on the thing as Dy-ar leaped out of its grip. A startled gleam jiggered in his pale eyes and a crazy look twisted his moonlike face.

The thing had dropped its loose bundle of flesh. Slowly it advanced on flexible hind legs, but were not. Maybe they were extensions of those loathsome tentacles. The other Skurgs shied away. They jabbed at it with goads while it crabbed back, uttering an inhuman screech, its black, sinewy, brine-glistening hide smoking. But it was not yet dead.

"Enough of this foolishness!" Dy-ar barked. Spittle flew from his lips. He sprang aside, rodent-like. "I want that specimen preserved! You hear me, preserved! It must be saved, you fools!"

But there would be no saving anybody or anything in that hell crib.

CHAPTER 47

I turned to blast that devil Dy-ar but he'd already scuttled aside like a mouse, hiding behind the protective armor of his momma Skurg.

Two of them lumbered at me. I felt the goad whirling toward my face, but I chopped it in half with quick blasts before it struck off my helm. Both mine and Marty's blaster fire careened recklessly about the pentagon of tanks, glanced off a Skurg's body armor and slammed into the nearest tank. The glass shattered, releasing more pale greenish brine in a gush of foul foamy steam. Two creatures followed with it. The larger, a cephalopod, was closest to me. Its rubbery body twitched and jerked out a slimy tentacle, whipping around my ankle. I fell, crabbing sideways, trying feverishly to get my barrel up. Another latched onto my waist. In an effort to save my life, I flung it off and blasted it with prejudice. It slapped on the floor, severed in two. Another tentacle reached for Marty. It pulled him into its rubbery body. A hail of blaster fire from my barrel sent the monster into a hundred, fleshy, rubbery parts.

Stray fire smashed into the last tank on the pentagon. A host of squid-like creatures were now squirming and twitching on the plated floor, unleashed from their loathsome captivity. Perhaps they remembered their age-old hatred of confinement. Smoke rose from the brine in greasy clouds. My blaster rays and Skurg green-glowing goads seared through it like sheet lightning, coating the air with a resinous, greasy smog. The squids were rendered in more nightmarish poise as they rose on their tentacle limbs and bounded toward us with a peculiar locomotive gait. It was disturbing to the eye and I could only think of the speed by which such creatures could purchase ground on those offensive members. An appalling and soul-disturbing sight.

I had to leap sideways to escape through the gap between a pair of Skurgs. The nearest whipped his goad at me and parried the barrel of my R1, sending my shot wide, but I twisted and smacked head first into his hip and sent him staggering back into the wide, gaping arms of the U-shaped device by the wall. There came a zap and a fierce yelp of electricity as the hulking shape shimmered from the world forever.

What the fuck? The Skurg'd just vanished, suit and all, as if he'd never been. Vaporized, as if snatched by a giant hand and teleported somewhere unimaginable.

I low-crawled over to Marty, gasping for breath. "We need to get the fuck out of here!"

He gave a jerky nod. Sweat sheened his cheeks. His eyes darted crazily about, still in shock from his near encounter with death. From waist down his suit was grimed with squid blood. Mine too, flecked with dark blood and gore. We made a blitz through the smoke and the death and confusion...dodged the slap of tentacles and the whirl of goads.

I almost missed the slumped form of Deidra lying on the metal grating. I knelt down at her side for a moment and held her hand. Her lifeless green eyes stared back at me through her cracked faceplate. The operative who'd killed her'd been scouting these halls, waiting in some cross corridor for ambush. Dy-ar's insurance policy. His special operative backup.

I recalled Deidra's words back in the ship as we lay in each other's arms—that we were going places and that we could 'do stuff'. *"Sometimes you have to take a chance, Rusco, because you reach for it too late, then tough luck, it's gone."*

I bit back my tears and clenched my teeth and dragged her along out of harm's way, cursing all the way. I bent to lift her over my shoulders but Marty grabbed at my arm. "Leave her, Rusco. She's dead! There's nothing you can do for her. You'll be dead too if you try." He plunged off into the gloom. Skurg goads slashed down and threatened to block my last path of escape.

I vaulted after him, uttering a cry of grief and rage. I kicked aside a goad, smacked R1 barrel into a helmet, hating myself for leaving her, hating Dy-ar, the *weave*, this evil ship, this whole stinking universe, the senseless injustice of a universe governed by demons.

Marty radioed Slapper on the safe channel. "Kid! Make ready to rendezvous at the blast hole! Get *Trident* online. We're coming through."

"It's mayhem over here, Marty!" Slapper called back. "There's ships flying from all angles—"

"Slapper, it's me!" I cried. "Meet us at the gap. Have the cargo door open."

"I'll do what I can." His voice cut out meekly.

We had to get off this damned Ring Station.

I scrambled through the inky darkness down the eerie main corridor. Marty was five steps in front of me. While the ominous rumble continued to vibrate the hull, we aimed for the air lock, plugging fire back at Dy-ar and his detestable minions who were forced to protect him. The rumble was bordering on a dull roar. Marty booted it back the way he'd come, with me close at his heels, both of us hoping to get out through that tiny break in the hull before it was too late.

I could do nothing for Deidra. I had to keep telling myself that, lest I turn my own blaster on myself.

We'd gone no more than half the familiar way there when the beams of a dozen figures flashed our way.

Bratts' men. Some Scags.

Marty pegged three of them down before they knew what was happening. The rest came at us like rats. We had to fight our way through the mob like berserkers. I laid fire into them like pepper bombs. The fools had no idea that an L19 Destroyer was about to bring hell on our heads. They were only too eager to make some silly claim and reap the rewards.

Scutzers from all camps were scuttling down the dusky alien corridors to plant their beacons and flags. They were caught in a gold-rush like fever, firing shots, killing rivals, enemy gang members.

No mercy. No one was a friend, every one a foe. Infected by some wasting disease that made them less than men.

I'd had about enough of blood and ambush for one day with the gut-wrenching death of Deidra.

Something in me snapped.

The events that followed were only a blip on my mind. I went kamikaze. An invincible, untouchable avatar, pure rogue. I charged ahead beside Marty, killing anything that moved. With blaster, gloved fists, boots breaking helmets. A blood, tooth and nail massacre, steeped in revenge and atavistic blood lust. So deep was my grief that I did not care whether I lived or died.

Such savagery was what saved us.

Disassociating from body, welcoming of death, I was no more Jet Rusco the man, but some fantastic agent of the *weave*. We sprinted from bulkhead to bulkhead, crouching in the shadows of cross-corridors, snipering down enemies, breaking skulls, then charging ahead down the main corridor when the way was clear. Snatches of scutzer talk broke through the general channel as I ran. *'Bagged us some bug ships... Oughta be worth something, eh Snead?...In scrap exotic parts at least...A house of horrors... Only in the Belt..."*

No more than noise, this chatter of insects.

The Ring Station lurched.

We plowed on through the final air lock with the funny blue beams.

Something had awakened in this ship, something alive, perhaps some ancient program of the ship's defensive system.

Perhaps the one life, Sharki's life, had been enough to trigger some defensive time bomb? Or doom.

My breath came out in harsh rasps. I took stock of our surroundings. The landing bay was as it had been before but with ten times the activity. I saw vessels had also widened the rupture in the hull with cannon blasts, and scutzer ships had flown in to deploy more men. Dozens of suited figures were angling our way from rover, scout craft and capsule hastily parked at the end of the hangar. Two such ships were parked before the portal we'd come out of at right angles to the aphid ships. One had a Scags' logo, the other was unknown. Possibly Dy-ar's ride. I swung my head around, glimpsed the streak of ships whizzing beyond the jagged gap in the Ring Station. Too many vessels to count. I did not like the look of the heavy-turreted Skurg vessels giving chase.

Marty gave a hoarse cry. He fired at the unidentified parked ship. I grabbed his arm. "Don't waste your shots. Let's get out of here, Marty—to the bender."

We scrambled in a defensive crouch behind the aphid ships. Marty loosed more shots into the fray as fire came toward us from ships that had landed in the bay. The bender was still where I'd left it. None of the fools had bothered to check behind those aphid ships.

I opened up the private channel to Slapper. "Slapper! we're here! Meet us at the breach."

We made a beeline the last few dozen yards toward the bender, exposing ourselves as we passed along the shadowy gap between the third and fourth aphid ship, opening ourselves up to attack.

The tremors hit the hull like an earthquake. Marty and I were knocked to our knees. We picked ourselves up, and staggered on, wondering if the walls were going to crumble down on our heads. Whether the convulsions were internal or external, I could not tell. We clambered aboard our bender with Marty crammed on the other side of me like a sardine. I lifted her above the aphid ships, then aimed the craft out the gap and toward open space.

Something had awakened in the ship. I had a hunch now why. The ship was powered by the life force of those organisms held back there in those tanks, particularly the central one, how, I did not know…I knew it was amplified by the wizardry, or the miscarriage of science, that alchemic technology the insectoid Mentera had developed.

Whatever events had gone down in the past to stop the flow of organisms or 'receptors' being fed to that sinister technology, had ended in the ship naturally shutting down. It had gone into dormancy. Possibly to sit for centuries in a state of hibernation...until now, when the fresh body of Sharki had been injected into the matrix...and now the ship was fighting back.

Our bender cleared the gap.

Into an airborne hell—a maelstrom of ships and the bright traces of cannon fire.

CHAPTER 48

Everywhere was chaos. Ships of all sizes darting about the space wrecks and each other.

Beyond, I saw two battleships looming high at two o'clock. Midships cannons rained a stream of death upon the many scutzer vessels that blitzed about like gnats in and around the cyclopean hull of the Ring Station. The destroyers were the only thing saving our ass right now. They directed the enemy scutzers and Skurgs away from our puny, gnat-like bender trying to escape the barrage of ion fire. Only the bravest and most foolish of scutzers were making sweeps for the gap in the Ring Station, trying to land their craft swiftly there and lay their claims.

My eyes registered the squat shape of *Trident* looming below near the bottom lip of the Ring Station. I saw bright flashes spit from her port guns as she snipered at ships that came into our vicinity.

I impulsed toward her, following the smooth curve of the alien hull, a speck of nothingness compared to the sheer mass of the Ring Station. With Marty squeezed next to me, I flew full throttle toward the U56 and her open bay. The gap lessened between us. Perhaps a short distance, but fraught with much peril. I dodged in and out of light trails arcing our way and caught grazing hits from both Skurg and scutzer as we were buffeted around like pebbles in a tin can.

A tail of fire caught our rear end just as we flipped sideways and clipped our way into the hold. The front bumper slammed into the far wall. We bounced back and the bender crashed to the floor.

I unpeeled myself from Marty. The hold ramp was closing. I saw through bleary-eyes, the monstrous hull of the alien ship receding.

Good boy! Slapper was drawing us away from that time bomb and ant trap!

I kicked open the bender door and we pulled ourselves out of the battered craft. We shook out our hurts and wasted no time stumbling to the bridge.

Slapper was at the helm, his face flushed scarlet, his eyes red, his matted hair dripping sweat. "Where's Dee?" he cried as he turned toward us.

I stalked over to the nav.

"Where is she?" he persisted.

"She's fucking dead, you ninny! What do you think? Leave it alone."

Slapper glared at us, his eyes glassy. His lips gave a little quiver, then he moaned. "She was a good person, a hell of a fighter."

"Yeah, she was." I stared, dismayed at the number of ships I saw in the viewport while knowing I didn't deserve someone as noble as her to come down and try to save my ass. "Should have been me who died," I muttered.

"But it wasn't, Rusco," Marty said. "So let's move on and survive. If we're lucky, maybe we take down some more of these fuckheads."

I pushed down the sinking hollowness in my gut. I nudged Slapper aside and took the captain's chair. "Take starboard cannons, Slapper. Marty, you man port. This is a full out war. They want a fucking dogfight, they got it."

I saw to my amazement Dy-ar's forces were impressive—an army of Skurgs, 100 or more sleek, spike-mantled ships and two battleships bearing the logo of Damocles.

It seemed as if every scutzer in the Vala system was out here to play, to pay tribute to the hallowed Ring Station. Hundreds of ships swarmed the air space like fruit flies. More were arriving still, weaving in and out of the floating ring, like misplaced moths. Some ventured recklessly into the center of the ring, looping about the 5-mile X-cross-corridor that connected the orb-like bridge to the outer ring. Warring gangs of scutzers were quick to rain fire on each other as they whizzed past.

The Damocles battleships sent golden globes of terror into the hulls of reckless scutzers, heedless of logo or affiliation. Surges of fire smote the hulls as they erupted in flame. The Skurg wildcards of Dy-ar and his Moon Temple ghouls fired indiscriminately at anyone within range.

The air-space was a clusterfuck. I wondered how any ship could survive. I saw scutzers and Skurg, cornered by enemies, collide with each other or the many space hulks scattered about. There seemed no end to the confusion and mayhem—an orgy of destruction—masses of random space battles—fought in a chaotic soup of fireflies that blinked in and out of existence. A chaos much suited to Dy-ar's plan, and I could see the smirk on his pasty, jowly face.

But the tide of the battle was turning. More and more scutzers were falling under the fire power of the destroyers and the sniper tactics of the Skurgs.

Ion bombs licked out from the nearest L19 and sent both Reaper and Bratts into oblivion.

Several Reaper craft were hauling ass away on sight of the oncoming battleships and the phalanx of Skurgs. Two dozen Bratts' ships too.

I balled my fists into whitened lumps and cried over the com, "Fight, damn you! You have to fight these bastards! If you don't, they'll terrorize you till the end of days."

A rough voice came barking back at me, "Who are you to tell us what to do, *Lodestar*? You want to die, go right ahead. They're too many of these damn Skurgs. Not to mention two destroyers on our ass."

"One of us is good for three Skurgs," I shouted back.

A stinging memory surfaced, of Skel and his band and the tooth-and-nail fight they'd fought and lost, the duty I'd promised him to fight against the Skurgs. A promise I'd forsook. A prickle of shame bit at my neck. I wiped the sheen of sweat from my brow.

Torn between fight or flight, I stared at the battle of the Ring

Station and my skin ran cold. I remembered the death of my friends long ago. I swallowed hard. "If I could," I muttered hoarsely, "I'd wipe them off the face of these worlds."

The voice came from faraway, from across the voiceless depths of the *weave. But you can't. And yet, you must.*

My gaze wavered and I caught a glimpse of the scout craft I'd seen by the air lock. She darted out of the gap in the Ring Station and veered up on an angle toward Dy-ar's fancy space yacht. The bastard had fought his way out with the last of his Skurgs, it seemed.

An indescribable wave of hatred and fury flashed over me. The loss of Deidra along with the chilling revelations of him and this silly fire and brimstone war over this alien craft. It plunged me into an abyss of no return.

"There's that tree weasel," I thundered. "Fire on the bastard!"

A squadron of Skurgs had flanked Dy-ar's scout craft and were now escorting her back to the space yacht. War ships with raised turrets and long-range cannons set well back from their heavily-plated noses.

The old fury had returned and with a snarl I turned on Slapper. "Fire! Now! Full cannons on Dy-ar's shitbox. We might as well take these adders with us if we're all going to die."

Marty and Slapper's fire rained hard and furious. But Dy-ar's Skurgs had blocked access and absorbed the brunt. Some of our trails ripped at their hulls with enough force to send them dropping out of formation. What was worse, I was forced to bank sharply to avoid facing a head on collision with Skurg ships as bow fire came rippling at our nose and port vanes. A swarm of them came honing in directly at us.

This fight was doomed. All I could see was death. The disheartening prospect of retreat became a reality. But we had to clear the roid field before we could hyper out of here.

And hyper with what? Some vestige of a working drive?

Gator was not an option either. She was so close, yet so far. No way we could get to her on that lonely roid without getting blown out of the sky.

Rainbow fire suddenly spewed out of the octagonal turrets of the Ring Station. It happened so fast, it was like something out of a dream.

Another round gushed out from the weapons' ports of the monstrous hull. But these did not fade and disappear as normal cannon blasts should. They stayed lit in the air like luminous icicles, like frozen spikes of doom that seemed to lance out to infinity. Any ship or roid struck by those shafts of energy, was instantly obliterated.

More spikes came arcing up from other turrets that had not fired yet along the sinister hull. The nearest battleship exploded in a massive fireball. Two dozen scutzer ships went up in flames. Like mosquitoes zapped in a garden lamp, ships poofed out of existence as if they'd never been.

The Ring Station was fighting back.

It seemed expedient to flee this chicken coop.

The Skurgs had decided likewise. But a score of them came pursuing us like a pack of bloodhounds. Under Dy-ar's orders? I knew in my gut the knave had escaped in that P3 scout back to his space yacht. I'd failed to kill him when I had the chance down in that macabre engineering room.

I banked and hurtled left and right, up and down, dodging space rocks and murderous Skurgs. I kept clear of the long death spikes that radiated out from the Ring Station, frozen in time like spears of a great army, or the poisonous spines of a sea urchin.

A dozen ships with long-range guns dogged our ass. I was getting mighty edgy.

"Fucking maggots!" Marty swore. He sent a stream of ion flares back to deal with them.

I swung *Trident* hard round, looping sharply over the prickly mess of an ancient space wreck. Bright Skurg fire missed our stern by inches.

I hissed a curse as a micro roid loomed in our path.

I swung away, nearly brushing its pale gray surface, vaporizing us then and there.

The nearest Skurg pursuer was not so lucky. His blunt-nosed craft went smashing into the roid's surface, grinding itself to pulp.

The remaining enemies were like sprites on our tail. Ever closer they dogged us. I could not dodge forever their combined fire which ripped into our stern. I quailed as I watched our shield strength dip lower and lower.

Dy-ar's gloating voice chimed over the com. "Will you join us now, Jet Rusco? Or will you die? I test the *weave,* by pushing the limit of the prophecies of the Screeds, the life strings of your destiny, even though you are the Chosen One. It is a risk I take willingly, a cosmic experiment."

I ignored the voice and concentrated on the perilous path ahead of us.

Drawing on the best of my piloting ability, I zigzagged through a minefield of miniature roids and sent *Trident* in a roller-coaster ride between the last of the outlier rock. I was amazed that we had survived this long. Behind us the Ring Station dwindled to a speck, a bright nimbus of ice-like spikes, radiating out like sunbeams. I saw, much to my awe and horror, the alien ship began to move.

We cleared the roid field. Our shields were at near zero. Ten Skurgs were still on our tail. My fingers danced over the nav's star chart. I made the preparations for the jump to Veglos.

But not fast enough.

A last withering charge of ion fire struck our tail, rear vanes turning red hot at a breach in our shields.

A monster electrical arc ripped across the bridge, sending me and Marty sprawling out of our seats. Slapper was jerked back in his straps in agony. Hands and face were burnt as the electrical surge passed through him and went on across the starboard weapons' console. He sagged in his chair. His left shoulder was charred, left strap burnt and snapped and he slid sideways, head and neck tilted toward the floor.

The ion bomb had hit hard on our starboard side. Our shields had plummeted to zero. And now the end was near…

Dy-ar's voice trumpeted over the com, "The *weave* beckons, ungrateful wretch. You can run, but you cannot hide."

An echo from the past brushed the hairs on the back of my neck. One from a very long time ago. When I was young and susceptible and malevolent forces were trying to recruit me into their secret cult. I jerked my mind away from the dark slide of memory and back to the present horror.

The blast somehow jad joggled our hyperdrive. *Trident's* varwol kicked in. We made the jump to light speed. How, I did not know, or cared. To where we had no idea.

Were we safe? I could only scoff, or laugh for joy.

But I did neither.

I rose to my knees and peered at Marty who lay sprawled on the floor. I reached out for him. "Marty, Marty, you still with me?"

He stared up at me, hand grasping the edge of the console. He tried to pull himself off the floor but was having trouble.

I staggered over to help him up. His hair was singed; his feet and limbs struggling to lift himself shakily from the floor.

Slapper did not rise. He would not be rising anytime soon. Had Marty been strapped in too, he'd have suffered the same fate.

Marty coughed. I saw flecks of blood where he'd wiped his mouth with his glove. "So—where we—headed—Rus?"

"We're flying blind, Marty, you know that! Fuck!"

The blood was pounding in my ears. My heart a puddle of molten lead. What could I say? How much had we lost? Deidra, her neck snapped back on the alien ship. Slapper, dead, burnt, his eyes staring up from his skull, stiff and blackened not six paces away before the weapons' console. How many more innocents would die as casualties of the *weave*?

It was an unfair conclusion. Was it the *weave's* fault? We all should be dead. For some reason, it had decided to spare Marty and me.

"Where the hell…we going to…Rusco?"

"Who cares, Marty…as long as it's the fuck away from here."

OTHER BOOKS IN THE STARSHIP ROGUE SERIES:

STAR RUNAWAY
STAR WANDERER
THETIS 3
STARHUSTLER
STARVENGER

https://innersky.ca/starship

ABOUT THE AUTHOR

Chris is a prolific author of fantasy, adventure, and science fiction. His writing spans many genres: heroic fantasy, sword and sorcery and speculative fiction.

Browse Chris's books at:

https://innersky.ca/books